P9-BTY-922

ROMANCE!
WAR!
HONOR!
ADVENTURE!

As vast as our nation's history, as magnificent as its destiny, here is the unforgettable story of the men and women who claimed America's "first frontier," the wilderness that lay at the heart of a new and untamed continent.

CONQUEST

The Second Unforgettable Novel in the Bold New Series from Berkley

Pontiac's warriors have laid down the tomahawk. The bloodshed has ended. But in their
hearts, the men and women of Fort Detroit know
that their peace could shatter at any moment . . .

OWEN SUTHERLAND. His plans to form a
great frontier trading company are threatened
by scoundrels and renegades and may come
between him and his bride . . .

ELLA BENTLY SUTHERLAND. A lovely
Englishwoman, she must prove herself as a
woman of the frontier and as Owen's wife . . .

ANGÉLIQUE MARTINE. She loves a renegade Frenchman, marked for death...

JACQUES LEVESQUE. His lust for vengeance leads him on the warpath with Pontiac...

PETER DEFRIES. A handsome Albany Dutchman, his brawn and wits save him from disaster...

MARY HAMILTON. She must escape the bitterness of her past in order to forge a new life for herself in Montreal...

JEREMY BENTLY. A boy who will grow up quickly in the wilderness of the Northwest Territory...

JUBAL SWAIN. A ruthless backwoodsman, he and his band of murderous renegades create havoc in the Northwest country...

BEN FRANKLIN. The great Philadelphia statesman, he saves his city from destruction at the hands of rebellious settlers...

NORTHWEST TERRITORY · BOOK 2

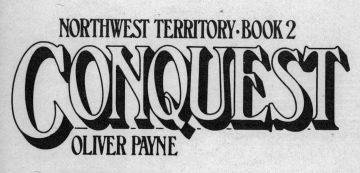

CONQUEST

OLIVER PAYNE

Created by the producers of
The Kent Family Chronicles,
Wagons West, **The Australians**,
and **White Indian** Series.
EXECUTIVE PRODUCER, LYLE KENYON ENGEL

BERKLEY BOOKS, NEW YORK

CONQUEST

A Berkley Book / published by arrangement with
Book Creations, Inc.

PRINTING HISTORY
Berkley edition / September 1982

Produced by Book Creations, Inc.
Executive Producer: Lyle Kenyon Engel
For information address: Berkley Publishing Corporation,
200 Madison Avenue, New York, New York 10016

ISBN: 0-425-05832-8

For all my friends at BCI

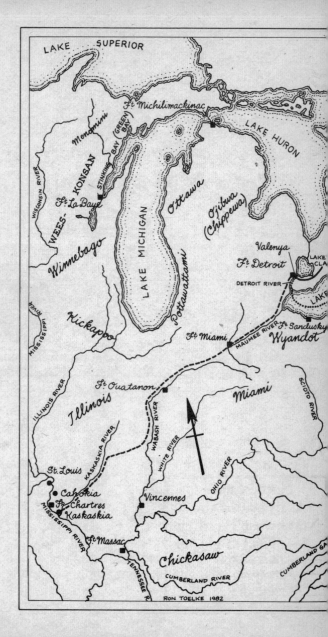

Sutherland's
Journeys in the
Northwest Territory
1763-64

...... to Philadelphia
— to Montreal
--- to Kaskaskia

0   50   100   150   MILES   © BOOK CREATIONS INC.   1982

"...the Indians now at Philadelphia are His Majesty's perfidious enemies, and therefore, to protect and maintain them at the public expense, while our suffering brethren on the frontiers are almost destitute of the necessaries of life, and are neglected by the public, is sufficient to make us mad with rage, and tempt us to do what nothing but the most violent necessity can vindicate."

—Remonstrance of Matthew Smith to Governor John Penn of the province of Pennsylvania on behalf of the inhabitants of five frontier counties ravaged by Pontiac's uprising.

"If an Indian injures me, does it follow that I may revenge that injury on all Indians? It is well known that the Indians are of different tribes, nations, and languages, as well as the white people. In Europe, if the French, who are white people, should injure the Dutch, are they to revenge it on the English, because they, too, are white people?"

—Benjamin Franklin, commenting on the attacks of Pennsylvania border settlers on peaceful Indian villages in 1763.

PROLOGUE

In 1763, the statesmen of Great Britain and France signed a treaty in Paris that declared an end to a bloody century of war in North America. These diplomats agreed on peace terms that gave Britain possession of the former French empire in America that stretched from Nova Scotia to the Appalachians, and from Pennsylvania west to the gathering of the Mississippi waters. Yet for all their sophistication, the makers of this treaty did not anticipate the power of one Ottawa war chief named Pontiac, a former French ally who refused to accept defeat.

As the infant British empire reeled in exhaustion from the worldwide conflict known in America as the French and Indian War, Pontiac called upon his sachems, his chiefs, and his warriors to strike a brutal blow against their traditional enemies. In the spring of 1763, this onslaught burst upon British America, and nine of eleven northwestern posts were destroyed. The vaunted British army was humiliated, and the western frontiers of New York, Pennsylvania, Maryland, and Virginia ran with the blood of settlers and soldiers. The Indians were victorious everywhere—except at the highly strategic posts of Detroit and Pitt, which held on through the longest sieges ever conducted in warfare between whites and Indians.

In August, however, the British narrowly won the battle of Bushy Run, shattering the alliance of Shawnee, Delaware, and Mingo, and relieving desperate Fort Pitt. And Pontiac failed to take Detroit, though he surrounded the fort with fifteen hundred fighters. With winter fast approaching, the Indians could not continue the war, for they had to follow the game south. Reluctantly, Pontiac agreed to a truce with the commander of Fort Detroit, and to many it seemed the siege was over.

Yet those who understood Pontiac were not deluded by his promise of peace. They knew that when spring returned, so would his warriors. The British government, nearly bankrupt from the wars in Europe and the New World, could not raise enough troops in America to protect those scattered settlers too brave to flee. In that winter of 1763–64, everyone—red and white—who had been through this uprising knew that the killing would begin again.

In western Pennsylvania the border settlers cried out for military protection that could not be given. During the cold months, the British and provincial governments struggled to prepare for two major campaigns against the hostiles in 1764, but there was too little money available, and too great a wilderness to pacify. And there were too many stubborn Indian warriors ready to fight to the death to hold on to their sacred lands—lands they believed no French diplomat had the right to surrender to the British.

Thus began the last great struggle between red man and white for control of the region then known as the northwest territory. For generations the two peoples would continue to fight one another, but none of their wars was as terrible as that known as the Uprising of Pontiac.

PART ONE

The Frontier Company

chapter 1

A WEDDING

Old Mawak beached his canoe near the deserted landing at Fort Detroit, ending a short journey from his lodge at the Ottawa village a few miles upstream. For all his uncounted years, Mawak's gnarled and sinewy body was still strong, and he climbed out of the canoe with the vigor of a young warrior, hauling the craft up on the shore. He moved quickly because he was excited, happy to be back at the English fort after a forced absence of nearly five months.

He turned to face the high stockade on the crown of a slope rising from the river, and he saw the Union Jack fluttering in the September-afternoon breeze. For a moment, Mawak wondered if Chief Pontiac was as wise as he claimed to be. Anyone who looked up at the strong walls and massive blockhouses of this place should see that no Indians could capture it by storm.

Standing at the water's edge, Mawak felt insignificant in the shadow of Fort Detroit, even though he wore his finest eagle-feathered headdress and had put on his best red shirt over four others of less importance. It did not matter that Mawak was a respected elder in his tribe of warlike Ottawa, nor that once he was first on the warpath and first in hunting buffalo. On the riverfront under the guns of the strongest fortress in the northwest, Mawak was just another redskin whose chief had sued for peace after leading the Indians in an uprising against the British forts of the northwest territory. The recent hostilities had lasted for five months, and Pontiac had agreed to a truce because winter was coming.

When Mawak saw a sentry wandering on the rampart at the top of the palisade, he stopped gaping at the fort and reached down into the canoe for a blue blanket, which he threw with great ceremony over his shoulders. The soldier stood watching Mawak now, and it was important that the Ottawa make a good impression on him from the start. Mawak drew himself up and strode solemnly up the slope toward the door in the fort's river gate, which was closed. He put out of his mind all humbling thoughts of how Pontiac and more than a thousand warriors had been unable to starve Fort Detroit into submission during the siege last summer. Instead, he thought of the Indian victories of the past five months—of the nine British forts that fell so swiftly, of the defeat of regular soldiers upstream near Parent's Creek, which the whites now called Bloody Creek. Even the French with all their power had been unable to defeat the British during the great French and Indian War. That fighting had ended three years earlier, in 1760, and the British had taken control of the mighty French region that once counted Fort Detroit as a western jewel.

Mawak felt intensely proud, and for a moment he began to wonder whether, after all, Pontiac might not have been able to take even Detroit by a massive frontal attack. Perhaps next year, when the weather became warm again, when the young men of the Ottawa, the Huron, the Chippewa, the Delaware, the Mingo, the Shawnee, and even the tribes of the Illinois Confederacy joined with Pontiac—perhaps then the fort would be captured. Then the northwest would again belong to the Indians, not the British Redcoats.

Mawak stopped at the sally port just below the young sentry, who scowled down at him. The pale-faced boy on the ramparts did not need to hunt, to travel many miles to find game. This boy would be helpless man-to-man against an Indian warrior his own age in a fair fight, but he represented a king who sent ammunition, food, warm clothing, and rum to his fighters.

Rum. Mawak licked his lips and felt thirstier than ever before. He longed for a good drink of rum, and he thought again of why he had come to Fort Detroit, when most of his people were packing up all they owned and traveling southward to the Illinois country, where game would be found come winter.

Mawak cried up to the young sentry, "Hey, soldier! Me come wedding! Me big Christian! You know Prince o' Wales?"

The soldier was a private in the 60th Regiment, called the Royal Americans and composed mostly of provincials. Mawak had never seen him before, although he knew most of the garrison by sight. This fellow was new, for he showed no recognition, but instead spat over the wall, aiming close to Mawak's feet.

Mawak did not stir. He cried again, "You know Prince o' Wales?" This was Mawak's English nickname; before the hostilities, everyone in the fort knew the Prince of Wales. But this soldier was ignorant of such things, Mawak realized, as another gob of spit came down, this time hitting the Indian's battered moccasin.

"Do I know the Prince o' Wales?" the soldier sneered. "Yeah, old man, I know 'im. 'As 'e been askin' for me again? Well, tell 'im sorry, but I'm too busy ter come ter 'is birthday ball this year! Tell 'im I'm protectin' 'is Majesty's American bloody empire for 'im. Tell the prince 'arry Tompkin's too bloody busy keepin' murderin' bloody savages like you from murderin' bloody farmers. Tell 'im that, yer lordship, an' get yer scurvy tail outa 'ere before I call the corporal o' the guard an' clap you in irons!"

Mawak drew out a white card with writing on it and held it up for the sentry to see. "Soldier," he said in his deepest, most gravelly voice, "Prince o' Wales come to fort for weddin'. Prince come for Owen Sutherland and squaw. Soldier, this Injun—" he thumped his chest once, hard "—this Injun sing in Rev'nd Lee choir, hear? This Injun name Prince o' Wales, hear?"

Now the soldier was confused. He looked Mawak up and down and shook his head slowly.

"You? Sing in the choir?" He stared at the shabby clothes hanging on Mawak's aged body. Mawak stood in silence, calm and proud. The soldier continued muttering, gave Mawak a dubious glance, and then finally cried down behind him, "Let this ragamuffin in, mate. Check the card 'e be carryin'. Says 'e come for the weddin'."

The sally port opened, and Mawak handed over the white card to a second soldier, who mumbled to himself as he turned it one way and then another. He was poor enough at reading in any case, but this writing was pure confusion. As he stared at the card, Mawak walked placidly into the fort. The guard grabbed him by the arm and shoved the card at him, saying,

"What the hell's this all about? It's Injun writin', if there be such a thing!"

Indeed, the card was covered with designs and pictures, which to Mawak said Owen Sutherland, the one the Ottawa called Donoway, had invited him to his wedding that day. With great dignity, Mawak held the card under the private's nose and pointed a bony finger at each symbol: "Donoway. Ella squaw. Marry. Mawak's sign. Come today."

Squinting, the soldier followed Mawak's explanation, then took the card and began to puzzle through it once again. Serenely, Mawak walked ahead, toward the broad Rue Sainte Anne, where a surging, colorful throng of every caste and type of human being in the northwest wilderness flowed around the log cabins and whitewashed clapboard dwellings of the little settlement. Mawak grinned to see the marvelous spectacle, and he stood even more erect to know he was in the very best of company.

There were British officers in scarlet coats, trimmed in white and glittering with gold adornments. Wealthy traders, British and French, paraded through the host of revelers, wearing fine fur caps or broad beaver hats adorned with amazingly large cockades of white tinsel ribbon. The merry *voyageurs*, most of them French and Indian half-breeds called *métis*, strutted in their gaudy finery, spangled with earrings and bracelets, feathers, and broad, red waist sashes. These men, who traveled the rivers of the northwest in their canoes to sell their goods, now seemed to Mawak more gloriously adorned than even the women, whether squaws, *métis*, or British.

The French *habitant* women wore explosive blues and yellows, costly gowns worth more than the very homes they lived in. Their curled hair cascaded down their backs, and nothing was spared of bright ribbons that tied their hair, their waists, their arms, and even their ankles. Though they were as poor as their broken fingernails were dirty, these proud folk loved a wedding, and they dressed far beyond their means for this great occasion.

The wealthier women, both French and British, wore the latest fashions from Europe, not more than six or seven months behind the times. Their families were connected to the great fur trade through Montreal and Albany, and their commerce with the far side of the Atlantic was so regular and thriving that they often had the latest news and styles before Philadelphia and New York. By the time European fashions became popular in those great colonial port cities, the leading ladies of frontier Detroit were ready for the next; they watched each other that none should have too much advantage before a husband or lover was scolded into procuring from Montreal the best their limited means could buy. The five-month siege had cut off normal channels of communication with the outside world, but these women of Detroit had charmed the officers of the newly arrived regiments into producing information on the most recent fashions that the officers did not even realize they possessed.

Thus for the wedding of the widow Ella Bently and trader Owen Sutherland, these leaders of Detroit's society felt confident that their dress did justice to their station as the wives, daughters, and sweethearts of prosperous merchants. The siege had halted all profits for the time being, but it had left its people desperate for a reason to celebrate.

Mawak waded into the gushing, laughing mob, saw old friends who knew he had not been in Pontiac's war band, and was welcomed among many he had thought not long ago were doomed to die. Somewhere in the fort Sutherland and his woman were being married, but where that was did not particularly matter to Mawak. He would congratulate them later, but first he needed to drink some rum, to wash away the sorrow of the past months and to honor the spirits of his ancestors.

Nodding and bowing as he went through the crowd, Mawak followed the fragrance of roasting beef and came out on the parade ground, where two whole oxen were spitted over fire pits. His mouth watered to look at such food, for it had been too long since any Indians had eaten well. The fighting had used most of their powder and lead, and they could not trade for more, so it was difficult to hunt. What food and ammunition had been captured was nearly gone, because Indians knew little of saving for cold weather and leaner times, so Mawak had eaten mostly wild rice and cornmeal for the past two months.

Now he gazed longingly at the roasting oxen, closed his eyes to smell the aroma, and knew in the depth of his heart that he no longer loved war. For all the white man's ignorance and rudeness to Indians, whites had much that the Indians craved and needed. Mawak considered himself well on the way to becoming like the whites, because already he was a Christian. Singing in Reverend Lee's choir of Indians made him a Christian, though not as big a Christian as the reverend or the

white members of the choir. But he was a bigger Christian than
the other Indians; they mostly came for the beer they could buy
with the coppers Lee gave out. Not Mawak. He had come and
listened when Lee told them about hellfire and the baby Jesus
and the angel Satan. Mawak was able to sing the melodies of
some of the hymns, and he had an idea about the words. And
no Indian was better at staying awake when Lee spoke about
the white man's god.

Mawak heard the bell ringing on the tower of the French
Church of Sainte Anne. He was borne along as the mob pushed
hard toward the big council house across the parade ground
from the church. He would have preferred to be at the far end
of the parade ground sniffing the roasting oxen, but he had no
choice. Then he saw why the mob had come this way.

The door to the massive building of squared logs opened,
and out came Sutherland and his new wife, Ella. The people
roared and threw rice and pieces of bright ribbon at them. The
bride, a pretty, fair-haired woman, was wearing a blue satin
gown and a linen cap, and she carried marigolds in a bunch,
which she threw in joy to the crowd. Somehow, the bouquet
wound up in Mawak's hands, and he was shoved and scratched
before it disappeared as magically as it had come.

To Mawak, Owen Sutherland looked strange. In the past
five months much had happened to this tall, clean-shaven Scotsman who had been adopted years ago by the Ottawa and re-
named Donoway—"Fearless in the Flames." Mawak thought
that Donoway was even lucky to be alive after his opposition
to Pontiac's war. As Sutherland and Ella walked smiling under
an arcade of crossed swords and past a rank of soldiers who
clattered to attention in their honor, Mawak noticed Donoway's
handsome dark-blue frock coat with a buff waistcoat and
breeches. These fine clothes were very different from the linsey
and buckskins he usually wore. As for the blue tricorn Owen
Sutherland waved to the crowd, it would never have belonged
to Donoway, the great hunter and fighter who always wore a
broad-brimmed, black beaver hat.

Certainly Mawak understood why Sutherland was so loved
by these people who were milling and singing in honor of the
newlyweds. If not for him, Fort Detroit might have fallen. If
Sutherland had not fought for the whites at the battle of Bushy
Run, Fort Pitt near there would have been lost. It was Sutherland who had gone to Pontiac and talked peace with him.

This truce, even if it would last no longer than the winter, was a glad and welcome respite for the besieged people of Fort Detroit, French as well as English. Most French had tried at peril of their lives to remain neutral, but Pontiac had grown weary of their reluctance to help him, and more than once had threatened them. Now the siege was broken, and when the hostiles returned next spring, the French would flee long before they found themselves again between two warring forces.

Mawak edged away from the crowd and walked toward a young woman directing the cooking of an ox. She was a lithe, slender French girl, raven-haired and with a fair complexion, one the whites considered very beautiful but whom Mawak thought too skinny to be worthy of being any Indian's squaw. This was Angélique Martine, daughter of the prosperous French trader Jean Martine. Mawak came to her and grinned broadly. In halting French he asked if he could eat. Sharply she told him the wedding party and choir would eat first, and he would have to wait his turn.

Angélique went back to arranging the long banquet table, which was spread with white linen and laden with every sort of food. There were pheasant, venison, bear steaks, roasted mushrooms, fruits, and vegetables of every kind that grew up and down the river in Indian town or *habitant* garden. There were sumptuous wild turkey, hare, whitefish, trout, and sturgeon, pâtés of potatoes, blood pudding, even a half-dozen roasted suckling pigs. As the petite French girl ran up and down at the table, giving orders and commands to a dozen other women, Mawak thought her a magician. Suddenly an empty table was burdened with bottles of brandy and wine, with sparkling glasses. In an instant, another table was set with a gloriously huge keg of beer. For the English, small half-kegs of rum appeared in a twinkling on a third long table, and they were augmented by crystal bowls brimming with rum and brandy punches.

Angélique Martine flitted here and there until someone shouted that the wedding party was coming. With that, she swept her linen apron away and smoothed her burgundy gown. She put a marigold in her hair and stood before the table, eyes alight with happiness for her friends.

The mob parted, and Sutherland and Ella came, hand in hand. Mawak stood in their path, and they welcomed him warmly, he and Sutherland speaking in Ottawa. The rest of the wedding party came next, with Reverend Lee at its head. The slim, bespectacled young Scots-Irish minister was beaming with satisfaction, and he nodded once to Mawak as he passed. The choir followed, garbed in long linen gowns and carrying English hymnbooks, even though a few of the dozen choristers were French Catholics.

Mawak watched the wedding party moving directly to the banquet tables, where some chairs were set, and he envied them for their fortune. He could almost taste the roast meat, and he thought the rum kegs must be leaking out their spirits, for he could feel their heady power already.

The wedding party arranged itself on either side of the newly-weds, in front of the table. On Sutherland's left stood the choir; on the right, next to Ella, was her brother, Major Henry Gladwin, tall and formidable in his scarlet uniform. Gladwin looked happy, but pale and drawn from the strain of commanding the fort during the siege. Next to Gladwin was the big Chippewa brave called Tamano, a close friend of Sutherland's and a fearless fighter well known to Indians all over the northwest. Tamano, too, had been sorely tried during the recent hostilities, but had decided once and for all to throw in his lot with his brother Donoway and join him in the fur trade.

Then a tousle-haired blond boy of eight appeared at Ella's side, and Sutherland drew him between them. This was Jeremy Bently, Ella's son by her first marriage to a provincial from New England who had died of wounds suffered in the long war against the French. It was clear from the look of the boy that he was glad to have Owen Sutherland for a father, and, judging from Sutherland's expression, the feeling was mutual.

Reverend Lee moved to the fore and raised his hands, one of them holding a hymnal and the other a Bible.

The crowd gradually grew still. Lee kept his hands raised for a moment as he began to speak in a ringing voice that carried across the parade ground.

"Ella and Owen Sutherland, dearest of friends to all of us who are gathered here to bestow our best wishes for a full and happy life, blessed by our heavenly Father in the coming new age of peace in our bountiful country . . ."

Lee went on, recounting the service Sutherland gave the army in the recent fighting, and describing Ella as his most gratifying conquest of all. She colored at this; Sutherland smiled a little, and Lee went on longer than he should have in praise of the newlyweds. As the minister spoke, Mawak saw his chance and moved closer and closer to the gowned choir, until he stood just behind them. Now, as far as he was concerned, he was a member of the wedding party and entitled to all its privileges. Reverend Lee ended his speech: "It gives me boundless joy to offer up this token of our boundless regard for both of you—a gift of song!"

Lee spryly turned to his choir, and its members raised their chins in anticipation, a few clearing throats and licking lips. Sounding his wooden flute, he gave a keynote. With a flourish, he removed his broad minister's hat, revealing a head thinly covered with hair. All eyes were on him, including Mawak's at the rear of the two rows of singers. Lee pushed the spectacles back on his nose and smiled at the choir. Giving a sharp, then sweeping, gesture with the flute, he led them in a Scottish hymn, much to the satisfaction of the Sutherlands, who stood close together, listening to the beautiful harmony.

Owen and Ella were not the only ones pleased with Lee's choice of hymns. Old Mawak was delighted, too, for it was one he knew thoroughly—in his own way. He rocked back and forth, closing his eyes and sensing the rhythm; unfortunately, he was much better at rhythm than melody. When he chose his moment to join in, he released a dull, grinding baritone, throaty and painfully loud. The choir's bright harmony faltered and began to deteriorate, and the singers—except for the happy Mawak—hesitated and looked over their shoulders at him. Lee froze, flute high in the air, face ghastly pale. The crowd began to laugh, but the Prince of Wales sang on.

A few months earlier at moments like this, Lee would merely catch Mawak's attention, politely hand him a few coppers to buy some beer, and dismiss him from the rehearsal room, with no one particularly troubled. But on this special day, when hundreds were in the audience, and when the hymn his choir had practiced so diligently and flawlessly for weeks was being destroyed by a coarse groaning that had no relationship at all to the song—on this day, Reverend Angus Lee forgot his Christian charity.

Trembling with fury, Lee stammered, "Y–Y–Y–You—you—*Indian!*" He was not heard by the sole person still performing, and Lee threw down the flute before advancing on Mawak.

But Ella, her hazel eyes alight with humor, stepped between

Lee and the Indian and touched Mawak gently on the arm. Opening his eyes and seeing her, Mawak stopped singing and smiled grandly, saying, "Donoway woman have much happiness. Many little ones!" He drew from a pouch at his side a thin string of blue-and-white wampum beads. Handing his gift to Ella, he rumbled, "First, Prince o' Wales sing, then big feast! Drink good lady health! First sing, eh?" He looked up at Lee, surprised to find the minister quivering with anger.

Sutherland stepped forward and put a hand on Lee's shoulder, smiling and saying softly, "He's a big man among the Ottawa, even if he can't sing so well, Reverend. You'll get your choir back, just wait a minute."

The Scotsman took the wampum from Ella, holding the string up for all to see, and addressed Mawak. "We thank you for your good wishes, Mawak. Your gift wipes away the bad feelings that have lately come between our peoples. In return, I offer this token of our respect and affection."

Sutherland handed his new tricorn to Mawak, whose eyes opened wide at such a fine present so worthy of his high position among the Ottawa. Proud of the honor done him, the old Indian accepted the hat and jammed it on his head, grinning with delight.

The bystanders appreciated this little ceremony, and they applauded with good cheer. Ella leaned forward to whisper something in Mawak's ear, and he beamed even more happily, folding his arms and standing between the newlyweds. Ella said to Lee, who was perplexed and still annoyed, "You may begin now, Reverend."

With some effort Lee gathered himself, gave Mawak a withering look, and went back to his choir. Once again he summoned their voices; after a few notes, he eyed Mawak suspiciously. But the man was silent.

Now the hymn rose in perfect harmony above the isolated fort, and Lee's good little choir sang with all their hearts. Behind the back of smiling Mawak, who stood once more with eyes closed, Ella and Owen joined hands. The hymn ended, and everyone was quiet. Then came a whoop from a Scottish Highlander and a shout from a French *voyageur*. The entire crowd roared, and Sutherland drew Ella against him.

"What did you say to keep the old fellow still?" he asked her quickly.

Ella giggled. "That the choir was singing in his honor!"

Sutherland laughed. "You'll make a frontierswoman yet, lass. Maybe even a diplomat to the Indians."

She knew he was joking, but what he said touched her more than he had intended. Ella Bently had known little of frontier life; certainly she knew nothing compared with the lovely Ottawa girl, Mayla, who had been Sutherland's wife and valued helpmate in his trading business before she was cruelly murdered a few months ago. But Ella Sutherland was determined to be a frontierswoman and a skillful partner for her husband in the Indian trade.

"I want to learn how to live here," she said with more intensity than she meant to reveal. "I mean, I want to be a help, not a burden, not an overcultured weakling who can't—"

Sutherland put a finger to her lips and kissed her, forgetful of the crowd that was dispersing and moving, with Mawak in the lead, toward the tables of food and drink. The audience laughed and shouted their approval as the couple kissed ever so briefly, and Ella blushed and smiled.

Sutherland looked down at her, but saw the insistence in her eyes, saw the urgency she felt about their future together. Warmly he said, "There's much to learn . . . for both of us."

Then he swept her away on his arm as the music started up into a Canadian reel. He spun her onto the puncheon floor laid out in the center of the parade ground, and Ella's heart lifted as they joined the dance.

In all its decades as a haven for whites living among the northwestern Indians, Fort Detroit had never seen such a celebration. Not even the feasting and dancing at the many great Indian councils had been as bright and gay and as heedless of what tomorrow might bring. The weight of warfare had been lifted, and with a shout of joy the people cast off tension and doubt and lived as bold folk have always lived—for the moment, and for the joy of life. For four hours Detroit rang with music, laughter, and song.

An hour before sunset, a pony cart—called a *calèche*—appeared in the Rue Sainte Anne, its animal frisking in nervousness. Other carts drove into the street, as though conjured by magic. Adorned like their masters in ostrich plumes and garlands of ribbons and flowers, these well-trained, shaggy ponies were the pride of the *habitants*, who loved to race them, no matter what the season, even over the ice of the Rivière Rouge. This was the first occasion anyone had to race since the Indian uprising began in May. Even with the truce, there was still the danger of hostile Indians waiting to ambush any whites who left the fort. Thus Major Gladwin had seen to it that his men had scoured the area outside the fort, and a number of soldiers kept watch along the racecourse.

Excitement ran through the people, and they hurried to the cluster of ten or fifteen two-wheeled carts blocking the street. The rules had been settled by generations of tradition. The race would be eight miles—four out and four back—between the fort and the great marsh to the south known as Grand Marais, where winter festivals and skating were always held. Henry Gladwin had been asked to fire the starting pistol, and for the fun of it he climbed up a ladder to the wooden cavalier high above the parade ground, where a small three-pound cannon had been loaded. As the major climbed, Jean Martine ran to Sutherland and Ella, standing on the log pavement near the starting line. The short, swarthy Frenchman asked Sutherland to do him the honor of driving his cart.

Sutherland glanced at Ella, and she said eagerly, "I'll go with you, Owen! Is that all right, Jean?"

Chuckling, Martine bowed to Ella's wishes, but when she said, "I'll drive! I often used to drive a pony cart in England!" Sutherland was dubious, because the French raced hard and sometimes dangerously.

Gladwin stood atop the cavalier, taking the lighted match from a soldier there. He raised the match, and Sutherland knew he had no choice. He and Ella dashed for the beautiful white cart, ornamented with the golden fleur-de-lis of France. They climbed in, and Ella slipped the reins between her fingers.

"Hey, Jeremy!" Sutherland shouted, beckoning for the boy to come. Without hesitation, Jeremy clambered between his mother and her new husband, who put an arm over the boy's shoulders. Suddenly the cannon boomed. The ponies neighed and whinnied in their fright, bumping together. Only one got off to a fast start—Ella's. As her two passengers and the crowd cheered, she drove the horse up the center of Rue Sainte Anne and whisked out through the open gate. Sutherland whooped for joy to see her drive so, and she laughed as dirt spattered up over them from the pony's pounding, unshod feet. The *calèche* clattered away toward the marsh, following the riverside track. Ella felt the wind in her face and the pleasure of going where she chose without fear of an Indian attack. Jeremy yelped in excitement, and laughed along with Owen, looking back to see a string of carts rapidly overtaking them.

They had too much weight aboard to win the race, and though Ella drove skillfully and sometimes recklessly, their cart was passed, one by one, by the rest. Each time they were overtaken, they heard a cry of *"Bonne chance!"* or *"Félicitation!"* or *"Bon mariage!"* and they saw smiling faces and waving hands. The other pony carts edged ahead until the Sutherlands were last, but they did not care.

Ella slowed the pony to a walk, and as they approached the stream called the Rivière Rouge, where cattails stuck up in vast brown hordes from the water, she drew the cart off the track. They got out, and Jeremy led the pony down a little slope, tethering him to a sapling where the grass was sweet. As the gray munched peacefully, Jeremy stroking his mane, Ella and Owen walked to the river's edge. Jeremy came down and sat behind them, and they looked across the mouth of the river, which opened into the straits.

Sutherland pointed to the rising bank on the far side, where the trees had been mostly cut down and the wind blew over a grassy meadow. "Just a few miles south of here, at the Ecorse River, Pontiac spoke to thousands of Indians last spring," he said. "Now he's had his uprising, but he hasn't won yet. I don't believe he ever will."

Ella leaned her head against Owen's shoulder and said, "I'd like to think the fighting's over . . . that the killing's over forever."

On their right, the sun was beyond the farthest reaches of the forest that stretched from these roaring straits to the distant prairie. The world was tinged with red, and the glory of a sunset seen from outside the walls of the fort was a simple but profound pleasure. At the top of the slope the returning pony carts raced by, their drivers and passengers shouting happily.

"Yes, Owen," Ella repeated, "I'd like to think the fighting's over."

Her husband did not answer. He knew Chief Pontiac and the British too well to say what Ella longed to hear.

When the sun rose over the northwest territory the next morning, summer was gone. The frosty touch of cold nights had flushed maples yellow, and here and there on the hillsides were pools orange and red. Many miles east of Fort Detroit, ghostly mists hovered over the lakes, and the Niagara River boiled and hissed through a deep gorge on its way from the mighty waterfalls to Lake Ontario.

On the crest of the Niagara's eastern cliff a flash of brighter red appeared among the autumn foliage, and like a scarlet snake it wound along the portage road on the edge of he heights. The steady roar of water rushing through the gorge and swirling into a great whirlpool called the Devil's Hole was punctuated by the rhythmic tapping of a snare drum. Through the mists rising from the steaming river far below, a long column of mounted Redcoats with a drummer on foot and a crowd of civilian teamsters in their midst were making their way from the upper landing a Fort Schlosser above the falls down to the lower landing at Fort Little Niagara. There were twenty soldiers, commanded by a mounted sergeant, escorting thirty muleskinners and bullwhackers weary from hauling military goods to the upper landing all the way from Albany far to the east.

To the right, the forest was thick and dark. It crowded the portage road close to a sheer cliff that fell dizzyingly down to the swirling, rocky river. Along this narrow defile these fifty men traveled in a straggling colimn of twos and threes, the soldiers on nondescript horses mingling among the men walking. As morning drew on, the column marched even more casually, because everyone was fascinated by the sight of the cataract foaming below.

Frequently, teamsters cried out to the sergeant that they wanted to rest near the cliff and look at the magnificent scenery. But the gruff leader of the detachment refused. "Keep moving! Close up ranks!" he shouted, even though he felt sure there was no danger of attack here. Throughout Pontiac's uprising, the only Indians from this region that had joined in were the fierce Seneca, westernmost nation of the Iroquois League. But they had struck toward the south, taking three British posts between Fort Pitt and Lake Erie. Indeed, in the south, hostilities were still raging, especially in the Susquehanna Valley west of Philadelphia; but here, close to powerful Fort Niagara, there had been only sporadic disturbances and a few random killings of white traders. Here, as in the vicinity of Detroit, Indian momentum was almost gone.

Pontiac had made peace in the west, so these soldiers felt their escort duty was tedious and unnecessary. The teamsters shambled along like so many unruly sheep; the sergeant accused them of being slower-witted than the oxen they drove.

The leader of the teamsters, a big, handsome fellow with blond hair and massive shoulders, shouted back with a laugh, "We can't be all that ignorant, Sergeant, or we'd be in the army, wouldn't we?"

The teamsters hooted, and the soldiers retorted with good-natured barbs of their own. It was a crisp, fresh day, and the civilians were cheerful. Once they got back to Fort Niagara later that afternoon, the big blond one, Peter Defries, would present his bill to the commander there, and he would collect their pay. Then they would all get good and drunk before starting back for Albany, where they could sit out the winter very comfortably with their earnings.

Like his men, Defries was in an excellent mood, fairly prancing along the bumpy portage trail, kicking rocks aside and over the cliff, and leaping like a child across fallen trees. It was no wonder he was happy—at twenty, he was about to make a small fortune as the leader of the supply column. Defries had used the ties of his Albany-Dutch family and the confidence of friends to bid for an army contract supplying the western posts, and now he had carried out his end of the bargain. The goods so desperately needed at places like Fort Detroit were now at the landing, waiting for a schooner from the frontier, and Defries had not a worry in the world. It had been a grueling, difficult trek from Albany, and in organizing and leading the expedition, Defries had proven himself a prodigy in the military-supply business.

Not only had he raised the capital to buy the goods, ammunition, and foodstuffs, but he had found the men and stock to cart it four hundred miles through rough terrain. For years Defries had labored as a hired teamster or bullwhacker for other men who made the real profits. He had been the best at his trade, well paid and respected even by the age of seventeen. But last spring when he heard about the western uprising, he went after a military contract with all his native genius and determination.

He won it, thanks in part to the influence of the most powerful man in Indian country: Sir William Johnson, Superintendent of Indian Affairs, adopted member of the Mohawk nation of the vast Iroquois League, and a friend of Defries's father.

All Sir William did for the young entrepreneur was to recommend him to military procurement officers. The rest was
Defries's own accomplishment. Even before the contract was
formally awarded, he had prepared a list of precisely the right
kind of goods and went from merchant to merchant in Albany,
placing orders and requiring that the merchandise be held in
instant readiness until he called for it.

Since no one else in Albany—the main supply source for
the northwestern posts—was then able to find additional goods,
the foresighted Defries was the only man who could readily
provide the army with what it needed. Sir William was as proud
as an uncle that the youth had fulfilled his contract with such
mastery and efficiency.

As the run of comical insults between soldiers and teamsters
swept up and down the column, Defries spoke to the boy who
walked beside him, tapping cadence on a drum almost as big
as he was.

"Listen to me, lad, and get that lobster coat off your back
quick as you can. Be a free man, like we are!"

"Why?" The boy's childish face already had hard lines about
it, the marks of a soldier's harsh life. "I got no taste to goad
oxen for a livin'."

Defries laughed as the soldiers nearby cheered the boy. Then
the big fellow said, "Rather goad the ox than let an ox goad
you, son! Right, Sergeant?"

The sergeant turned in his saddle to give Defries an obscene
gesture, but before the man had finished his motion, the forest
came alive. The trees exploded in a roar of fire and smoke,
and the happy world of Peter Defries burst apart in shrieks and
blood. A shining blade whisked past his head, and he ducked
instinctively, turning to see a painted Seneca warrior swing the
tomahawk again, leaping in and screaming for his enemy's
death.

Defries roared and shouldered into the warrior's gut, ramming him back, at the same time grabbing for the elusive
tomahawk hand. The slippery, bear-greased Seneca threw his
free arm around the teamster's neck and tried to drag Defries
down, but the Dutchman was too strong for him. With a shout,
Defries lifted the Indian into the air, staggered three steps to
the edge of the cliff, and hurled the screaming warrior over.

He turned to fight again, but he saw ten Indians for every

white man. The portage road swarmed with redskins dragging soldiers from their horses, killing teamsters writhing beneath crowds of attackers. Defries had that split second to choose— fight and die, or escape over the cliff.

In the next instant, he glanced down at the river far below, and knew he would die that way, too, as several had already died in desperate attempts to escape. But then he saw trees growing a little way down the steep slope above the dropoff, and he realized they were the only possibility.

A weight crashed against him, nearly bowling him over. He turned to see a big Seneca lift the boy up by his drum strap, raising a tomahawk before the boy's terrified eyes. Defries slammed against the Indian, causing him to drop the boy. He wrenched the tomahawk away, and with a swift blow, Defries killed the warrior.

The drummer had fainted. Defries dragged him over his shoulders, took a quick look down the cliff, and went over, sliding much too fast down the steep embankment through bunch grass and gravel that tore away beneath his feet and broke free as he clutched for a handhold. The boy was under his left arm now, and the added weight made it hard for Defries to stop the slide. He skidded toward the brink. Beyond was air and a vision of the spectacular gorge and foaming river. He fought to slow down, but with only one hand free he could not. He dug in with his legs and feet, jamming them hard, but the edge of the precipice gave and crumbled. Then a twisted, skinny cedar tree was in his path, and he grabbed for it, feeling some roots pull out of the soil as the tree bent under the sudden weight. His feet kept skidding until he was over the brink, kicking at air. But the tree held—for the moment—and he stopped with a jerk. The burden of the unconscious boy strained at his arm, and he pulled him up and lay with him just above the tree. Gunfire, war whoops, and terrible screams of agony echoed through the gorge, and Defries looked up at the top of the cliff to see whether any Indians had discovered him yet. None had, but it would not take long for them to finish their murderous business and look around for a few more unclaimed scalps.

Defries heard a whimper, then a wail of fright. The drummer, conscious now, tried to scramble up the slope. Defries dragged him back, snarling at him to keep quiet or they would be found. The boy's eyes were wide with terror, and he trembled from head to foot. But for now, he obeyed.

They had to get under cover, though none was to be seen as they lay inches from the sheer drop. Directly below was water. That was better than stone, although the water swirled white, and might guarantee death just as well as rocks would. Yet there was no other choice. If the Seneca warriors looked over, they would see these two and shoot them.

They had to jump. Defries motioned to the drummer. The boy shook his head, his eyes wild, and tried to crawl away again. But Defries held him down, then looked over the side once more. He finally spotted another way—right below the overhang was a shelf of rock. It did not extend out far enough for him to drop straight onto it, and it was at least fifteen feet down. But if he twisted his body the right way and swung his feet under the overhang, he might—just might—get onto that shelf with the boy, and they would be out of sight from above.

There was no time to think twice. Defries let his legs dangle over the brink and drew the frightened drummer boy toward him. But the boy whined and tried to get away.

"You want to live?" Defries hissed, and the drummer steadied, biting his lip and trying to control himself.

Defries took the boy against him and whispered, "Close your eyes, then."

He eased over the edge, using the bent cedar as his ladder until he hung by one hand that slipped slowly down toward the thin top of the tree. Straining to get his feet in position to swing under the overhang and onto the shelf, he tried not to look down at the fearsome drop to the river. Grunting and sweating, Defries went as far as he could on the tree, and his strong hand was torn and blistered. He was almost in position when the boy could stand no more. He looked down and moaned. Then he fought Defries, trying to climb back up the tree. Defries held him, but the drummer was too frightened. He kicked and scrambled out of Defries's grip, but not quickly enough. The tree roots ripped and snapped. The cedar gave, in a sudden yielding burst of earth and stone.

Defries was in the air. He heard the boy scream. He could do nothing at all to control himself, but he fell for only an instant before landing heavily against stone, his body bending and pain shooting up through his right leg. He recovered quickly and found himself on the shelf of rock. But the drummer was nowhere in sight.

There was still fighting up above, and Defries risked being spotted by looking out of the cleft in the rock, fearing he would see the boy's broken body far below. He peered over the brink and was surprised to see the boy no more than five feet under the shelf, hanging by the drum strap from a scrub oak. Still conscious, but too shocked to speak, the boy stared at Defries, his eyes pleading.

Defries went after him. He put one leg over the side, wedging his foot against small outcrops. He managed to lean over far enough to grasp the boy's belt. The drummer gathered his wits and gripped his rescuer's shirt. Now the tremendous strength of the Albany Dutchman was called up. With one hand on an outcrop, he hauled them both to safety, and in a few seconds, they lay panting on the ledge.

There was a fierce commotion above, and Defries heard the familiar voice of one of his men cursing the Indians. A small avalanche of stones poured over the front of their hiding place, and Defries watched with fascinated horror as one of his boyhood friends flew out into space, shrieking angrily at the Seneca. Defries lurched to the edge of the rock shelf and saw the man splash into the water, bob up and down for a moment, and then vanish in the white rapids dashing toward the whirlpool a hundred yards downstream.

Unable to look away, Defries stared at the river. The sounds of battle overhead were gone now. The drummer boy was sobbing, his face pressed upon the rock floor. Defries sat up and leaned back against the wall of the cleft. He felt very weak. His strength was spent, and the pain from his knee shot up to his hip whenever he moved.

Defries told the boy, "We'll be all right. Soldiers from the Eightieth must have heard the gunfire. They'll be along soon." Defries knew that a company of a hundred soldiers of the 80th Regiment of Foot was camped a mile and a half away at the lower landing. Those specially trained wilderness fighters were the pick of English troops in North America, chosen for their skills at combat in the forest with Indians and French.

The drummer wiped away tears, his face streaked with dirt. He looked ashamed to be crying and struggled to compose himself. Then he whispered, "There's too many Injuns here. Those lads won't have a chance if the Injuns lay for 'em."

The boy was right, but what could they do about it? Defries

pursed his lips, then said, "When we hear 'em comin', we'll warn 'em."

That seemed to make the youngster feel better. He straightened his dirty, sweaty uniform, and a light came into his eyes—the light of determination. He had been humiliated as a soldier, but now he would redeem himself by warning the reinforcements before it was too late. Defries recognized this urgency in the boy, and he prepared himself for it, knowing that heedless courage at the wrong time could mean death for both of them.

For the next ten minutes they huddled in the cleft of rock, listening to the movement of the Seneca above. There was much hoarse shouting and laughing, and occasionally a cry of pain. Then everything was silent save for the sound of the river rushing far below.

"They've gone," Defries said softly. "Or they know we're here and are playing cat-and-mouse with us."

Listening like a hunted creature, the boy pressed back against the rock, fear still haunting him. Then he held up a quivering hand, whispering, "Listen!"

In the distance a drum rolled the charge. The soldiers from the lower landing were on their way—too late—to the rescue.

But those soldiers should be approaching carefully, not charging headlong up the portage road. They would end the same way as the teamsters and the escort.

"I've got to warn them!" Defries scrambled to the edge of the shelf.

The drummer was close behind him, terror now gone from his eyes. Defries looked closely at him as they prepared to leave their shelter. The boy was calm and steady. Defries nodded to him.

"You'll make a soldier, lad. Never mind what an ox goad like me says!"

He clapped the boy on the shoulder, and together they began the dangerous climb up the wall of rock. With each struggling pull from handhold to foothold, the sound of the drum grew louder. Defries's anxiety mounted. They had to get up before the soldiers walked into an ambush, but it was hard going. There were only a few narrow ledges underfoot to keep them from plummeting to their deaths. When Defries glanced back to find the boy, he saw that terrible fall. He closed his eyes and pressed against the cliff face to catch his breath.

The boy found an easier way, and his lighter weight made him more agile and quicker than the burly Defries. In a moment, he was above the teamster and near the top.

Defries whispered, "Careful, lad! Go easy until the troops are near enough, or the Injuns'll get you first."

The boy stopped climbing just a few feet below the brink of the cliff and waited until Defries came up. The drum sounded less than a hundred yards away, but the soldiers were still too far off to be warned. Another twenty seconds . . .

"Stay under cover!" Defries ordered. "I'll go!"

"No! They're my mates! I'm—"

A blistering fusillade erupted up above, shattering the stillness, followed by war whoops and shouts of the soldiers. The snare drum abruptly stopped. A ragged volley of muskets told that the soldiers were trying to fight back.

The boy clambered toward the crest. Defries reached out and stopped him short.

"Not yet!" Defries cried. "It's too late—"

"Let me go!" The boy tore away. Defries tried to stop him, but the boy yanked his leg away. Defries went after him, and both of them climbed over the top, but when they got there, they stopped short.

The road was blanketed with dead soldiers and teamsters. A little farther away, the rescue party was a confused mass. Men fell in clusters with every Indian volley from the cover of the trees. The horror and carnage were redoubled in that instant, when the Seneca charged out of the woods and hurled themselves upon the light infantry. The entire detachment was seconds away from annihilation.

Numbly, Defries and the drummer gaped at the slaughter. It was then the Seneca saw them. A few whirled and charged. Defries started back down the cliff, but the boy was transfixed. Defries shouted to him and hesitated—the Seneca were only yards away. He pulled the boy over the edge. As they slid down the slope, curdling war whoops pursued them. This time there was no chance for a careful descent. The loose slope gave way under their feet. A bullet whizzed close by. They skidded on their backs through low brush, frantically trying to get a handhold. The brink came up at them. Then the edge was there, and they had only an instant to think.

"Jump out!" Defries screamed. He churned his legs on the slope and sprang with all his might away from the precipice, trying to keep his feet below, praying he would land in water.

They fell, fell through space, and all around glowed the warm and brilliant colors of a perfect autumn morning.

chapter **2**

PARTNERS

In their small cabin near the commandant's garden at the northeast corner of Fort Detroit, Ella and Owen Sutherland sat down to breakfast. The small table near the room's only window was covered with a red-checked tablecloth; bright sunshine gleamed on a jar of English marmalade in the middle of the table near a butter dish, teapot, and a cheese board. Ella was content as she poured tea for her husband. The day was as bright as her own happiness. They had risen late because they were alone in the cabin—Jeremy had spent their wedding night with the family of Garth Morely, next to Sutherland the most important British trader at Detroit.

Both Ella and Owen felt as though they had been married for years. Neither needed to speak at all. As Ella poured her own tea, Owen recalled that first day they met, on the stranded whaleboat in the straits back in April. Trapped during spring flood, Ella, her son, and their traveling companions were in danger of drowning when Sutherland and the Chippewa Tamano came along and got them to shore safely. Those days seemed so very long ago. Sutherland was happily married back then, but he had noticed Ella's warm beauty from the start.

He had thought little more about her than that she was the widowed sister of his close friend Henry Gladwin, the post's commander. Ella's first husband had died several years earlier, and she had come to Fort Detroit to be with her brother and to go with him back to England. It had been Ella's intention to start life over again at the family's home in Derbyshire. As a woman of the upper class, she had a future in England, where Jeremy would have been raised as a gentleman.

Then Mayla had been murdered by a French renegade, and Ella had comforted Owen, had fallen in love with him, and he with her. It had all happened much faster than either thought possible, but now it had come to marriage and a new beginning.

Ella put down the heavy teapot. A beam of sunlight sparkled honey-gold in her hair. Owen smiled at his radiant wife. He knew now how ready he was to begin life anew.

He was determined to put aside his past completely—a past once shadowed by a false accusation of misconduct when he had been an officer of the famed Black Watch Highland Regiment fighting in Europe. Sutherland had resigned from the army in disgrace back then—eighteen years earlier—and had come to America to take up life as a fur trader in the northwest. He had been captured by the Ottawa and tortured by fire. In that awful ritual he had been silent at first, then scornful and insulting to the warriors who tried to break him. At the height of the torture, the great chief named Pontiac stepped in and claimed Sutherland for his people, naming him Donoway and sending him through a cleansing ceremony to wash away his white blood.

But Ella had changed all that. She had revived his white spirit and had kindled his blood with a fire he had never known before. For all his happy years married to a beautiful and courageous Ottawa woman, Sutherland was a Scotsman in his heart once again. What Mawak had seen at the wedding yesterday was true—Donoway's soul had very nearly left the body of Owen Sutherland.

A few weeks ago his reputation had finally been cleared— a dying English officer had admitted guilt in the long-ago affair that had cost the British a battle and many lives. Sutherland would never again rejoin his old regiment, now stationed in America, but he had fought alongside his former comrades in the crucial battle of Bushy Run in August. He had advised the British commander of the best tactics to defeat the massed forces of Shawnee, Mingo, Ottawa, and Delaware that surrounded them. It was that victory which had proved the power of the British army to the Indians, and had caused Chief Pontiac to call for a temporary halt to the uprising.

But it had torn Sutherland apart to fight against Indians, because he desired to abandon war forever and take up again the life of a trader with white and red connections in the rich fur trade. He wanted that life in the vast wilderness and he wanted it with Ella and her son Jeremy—a boy he loved as though he were his own blood.

When Owen realized Ella was watching him, he sat back and gazed at her without self-consciousness. He understood Ella's own intentions to be a woman of the frontier, capable and knowledgeable in the fur trade. He also knew she feared she might not be strong enough for frontier life.

A soft knocking came at the door, breaking the spell.

Sutherland rose to unbar the door, and in came Jeremy, reluctant and uncertain.

"I—hope I'm not . . . I mean, I hope it's all right if—"

"Get in here, laddie!" Sutherland rumbled and picked the boy up, tossing him like a bale of fur onto the four-poster bed. "You live here, too, now!"

Sutherland wrestled with the boy on the bed, and Ella scolded them for soiling the coverlet. She chased them off and showed Jeremy the trundle bed underneath the four-poster.

"At night we'll pull this out, and you'll use it," she said. "But this cabin's too small to let it stay out all day."

Sutherland led the boy to the table. "When we go back across the river to Valenya, then we'll have a good house. My place there has plenty of room, and next spring we'll build another lean-to onto it for you. We'll cut the logs this winter!"

Jeremy dug into a breakfast of bread, cheese, and marmalade as Sutherland spoke fondly about his big cabin a little way up the straits. He and Tamano each had a house there, nestled among a number of massive standing stones. The wind sometimes whistled through the narrow gaps between the stones, and the Ottawa called them the Singing Stones.

Jeremy and Ella were anxious to see Valenya. They had been unable to leave the fort all summer, but Sutherland promised to take them when the Ottawa had all left for Illinois country. Although there was a truce, it was still wisest for the women and children not to leave the fort until the younger Indian braves were well out of the area.

Jeremy devoured his food, listening to Sutherland talk of the future. The boy had admired the frontiersman from the first, and he was utterly delighted that he was now his father. Sutherland, who had been educated at Edinburgh University, promised to teach him his letters as well as the ways of the

forest. Tamano would also help make him as good in the wild
as an Indian.

When Sutherland finished talking, the three of them sat
quietly for a little while, enjoying the warmth of the fall sunshine, and that was enough just then.

Defries kept his feet below him as he fell, and he crashed into
the water upright, but the shock stunned him. He sank into the
torrent, gulping water, crashing against boulders, and swirling
away in the strong current. It took all his willpower to fight
to the surface. For an eternity he was unable to take one breath.
He wheezed and coughed, bobbing and thrashing for air, crashing brutally into rocks. Finally he struck one chest-first and
managed to hold on. The river pulled at him, trying to rip him
loose, to suck him into the whirlpool just a few yards downstream.

His head spun as he clutched the slippery boulder for his
very life, gasping the icy air. But his respite did not last. He
lost consciousness for a moment, and again he was torn away
into the torrent. Defries struggled desperately, but he knew that
in a moment he would be swallowed by the whirlpool.

Just as his strength gave out, he was jerked to a wrenching
stop, his clothing caught on a submerged log. It was enough,
and he regained control, holding on to the log until his lungs
took in sweet air once more. Wheezing for breath, Defries
studied his situation. He was facing downstream. Off to the
right floated more driftwood. It was his only chance. Holding
his breath, he struck out mightily, and this time the current
aided him. He was swept into the driftwood, and with trembling
arms he heaved himself out of the water.

He lay on his back, dizzy with exhaustion. After a while
he looked up at the top of the cliff. It was very far away. He
wondered how he was still alive. What about the boy? He sat
up painfully and searched around the gorge. The drummer was
nowhere in sight. He peered downstream at the roaring, eddying
whirlpool. No one could survive that. He lay back again, gazing
weakly up at the precipice. No movement there at all now. The
massacre was finished.

When he could, Defries crawled across the driftwood to
shore. His shoes were gone, his clothes torn to shreds.. The
agony of his right leg asserted itself, and it was with great
difficulty that he got up and walked along the shore below the

steep cliff. More than once the knee gave way and he fell. But on he went. He had to get downriver to the fort, and he had to do it without running into a roving scalping party.

The only way to get there was to climb back up the cliff. Inch by inch, every muscle in his body shaking with exertion, Defries went up the side of the gorge. Here and there he could walk along ledges, but more often he found himself pressed against a wall of stone, prying at rock for the next handhold. Every now and then he would stop to rest. Often he scanned the gorge and the river's edge for some sign of the drummer boy. But there was nothing to be seen.

In the storeroom of the long, low trading house of Garth Morely, where Indians and soldiers came to buy or sell, three men sat around a table—Owen Sutherland, the grizzled and black-bearded Morely, and the Frenchman Jean Martine. They were contrasts to one another, these three, but that was why they were friends. Sutherland, the adopted Ottawa, could go any-where on the frontier, counting on his courage and woodsman's skills to survive. Morely, who always wore a black coat and black smallclothes and spoke with a north-of-England accent, was a crafty and knowledgeable trader. He had a way in bar-gaining that left those he dealt with feeling satisfied, but they seldom got the better of this man, whose sharp eyes never failed to size up trade goods or a customer.

Jean Martine, clean shaven and well dressed, wore the red stocking cap of the *voyageur*. Born in Normandy of fisherman stock, he had come to America twenty-five years ago as a teenager bent upon adventure. For fifteen years he had been trading from Fort Detroit, and no man in the French community was more respected by the English. The French and *métis* also held Martine in high regard, even though it was rumored he had secretly supplied the besieged garrison with food during Pontiac's rising. Martine was important to Sutherland, for the Frenchman could assemble a crew of *métis* or French *voyageurs* at a moment's notice. He had close connections with the French merchants who had stayed on in Montreal after the British takeover. As he sat placidly smoking a long-stemmed, white clay pipe, his eyes were half-shut, but a gleam in them told he was aware of everything being said.

Sutherland was making a proposition. "Even though the army has forbidden us to go out to the villages this winter, there's a way to get furs. The Indians need everything possible we can bring to them, and the first traders to do it will make a fortune. They'll pile the finest furs into the arms of a trader who brings them what they want."

Morely sat back, shaking his head. "We can't bring them what they want, Owen. The bloody army says traders can't leave the posts. The Injuns who trap this winter'll have ter come in ter us. Nobody'll make no fortune goin' ter the villages if 'n the army confiscates their furs."

"It would be dangerous to go out, my friends." Martine had learned his excellent English while trading illegally between Albany and upper Canada. That trade had diverted goods and furs around Montreal, where a corrupt governing *intendant* had ruled with an iron hand and taken graft with a grasping one— cause enough to turn honest traders into lawbreakers. "Any English going among the villages so soon after the fighting . . ." He drew the stem of his pipe across his throat.

Lettie Morely appeared from the far side of the room, carrying a pitcher of beer and pewter mugs. She set them firmly in the center of the table and wiped her chubby hands on an apron. "Owen," she said, "if thee be thinkin' my man can traipse about in them woods, riskin' 'is neck while them Injuns ain't pacified yet, thee be a-thinkin' muddleheaded."

Sutherland smiled. "We'll need Garth here at Detroit, Lettie, not in the woods—"

"We?" she asked. "Who be 'we,' then?"

"The company, lass," Sutherland replied, looking at the two men. "The new company—the only organized company of traders on the frontier!"

At that moment, the door opened, and in came Ella Sutherland and Angélique Martine. They had just finished shopping at the weekly market. Without removing caps or shawls they both asked in unison, "What company?"

Sutherland was enjoying the suspense. "Listen, who has the money and the goods to supply the trade? The British! And who has the manpower and ability to get the goods to the outpost and the furs to the city? The French!"

Angélique sat down across the table from Sutherland. She had the handsome features of her Norman father, and the sultry beauty of her Huron mother, who had died giving birth to her. She said quickly, "But the army has ordered both French and British to stay out of the villages—"

Sutherland held up his hand. "They can't order the Indians to stay out of the villages. They can't order Tamano—"

Garth Morely slapped the table and laughed. "I begin ter see what thee be gettin' at, lad! Tamano trades our goods ter the Injun trappers in the wild, Martine here organizes the manpower, thee an' I put up the funds an' goods—" He slapped the table again. "Blin' me if it ain't a colorful notion!"

They began all talking at once. Even Ella, with her limited knowledge of the fur trade, knew that no one else had ever organized an effective company to control the lucrative Indian peltry. Under the French, the government of Canada had ruled the trade to profit the king and his favorites. Now, under the English, the trade was wide open; only the hostility of the Indians prevented wholesale competition.

Sutherland said, "When the troubles are over, the frontier will be mobbed with traders—British, provincial, French—all underselling each other, trading cheap rum and worthless merchandise, and debauching the Indians."

Morely and Martine nodded. The worst sort of traders would bring barrels of rum or high wine to the Indians, get them drunk, and then cheat them when they were helpless. It had happened before, and that was why the British were determined to keep the traders to the forts. If unscrupulous traders were permitted to travel freely among the Indians, the commerce in furs would be ruined—and the Indians would be made even more savage by their drunkenness and poverty.

But if a company of the best traders dealt fairly with the most reliable Indians, then the fur trade would be enhanced, controlled, and developed to its fullest potential. Sutherland proposed that the Indians be given goods on credit in the fall, before the best trapping season, and when they came in with furs after the winter they would pay their debt, and the value of extra furs would be given to them in goods—blankets, fowling pieces, fabric, supplies of food, clothing, ammunition, and traps. If the new company's reputation among the Indians was good, then the best Indians would join it, guaranteeing better profits and the welfare of the nations.

"There's more," Sutherland said, pouring beer into his mug. "I propose that a certain number of shares be distributed . . . shares in the company. The three principal partners get the largest number, then any additional partners—such as Tamano and our agents at Montreal—get smaller blocks of shares. Finally, even the lowest *voyageur* who joins up gets shares. That way, everyone profits when the company profits! Everyone belongs, and no one is just an employee."

"And," said Angélique Martine, "we form this company in secret, before anyone else knows about it! We must organize before winter, so that Tamano will be the first trader to visit the far country, where the best furs are."

Angélique was as astute as her father in the trade. He was the bargainer, but she knew what sort of trade goods to order, having kept his accounts perfectly ever since she was a girl. Often, when other traders were failing, Martine's house throve because of Angélique's ability to purchase just what was needed without overstocking or buying poor merchandise.

"But there's something I object to," she said. "Rum. Brandy. They are trouble here! Drink has been the bane of *sauvages*. Our new company must not deal in rum, not brandy—not at all!"

The others fell quiet. Angélique was asking for much. Without alcohol, a trader was lost. The Indians had an unquenchable thirst for firewater, and it was always used in ceremonies of friendship between trader and redskin. Any trader who refused to sell it could forget about profits.

Jean Martine shook his head and sighed. He had often heard this argument from his daughter, and it wearied him to hear it now. He said slowly, "*Chérie*, must you talk so?" He changed to French. "Without drink there is no trade. Without trade there is no house of Martine. I would rather go back to Normandy and fish than scratch the soil out here for a bare living."

"But the Indian has been drowned by French brandy and English rum!" Angélique replied. "It's all the same. It's all destruction to the Indian. They get cheated or go mad and murder their wives and children. Of course, they are sorry for it in the morning, but then we come with another keg—"

Martine threw his pipe to the floor, where it shattered. "Perhaps you would rather be the wife of a *habitant* wood-chopper or a poor *voyageur*, eh? No trips to Montreal or New Orleans, then! No Paris lace! And no dowry when you marry your ignorant *voyageur*, let me warn you! No drink, no trade! Don't forget that, daughter!"

There was an embarrassed silence until Ella spoke: "If the company can be formed as we think it can, friends, then the life of the Indian will be improved, not ruined. Angélique is right. We should not make rum our main ware, and it should not be given in any quantity until after the trading is done."

Angélique said quickly in English, "And all our partners should accept this as a regulation! No rum until *after* business is complete. A drunk is a fool, and no fool can trade well!"

Silence once more.

Finally, Garth Morely said, "It be much to ask, ladies, but my peddler's sense tells me it be a right notion. If'n we dole out rum as a gift—*after* the tradin's done—then a right lot o' Injuns'll flock for it." He stroked his stubbly beard. "Aye, an' they'll know they ain't ter be cheated by us, for we won't trade with 'em if they be drunk. Aye, friends. This trader be likin' it better an' better!"

For two more hours they talked and planned. They would pool their entire capital into buying the best goods from other traders at the fort. Tamano would take the goods out that winter, and he would bring back a huge harvest of furs—perhaps the only shipment that would reach Montreal the next spring. Pontiac's uprising had caused a complete halt in the fur trade, and British furriers were desperate for peltry, so the prospects for the new company were bright.

Finally they shook hands and prepared to drink a toast of Morely's choicest port. They raised glasses, knowing that all they owned would be risked in one massive shipment. Failure meant utter ruin for all of them. Success meant the start of a mercantile empire that would stretch a thousand miles from Montreal in the east to Rainy Lake in the west.

Morely said, "To dreams and a company." He held his glass higher. "To the newest company on the frontier!"

Sutherland said, "To the frontier company!"

It was a good name—the Frontier Company. It was the name for a bold adventure, the vanguard of a new era in the great northwest . . . if the Indians did not rise again.

chapter **3**

GOING ON

At dusk Peter Defries limped warily out of the trees and approached Fort Niagara. He was cold, wet, and miserable, and his right knee ached badly. Twice he had almost been caught by war parties scouring the woods.

The big stone fort seemed deserted. For an instant, he feared it had fallen, but a sentry called down from the wall near the main gate, and the sally port was opened. Defries was brought to the regimental surgeon to have his injured knee firmly bandaged. He was anxious to tell his story, but the officer of the day and the surgeon knew even more than he did. The sergeant commanding the teamsters' escort had escaped on horseback to warn the doomed detachment of light infantry, which also was wiped out almost to a man. Word of these attacks had come in to the fort's commander, Major John Wilkins; he and most of the garrison had gone out to meet the enemy.

When the garrison returned before dark, gloom deeper than twilight shrouded Niagara. Defries found the major in a small candlelit office that overlooked the lake. The man was haggard and dismal, his face drawn, eyes so dark that candlelight failed to penetrate.

Wilkins's voice quivered on the verge of breaking. "More than a hundred and twenty men are dead or missing. And not a single Seneca to be found from here to Devil's Hole."

Defries said carefully, "Sir, there was a drummer boy from the escort—"

Wilkins, removing his wig to reveal short brown hair, sighed and seemed to recover somewhat. "Well, then, my friend, there is some good news for you. Drummer Tom Kirk was found alive at the bottom of the gorge. He was trapped on some driftwood, half-dead. But he's all right now . . ." The major's voice faded, and he gazed out the open window at the blackness. "He's all right . . . I only wish this—this had never hap—"

The strain of having lost half his small command in a few hours was too much for him. The major was speaking softly to himself. "This uprising is far from over . . . far from it."

"I'm afraid you're right, sir," Defries agreed. Hesitantly he continued, "Major, I'm sorry to have to put this to you now, but there's a small matter of my compensation for the goods I brought to the upper landing."

Wilkins looked at him blankly. Then he said, "Yes. Yes, my man, life goes on, does it not? Life goes on . . . you must be paid . . ." Then the shaken officer sighed again and gathered his senses. He took a piece of paper from the drawer of his desk and dipped the quill in the inkwell.

Wilkins wrote quickly, and his voice sounded stronger but more brittle. "Life goes on . . . What did you say your name was?"

Peter told him, and he finished writing, sprinkled sand on the letter, and folded it. He applied the sealing wax, then said gruffly:

"Life goes on, and you will have to go on for your money, my friend. This is a letter warranting receipt of your precious goods. Take it up to Montreal, and—"

"Montreal?" Peter was dismayed. Montreal was hundreds of miles away; going there first would double the distance to his ultimate destination—Albany.

Wilkins glowered at him. "Yes, Montreal! We don't have that kind of money lying around here! The paymaster there will see to it you get what's coming to you." He began to address the letter, saying with a sneer, "Too bad the families of those poor fellows you hired won't see any of the money. Well, that's not my business—"

"What do you mean by that?" Defries had every intention of paying the families of the dead men; many of them had been friends. His fists clenched as he stared at the major.

Wilkins refused to look up at him. He held the letter out, and said only, "Life goes on."

Defries snatched up the letter. "I'll pay all of them, Major," he said. "Which is a sight better than the army would do in the same circumstances!"

He wheeled and slammed the door as he left the room. Peter Defries despised the attitude of officers like Wilkins, who looked down on the rest of the world, particularly on American provincials. But supplying the army was the trade he knew best, and he was well on his way to making himself extremely successful at it—despite his dislike of smug officers.

As he limped through the courtyard of the fort, his leg aching, he thought about Montreal. He knew that city well enough, having been there a number of times on supply trains for the British army. There were plenty of pretty, willing women there, and he had developed a taste for French brandy. Being in Montreal would not be so bad, but how long would it take for the paymaster to get around to paying him? Would he have time to get back to Albany before winter set in?

There would be more military contracts soon, and he wanted to be ready. He intended to visit his mentor, Sir William Johnson, to learn about any planned campaign against the hostiles. There was a fortune to be made supplying that army.

First to Montreal, by boat. There he would see a good doctor to get his leg attended to. A man couldn't trek through the wilderness if his leg went bad, and Defries intended to do a lot of trekking at the head of the greatest baggage convoys the northwest territory had ever seen.

The meeting at the Morely trading house had gone on through supper. It was still going on when Angélique and Ella tired of it. The Morely boys, both about the same age as Jeremy, were bundled off to bed, and Jeremy, who had been playing with them, left with his mother and Angélique.

They went outside into the crisp, bracing evening air. The fort was dark and quiet now; faint strains of a cheerful fiddle drifted on the wind. Here and there yellow light shone at windows, and the world was peaceful beneath a starry sky.

As they strolled down the street, Ella asked her friend a question that had been turning in her mind for some time.

"Angélique, exactly how dangerous is it for the British to go into the Indian villages now?"

The Frenchwoman glanced at Ella, realizing why she had asked. Though Sutherland had not said he would go out with

Tamano against the regulations of the British administration, both Ella and Angélique knew that Sutherland's status as an adopted Ottawa might justify his breaking that rule, and there was the distinct possibility he might try just that.

Angélique thought a moment before saying, "It is very dangerous—for *some* British." She paused, then said, "Do not worry about your man; he will go out if he likes, danger or not."

Ella nodded, still looking at the dark ground. They walked past a window where soldiers were laughing, playing cards, and drinking. From the room they heard the squeal of a woman's voice and more laughter from both men and women. Ella pushed the curious Jeremy ahead, then thought once more about her question.

She said, "I can see that whoever gets to the Indians first will get the best pelts and the best prices, but wouldn't it be better to wait until it's safe? I mean, what is it all worth if—if someone is . . . ?"

Angélique touched her arm, saying softly, "Ella, you know the kind of man you married. Mr. Morely is that way, and so is my father—and so is . . ."

Ella waited for her to go on, but Angélique merely sighed and looked away for a moment. Ella had heard of the girl's infatuation with a dashing young Frenchman, but the fellow was said to have joined Pontiac and to be fighting as a renegade now. Certainly that was reason enough for Angélique to hesitate.

Then Angélique sniffed and turned back, the light from a nearby window showing a tear in her eye. But her voice was steady. "Ella, if they were the kind of men to wait until all danger was past, they would not be where they are. And perhaps your man would not have won you, eh?"

Ella smiled and the two friends linked arms.

Angélique went on. "In this country, a woman must fight sometimes to keep her man, and sometimes she must fight at his side to survive. There are times when she has to oppose him because she knows he is wrong—but she must never oppose him simply because what he wants to do is dangerous. No. Remember that, Ella. There isn't much out here that is not, one way or another, dangerous."

• • •

They parted at Angélique's door, and she entered her own temporary home. In normal times, the Martines lived in a grand house outside the fort, but because it was in the no-man's-land between the Indians and the fort, they had been forced to take refuge in this small cabin. Angélique had not been involved in any transactions between her father and the army during the siege, but she suspected that the rumors were true—that her father had secretly supplied Major Gladwin's troops with food. That fact, Angélique presumed, was another good reason for moving to the fort, where the soldiers could protect them against any Indian reprisal.

She closed the front door and walked in darkness toward the narrow stairs to her garret bedroom. Quickly she climbed the creaking steps. She would go right to bed, but her mind was full of the day's talk, and she doubted that sleep would come soon.

She was excited about the company, not only because it was a sound and wonderful plan, but also because it would incorporate many of the best French and *métis* in the country as partners. Since the British victory in 1760, life for the French had been a struggle. The British governor had tried to bring them into their rightful place alongside the British coming to Canada from overseas and from the colonies, but it was difficult. The newcomers had the money and the political control. The French economy had been in a shambles for years, even before the end of the war. People were hungry and forlorn, and daring ventures such as the Frontier Company were needed to revive French hope and economic strength. A powerful trading company of mixed partnership was the best way Angélique knew of guaranteeing the French a voice in government and society.

As she entered her room she heard a scuffling noise in the darkness, likely a mouse. She stopped near the cabinet where the tinderbox lay. The noise came again. This time, she knew it was no mouse. She felt a presence. She turned slowly. Her breathing stopped. She eased backwards to the open door, making hardly a sound.

"Angélique."

She gasped, her hand to her mouth. Fear flooded away, but anguish mingling with joy filled her. "Jacques! *Mon dieu*, Jacques!"

He was with her, arms around her, holding her against him,

and she trembled. The voices of drunks singing in the street drifted up to them, and the fiddler was now playing a melancholy tune. Angélique held Jacques Levesque close, and she wished from the bottom of her heart that their lives had been different, that they could have let their love blossom. But it had been only a wonderful promise until the past spring, when Pontiac called on all Frenchmen to join his war band and fight the hated English. Jacques had gone, and now he was hunted, with a price on his head. Angélique had not seen him for two months, since just before she and her father abandoned their house for the fort. Jacques had spoken privately with her father then, and she suspected it had been to warn Martine of Pontiac's plan to punish him for helping the British.

"Mon dieu, mon dieu," Angélique murmured as he held her, his arms lean and hard, his breath coming quick like hers. "You should not be here, Jacques. My father will be home soon. You must—you must go!"

"I came to talk with you, Angélique."

In the darkness, she could see only the glint of his eyes. She reached out and touched his face. There was a beard now, and she felt what seemed to be a scar on his forehead. He was only twenty-six, but his voice sounded old as he said, "I am going away."

She kissed his face, losing herself for just a moment in her love for this man.

He wrapped his arms around her. She trembled again, and he caressed her hair, kissing her neck and cheek until she calmed down. It was no surprise to hear that Jacques would leave the country—but to hear it from him, and to hear it while in his arms . . .

In the faint light from the garret window they sat down together on the edge of her bed. She was careful now not to touch him, for she knew that she was weak in his presence, and she was a virgin. Angélique Martine would keep herself for the man she loved, the man she married. How she wished it could have been Levesque!

For a full happy year he had courted her, and they were in love. Both of them had seen much of the world. He had worked for her father in the illegal trade with Albany starting as long ago as 1750, when he was just a boy. It was then that he, like the Martines, had learned to speak English.

The war began in 1755, and a year later, Jacques had left

the merchant house to fight against the British. He had been
an officer at the great battles of Ticonderoga and Oswego, a
brave and honest commander who rose rapidly to become captain of provincial troops. But the French defeat had embittered
him. He escaped from the fall of Montreal with a band of
western Indian allies, and he had continued to fight until out-
posts like Detroit were surrendered to the British without a shot
in 1760. After the war Jacques was recognized as a leader
among the *voyageurs,* and he had been ready to step into Jean
Martine's company as first assistant. Jean had been proud,
then, to call him the future husband of his daughter—but all
that had changed.

For the three years between 1760 and 1763 Jacques had
struggled within himself, trying to make peace with the British,
but he could not. Pontiac called, and he answered along with
scores of other brash and wild young men. In the first years
after the fall of Canada, Jean Martine had encouraged Levesque
to start again. But this past spring, when Levesque could not
abandon his hope that the French empire would send armies
to reconquer his homeland, Martine lost his temper and told
the young man whom he cared so much for to leave and never
see Angélique again.

Angélique loved him. She would have gone away with
him—anywhere. But Levesque intended to stay in the northwest, to join the warriors, to fight on. That, Angélique could
not accept, and she had rejected him, though it crushed her
innocence and her youthful exuberance.

Yet here he was once more. She had not seen him in much
too long. She knew again how fiercely she loved him.
Angélique sat on the bed, waiting for him to speak, willing to
join him once and for all. If . . . if he would give up his crazy
dream. Had he learned yet that a peace treaty had been signed
in Paris between the British and the French? Could he admit
finally that the rumors of returning French armies were the talk
of fools and belligerent zealots?

She prayed that his hands were not covered with English
blood. She knew he was no murderer, but she also knew the
warlike ways of the Indians, and she had heard that many
French had cooperated in their savage cruelty. She thought all
these things, yet she would not ask. It was for Jacques to speak
first.

When he did, his voice was hoarse and hesitant. "I am

leaving—for the winter, Angélique. I leave tonight. Ah, Angélique, how I wish I could see your face!"

They held hands, and she kissed his. He went on: "Come with me, my love."

Angélique trembled again and whispered, "Where?"

"South to the Illinois country."

"That is British territory now, Jacques. They will find you there, too."

His voice was angry suddenly, and it shocked her. "It is French! Until the British bring the troops to take it from us, it will remain French! And the day will come when loyal Frenchmen will take back what is theirs instead of—"

"Stop! Please stop, Jacques!" She let go of his hands.

"Come with me, Angélique!"

"To New Orleans? Then, yes, oh, yes! I'll go there with you! Tell me we'll begin again there, and we'll have babies and love and happiness—and no more, no more war!" She whispered, "Tell me, promise me, no more war and no more death, Jacques."

He stared out the small window at the night sky.

"Tell me that, please." She took his hands again.

Levesque looked back at her. "I can't say that, Angélique. I have begun something, and it will be finished, one way or—"

"And what shall I do, if it is the other way? What shall I do with your child in my womb with you lying—"

"This is my homeland!" he said, too loudly. "This," he went on more quietly, "is our country. It is the land of my fathers, and it was ours before the Redcoats came, and it will be my children's country after the Redcoats are driven out!"

Angélique did not respond. She had heard him like this before.

Levesque said, "I don't want hot swamps like the people who were driven out of Acadia to New Orleans before us! I don't want the mud of a tidal flat! I want the lakes, the forest where a man can hunt and be free! Don't you understand?"

Both of them were silent.

He asked, "Do you love me?"

Her voice broke. "So very much!"

"Then come with me!" He was on his knees before her, holding tightly to her hands.

"To fight in an Indian war?"

"Not an Indian war!"

"It is an Indian war!" she cried out, not caring who heard. Then, realizing the danger for Jacques if he were caught, she went on more softly. "Jacques, my father will come! If the British knew you were here..." She could not bring herself to say they might hang him.

Levesque stood up slowly. "It is more than an Indian war, Angélique. It is a war against the invader."

Once more she did not respond. He touched her chin and lifted it until they could vaguely see one another.

Carefully, she said, "The great war is over, Jacques. Can't you see that?"

He took his hand from her chin. "I only see how you and your father are living as servants of the Engli—"

She stood up and smacked his face hard, a stinging blow. Then she was in his arms again, sobbing and shaking. "Don't say that ever again! Please!" After a moment, she pushed back from him and said, "Canada needs you! You have to return to us! Come back and face the authorities. Make a new beginning. Your people need men like you."

He turned away from her, going to the window. "Do not ask me to accept defeat." She sat down uselessly on the bed again, her face in her hands. He said grimly, "I will not accept defeat until I am totally defeated. Until—"

"Until you are dead!" She did not look up, but spoke through her hands covering her face. He sat down on the bed beside her. They had little time left. She gathered herself and said in a quavering voice, "I cannot go with you unless you swear our children will live in peace. Promise me that, Jacques." He gazed through the dimness at her, and she implored him: "Promise me that, and I will go with you now, anywhere you say!"

They heard footsteps in the street. Her father. The door handle rattled, and he came inside the house. It was dark, so he must presume she was sleeping.

Jacques was on his feet, soundless as a cat.

Angélique rose, the boards creaking underfoot so that her father called up, and she cried good night to him. He walked heavily to his chamber, for he had drunk too much English beer that exuberant day.

"Until we meet again," Jacques whispered and held her close.

Then he was gone, through the window, where a cold wind fluttered at the light curtains.

Owen Sutherland returned to his cabin late that night. In the small, rough room, a single candle burned near the bed where Ella lay watching him as he took off his shirt. Nearby, Jeremy slept soundly in his trundle bed.

Sutherland came in beside Ella and kissed her. "You've had a long day," he whispered. "I thought you would have gone home much sooner than you did. Are you so interested in the fur trade, then?"

"Yes," she replied and kissed him back. "Even more than I expected I would be. Talking with Angélique shows me that a woman can do much in the trade."

He yawned and lay down. He looked thoughtfully at her and said, "You can learn a lot from Angélique; she knows all there is to know about keeping accounts, ordering goods, and helping Jean decide where and when to sell his peltry. One day you can go with her to Montreal and see that end of the business."

Sutherland warmed to the subject and began explaining how furs were sorted by type and quality, and baled for shipment to Montreal or Philadelphia or Albany. Canoes did most of the freighting, but he envisioned a day when successful traders would own small sloops or even schooners to haul goods all the way from Stinking Bay—the one sometimes called Green Bay—on Lake Michigan to Niagara and on to distant Montreal in the east.

"Aye," Sutherland continued, "but the people who manage the company's storehouses and offices are just as important as the traders in the Indian villages—"

"As long as they know what the traders in the villages need and what conditions they're facing."

"Yes. You'll be able to learn all that by asking questions, by listening to traders talk, and—"

"By going with you into the woods."

The candle crackled as a moth struck the flame and fell to the floor. Jeremy's breathing sounded loud in the quiet room. Sutherland looked at his wife, and she held his eyes until he looked away at the ceiling.

"So," he said thoughtfully. "You want to go into the woods with me."

Ella leaned up on one elbow and said, "I do. If I'm to understand the trade thoroughly, I have to see firsthand what it's all about, don't I?"

He turned on his side away from her without answering.

"Well?" Ella pressed. "Don't I? Is there any other way, really . . . ? Owen! Do you hear?"

The reply was a snore.

Ella shook him, knowing he was teasing her, but she was determined to have it out with him.

She slapped his bare arm. "Owen!" He snorted and snored louder. "Owen Sutherland!" She bit him hard on his shoulder, and he yelped and caught her roughly, pulling her over to him. She laughed in spite of her annoyance and found herself kissing him and struggling playfully. Then she fought him off and sat up, looking to see if Jeremy had been awakened. But the boy continued to sleep soundly.

"Listen," Ella said firmly but softly, "I mean what I say. Don't tease me in this, or—or I won't forgive you!"

He took her hand and kissed it. "I understand." He tried to think of some way to tell her that she was not made for the wilderness, that she did not realize how hard it could be, how ruthless and merciless. Sutherland knew she would not give up this idea easily.

"Owen, I want to come out with you. That way I'll learn more in one trading season than I would in ten years of staying at the post. And—and there's more than that to why I want to come."

She bit her lip and looked away at the flickering candle. He reached up and brushed her hair back, caressing her neck.

She said in a rush, "I don't want to have you go out and never come back to me. I want to be with you!" She looked at him and kissed his hand. "I want to be with you now, when it's so dangerous out there! I won't stay home and let you die . . . alone."

His fingers touched her cheek. He was thinking of how she had lost one husband whom she had loved dearly, and he knew now why she was so insistent on going into the wild with him.

Sutherland said gently, "Lass, life out there is hard. It's something you've never experienced before. It can break a strong man, and you—"

"I can learn!"

He was angry. "I don't want it to break *you!*"

"Give me that chance! Don't be so sure it will break me!"

Sutherland sat up. "Look, Ella, the wilderness isn't anything like the poems the naturalists are writing! It isn't anything at all like their charming realm of sweetness and innocence! The Indians aren't noble savages any more than you and I are great crusaders for a divine cause! They're people, just like us! The forest is just that—a forest! It's deep and it's dark. And it's dangerous if you know it, deadly if you don't!"

"I said I can learn!"

"You don't have to learn!"

Jeremy stirred and turned over, and Ella lowered her voice.

"I do have to learn! You say you understand what I'm feeling. Well, then, if you do, you'll admit that it's my place to go with you!"

"Ella . . ." He was exasperated now, and he lay back, staring straight up. "The wilderness is no place for a woman like you—"

"Mayla went with you!"

He looked at her in surprise, in guarded dismay. She wished she had not referred to the Ottawa woman whose death had nearly crushed him. The pain of Mayla's memory still smote him, and he was at a loss for words.

Ella took a shaking breath and looked away. "I'm sorry," she said softly. She faced him, but he was staring at a dark corner of the room. She touched his shoulder. He was like stone. "Owen."

He looked back at her. After a moment he said, "It means everything that you want to come with me." He saw the love in her eyes, and he touched her face. "We can talk more about this tomorrow, if you insist. But mark me, Ella, I won't risk your life in the forest. You're no Indian woman, and you never will be. I didn't marry you to make you an Indian woman. I don't want you any different than what you are, not for what you think you should become."

He stared at her until she said, "What I become, my darling, is for me to decide."

Sutherland smiled a little and slid his hand behind her neck again. "And who goes on my trading expeditions is for me to decide—"

She cut him short, hurling herself upon him and kissing him

eagerly. He responded, and she whispered, "I don't want to argue the day after our wedding. Let's wait at least another day, like respectable folk."

He laughed softly. He pushed her back and blew out the candle, ignoring for the moment that Ella was just as stubborn as he.

chapter **4**

TROUBLE IN
PENNSYLVANIA

Long before dawn Sutherland lay awake. Beside him, Ella slept soundly. He thought of all that had been discussed at Morely's yesterday, of the plans for the new Frontier Company, and he smiled at how ambitious they were. Those plans could work if the right people carried them through; and he had the right people in Morely, Martine, Angélique—and beautiful Ella. They would only work, however, if certain other conditions were just right, including the ending of the Indian war with Pontiac and the recognition once and for all by his followers that their best course lay in coming to terms with British rule. Their only hope was in exercising power diplomatically through economic ties with the British, and spurning all efforts of rebellious French to keep them fighting.

Next summer would be critical for the Indians of the northwest—indeed, of all North America. Plans were being made even now for the British army, led by such proven commanders as Colonel John Bradstreet and Colonel Henry Bouquet, to come to the wilderness, to force the Indians to give up their white hostages and to compel them to attend Sir William Johnson's peace council.

Sutherland and his friends were on the right path as long as the Indians were peaceful, the direct trade in the villages was reopened, and the company's limited funds were not squandered through error or mishap. The others would trust his judgment at the start, but if anything went wrong—trade goods lost somehow, or peltry stolen by hostiles—there would be no way to recover their losses. The company would go under as soon as it was founded.

Tamano would go north and west when winter began, and there he would trade. He would return with his harvest, and Sutherland would see that it reached Montreal before anyone else brought pelts out of the lake country. The first furs down to the city would get high prices. He could demand enough from eager merchants to put the Frontier Company on a strong, solid footing. At the same time he would establish a good business relationship with the top fur merchants in Montreal— or Albany if the Montreal merchants were not cooperative. But he was determined to establish an office in Montreal, and he knew who might serve well as the firm's agent there: Mary Hamilton.

He thought about Mary for a moment, recalling how she had impressed him with her inner strength last summer when he had encountered her during the return of Indian prisoners at Fort Pitt. She was the daughter of a trader murdered by the Indians, and the sweetheart of Sutherland's close friend, Duncan McEwan. McEwan, an ensign in the Royal Americans, had been killed in the fighting, but he had left Mary pregnant and she had gone up to Montreal. For the sake of the girl and her baby, and because of his close attachment to McEwan, Sutherland intended to ask her to take charge of the Frontier Company's Montreal operations. She was experienced in the trade, and through her father's reputation she had connections with the English and provincial merchants dealing in that city. Yes, Mary Hamilton might be just right as the new company's agent—although, as a woman, she would have to struggle that much harder to establish herself.

Sutherland felt more positive than ever about his plans. They would be novel and dynamic, and by the time others caught on to the idea, there would be no overtaking the Frontier Company. Its network of trappers and traders, *voyageurs* and suppliers, would challenge even the long-established Hudson's Bay Company, which was chartered by the king to trade in the far north.

He rose and dressed in his woodsman's clothes—a linsey shirt under a fringed doeskin hunting smock, light breeches beneath buckskin leggins. He slipped on his moccasins and went outside into the predawn darkness. The fort was stirring, and the guard near the water gate was changing. He breathed deeply; the wind had turned around to the southeast, bringing the scent of rain. A detachment of sentries marched past, the ensign in command giving him a polite nod, and Sutherland bade them good morning.

He was content with his world, happy as never before. He was anxious to get out into the backcountry soon. As Ella had suspected, Owen meant to do some of the trading himself. Except that it meant leaving Ella for weeks and months at a time, the life of roving the forests, meeting danger and adventure every day, thrilled him.

Sutherland gazed up at the sky, a pale reddish haze burnishing the eastern horizon, the rest still dark blue and starless. Inside the cabin, Ella stirred and called his name. The scent of woodsmoke, the aroma of someone cooking bacon, came to him, and he felt hungry.

Back in the cabin, he sat on the bed next to Ella. She had fallen asleep again, and he saw once more how remarkably lovely she was. Her high cheekbones, large eyes, and wispy but full hair that never obeyed her brush . . . It would be difficult to go into the forest and leave her behind, but surely she must grasp the reality of things.

He thought of how he would one day build a big white house at Valenya, on a slope overlooking the river. That dream would be given form in time. Ella would get over this urge to prove herself in the wilderness. She would love to have a house like that, where she could raise the children and play her spinet to her heart's content. Ella came from the English upper class, and life in a fine house was right for her, whether she admitted it or not.

She stirred and moved close to him, taking his hand in her sleep. It would be a good life, and soon he would not need to go into the forests for very long—just enough to please himself and to teach his children about life out there. Then he could turn to other things—to his poetry, to reading and scholarship. There were so many new ideas abroad in the world these days. Even out here in the wild he had heard of Voltaire, Rousseau, Benjamin Franklin, and Samuel Johnson. Their ideas and philosophies fascinated him.

In the coffeehouses of Europe and America, thinking men were changing the world. It was the age of reason, some said; reason was triumphing over old bigotry, ignorance, and fear. People were thinking for themselves, reshaping man's understanding of the universe and nature.

Sutherland felt restless again, and he went to the door of the cabin. For a fleeting moment, the fort and even the wilderness seemed confining, restricting, without the inspiration of educated genius that other cultured men encountered in the coffeehouses and universities. Yet Sutherland had many close friends out here, and he would never exchange one of them for an intellectual who could not put grand theories to use in real life. To him, an Indian following the trail of a wounded buck was philosopher, magician, and hero all in one. The soldier who risked his life for his comrades, the women who brought up children to be honest and strong in the face of massacre and warfare, meant more to him than an army of clever intellectuals.

But on this chilly morning, he felt the need for another inquiring mind, one that was kindred with his own. He wanted to talk about the clouds, the stars, the wind from the southeast that brought rain. He longed to hear more about Ben Franklin's remarkable experiments that linked lightning and electricity. And what were the fundamental, natural rights of a man? Did God give kings a divine right to rule? What did that mean? Did that question really matter anymore? Did King George really believe that it was his God-given right to tax Americans in the American provinces? Or was that Parliament's right? And what was an American? Was an American British, or was he different? Different, probably. Were these British soldiers Americans in their hearts, even though they were here by order and not by choice? Were Indians Americans? And what about Owen Sutherland?

He shook his head to clear it, and chuckled softly. Yes, all these questions and many more often tumbled in his mind on those long canoe trips and on the endless trails. They were questions that men and women like Sutherland were asking all over Europe and in the colonies. Sutherland had Henry Gladwin to talk with, and Gladwin was deep and well educated. But when it came to philosophical questions, to the subtler values, there Henry Gladwin was languid, uninterested.

Ella, like her brother, did not enjoy theorizing and philosophizing. With her optimism and serenity, she seemed, to Sutherland, to be above such things. Still, like her husband, who wrote poetry to relieve the inner struggles, Ella needed a respite from everyday cares. For that she had the blessed gift of music. Whenever it suited Ella, she would go down to the big council house and play the spinet Henry had put there for her.

Sutherland went back inside. She was sitting up, holding the covers to her breasts, watching him. The glow of a red dawn tinted the room. He smiled and so did she. For all his thinking and puzzling about life, Sutherland could find rest with Ella, find a certain peace and tranquillity that even Mayla had not brought him. Now he understood as he gazed at her that Ella gave something special to him—some kind of comprehension that life need not be as complicated as he sometimes made it.

"What are you thinking?" Ella asked.

He smiled and came to her and sat on the bed. "How many children we'll have."

"Oh? How many, then?"

Still smiling, he said, "Three more than Jeremy."

She quickly calculated, then said, "If we have one each year, I'll be thirty-five with the last one. Isn't that a bit old?"

"All right, only two more. A boy and a girl."

"Well, perhaps we'll need an extra girl to keep the boys in hand."

"We'd better get started, then," he said.

The following week, the schooner *Huron* sailed up the straits to Detroit with a contingent of soldiers as replacements for the garrison, with supplies, and with the post. This recent trip to Niagara and back was the first that either of Fort Detroit's two supply ships had made in the past five months without encountering any hostiles during the voyage—although the men on board had been vigilant every mile of the way.

Well before the *Huron*'s cargo of foodstuffs and ammunition was unloaded, the mail was distributed to the civilians at Morely's trading house. Military expresses were delivered to Gladwin, who immediately sent an orderly to fetch Owen Sutherland.

When Sutherland entered the commander's whitewashed clapboard house facing the parade ground, he saw his friend sitting at a desk, his expression strained. Gladwin had intended to turn over command of the fort and return to England this fall, but Pontiac's uprising had changed that. He would not be able to go home to his wife until winter was over and a replacement was found for him. But something else was clearly troubling Gladwin, and apparently it had to do with Sutherland.

"Sit down, please, Owen," Gladwin said, looking up and motioning to a chair beside the desk. "We have a whole new development here." The major handed over a letter that bore the wax seal of Colonel Henry Bouquet.

It was addressed to Sutherland. Before he broke the seal, he asked, "Do you know what's in this?"

Gladwin nodded. "Colonel Bouquet sent me a copy. But read it first, then we'll talk."

As Sutherland read the letter, he understood why Gladwin was uneasy. The major knew Sutherland wanted nothing more to do with military affairs, but this letter was an urgent request for Sutherland's assistance in the province of Pennsylvania.

Bouquet was in command of the military's Pennsylvania and Ohio Valley department, and as such was responsible for protecting Philadelphia and the scores of vulnerable settlements west of the city. Last summer at Bushy Run, Bouquet had been successful—with Sutherland's help—in putting down the massed forces of hostile Indians. Demoralized, the Indians could not now put a large, coordinated group of warriors into the field. But they still were spilling blood ruthlessly up and down the Pennsylvania frontier from Fort Pitt on the Ohio all the way to villages just outside Philadelphia itself.

As a result, the backwoodsmen were up in arms; some had sworn to drive out or kill every Indian within reach. But the strongest political force in the province was the pacifist Quakers, so Pennsylvania was slow in approving fighting men to patrol the borderlands, where the population was Presbyterian. A further complication was a struggle between Pennsylvania's governor and the majority of the people. The governor represented the Penn family, which ruled the province by charter from the king. The people wanted to get rid of the Penns and rule themselves without the restrictions imposed by a family that saw the province as a business rather than as a democratic community.

The result was a state near civil war, according to Bouquet's letter.

". . . because of the unnatural obstinacy of the government of Pennsylvania, which has refused to produce troops and supplies, the entire burden of this war falls upon us, the regulars. As a former soldier yourself, Mr. Sutherland, you well understand how difficult it is for troops to defend the border counties against an enemy who chooses where and when to strike.

"As a frontiersman, sir, you also know how much hatred exists between whites and Indians in this country, further complicating the army's duty of determining whether the continuous hostilities are being perpetrated by whites or Indians. You see, Mr. Sutherland, we face the unfortunate prospect of having a number of peaceful Indian communities wiped out utterly!

"Forces of borderers—otherwise brave and honest folk— are gathering to strike a terrible blow at the hundreds of peaceful Indians who live among us. Already, several families have been attacked in the night and murdered cruelly, children included. We face the obliteration of a whole society of peaceful, often Christian Indians unless someone can stop the borderers.

"Yes, Mr. Sutherland, Bouquet is calling upon you once again, but it is not a call made routinely or without sober reflection, for I know you, and I realize how reluctant you must be to go so far from your home again to risk your life. But, sir, you are well known among the borderers ever since your glorious success leading them at Bushy Run, and I believe a man with your abilities can influence them, can reason with them, and compel them to return to their cabins instead of attacking innocent Indians whom they unjustly accuse of doing them ill. It is with the greatest reluctance, but also with the utmost urgency, that once again I seek your assistance in this dark time."

His heart sinking, Sutherland read on. Bouquet was obliged to leave Philadelphia in late autumn to attend to military matters at headquarters in New York. He would be away for some time, making plans for the next summer's campaigns, when Pontiac would no doubt return to the warpath. Bouquet was thus counting on Sutherland's knowledge of the borderers— most of whom had Scottish blood—and on his willingness to place himself between them and the peaceful Indians if attempts to reason failed.

"A mob has threatened to march on the city of Philadelphia itself," Bouquet's letter went on. "Believe me when I say that such a calamity is in the making at this very moment. The borderers despise the Philadelphia Quakers and accuse them of loving the Indians more than they care for the borderers (which may be true). If this rioting and murdering is not stopped, it will lead to civil war and bloodshed. In New York, I hope to convince our new commander in chief, General Thomas Gage, to give me the troops I need to defend the city.

"If you accept this responsibility, please send by the next post a confirmation to the Honorable Dr. Benjamin Franklin, who awaits your reply as my representative and your host in Philadelphia."

Franklin! Of everything Bouquet had written, only one thing had inspired Sutherland, and that was the line declaring that Franklin himself awaited his reply.

Gladwin interrupted his brother-in-law's thoughts. "Colonel Bouquet asked me to do all in my power to persuade you to go to Philadelphia." He leaned forward a little. "I don't like having to sway you in this, Owen. I know what you have done already, and I want only happiness for you and Ella."

Sutherland sighed and sat up. "I've heard about Pennsylvania's difficulties governing itself. Their elected assembly can't clean the streets without permission from the Penns. No money, no way to fight the Indians—and the borderers have suffered, I know, because I saw it this summer."

No Pennsylvania militia had been called up because of the political infighting. The borderers sent out their own patrols, built small forts here and there, and fought a bitter, dirty war against an enemy who kept them in constant fear. The same thing had happened years earlier in the French and Indian War, when the assembly and the governor had struggled over the means of organizing a military force that was slow in coming to the aid of the settlers under attack. At one point, borderers loaded a wagon with their dead kinfolk and marched through the streets of Philadelphia before the government did anything to counter Indian raids.

"There's other bad news, Owen," Gladwin said. "The commander of Fort Niagara sent a dispatch on the *Huron* to inform me that a detachment of army regulars and teamsters was massacred by Seneca near a place called Devil's Hole."

So despite Pontiac's truce and the coming of winter, the Indian uprising was still in force! It seemed there would never be peace in North America until, one way or another, the Indians were conquered, once and for all.

Sutherland got up slowly, folding Bouquet's letter and slipping it into his fringed shirt. "I'll talk to Ella about all of this, Henry." He turned to leave.

Gladwin said quickly, "Bouquet has dispatched an officer and an escort to Fort Pitt in anticipation of your arrival there . . . if you go, of course. And I'll send an escort along as far as Pitt."

Sutherland looked his brother-in-law in the eye, then Gladwin said, "Listen, Owen, I won't let even you—adopted Ottawa or no—go out to trade with the villages against regulations this winter, so you can get that straight. If you go, it's my duty to fine you and take your license away, just as I would anyone else; friend or not. So if you don't go to Philadelphia, be prepared to play a hell of a lot of chess with me this winter."

Sutherland knew Gladwin was making a strong point in favor of Bouquet's summons. Before leaving, Sutherland said with a wry smile, "Jeremy's learning how to play chess. *He'll* keep me amused all winter, if need be. He can almost beat me already."

When Sutherland told Ella about the letter, she did not know what to say at first. He had found her in the commandant's garden, where the vegetables and flowers had withered, save for a few of the marigolds that had served to brighten Ella's marriage garb. Without answering, Ella knelt to dig out a tulip bulb that was too close to the surface and needed replanting. Her hands shook a little as she wielded the trowel, and she split the bulb in her clumsiness.

"Now look what I've done!" she muttered to herself, wiping her face so that the dirt streaked her cheek. Owen knelt at her side and took her hands in his. She smiled shakily and rubbed dirt from her fingers, dropping the bulb. He picked it up.

He said, "I intend to go, but I'll be back well before the end of winter. I have to be here when Tamano comes in with the furs. Then I'll take them east to Montreal."

"You'll come back through the snow?" she asked, taking short breaths as she spoke. "How can you come back all that way through the dead of winter, and then go out to Montreal?"

"I have a way. The Indians in the north country use sleds and dogs to travel in the winter. I'll arrange for a team of dogs and a sled to be taken down to Fort Pitt. The commander there can ship them right to Philadelphia. I can leave Philadelphia anytime I want, in any kind of weather with sled dogs and snowshoes!"

In Massachusetts, Ella had seen Indians with sleds, and

many white trappers used them farther north, she had heard. But few of the tribes of the northwest had more than two or three dogs to pull their sleds, and they seldom traveled farther than their line of traps. Owen's idea was a good one, and when he said the army would have to pay for the dogs, sled, and their shipment or he would not answer Bouquet's call, she realized that he very well could return in winter. But she still feared for his life, stepping into this dangerous conflict in Pennsylvania.

She looked closely at him, wishing he would not go, knowing she could not ask him to stay here for her sake. "Do what you think is right, darling. Whatever you decide."

Sutherland thought of something, then he rejected the idea. Then he considered it once more. The plan might be foolhardy, but he knew Ella was serious when she said she wanted to go into the wilderness with him.

He tossed the tulip bulb up and down. "If I said you could never come into the woods with me, what would you do?"

She looked at him a little sharply, wondering what he was getting at. "Are you saying that with finality?"

"No." He rose. "But if I did?"

"Owen." She was exasperated, and stood up. "I'd find a way to learn. I'd go with someone who would teach me, and you could never refuse me again after I knew enough. Is that what you wanted to know? If it makes you angry, I'm sorry, but—"

He brought her face around to his. "How would you like to go with me to Philadelphia?"

Ella's eyes widened. "Owen!" she gasped, and threw her arms around his neck. "Owen, I'd love it! I mean—" She struggled to regain her composure, to make it obvious that she was not giddy, that she was aware of the gravity of what he was offering. "I'd—I'd love to. I'd—Owen! Yes!" She hugged him again, and he squeezed her close.

She said hurriedly, "You'll see. You've not made a mistake! I'll keep up, and I'll learn quickly as we go. Philadelphia! Oh, Owen!" Then her face changed from ecstasy to doubt, and she said weakly, "Philadelphia. You'll be invited to receptions, balls. There'll be gentlemen and ladies, won't there?"

"Of course! Won't that be half the fun of going there? Why, we'll be the guests of the military command, and of Dr. Franklin himself!"

Still weakly, Ella said, "Dr. Franklin." Then she looked confused. "Owen, on the journey we'll be wearing woodsman's clothes, yes? Buckskins, linseys—"

"Blanket coats, leggins—of course."

"Of course." She was struggling with something that Owen could not understand. Then she said, "But—but I can't go to the balls in—in buckskins!"

"No," Owen said solemnly, comprehending now. He stepped back, thinking hard, trying not to laugh. "The ladies and gentlemen of Philadelphia are the finest in the colonies." He shook his head. "Philadelphia's the greatest city in the British Empire, after London! No, indeed, leggins are no longer fashionable at Philadelphia balls—"

"I don't care!"

"About what?"

"About Philadelphia balls!" She carelessly rubbed dirt from her hands onto her apron. "I'm coming anyway, and you can go about your social business alone. I'll need a few weeks' rest there anyway after all that traveling through the woods!"

Sutherland laughed and pulled her against him. "Don't worry, Ella. They still have dressmakers in Philadelphia!"

chapter 5

MONTREAL

A few days later, a young woman in Montreal turned over in bed and felt the baby in her womb. It had just moved—for the first time the baby had shown itself to be real. Mary Hamilton sat up in the dimness of her small bedroom and looked down at her tummy, lifting her nightgown and touching where she had bulged so amazingly in the last four months.

The baby moved again, and Mary gave a faint exclamation, not knowing whether to be excited or afraid. She closed her eyes and tried to remain calm. For the sake of the child she would remain calm throughout her pregnancy and deliver a beautiful baby, one Duncan would have been proud of.

Tears came again, even though she fought them back. She thought of Duncan McEwan, father of the child in her womb. It seemed ages since they had met. She remembered those brief moments together when, as prisoners in a Chippewa village, they had fallen in love. It was the most terrifying and most beautiful time of Mary's life. She had conceived in that village, and Duncan had escaped, unable to take her with him. He had searched for her all over the wilderness, following Mary and the Delaware war chief who had taken her as his slave. That chief was later killed in a fight with Owen Sutherland, and after the Delaware were defeated at the battle of Bushy Run, Mary was returned to the British. But by then Duncan was already dead.

Now she was alone, for her trader father and both her brothers had been murdered by the Indians when she was first made a prisoner. Lying there in the faint luster of a gray dawn, Mary tried to block the memory of that horrible time of imprisonment with the Delaware who had tried to force her to be his wife. He had failed. She thought instead of the love she shared so briefly with Duncan. For all those weeks of captivity, she had risked her life, dared the war chief's wrath to keep herself for Duncan, only to learn at her moment of liberation that he had been lost.

Mary lay for a long time, hands on her womb, conscious of the baby. Light filtered gradually into the room, which was small but elegant: the maple panels covering the walls gleamed rich and warm in the first sunlight. She was a lodger in the home of a merchant family named Cullen, who must be very wealthy to have bought this house, one of the finest in war-ravaged Montreal. Much of that wealth, she knew, had come to the Cullens because of their dealings with her dead father. He had formed a partnership with Bradford Cullen, and had been owed some money by Cullen before being murdered by the Indians up on Lake Huron. To repay that debt, the Cullens had taken Mary in a month ago, but they had offered her little in the way of compassion or love.

A strict and austere family, the Cullens had come to Montreal from Boston soon after the French capitulated in 1760. Here they had increased their wealth by taking full advantage of the terrible famine afflicting the French, and they had also profited by selling to the soldiers the great number of necessities the army did not provide. Throughout Montreal the Cullens were despised by the French and British lower classes, who were forced to pay high prices for bread, shoes, clothing, and other essentials of life.

The Cullens were purse-pinching folk, strict adherents of the worst kind of bigoted Puritanism. They could have paid Mary off in cash—they owed her father no more than forty or fifty pounds—but they offered instead to put her up for a time, giving her room and board for the winter and spring. They did not know she was pregnant, though; if they had, she would have been thrown out into the street, to beg for what the Cullens owed her.

Mary had no bargaining power when first she came to Montreal, exhausted from her imprisonment and suffering from the anguish of losing Duncan. She had accepted their meager offer, and even signed a formal contract they drew up to make their

terms explicit and binding. She was to stay with them until
next spring as long as she lived "with the accepted moral and
social propriety worthy of her class" as the daughter of an
influential merchant. Time and again Mary regretted the arrangement. But there was nowhere else she could go.

The Cullens had been civil enough at first, though the fat
old man was stuffy and narrow-minded. Helen Cullen, the
wife, was a prune of a lady in her early fifties, ten years younger
than her husband. She was always cool and short to Mary, and
the girl suspected it was because Linda, the Cullen's only child,
who was almost twenty—the same age as Mary—was rather
homely, with thick features and a prominent nose. As jealous
as her mother of Mary's striking beauty, this dreary young
woman never missed a chance to criticize Mary, whether it
was how she wore her blond hair or how she too often was
dressed in a drab linen dress and natural wool shawl.

Mary knew Mrs. Cullen suspected that something was amiss
with her lodger. The woman had been asking about the sickness
that came on every morning—a queasiness that often compelled Mary to leave the table. For all that she tried to control
the nausea, Mary seldom lasted through breakfast. She was
fine over the tea and toast, but when Linda feasted on her
regular fare of mussels and pickled herring, Mary could not
abide the smell.

Thank heavens for Emmy, the black kitchen slave, who had
become Mary's only friend in the household. Emmy knew
Mary was pregnant. She watched each morning from the
kitchen, and when Mary got up, the maid opened the door and
let her in, handing over a bucket of water to catch her sickness.

Perhaps Mrs. Cullen might have dismissed Mary's abrupt
departure from the table at the same time each morning as a
strange, impolite habit. But the other morning, Mary had failed
to get to Emmy's pail in time. She had become sick all over
Linda's new nankeen slippers.

Mary giggled as she lay thinking about that awful but funny
morning. Linda was dumbstruck; Mrs. Cullen, shocked, had
inhaled her tea and could not speak for coughing. Through it
all, nearsighted Mr. Cullen had blustered and dithered, not
knowing whether to slap his wife's back or wipe his daughter's
feet.

The baby moved again as Mary laughed to herself. The fear
and loneliness that had awakened her were gone now. She held

her small burden between both hands. Soon it would be large.
Sometime in March the baby would be born, and no matter
what Mrs. Cullen or anyone else thought about it, the child
would be wonderful! The child would be hers, and the memory
of Duncan would live in it. Alone or not, Mary Hamilton was
glad to be with child. That was her responsibility for now, and
she accepted it.

On the floor at the foot of the bed, the mongrel Toby
stretched her legs and tail. The brown-and-white dog had awakened with Mary's quiet laughter, and she lay gazing at Mary,
waiting for the hint that they would take their morning walk
down to the waterfront. Mary spoke to Toby, who got up and
came to her, nuzzling against her arm. She, too, was a reminder
of Duncan, who had found the puppy at a burned-out British
fort in the wilderness, and had carried her while he searched
for Mary. Owen Sutherland, who had told Mary about her
lover's death, had given her Toby, who was about four or five
months old now. Toby had a pretty face, and there were moments when Mary was sure she understood her. She whined
and then backed up, about to bark.

"Ssh!" Mary said and sat up. "You'll wake them all!
Don't—"

But Toby did. She was excited, and she yelped and barked
and whined, then jumped at Mary when she stood up. Mary
grabbed her and held her still. "No, Toby! We'll go out, but
quiet!"

Toby wagged her tail, and her entire body wiggled. Mary
let her go, and she went to the door, scratching for it to be
opened. Warm sunlight fell in bright rectangles on the floor,
and Mary hurried into her linen dress, first washing up at the
pitcher and bowl on the small table near her wardrobe. Toby
stretched again and gave an impatient yip. Mary poured a glass
of minted water and rinsed her mouth, lifting a finger to the
pup. Then she snatched her starched white bonnet from a hook,
picked up her sabots—heavy French clogs—and went barefoot
out of the room to the stairs. Partway down, the urge struck
her, as it usually did at this point on the stairs, and she threw
a leg over the banister, sliding all the way down on her stomach,
feet first.

As she dropped lightly to the floor of the hallway, Mary
saw the kitchen door open, and the motherly black face of
Emmy poked out at her.

As Mary waved and opened the front door, Emmy whispered, "Missy, don't you go doin' that on them banistairs, hear? Don't go crampin' up that little one afore he's got a chance to grow! Hear?"

Mary smiled at the middle-aged servant and blew her a kiss. Slipping into her sabots, Mary waved and hurried away, closing the door softly behind her.

Emmy smiled to herself, proud of the girl's cheerfulness at such a difficult and lonely time. She shook her head and went back into the kitchen, remembering her own pregnancy and her own children. They were all gone now—dead, or sold to another master—but the memory of them was warm rather than sad; Emmy compelled herself to be that way. She thought of her motherhood and remembered those days when she was the happiest slave in all the world.

Out on the street, Mary ran with Toby at her side. Her clogs clicked on the cobblestones as she ran through a narrow side street leading to the waterfront. Men carrying bricks to repair a building damaged in the British bombardments of three years ago turned to watch her run, her blond hair flying in the breeze.

She was a beauty, and whoever saw Mary Hamilton admired her. Soldiers called to her as she passed, and aged fruit sellers pushing laden carts to market thought of younger days—when Canada was French, and women thrilled to the sight of soldiers in Bourbon white.

Mary ran a little farther, then she realized what day this was. It was the morning of her appointment with Dr. Devalier, an elderly Frenchman who spoke English and had agreed to take her as a patient. Mary stopped running, but Toby bounded ahead through the crowd near the busy waterfront. She took a deep breath. No one else in Montreal but Emmy, Devalier, and his kindly wife knew about Mary's condition. They had scheduled this examination some weeks ago, but Mary had forgotten all about it until now, when she was near the alley where he lived.

On a small chapel nearby the clock struck seven. Mary had an hour before her appointment. She would miss breakfast at home, and she had forgotten to make up some excuse so the Cullens would accept it. Well, it was just too bad if Mrs. Cullen objected to Mary's coming and going as she pleased. Now she would stroll with Toby down to the harbor to watch the ships being loaded and unloaded. Ships fascinated her. They symbolized freedom and excitement, told of travel to distant lands and of the gay adventure her father had always promised.

Toby barked at her to run, but she wanted to be clean for Dr. Devalier, so she ignored the dog, who plodded back and settled for trotting circles around her mistress as she walked.

In a whaleboat under sail in the Saint Lawrence River, Peter Defries shifted his sore leg and watched the pretty scenery passing by. With the wind at their backs, and riding with the river's current, the dozen soldiers, traders, and merchants in the boat had made excellent time in their passage toward Montreal. A mile away, the city was in view, bordering the river at the base of a sudden steep hill called Mount Royal. Located on a thirty-mile-long island in the middle of the river, Montreal had between three and four thousand French inhabitants, along with a few companies of British troops, numbering fewer than two hundred. This city was still a frontier town in many ways, unlike Quebec a couple of hundred miles downstream, a seaport that had been the capital of New France. Yet Montreal received a goodly share of important oceangoing trade, and its harbor was constantly busy.

Between the river and the heart of Montreal was a low stone wall, and behind it were a few hundred buildings of natural stone and slate roofs. All around the town were tilled fields, gardens, and orchards. As far as Defries could see on both sides of the white river, *habitant* farmhouses ran like beads on a necklace close to shore. Here and there, where streams emptied into the great Saint Lawrence, stood massive stone mills. Every few miles the spire of a small parish church rose above the dark line of conifers planted to mark the river roads.

Defries was glad his journey was almost over. The tillerman heeled the craft toward the city's docks, and another boatman prepared to haul down the sail. It had been almost a week since Defries left Niagara. He was anxious to find the military paymaster, but he was also intent on getting to a good French doctor someone had told him about. His leg troubled him; the knee was badly swollen, showing bluish from shin to thigh.

The boatman steered the craft alongside a jetty, and the men at the oars guided her in. Defries tugged on his short blue coat and took his kit bag from the floor of the boat. He wasted no time lingering about the swarming docks. It was late in the

season, and the last ships to leave Montreal before winter were
hurriedly loading. Half a dozen vessels lay at anchor in the
channel, and three more, crawling with longshoremen and sailors, were tied up at the jetties.

Defries adjusted his hat and looked longingly at the oceangoing brigs anchored like princes in the midst of lowly fishing
smacks and sloops. Painted smartly, crisply lined with white
and red trim, their pennants fluttering in the breeze, these ships
spoke to Peter as they spoke to Mary, telling of foreign cities,
and of great cargoes worth thousands of pounds. Looking across
the windy, sunny harbor, Defries wished he could send such
a ship abroad laden with his own merchandise. No, not send,
but *go* with such a ship and make the world his marketplace.
That, he thought, would be a fine life for him!

He limped along the stone jetty, looking up at the city before
him. In those first visits to Montreal, Defries had been a common teamster, feasting and spending like the others, chasing
girls and staying drunk as long as possible when there was no
work to be had.

That had changed. Now he was a businessman with responsibility to the families of the men who had died at Devil's
Hole. Before he could celebrate, he had to collect the money.
He gazed at the city, seeing that some of the damaged buildings
were finally repaired. Though it was apparent by the sight of
the ragged French in the streets that poverty still reigned here,
Defries sensed that life was improving a bit.

Pony carts clattered rapidly back and forth, and the streets
were a jumble of well-dressed Redcoats, *habitants* in baggy
homespuns, hooded Récollet monks in brown soutanes, Jesuits
in black, and Indians and frontiersmen in buckskin and feathers;
small groups of men obviously from the British provinces were
walking and talking over the business they had taken from the
stricken French economic structure. Nearly every man favored
the inevitable clay pipe of the *habitant*.

Few women were to be seen, for the waterfront was inap-
propriate for any but the roughest of squaws in their knee-
length fringed dresses. But Defries knew where to find girls,
though that matter would have to wait until he had seen the
paymaster and had his leg tended to.

Though it was early, the day was already warm. As he
walked across the cobbled pavement, Defries noticed that every
corner was thronged with idlers, most of them off-duty soldiers.

They talked loudly and traded insults with one another, often blocking the sidewalk so that more discreet folk were compelled to detour around them instead of confronting a drunken bully head-on. Not Defries, however. He was big enough and cool enough to shoulder through knots of men, and they always made room for him to pass.

As he walked he tried to read the street signs fastened to the corners of buildings. But he was hopeless at reading. Defries was the only member of his large family who had never learned to read or write. He could add and subtract, and his mind was uncannily quick with figures when money was involved, but he had rebelled against the discipline required to learn his letters.

After asking for directions, Defries was making his way to the doctor's office when he heard a woman shouting and a dog snarling up ahead. In the middle of a group of soldiers, men were swearing and laughing, and the sound of the woman's voice told Defries she was furious.

Well, no respectable woman would be at the waterfront, so it was likely some whore in difficulty with her customers. She would be all right after a little teasing, he thought, and decided it would be prudent to cross the street instead of mixing into potential trouble. He hobbled over the street, where a crowd of onlookers was pointing and laughing. There, among the soldiers, a big sergeant was struggling with a brown-and-white dog that had him by the cuff. The fellow was shouting and slapping at the dog. He was strong enough to lift the animal off the ground and swing it through the air, but the dog did not let go of his forearm.

It was funny to watch, but Defries had other business, and he walked ahead, glancing back now and again to see whether the dog still harried the soldier. The shouting woman threw herself at the soldier, and Defries saw her try to separate him from the dog. The woman's long blond hair flew in the soldier's face, and the fellow grabbed it, yanking hard, and throwing the girl to the ground. That stopped Defries. Even a whore should not be treated like that. He hesitated and saw the man shake off the dog, aiming a savage kick at it but missing.

Defries was only fifty feet away, close enough to hear the man growl angrily at the girl, "Now I'll teach you something, little witch!"

The soldier reached down to drag the girl to her feet, but

the brown dog was back. The man roared in pain when the dog
fixed its teeth to his inner thigh. His friends shrieked in delight,
and the girl got up quickly and began pummeling the fellow,
but once again he grabbed her lush hair and threw her down.

Unconsciously, Defries had moved forward so that he was
only a few feet from the trouble. He saw that this girl neither
looked like a whore nor dressed like one. She was bravely
fighting, and Defries admired her. Again the soldier freed himself from the dog, and in a boiling fury came at the girl. He
kicked at her, and that was all Defries could take. Tossing his
bag aside, he threw himself at the man, lifting him off the
ground by his tunic front and hurling him savagely against a
wall.

Defries knew what would happen next, and he turned as a
second soldier came at him. The fellow ended up with a cracked
head, propped upside down against the same wall where his
sergeant sat stunned. Another and another soldier jumped on
Defries, who forgot about his sore knee and wasted no time
pulverizing five of His Majesty's 17th Light Dragoons. So
effortless and remarkable was the Dutchman's mastery of these
toughs, that the watching crowd applauded as the last soldier
fell to his knees, being throttled.

Someone shouted for Defries not to kill the man, but his
blood was up, his anger so intense that he barely felt the hand
on his shoulder. He saw only the strangled soldier's contorted
face.

Then blond hair appeared in front of him, and he found
himself looking into the most hypnotizing eyes he had ever
seen. He forgot his victim and his grip, letting the man drop
gasping to the ground. Defries stared at Mary Hamilton as
though he had never in his life seen a woman. Indeed, never
before had he seen anyone so beautiful. She was saying something, and he forced himself to listen.

". . . please, not for me, sir! Please don't kill anyone,
please!"

"Kill?" Defries asked vaguely, then came to his senses.
"Kill? Me, kill somebody?" He looked around at the battered
soldiers, one of whom was trying to crawl away. "Why, miss,
I—ah—I wasn't meanin' to kill any o' these scoundrels." He
felt dirty in her presence, like an animal rather than a fellow
who had just rescued a pretty girl from danger.

They stared at one another, oblivious of the crowd's shout

of satisfaction as Toby nipped the rear end of the soldier trying to scurry off on hands and knees. Looking into Mary's eyes, Defries could say nothing.

She smiled. "I am in your debt, sir."

As she dropped her eyes shyly, Defries knew this was no woman of the streets. She wore no makeup, and her clothing was too simple to be that of a . . . He could not even bring himself to think of that term in her presence.

Suddenly someone shouted that the watch was coming. Defries realized they had to get clear of there before they were arrested. Redcoats were already dragging the unconscious men away, and the crowd was quickly melting. In the center of it all, Defries and Mary stood looking at one another, with the pup Toby prancing proudly nearby.

Defries said, "We—I—we have to go, miss." He looked around and heard the crunch of soldiers' boots running not far away. "We have to go before the watch . . . What's a girl of your kind doing on the waterfront? I mean . . ." The sound of boots was louder.

Mary smiled at him, seeing how his shirt was torn, and knowing she must look ragged and rumpled herself. "We'd better go first and talk later," she suggested.

"Do me the honor, miss, an' I'll escort you out of here!"

"My pleasure," she said and took his arm. He picked up his hat and bag, and they walked away, turning down an alley just in time to avoid the soldiers of the watch, who doubletimed down the waterfront street in search of a disturbance that had magically vanished.

As they walked arm in arm, Mary told how the trouble began.

"It was my own fault, really. As you said, I was foolish to come down here alone—"

"Foolish, miss? Well, I wouldn't go so far as to say you're foolish; I mean—"

"No, foolish is the word all right. I came down here to watch the ships being loaded. I was passing those men when they insulted me, and I got angry and spoke back to them, and that's how it began. They hadn't counted on Toby being as determined as she was." She laughed a little to think of it.

Defries laughed with her, the sound echoing through the narrow alleyway. "You better keep an eye on your Toby, in case she gets sick after bitin' that dirty Redcoat."

They continued walking and joking, and paid no attention at all to where they were going. Then a clock chimed eight, and Mary remembered her appointment.

"Oh! I have to be at my doctor's office now—"

"Are you sick?"

"What? Oh, no! Not sick, just—just something personal." She smiled, and he knew enough not to stick his nose into a woman's business.

When he said he was looking for a Dr. Devalier on Rue Madeleine, she cried out that they were going to the same place. It was nearby, she said, adding that the doctor was a wonderful man.

"Do you speak French?" he asked.

"A little. But the doctor speaks English. Do you? Speak French, I mean."

Peter grinned and shook his head. "I know a few cusswords in French an' Dutch, an' I can speak some American an' even a little English if I have to."

Defries told her about his knee, and before they realized it, they stood before the narrow green door of the doctor's residence. It was a building with several doors on both sides of Devalier's, each the entrance to a dwelling of two stories. Mary told Toby to sit and wait for them, and she was about to tug the bellpull when Defries could hold back a question no longer.

"Mary, are you married or going to be married or are you in love with someone?"

Unprepared for so direct a sally, Mary laughed a little shyly. "Why, Mr. Defries! Don't the Albany Dutch teach their sons how to be discreet and polite like other folk?"

Defries took off his battered tricorn and held it at his chest. "Well, I know it ain't my business. Yes, Albany Dutch taught me manners, but I never use 'em when I'm in Montreal only long enough to say hello an' good-bye to a pretty girl! Takes too long to meet a body when you get hog-tied by good manners. Don't you think?"

"You mean there are too many girls in Montreal for you to waste your time charming me if I'm already—attached?" She was smiling.

"Let's not beat around the bush, Mary Hamilton. What you say is the long an' the short of it, but not the middle. You see, I asked that impertinent question because you're a lot different than what I'm used to in a—ah—pretty girl that I meet at the—I mean—"

"Waterfront." Her laughter was music to Defries. "If I were attached, would you want to spend your precious time with me, then?" She did not know why she felt so bold and playful with this handsome, kind fellow. But she did not care just then.

Peter's honest face showed his inner struggle. Then he looked closely at her and said, a little befuddled, "I have to say no! I wouldn't want to see you again if you were attached, Mary Hamilton, because I couldn't bear to—" He grunted and slammed the hat back onto his head. "Sorry! I won't blab on so! Here's the office, an' I guess we better go in an' have the doc fix us up—fix me up, I mean, an' whatever he has to do to you!"

He yanked the bellpull, and it rang faintly behind the green door. Mary liked him, and she said, "I owe you something, Peter. So I'll answer your question briefly: No, I have no one I love, am engaged to, or am married to. I'm not attached, Peter."

They smiled warmly at one another, and Defries took his hat off once more, turning to face the door being opened by an elderly little Frenchwoman.

As they entered the vestibule of the house, Marie Devalier welcomed them, recognizing Mary from the earlier visit. The bent old woman said in English that the doctor would be with them in a moment. She led them up the narrow stairs; she was spry and agile, despite her age. She took the steps easily, then directed them to an airy, bright waiting room with walls full of paintings.

Mrs. Devalier went out a door at the far end of the room, and the couple strolled about, looking at the commendably skillful artwork. The paintings depicted scenes on the Saint Lawrence River as well as colorful street scenes in Montreal and Quebec. There was even a painting made near Albany, where the Mohawk River empties into the Hudson, and Defries knew the spot immediately, having fished and swum there often. On the lower right corner of each painting was the signature of Michel Devalier.

Mary was thinking that many of the buildings in the painting of Montreal had been destroyed in the fighting of the last war. She was about to comment on this when the door opened and the doctor came in.

He was a very short man, broad and chubby. He wore a white goatee, which lent a pixie quality to his smiling face. When he entered the room, it was as though a burst of energy had come in with him. Dr. Devalier bowed low to Mary, and as he straightened up, he peered very closely at her. She began to introduce Defries, but Devalier raised a pudgy finger to his lips. With twinkling eyes he stepped back and looked her over from head to toe. At her right Defries was just as intently observing the lively little doctor.

Devalier beamed and turned to Peter, who wondered what would happen next. The old man said with a friendly grin, "Well, my friends, it's no doubt your child will be blond, with blue eyes!"

Defries and Mary both stumbled for words, until Defries got out, "We ain't married, Doc!"

Devalier stepped back farther, a look of surprise on his face. "No? Then you are a very unfortunate fellow not to have the good sense to make this lovely girl your wife! Does no one these days have any sense of responsibility?"

Mary tried to speak, but Defries said first, "I ain't responsible for anythin'!" He looked at Mary, not understanding. Mary looked away. Defries still had not penetrated the mystery when he said, "I'm just a friend. I mean, we just met each other!"

"Sacre bleu!" Devalier exclaimed and slapped his forehead. "Forgive me, monsieur! Forgive me, please! It is just that I thought you make such a fine couple, and naturally, with Mary's condition, I foolishly presumed you were the lucky father. Once more, monsieur, forgive me!"

Smiling, Devalier directed Mary into his office and closed the door, leaving the stunned Defries standing in the center of the waiting room, his mind awhirl.

For the next fifteen minutes, Defries sat glumly outside Devalier's office. His knee was very sore, and he tried every position he could think of to ease the pain, but none worked. Over and over in his mind he tried to puzzle out just what Mary was all about. What kind of lunkhead would have got her this way and then left her? Not someone she did not love, that was sure! But then why had she said there was no one, that she was unattached?

The more he thought of how some perfumed dandy with scented armpits and probably a shiny uniform might have seduced Mary, the angrier he became. He did not hold it against her, because he understood how that sort of thing could happen in a garrison city. Defries had done his own women-charming here, but none of the girls he caught were like Mary. They had been worldly-wise and experienced. He knew Mary well enough to see she was no wanton.

He resolved to confront Mary later, when they were alone. She attracted him, and she had told him there was no one else. That gave him the right to ask her about what otherwise would have been none of his affair. He wanted to talk more, if she were willing. He would not give up without a try.

He moved his stiff knee again. It had swollen further from the strain of fighting, so he undid the button holding the leg of his breeches closed. The door to the examining room opened, and he stood up clumsily. Devalier appeared, rubbing his hands and smiling a little stiffly.

"Please come this way, monsieur, and we'll have a look at that leg of yours. By the way, the young lady sends her compliments and her profound apologies." Defries stopped short in the doorway and turned, towering over the small man, whose aged face was a vision of wisdom. "She asks most sincerely that you forgive her for any misconception you might have had with regard to her, and for her departure without saying *au revoir*."

Defries's heart sank. He hesitated in the doorway, and Devalier said with sympathy, "She knows you will understand, Mr. Defries."

Peter went into the examining room, where cool northern light fell from the high window over sparse but comfortable furnishings—a desk and a few chairs, a long table with a blanket spread on it, some shelves with jars of herbs and potions. Glumly, Defries sat down on the table as the doctor directed him. He let his mind rove while Devalier lanced the swelling and bandaged the leg. He tried to think of Albany, of military supply contracts, of anything but Mary Hamilton. It was useless. He talked to Devalier about the massacre at Devil's Hole and about the changes in Montreal. But always he broke off, thinking about the girl, and wondering whether he would see her again.

Defries probed, trying to persuade the physician to tell where she lived. But Devalier declined, politely.

"She is a fine young woman," Devalier said, pulling Defries's breeches over the thick wrapping. "Very independent and courageous."

For a chilling instant, Defries wondered if Mary had come

to Devalier for an abortion! Was this man, sitting so placidly before him, actually guilty of the death of Mary's child? That thought repelled Defries, but he tried to find out, saying he hoped he would still be in Canada when the child was born. "In January, is it? She told me, but I forgot."

Dr. Devalier looked with placid, penetrating eyes at this young man. Defries held the other's gaze and went on, saying, "You know how she can be, Doc! She wants to go through all this alone, but I intend to stick to her side if she'll let me. Even if she's too proud to accept my help, I'll be there if I can. An' if you give me an idea of when the baby's due, I'll be here, come hell or high water! I will, Doc!"

Devalier grinned, beaming once more. "January? Well, son, the baby will come after that, sometime in March." His voice was compassionate. "Mary wants that child very much, as you must know."

"Yes, of course, Doc."

"And you are correct, she will need friends around her—"

"That's why I got to know where she lives! You see, Doc, she's too darn proud to tell me! You know, she don't want me—ah—scandalized!"

Devalier sat back in his chair, hands folded on his ample stomach. "She is like that, yes."

"So if you would just tell me where she lives, I'd be obliged, Doc."

Devalier thought there must be good reason if Mary had not told the young man where she lived, so he smiled and shook his head. "I'm afraid that is not possible, my friend. Now, let us set another appointment for you, and we'll have that leg repaired well enough for you to skate all the way back to Albany."

"Skate? I'm goin' before ice sets in!"

The doctor continued to smile. "But, my boy, you just said you'd be here when Mary Hamilton's child was born! Anyway, you will indeed have to stay in Montreal until the leg heals if you wish to avoid permanent damage. That's not so bad—one never knows, you might meet Mary Hamilton again!"

chapter **6**

YOUNG FOLK

The Morelys had offered to take Jeremy into their household for the two or three months Ella and Owen Sutherland would be away, and he was bravely, though uneasily, willing to stay behind when they left. At one point, Ella had decided it might be better if she did not go, but Jeremy proved himself more mature than his years by insisting that she accompany Owen. He understood the gravity of what Sutherland was asked to do in Pennsylvania, and he also knew how much his mother longed to go on the journey.

For the ten days before they were to leave with a score of soldiers in whaleboats, Ella and Owen spent as much time as possible with the boy. They even thought of taking him, but that would have been too difficult for Jeremy, who was not yet nine years old. Instead, Owen planned how the boy would be kept busy during the months when they were gone. Collecting books of his own and from friends, Owen put them on the table one night and sat down with Jeremy.

The three books he thought would be most interesting were Swift's *Gulliver's Travels*, Defoe's *Robinson Crusoe,* and an edition of *Aesop's Fables*. In addition, Sutherland had collected from merchants in the fort a number of inexpensive peddler's copies of children's books from the English bookseller John Newbery. These last included stories of Jack the Giant-Killer and Tommy Truelove. Jeremy was already an eager reader, as Sutherland had discovered, and this pile of books on the table would serve to engross the boy for weeks to come.

Jeremy quickly chose Daniel Defoe's book about a sailor shipwrecked for many years on a deserted island. In the days that followed, Sutherland read with the boy whenever he could, helping him master key words, amazed at how quick to learn Jeremy was. By the time his mother and Sutherland were ready to go, Jeremy was well into *Robinson Crusoe* and could read without too much difficulty. This dog-eared book that had pleased Sutherland so much every time he read it became Jeremy's passion—so much so that Ella wondered whether he would even notice when they left.

Jeremy often would read late into the night, and then he would get up before dawn and light the fire so he could read before going to Reverend Lee's school in the morning. Ella and Sutherland, watching the boy devour the book, were glad for his love of reading.

One day, after the morning chores were done, Jeremy went to school in Lee's converted barracks, reading the book every step of the way. Stumbling and bumping into things, but not giving up the episode of Robinson's fight against the cannibals, he tripped up the steps to the barracks. He walked blindly into the classroom, stopping at his desk and standing as he kept on reading.

"Master Bently!" Jeremy had not noticed the minister approach him; Lee was tapping his foot, ruler in hand. The boy whipped the book down behind his back, trying to smile. His friends tittered from their seats at the school's two long tables. "Are you quite finished? You're already late this morning, but you seem to think that doesn't matter!"

Jeremy eyed the ruler, gave a wan smile, and sat down, tucking the book behind his back. He was one of six boys his age and younger at a long oaken table that faced the minister's dais and tall stool. At another table behind Jeremy's were the older boys, aged ten to twelve. Lee rocked on his heels a moment, gave a warning snap of the ruler on his palm, turned, and strode to his desk.

As teachers went, Lee was not very strict or severe. He demanded obedience, but he did not overuse the ruler or the birch switch that leaned menacingly against his podium. In his six months at Detroit, he had used the birch only once, and then simply to brandish it to quiet the youngsters during one of his first days as a teacher. That hollow, whistling sound it made was more than enough to bring home Lee's point. Since then, only an occasional tap with the yardstick had been needed to jog a student's memory or get his attention.

Jeremy liked Lee very much, for the slender fellow was a frequent guest in his home, but at that moment, the boy was restless and impatient. Seven-year-old Tommy Morely—the elder of the two Morely boys—handed out battered copies of a gloomy book written by a James Janeway. The books had been sent as a gift to the children of the fort by a New England preacher who believed children on the frontier should learn religious morality as they learned to read. The boys opened their books, titled *A Token for Children, Being an Exact Account of the Conversion, Holy and Exemplary Lives and Joyful Deaths of Several Young Children,* and Jeremy leaned his open *Robinson Crusoe* against the edge of the table, standing it on his lap.

"Follow along, students," Lee said. "We'll find a chapter that tells us about some children in whom the fear of God was remarkably budding before they died. Those happenings took place in several parts of New England. Now then . . ."

From most of the children in the room, a sighing, barely audible groan went up. They knew this book only too well, and they hated its wordy, passionate tales, such as the one about two young babes who chided their parents for not praying enough. When the children died, they had ecstasies of delight because now they were able to pray ad infinitum.

Lee was convinced Janeway could inspire piety, and there was little enough piety on the frontier. He began to read in a lilting voice, and had not gone very far when Tommy Morely yawned loudly. Lee caught him and gave an angry glare that threatened to wither the boy. Jeremy did not notice, because he was wondering just how Friday's old father had been taken prisoner by the cannibals.

"The next boy who yawns, slouches in his chair, or in any other way disturbs this reading will feel my birch switch." As though by magic, the birch was in Lee's hand, and it cut at the air with what appeared to be its own malevolent power.

Then Lee went on reading. The boys grew rather drowsy, all except Jeremy, who read about swordplay, pirates, and tropical islands. Lee finished a long excerpt and closed the book with a loud snap. The dozing Morely boy jumped awake and struck the table with his knees, so that Jeremy's book banged to the floor.

The room was silent. Lee stared fiercely at Jeremy, who sank into his chair. He kicked the book a little underneath himself, hoping Lee would not see it, but he was too late.

Slowly, deliberately, the minister left his dais and walked to Jeremy. He placed one hand on the table, leaned forward, and held out his other hand for the book. Jeremy, his eyes on Lee's, trying not to tremble, reached down for the novel and gave it up.

Without looking at it, Lee said, "Of course, you know what this means, Bently."

Jeremy knew very well.

Lee glanced at the book's title and then at Jeremy, then quickly back at the book. He opened it, then stared in surprise at the boy. *"You* were reading this?"

Jeremy did not know what to say, except, "Y–Yes, sir."

"Do you mean to tell me you can *read* this book?"

"Y–Yes, sir."

The entire class hung on Lee's next words, expecting an explosion of wrath. But instead, Lee rubbed his chin, tapped his foot a few times, and muttered to himself. Staring at the book as he walked back to his dais, Lee absently reached down for the birch switch.

At Lee's summons, Jeremy got up, trying not to show his fear; he walked bravely forward. Lee paced back and forth, the birch and the closed novel held behind his back. Then he spun and approached the boy.

Raising his chin, Lee said, "Six of the best is what you get, Bently. I promised—and I warned you."

Jeremy pursed his lips and held out his hand. He did not want to close his eyes, so he stared hard at the wall, his back to his classmates. Lee prepared to deal out the punishment. Then he said with annoyance, "All right, only three this time, because you were not intentionally disrupting the class."

Three stinging lashes of the birch hurt terribly, but Jeremy did not flinch. When he was done, Lee tossed the birch aside as though it revolted him. Then, rocking on his heels again, he handed the novel back to Jeremy, who took it with his unhurt hand.

"All right," Lee said, and Jeremy began to turn away. "Not so fast, Bently. This is the first I knew that *Robinson Crusoe* was anywhere within a thousand miles of this fort. What part were you reading?"

"A—About the cannibals, sir, and the father of Friday. It's the part where they have to fight the cannibals to save Friday's father."

Jeremy went on telling the story, and the children were immediately enthralled. Lee noticed their response, and he made up his mind quickly.

"Right, Bently. Read it to us. Start where you left off, and these other sluggards here will have to learn their letters if they have any hope of reading the book's opening chapters."

Jeremy was dumbfounded. "Read it? Me?"

"*I!* I mean, yes, you!"

Jeremy tried to speak, but changed his mind and opened the book. Turning toward his friends, he cleared his throat. Before beginning, he cast a dubious, sidelong glance at the minister, who was seated on his stool, gazing out the window.

At first Jeremy's voice was awkward and hesitant, and several times he blew into his sore hand to soothe it. After a few paragraphs, however, the story captivated him, and he read without the slightest self-consciousness. The boys listened, eyes wide, and Reverend Angus Lee leaned back, his own eyes closed, hearing once more the story he loved most in all the world.

In Montreal, the coming of night found Mary Hamilton sitting alone in her room, not sure whether to laugh or cry. She had been through a terrible time with the Cullens this evening, having been blamed by Mrs. Cullen for shaming her daughter in the street. Linda, for her part, had accused Mary of enticing some young artillerymen they had encountered that afternoon.

The two girls had been walking home from shopping, when four young officers met them and introduced themselves. They were polite at first, charming enough to easily overwhelm co-quettish Linda, who had not noticed they were a little drunk. Mary realized it, however, and she wanted to walk on home. Besides, thoughts of Peter Defries still troubled her mind, though it was several days since their meeting.

Mary had tried to pry Linda away, suggesting that the gentlemen might call at home if they wished to advance their relationship with Linda. At that, one of them put his arm around Mary, whispered they liked her best, and then said something lewd. Mary kicked him in the shins. This angered the fellow, for the drink was rising in him, and his friends were laughing.

He swore at Mary, whereupon she hit him squarely in the face with her heavy-laden reticule, flattening him and bloodying his nose.

The other men roared with laughter at their stunned friend, and it seemed the only upset onlooker was Linda. Anguished, Linda went to the dazed artilleryman and tried to help him up. By now a crowd was gathering. Laughter was mixed with expressions of outrage and surprise to see Linda's indiscretion.

Angry, Mary stood over the soldier, her bag ready to fell him again if he had any more rude intentions. Linda fussed and chattered to the fellow, then she screeched at Mary to stand back and leave the poor boy alone. That got a laugh from the crowd, but the proper folk who knew Linda's family could bear no more. Appropriately scandalized—and equipped with plenty of juicy gossip—these people made a correct and delicate exit. It would not do to linger too long and be accused of gawking.

Another soldier complained to Mary, telling her not to be so touchy. His friend would leave her alone, if that was what she wanted. Then, as he picked up the other artilleryman, he sneered about "bitches," and without thinking twice Mary aimed a swing at him, too. With a scream of horror, Linda jumped in the way and took the force of the blow on her chest. She fell backwards over the first artilleryman, he shouting in anger, she shrieking, her legs and petticoats high in the air.

Mary stormed home, barging through the door and past the prune-faced Mrs. Cullen. She ran up to her room, where Toby waited for her, but the girl had not been in the house more than two minutes when she heard a pitiful cry of dismay downstairs. Linda was home. The cry was Mrs. Cullen's. It was followed by a sobbing, croaking sound—that was Linda telling the entire, mortifying tale.

Before the howling was done, Mr. Cullen came home, and the groaning began all over again, punctuated by the rotund merchant's gasps of "By Jove!" Just when it sounded as though the Cullen family would don war paint and rush upstairs after Mary, Emmy tinkled the dinner bell.

Mary was hungry, and she wanted to get the confrontation over with, so she came down immediately. The Cullens glared at her. The kitchen door opened a little, and Emmy peeked out, fear in her eyes. Mary stopped halfway down the stairs, ready for the barrage.

Mrs. Cullen was seated in the hall, cradling Linda's head in her lap. "Well, Bradford," she said, "*will* you tell her?"

Bradford Cullen cleared his throat and looked up at Mary. He cleared his throat again and winced when his wife blared, "Tell her! Tell her!"

Cullen raised a pudgy hand. But he was not quick enough. Mrs. Cullen, her face purple with rage, threw her moaning daughter aside and stamped to the foot of the staircase.

"You—you—"

"Helen—" Bradford cautioned.

Wagging her finger, Helen Cullen said, "You will leave this house by the end of the week, do you understand? On Sunday you will be gone! That's five days!"

Mary showed no emotion, but her bottom lip twitched. The door to the kitchen closed quickly. Mrs. Cullen let her fury go: "You will be gone, and I don't care where you go! You have disgraced our daughter, and you have disgraced our good name. Your vulgar behavior has voided our contract! After Sabbathday you'll not show your face here again. Is that clear?"

Mary spun to go back to her room, but Linda's sour voice pursued her. "And Father knows exactly where you went the other day!" Bradford Cullen, a look of pain on his face, tried to still his daughter. She ignored him, seeing Mary hesitate and look down. "You were at the doctor's because your Indian husband made you pregnant!"

Mary's first instinct was to run down and slap the girl. But she felt the baby move suddenly, and she put her hands to her middle. Wavering between anger and worry, she got control of herself, turned, and ran upstairs, slamming the door to her room.

But now, hours afterward, Mary felt as though a great weight had been lifted from her shoulders. She had disliked living with these people, and now she would be free again. How she would live, or where, she refused to consider just then. She was too concerned with being calm for the sake of the baby. Furthermore, every time she thought of Linda tumbling back onto the helpless artilleryman, Mary started giggling. She laughed so hard that she had to bury her face in a pillow. Lying at the foot of the bed, Toby did not know whether to wag her tail or put her head down and be glum. Mary soon fell asleep.

• • •

Two hours later there was a soft knock at the door, and it opened before she could answer. Emmy, dressed in a gray nightgown, slipped into the room. The maid was carrying a silver tray covered with a white linen cloth.

"Here, missy, I got dinner all cooked special. Better'n what those old fogies ate tonight, hear?"

She uncovered a platter of Mary's favorite food—fried mushrooms in a butter sauce. There was also a dish of green beans, and the largest plate held roast partridge. There was even a dessert of maple sugar and a small pot of hot coffee. Toby sniffed and frisked about in anticipation.

Hungrier than she realized, Mary hugged Emmy and sat down to eat. The maid stood nearby, her hands folded in front. Mary tucked a napkin into her nightgown and turned to the woman.

"Sit and join me, Emmy! There's more than enough for—" Mary saw a hint of tears in Emmy's eyes. "Now, Emmy, what's this all about? Don't . . . please . . ." Mary stood up and felt her own tears coming. She hugged Emmy again, and they stood that way awhile, wetting each other's shoulder. Then Mary pushed the woman back, and they wiped their tears away, half-laughing, half-whimpering.

"Oh, Emmy," Mary said, "it's not as bad as all that! You and I will still see each other, and I'll be fine!"

Emmy dried her hands on her nightgown front and said, "Hear me, missy! You can stay at the Grey Sisters' convent until your time's on you! They take girls in, and they're kind, it's said. Say you'll do that, and I won't worry about you so!"

Mary assured her friend that she would be all right, though she could not think of anything more unpleasant than the strict, cold Grey Sisters' residence for women who were alone and in need of help. Before long, they were seated across from one another at the dresser, eating heartily, and Toby on the floor joined in. As Mary divided the maple sugar she told Emmy how Linda had acted that afternoon, and Emmy nearly choked with laughter. Covering her face with a napkin, the maid stifled her hilarity so the Cullens would not hear, and she got up, went to the bed, and fell flat on her face. Feet kicking, her face buried in the pillow, Emmy laughed and laughed. Every time she steadied herself, Mary would tell her something more, and both of them went off again, giggling until they were weak in the knees.

• • •

At that moment, in a waterfront tavern best known for its shattered mirror and bloodstained floors, Peter Defries was trying to get drunk. He was furious, the more so because it seemed the rum was doing nothing to obliterate his fury. He ordered another glass, and when it came, he slurred something about the rum being weak. Knowing better than to dispute his guests, the tavernkeeper muttered that Peter had not tried to stand up for a while.

Defries scoffed at that and looked at his half-dozen drinking mates who were singing and laughing, crowded around the table. They were tough but honest laborers and soldiers. Defries wished the secretary for the army paymaster was half the man these simple fellows were. That was why he was so angry. That was why he was trying—apparently unsuccessfully—to get drunk.

For the past few days he had gone regularly to the office of the paymaster, each time to be put off by one Mortimer Gillis, a prissy fellow who guarded the door to the paymaster's inner chambers. Gillis, scented and frilly in fashionable clothes and an enormous wig of white curls, obviously despised all provincials. He accepted the letter authorizing payment for Defries, but told him to come back the following day. The next day the paymaster was terribly busy with government matters relating to the Indian war and was not be able to see him that day either.

Defries had demanded an interview with the paymaster, but Gillis had warned him not to be so rash; all would be carried out in due time. These things could not be accomplished overnight, particularly for a sum as large as a thousand pounds. The Dutchman longed to pick Gillis up and throw him through the wall, but he knew the secretary was probably influential with the paymaster. He would just have to be patient a little longer.

But, for all his other good qualities, Defries was not a patient man. Confused at whatever was behind the paymaster's stalling, he was determined to get blind drunk and wipe out all thoughts of the secretary, who spoke like such a fop: "Well, strike me blue!" or "Stab my vitals!"

From time to time Defries muttered one or the other phrase, laughed derisively, then grew angry again. Then he would start all over trying to rid himself of the memory of Mortimer Gillis, but he could not do it for long. When he did manage to do it, a vision of Mary Hamilton came to him, and that was worse. He wished he could find her, but seek as he would, it seemed she had vanished.

As the evening wore on, other men took on his unhappy mood, and before long the singing and joking stopped, and there was too much grumbling and complaining. Disgusted with his company for lacking good cheer, and angry that he could not get drunk, Defries downed a last swig of rum, tossed some coppers on the table, and got up.

"Leavin' early, mate?" someone asked.

Defries tried to answer the fellow and at the same time to jam his tricorn onto his head, but for some reason he missed his head and could not speak very well. Deciding against either putting on his hat or answering, he turned to go. Unfortunately, the floor tipped sideways all of a sudden, and Defries fell, his ear banging hard against the edge of the table. It was a wicked knock, but strangely he did not feel it. He wanted to ask who the hell tipped the floor, but if he had been able to get out the words, he would not have been conscious long enough to hear an answer.

"So, my boy, you were not satisfied to have only one injury," mumbled Dr. Devalier as he swabbed the torn ear with spirits. Defries winced in pain, but he did not complain as the doctor stitched him up. He had come this morning for the appointment to care for his leg, but Devalier said the injury his ear had suffered the night before needed bandaging.

"This will heal in a couple of weeks if you take care of it." Brandishing a large hollow lancing needle, he said, "Now, let us see to your leg." He stuck the needle into the knee and let fluid drain into a tin bowl on the floor.

When the lancing was finished and the leg bandaged again, Peter hobbled to the door. Throwing it open, he stopped short.

In the waiting room, Mary stood up quickly, as surprised as he. Their eyes met and held until the voice of Mrs. Devalier broke in.

"The best and perhaps only true French coffee in all Montreal is being served in the sitting room, children. Won't you join us?"

Standing bright and cheery in the doorway to her living

quarters, Mrs. Devalier could see the bloom in Mary's cheeks and the light in Peter's eyes. She repeated her offer and beckoned to her husband, and they all went into the spacious sitting room. The aroma of coffee was in the air, and a fire crackled brightly in the iron hearth.

As she and Peter walked across the room, Mary whispered, "Was this your idea?" When he shook his head, she glanced at Mrs. Devalier, whose face was aglow. Mary gave a little laugh and looked at Peter once more. He thought she was incredibly lovely.

The doctor waited by his chair at the cozy table, where a china coffeepot and matching flowered cups were prettily set on the white linen tablecloth. The young people sat down next to one another, and when her husband was seated, Marie Devalier went around the table, pouring hot coffee.

For the next half hour, the two couples lingered, thoroughly enjoying themselves. Mrs. Devalier had baked special cakes for the occasion, and it was hard for Defries to keep from eating them all. However, he did not gobble them up, duly impressing Mary with his table manners. He and the doctor talked of painting and travel, and they all discussed the changes in Montreal. Mary's condition was not alluded to, and her abrupt departure of a few days ago was not mentioned. But an understanding was reached without direct talk. All the while, Mrs. Devalier observed Peter and Mary closely; every time they smiled at one another, she sighed happily.

When the couple left the Devaliers', Toby joined them as they came into the alley. They strolled to the main street, where they stopped, neither knowing which way to go. Mary's face colored, and she looked down at the ground. Toby came to her side as a two-wheeled *calèche* rattled toward them. They stepped clear to let it enter Rue Madeleine, and Mary's eyes came up to Peter's.

He asked, "Why did you leave that way last time?"

She looked down at her hands and tugged the woolen shawl closer about her waist. "I—I supposed it would save you the embarrassment of leaving *me* that way, since you knew of my—my situation."

For days Defries had thought of what he would say if he found her again and could ask that question. He had even anticipated her reply, so without hesitation he said, "Mary,

I've been thinkin' about you almost all the time, an' wanted to see you!" The rest of the planned speech was jumbled in his mind and never spoken. He was too much drowned in her eyes as she stared at him.

He smiled and said, "At least give me the choice of leavin' or not. But if I do leave, it won't be because of your condition."

His words were spoken with such sincerity that Mary's lip trembled, and she laughed to hide it, putting up her hand and looking at the *calèche* disappearing down the alley.

She tried to speak, but could not. He took her arm firmly and said, "I know a nice quiet place where Toby can run an' we can talk. It's as nice a spot as I've seen in this Frenchy country. It's just outside town, an' it overlooks the river. A lot like Albany, but the Saint Lawrence here sure beats the Hudson at Albany for width, I guess. How about it? You'll be home in time for supper!"

She nodded and smiled.

He said, "Okay! We'll buy some bread an' cheese for lunch, an' maybe some wine. You like Frenchy wine? It's as good as the bread an' cheese they make, an' that's somethin'! Let's see. *Vin! Oui, fromage! Et du pain!* Not bad, eh? I've learned more than just cusswords."

They walked into the surge of morning traffic near the quay, and Peter cheered her up with his talk of winning an army contract. Since she had been involved with her father's trading business, they had much in common to talk about. Peter and Mary did not speak of emotions, or romance, or feelings. Instead, they discussed freighting, canoes, army supplies, and the relative cost of merchandise in Montreal and Albany.

Their personal attraction complemented their business interests, and they hardly noticed the fifteen minutes it took to buy food and walk to a windy bluff just east of the city. Defries was glad for the rest there, because his leg hurt. Toby scooted through the long grass, yipping and yelping, scaring up rabbits and pheasant.

Meanwhile, Mary and Peter sat on his coat spread in the browning grass, and ate their bread and cheese. Peter told her about himself and his experience as a teamster. She, in turn, told about her captivity, her romance with Duncan McEwan, and her intention to raise the child rather than give it away for adoption. He liked that.

Then they sat next to one another, neither speaking. Their

shoulders touched, but they did not move apart. Toby tired of the chase and came back, her tongue hanging out, and lay beside them. Peter rubbed the pup's head.

He walked her home that afternoon, getting there long before suppertime. As they approached the door, Mary noticed curtains upstairs in the Cullen bedroom move as though someone was behind them. Peter bowed the very best he could and asked to see her the next morning.

"Let's meet at the bluff," she said, and he agreed, then kissed her hand. He was unpracticed, but he did it well enough to impress anyone spying from the windows. Besides, Peter Defries was such a handsome fellow that Linda or Mrs. Cullen was probably already beside herself with jealousy to think that Mary had met him.

That night as Peter lay abed, he thought about Mary and her predicament. Somehow he had to help her. Never mind the fact that she attracted him beyond all reason. He would help her without asking anything in return. Defries did not think about enduring relationships as he puzzled through a vague plan to assist her. He thought simply that this girl needed help, needed assurance that she would not have to have her baby at the Grey Sisters' home for poor, unwanted women.

It did not take long to formulate a clever but dangerous course of action. It meant prison if he were caught, but for Mary he was willing to risk it. His plan would get even with both the paymaster's secretary and the Cullens in one stroke. And it would bring Mary the money the Cullens owed her.

chapter 7

ALBANY CRYSTAL

Very early the next morning, before the Cullens were up, Mary hurried shoeless downstairs on her way to meet Peter. When Mrs. Cullen shrieked her name from the second floor, Mary looked up to see the woman, cloaked in a nightgown, her head covered with a gray flannel nightcap. Mrs. Cullen's eyes were swollen from sleep but she came down the steps.

"Mary Hamilton! Where do you think you're going?" She rubbed her eyes and paused on the bottom step.

"Why, I'm going for a walk, and then to meet a friend."

Toby barked at the door, her tail wagging. But when Mrs. Cullen took that last step and confronted Mary, the pup quieted and huddled close to its mistress.

"To meet a friend, are you? You mean that ruffian who brought you here yesterday?"

"He's no ruffian—"

"No? Then what *would* you call a man who isn't good enough to be brought inside to meet your guardians?"

"As of Sunday next, you are no longer my guardians."

"Until then, we are your guardians, and we have the right to forbid your associating with someone who is no better than—"

"Mrs. Cullen, please!"

But the woman cut Mary off by stamping her foot. Unfortunately, she nipped Toby's tail, which sent the dog charging about the hall, howling in pain and shock.

"Oh, Toby!" Mary exclaimed, trying to catch the pup as she bounded past. "Toby!"

"Stop that dog!" squealed Mrs. Cullen, lifting the hem of her nightgown and kicking at the pup. Toby was frightened now, and hurtled by, nearly knocking her over.

The kitchen door burst open, and out came Emmy, eyes wide and holding a big spoon. When she saw it was Toby causing the fuss, the maid crouched to intercept her. The dog crashed against Mrs. Cullen again and swerved for the kitchen; when the dog was almost upon her, Emmy roared "Stay!" The terrified Toby spun in midair, desperate to change directions. But her momentum was too great and the floor too well polished. She slammed against Emmy, bowling her over in a tangle of arms, legs, and petticoats.

"What in heaven's name is going on here?" thundered Mr. Cullen from the top of the stairs. Dressed in his red nightshirt, he lost a slipper as he came down quickly.

"It's all right, Toby," Mary was shouting, trying to get the pup's attention, but to no avail. Toby quailed at the sight of both furious Cullens and scampered past Mary into the sitting room. She hit a small rug and skidded on it across the floor, ending her slide with a clatter against a small Chippendale table. Mary, the Cullens, and Emmy all gasped in horror as the table teetered, then fell over; with it went a blue china bowl and a silver candlestick.

Mrs. Cullen howled even louder than her husband, and from upstairs came Linda's cries of fright. Toby ran back to Mary, who whipped open the door so she could flee. Unfortunately, Mr. Cullen was too close to the door, and it hit him full in the face.

Stunned, he sat down heavily on the steps. With Linda screaming and Mrs. Cullen's mouth open but finally speechless, Mary darted outside, carrying her sabots, her cloak trailing behind. Mrs. Cullen shouted, "Come back, Mary Hamilton! Come back! Come back or else!"

But Mary was far away, racing down the street, Toby loping nonchalantly at her side.

After running through side streets in the dull light of a chilly dawn, Mary slowed down, her heart pounding out of control. She realized she was risking the child by such extreme exertion, and she stopped running, trying to catch her breath. She was responsible for the baby, and she had to be calm.

Soon she was at the outskirts of town, passing through a small gate in the city wall. Out here, it seemed easier to breathe. There were a few farmhouses along the way, and whenever she walked past one, the farmer or his wife waved a greeting to her. Toby visited with friendly dogs, sticking her tail up as though each farmyard were her own, once insolently prancing off when an angry husky strained at a rope, snarling and barking.

Vegetable gardens were being absorbed by black rows where the soil had been turned in anticipation of winter, the carrots, potatoes, and cabbages mostly harvested by now. The neighborhood Mary passed through was tranquil and restful; the only movement was the drift of a cow herd through meadow or the passing of a cart loaded high with hay.

Behind her, Mount Royal loomed steep and regal over the city that bore its name. In front and to the right were windswept fields of dark grass and clusters of graying apple and peach trees, whose leaves were almost gone.

Mary turned down a lane toward the river. Bounded by a stone fence on the left and thick underbrush on the right, the narrow road shut out everything but a strip of leaden sky overhead. Toby ran playfully in and out of the thicket, and Mary was calm by now.

She was only a few moments from meeting Peter on the bluff. Already her heart lifted to think of being with him again. She was not really in love with him, though she liked him very much. Love, so soon after the loss of Duncan, was too much to consider. It was more than sufficient to say she enjoyed Peter and felt good in his company. He had asked for nothing more than that, and until he did, she was content.

The lane climbed to a little rise until the Saint Lawrence appeared on her right, to the south. The sky was heavy with clouds, yet it did not feel like rain. The deep green flatlands and dots of white French cottages at the edge of the river made a wild and picturesque sight. Mary stopped and let her eyes rove, not focusing, simply moving and taking in nature's beauty.

Then, to the right, she saw Peter, waving from the knoll, silhouetted against the cloudy sky. She left the road, and Peter ran to her, Toby already at his heels. She felt like running to meet him, but that would not do—not just yet, not before she knew him better. Then he was at her side, his arm hooked in hers as they walked through the long grass to the top of the knoll.

Peter had spread out a clean blanket borrowed from the inn. On the blanket was a basket of food and a bottle of wine. Neither was hungry enough to eat yet, so they sat quietly for a little while. On every side was a pretty view. They could see the river and across to the plains. The city was behind and to the right, massive Mount Royal beyond.

Peter said, "Would you like some wine?"

She looked at the bottle as he took it from the basket, and recognized the vintner's markings. "Not for a while. How did you get that bottle? I thought none as good as this had been imported from France since the war ended."

Peter grinned and turned the bottle in his hand. "Well, after I left you yesterday I took a little trip to that paymaster's secretary—you know, the one always sayin' 'Stab my vitals!' or 'Strike me blue!' Well, he still ain't settled anythin' for me with his boss, an' he didn't seem to care much about it. He just snorted some snuff an' told me to come back again. Well, since that slim-waisted bootlicker owed me an apology which he didn't deliver, I took it upon myself to make amends." He scrutinized the bottle, then looked at Mary. "You say this is real good wine, eh? Well, that's fine with me! At least that perfumed armpit has somethin' right about him. He's got good taste, even if he don't know a damn thing about where to hide it when someone who doesn't like him comes visitin'."

Mary laughed. Peter leaned back on his elbow, toying with the cork of the bottle. Then he said, "Did the Cullens agree to pay you what they owe?"

Mary felt gloomy suddenly, wishing he hadn't mentioned them at such a happy moment. "I—really haven't asked yet."

Peter thought for a little while, then sat up. "Listen, Mary, the only way you'll get what they owe you is to hire a lawyer, an' then a lawyer will take a good chunk of what you're due— if he gets anythin' at all from 'em. How much do they owe you?"

"I'm not exactly sure, but it's probably around forty-five pounds. They have all my pa's records now."

"Hmmm," Peter said. "Forty-five or fifty pounds, eh? Why, that can't be much to people rich as they are, but it'll keep you an' the baby in grub for half a year, I guess."

"I'll ask them for a settlement when I go back."

Peter grumbled, "They won't give you a farthin' if they can get away with it, an' they'll try to get away with it. But, listen, I have a plan. Hear me out, an' you'll see that they won't get away with it any more than that snuff-sniffin' perfumed armpit will get with chiselin' me!" He asked probing questions, such as whether she was legally heir to her father's small trading house—she was, according to her prudent father's will, which she had safely packed. He asked if she had the power to sign away her father's business, and she again said yes.

Then Peter explained his plot. Mary thought it outrageous and brilliant and very dangerous if he were caught. When he finished, he dug a corkscrew from the picnic basket.

"Well, it may be too early for you, but it ain't for me!" He popped out the cork and searched the basket for glasses, but there were none.

Before taking a drink, he offered the bottle to Mary. She was thinking about his plan, and it excited her. Preoccupied, she took the bottle and drank deeply. Indeed, the wine was delicious.

Defries chuckled. "You've drunk like that before."

She nodded. "I went traveling with my father a lot. There were often bottles but no glasses."

He raised the wine and said, "Here's to the sixty pounds they owe you!"

"Sixty? I said forty-five!"

"That baby's gotta eat, an' so does its ma! Can't always count on good French wine to fall in your lap when you least expect it." He handed over the bottle, and Mary giggled before she drank it, just a sip this time, because she had to think of the baby.

They walked back to the city, and Peter left her at the door of the house before going off to set his plan in motion. Mary entered, but as soon as she was inside the door, she saw everything she owned piled in three tow sacks at the foot of the stairs.

In the sitting room, the Cullens were waiting for her. When Mr. Cullen called Mary, she went to them, ignoring Linda's smug, gloating expression. Mr. Cullen was standing behind his wife, who sat in a chair, looking prim, proper, and indignant.

Mr. Cullen harumphed once or twice, as though to talk; but

it might as well have been a signal for his wife to take charge, as she did. Mrs. Cullen enumerated the reasons Mary had to leave at once, this very day. Mary stood looking down at the floor, saying nothing. The woman said Mary had soiled their good name, shamed their daughter, and injured her husband. Mary looked up and saw the bruise around Mr. Cullen's swollen left eye.

"Furthermore, and more important than the rest, is our learning of your scandalous condition!" Mrs. Cullen pronounced those last two words with a scorn intended to cut Mary to the bone. Instead, Mary lifted her chin and looked the woman straight in the eyes. Wavering, Mrs. Cullen looked away and began to huff about Toby having destroyed fine china and damaged tables and chairs in her rampage that morning. Hearing her name spoken so harshly, the dog lay down at Mary's feet and pretended innocence.

At last Mr. Cullen spoke up. "Mistress Hamilton, our company's records show that we are obliged to your father's house for approximately twenty pounds. Now the damage your cur did today far exceeds that sum."

Mary was about to protest, but Mrs. Cullen cut her short. "Don't think we'll put you out without a penny! No. Out of the kindness of our hearts we will give you enough to see you through until—until—" She gave her husband a quick little flick of her hand. "Let her have the money, Bradford."

With much pretentious exaggeration, Mr. Cullen took three pound notes from his thick pocketbook and handed them over to Mary. She longed to refuse them, but she could not. That money represented all she had.

Mrs. Cullen magically produced a receipt for the money. "You will sign here, showing our commitment to your father has been fulfilled."

Mary glanced at the receipt, looked back at Mrs. Cullen, whose face was devoid of all feeling, and then tossed the pound notes lightly into Mr. Cullen's chubby hands. Ignoring an exclamation of surprise from the Cullens, Mary left the room with Toby at her heels. She picked up two of the bulky tow sacks, struggling for the third. Before the Cullens could speak, Emmy appeared at Mary's side. She was dressed for shopping, and cried brightly to her masters:

"I'm goin' her way, Mr. and Mrs. Cullen. Be back with dinner groceries directly!"

Without a wasted movement, Emmy took two bags, and in

a moment, before the Cullens gathered their wits enough to command the maid not to help, the two women and Toby were hurrying away.

With tears welling in Emmy's eyes, the two friends walked a few blocks to the massive, brooding Grey Sisters' convent. At the main door, saying little more than that they would see one another again, they parted. After Emmy left, Mary looked up at the convent's steeple, where a great bell began tolling sadly. Then, as she bent to pick up her bags, Mary noticed Emmy had left the shopping basket at her feet. Toby was sniffing at the white cloth covering it, and when Mary looked inside, she smelled the aroma of roast partridge and mushrooms.

The office of the military paymaster's secretary was a large room, comfortably furnished with the finest chairs and desk available in Montreal. The slim little secretary looked like a boy sitting behind an adult's desk, and when the fellow glared with anger at the reappearance of this most pesky visitor, Peter Defries had to restrain the urge to pick him up and toss him through the window.

The smell of perfume made Defries wrinkle his nose, but he stepped cheerfully into the room and closed the door. With an exasperated snort, Mortimer Gillis rose to his feet, looking even more like a spoiled brat playing at public official.

"Mr. Defries..."

"Mr. Gillis!" Defries exclaimed, pulling his hat from his head and holding it behind his back. "Honored that you remember the name of such an ordinary, simple soul as me! At your service, sir!"

Without further preliminaries, Gillis swept into a rushed explanation that the paymaster was still very busy with many more important matters. He came around the desk, his yellow frills and brown satin waistcoast fairly glowing. As Gillis tried to edge Defries toward the door, he looked the epitome of everything the Dutchman despised in military bureaucracy: spindly legs in skintight breeches and stockings of fine white silk; a curly wig that hung down to his shoulders. Even the way he opened the door with a self-important flourish made Defries steam inside with anger, but he forced it to dissipate, and began his plan.

Interrupting the secretary's tirade, Defries looked back at

the large desk and declared, "Oh! You have such a magnificent snuffbox, Mr. Gillis!"

He reached over the desk and picked up the small silver cube. Gillis snatched the box away, but not before Defries had opened the lid and touched a fingertip to the mixture of tobacco and spices used as snuff.

Gillis returned to holding the door open, but Defries hissed "Wait!"

"Why?" Gillis was angry now.

"Because, my friend, you are a lover of fine snuff!" Defries closed one eye and wagged a finger at the secretary, who really wanted none of this at all, though it was true that he was addicted to snuff. "If you close that door, I'll let you see some Albany Crystal!"

Gillis was stumped. He even almost closed the door, then thought better of it; but he was intrigued by the small wooden snuffbox Defries now held before him.

Defries said, "This here's somethin' I figured a fellow like you'd appreciate, an' when I got a whiff of that fine snuff in your box, I knew I was right. This box has a load of Albany Crystal, an' it's made from a secret recipe that the old Peter Stuyvesant and Peter Minuit down in New Amsterdam kept secret till the day they died."

"Albany what?" Gillis tried not to let on that he was attracted to Defries's story, but the fact was that no one knew more about good tobacco than the Dutch. "Are you trying to tell me that any snuff from Albany could be special?"

"Albany Crystal, Your Highness, an' I ain't surprised you never heard of it, 'cause not too many folks have. You see, it's kept secret—"

"Come, come, man." Gillis held out his delicate hand for the snuffbox. "There isn't a snuff in the civilized world that I haven't tasted."

"That's just it, this ain't *civilized* snuff! This here Albany Crystal ain't for everyone or anyone. It's specially mixed for *uncivilized* men! How do you think the Dutch bought the island of Manhattan for just a few trinkets an' some whatnot? Well, Your Honor, this was the whatnot!"

Defries had him now, and using the box as a decoy, he guided Gillis away from the door, handed him the closed box of snuff, and prodded the door shut with his foot. Gillis walked behind his desk and carefully opened the box. But he got just a brief look before Defries snatched it away from him. Gillis cried out, but Defries seemed reluctant to give up the box, as though arguing with himself about whether Gillis should have it.

Annoyed but amused, the secretary sighed and waited.

"Listen, Your Worship, you've never seen snuff this color before, right?" Defries held open the box and revealed a reddish, white-speckled substance inside. Gillis reached for it, but Defries once more withdrew it quickly.

"As I was sayin'," he continued, "this Albany Crystal was concocted after years an' centuries maybe of Injun councils! Listen! You know Sir William Johnson?"

"Of course! What does he have to do with—"

"An' you've heard of how he parleys with the Iroquois and sweeps 'em right off their callusy feet? Well, do you know how he gets 'em where he wants 'em so's genteel folk like yourself an' the paymaster can walk right up to 'em an' actually feed 'em without gettin' bit most of the time?"

The secretary guffawed, saying, "Of course! Sir William plies them with rum and sleeps with the daughters of their chiefs—maybe even with their wives and mothers, too!"

Defries had his eyes closed and was shaking his head. "More than that, Your Highness!" With a hint of condescension in his voice, Defries said, "The king of the British Empire, with Sir William Johnson as his honest an' humble tool, won over the warlike Iroquois—most of 'em, anyway—with Albany Crystal!"

Before Gillis could speak, Defries went on. "Enough excitement in one pinch to quiet the savage heart! Enough power in a second pinch to make the red man love the Englishman! Enough whatever in a third pinch to rile 'em up an' send 'em screamin' an' whoopin' through the piney woods after them Frenchies!"

Gillis smiled weakly, and motioned to see the box once more.

Defries held it out to him. As he did so, his long waistcoat fell over the paymaster's official silver stamp used to imprint the paymaster's red-wax seal on official correspondence and documents. "Look close," Defries whispered, and Gillis took the box.

The secretary shrugged. "I've never seen snuff like this before."

Defries, still leaning over the desk, exclaimed, "How d'you think Sir William kept it up at all 'em Injun councils—dancin' an' speechmakin' all day an' most of the night through?"

"Very well," Gillis mused. "Let me try some of this Albany Crystal, then."

"All right, sir," Defries said, cautiously handing it over. "But don't hold me responsible if it don't sit right with you. There's more'n one Injun chief lost his sense of time an' place by overindulgin' in Albany Crystal—though I admit they always come back for more."

"You don't say," Gillis replied with a laugh of mockery. He sat back in his chair and looked over the snuff. He licked his finger and put a tiny bit in his mouth. "Strange, but this is familiar, somehow. Strike me blue! Yes, rather like the Brazilian I had down in Martinique during the war." With that he took a solid pinch and deftly drew it up both nostrils. Defries stood with his mouth open.

Then came an enormous sneeze. Gillis staggered from his chair and sneezed again, stumbling backwards across the room. In the fit of sneezing and coughing that followed, the secretary fell to his knees, half-blinded by tears. Clucking sympathetically, Defries helped him to the couch.

"Oh," Gillis groaned. "My word. What happened? How did that—"

Defries shook his head. "Strike me blue, Your Worship, I hadn't finished explainin' the technique of snortin' Albany Crystal! Never, never take it in two nostrils at once! An' *always* start with the left nostril first. You started with the right, sir, an' that's why you had such a misunderstandin' with it. I should've told you! It's all my fault, Your Excellency, but then I hadn't figured you would want to actually try it right away without thinkin' some about it."

Defries picked the snuffbox from the floor. "I'll just take this cruel stuff back to—"

"No!" Gillis held out one hand and dabbed at his eyes with a handkerchief in the other. "There isn't a snuff made that I can't handle. Set it on the desk there. I'll pay you for it next week—say Wednesday—when you come for your appointment."

"Appointment?" Defries showed his delight.

"With the paymaster. By this time on Wednesday, everything should be in order. But I insist on having the address of the manufacturers of this Albany Crystal. Stab my vitals! I have a few friends who would like to try it." He giggled. "But I won't tell them which nostril first! You did say left first, did you not?"

"Right! I mean, correct, sir. Left first. You can always remember that by thinkin' that Albany's on the left side of the Hudson River." Defries was backing out of the room, one hand holding his waistcoat tightly closed. Bowing politely, he said, "Albany's a nice place, sir. You should go there sometime. Not too many English there, you know."

Once in the street, Peter Defries felt better. He shifted the paymaster's official seal to his waistcoat pocket, where it was safe.

Then he chuckled. Probably no need to hurry. It wasn't likely Gillis would notice that the seal was missing that afternoon. He would not be able to see very clearly until the mixture of cayenne pepper and salt in his nose lost its fire.

chapter **8**

I WOULD THAT
THE WARS WERE ALL DONE

The journey by whaleboat from Detroit to the southern shore of Lake Erie took four or five days. Ella had stopped counting by the time they arrived at the mouth of the cove where Fort Presque Isle had stood—she had been too overwhelmed by the beauty of the wilderness in autumn. There was always something wonderful to observe, whether it was clouds of golden leaves fluttering to the ground all around their camps, or slender wedges of honking geese high in the deep blue sky.

The three whaleboats had skimmed before a smart wind the entire way from the straits, giving not the least cause for complaint among the eight boatmen and the thirty soldiers escorting Ella and Owen down to Fort Pitt.

The easy trip had given Ella much time to think of her difficult parting from Jeremy. She had tried to be brave and encouraging so he would not sense her worry, but the effort was unnecessary—when she was halfway through her talk, she noticed he was fingering *Gulliver's Travels* in his jacket pocket. With that she cut her speech short and hugged him, leaving the boy in Lettie Morely's care. Henry Gladwin would also be looking after his nephew. There was no need to worry about Jeremy.

The news of the continued hostilities in the east—especially the massacre at Devil's Hole—worried Gladwin, though, and he assigned a strong escort to this trip. There was always a chance of an attack on the overland trail from ruined Fort Presque Isle to Fort Pitt.

Ella closed her eyes and let the sun soak through her. A cool breeze contrasted delightfully with the sunlight. The soothing rhythm of the whaleboat scudding along relaxed her mind. Certainly there was peril in the wilderness, but Ella felt secure among these men. They were kind and considerate toward her, and Owen never tired of explaining things.

Already she could recognize beaver lodges along the shore, and she knew to look for them in the flooded marshland where their dams had backed up acres of water. Her eye could discern a moose standing motionless, watching them from the water's edge. She could tell a black spruce from a tamarack, and she knew that large stands of evergreens were hunting preserves of Indians, who burned them off periodically in order to keep growth low and thick, where deer liked to browse.

She quickly grasped the essentials of setting up camp, although the soldiers gladly put up a tent at night for her and Owen and took it down in the morning. In return she prepared treats to supplement the soldier's plain food, baking them over the campfire in a heavy kettle. The men looked forward each evening to Ella's contribution, whether it was sweet bread or a raisin cake. She had never had such enthusiastic guests at table as these rugged, easygoing soldiers and boatmen.

Owen called out that Presque Isle was in sight. Ella studied the shoreline, her hand shading her eyes. They were inside a sandy spit that curled from west to east, then sharply southward. Sails were dropped and the whaleboats came under oars into the small harbor. The trees were an explosion of bright orange and yellow, with dark pines standing here and there. Then Ella saw what she thought was a grove of pines—a mass of shadows among the broadleaf trees.

But her heart skipped when she realized this was not a grove, but all that was left of Fort Presque Isle. Charred timbers—The three whaleboats floated in to shore near the desolation. There was an uncanny silence. The only sign of life was a rat that leaped from the remains of the destroyed blockhouse where the little garrison had fought hopelessly against two hundred Indians. Only two of the twenty-eight defenders managed to escape the capitulation, and the rest were killed or taken prisoner.

Ella shuddered to think of what had happened at this dismal place, and she knew the same—perhaps worse—had happened at the other two tiny forts between Presque Isle and Pitt. They would pass by those ruins also on their journey, so Ella steeled herself for the eerie confrontation with death that Sutherland had experienced making this same journey during the summer. Her whaleboat was pulled ashore, and men spoke softly. Orders were given by young Ensign James Parker, who would command the escort as far as Fort Pitt, and they moved to the left, away from the skeleton of the fort, and settled down to make camp near a creek that emptied into the bay.

Even the warm beauty of autumn and the brightness of the sun did not dispel Ella's uneasiness. The entire party seemed to feel the same. Men went about their chores, stacking firewood, filling wooden buckets with fresh water, putting up canvas tents, and piling supplies and equipment to be covered with oilskins, but no one seemed interested in speaking.

Immediately Ensign Parker sent a patrol of seven men out to scour the area for signs of Indians. This had been done at each of their campsites, but nowhere else had it seemed so urgent a duty. Ella could not help strolling to the sandy beach and gazing across the spit to the blue expanse of Lake Erie. She needed a wider perspective. The wind swept across, ruffling the water of the bay, and helping to soothe her. She turned to look at the ruined, roofless blockhouse. The terror that had visited this pretty little cove still lingered here. With another shudder, Ella envisioned Fort Detroit lying in ruins, a hundredfold more hideous in death and destruction.

The woods were quiet, save for the clatter of tools as the men made camp fifty yards away. The wind rustled through the trees, and gentle waves lapped at the sand. Ella was glad when Owen came walking along the shore toward her and put his arm over her shoulders.

She turned away from the ruins and looked out at the lake. "It's an awful place," she said. "A beautiful, awful place! I wish we could have camped somewhere else."

He gave her a squeeze. "We can pass by Fort Le Boeuf, because it's only a half-day's march from here. Some of the lads there got away, but the next one, Venango, is worse than this. We'll pass them both by. The men don't want to camp near them any more than you do."

They strolled back to camp, and Ella felt stiff and sore from sitting hour after hour in a whaleboat. She wondered whether marching along the trail would be as difficult. In the weeks before they left Detroit, she had made an attempt to condition herself by taking long walks whenever possible, and she had tried to continue that recently whenever they made camp. Tomorrow they would set off down the trail toward Pitt, and she would learn just what strength it took to travel in the forest. At least her clothes were comfortable: shoes that were well broken in, an Indian-style doeskin dress, and a short burgundy cape and hood.

She went to her tent to direct the placement of its sparse furnishings—spruce branches overlaid with blankets as their bed, a couple of folding chairs. When the soldier arranging the quarters departed, she lay down gratefully on the bedding. The tent flap was closed, and her small world was a wash of natural light. Shadows of leaves danced on the canvas above her, and she heard someone tune up a fiddle. Another man was singing to himself, and soon a few others joined in. The men were determined not to be depressed by the dreary atmosphere of this place.

In a little while, as Ella was almost dozing, she heard a dozen strong voices singing a popular war song called "Hot Stuff." It was about the capture of Quebec by the British, and its verses were sometimes rude and vulgar—she knew because Lettie Morely had sung them to her with many a giggle when the men were not around.

Now the soldiers began singing a more mellow song—"I Would That the Wars Were All Done." She began to fall asleep as the words came in gentle harmony to her, and she heard Owen's voice among them:

> In the meadow one morning when pearly with dew
> A fair pretty maiden plucked violets blue.
> I heard her clear voice making all the woods ring,
> "Oh, my love is in Canada to fight for the king.
> And I would that the wars were all over,
> Oh, I would that the wars were all done."

As Ella slept, Sutherland sat by the campfire, cleaning his Pennsylvania rifle. One of the few of its kind in the northwest, the gun was rifled with spiral grooves inside the barrel, which gave it great accuracy. A pot of water was on to boil, and the bustle of the camp slowed as men took their rest in the eight tents pitched about the clearing. Sutherland noticed that this must have been where the lost garrison of Presque Isle did their laundry and fetched water, for the ground was flattened hard from all the walking over it. He wondered absently what had happened to those men. He knew two had managed to flee through the woods to Fort Pitt; some were prisoners, and others had vanished. A few had been given up when Bouquet defeated the Shawnee and Delaware at Bushy Run, but out in the forest there must still be British soldiers captured by the Indians, no better off than slaves, perhaps, and at every moment in danger of death.

It was the same story from Michilimackinac in the far northwest to the Cumberland Gap down in the Alleghenies. Whites were captives by the hundreds; everyone living on the frontier had a story to tell and a friend or relative lost in the fighting.

No wonder the borderers of Pennsylvania were up in arms. No wonder even peaceful Indians were in danger of retaliatory attacks by men hungering for vengeance against redskins.

The sun was low in the sky, and the men were preparing for the evening meal. A side of salt pork was sliced into chunks for boiling over the fire; a boatman was dividing up the last of a small keg of pickled olives, and dried peas were soaking in barrels of water before being boiled with the pork. Here and there a man opened his knapsack and took out what spices and flavorings he favored—vinegar, celery seed, mustard seed, all of which were potent antidotes for scurvy. It was simple fare, but filling. The men expected nothing more from the army.

They were paid only eightpence a day—less than enough for anyone to survive, let alone a man with a family. And even most of that meager sum was kept back as "subsistence" totaling sixpence a day. This money went for food, shoes, stockings, gaiters, medicines, and soap, and to repair the soldier's equipment. Furthermore, another penny a week was kept aside as a fee for the regimental paymaster and surgeon. Also, one full day's pay was taken off each year as hospital payment—for the solider's right to be admitted to Chelsea Hospital in his old age.

Like the others, young Ensign Parker was nearly destitute. Though he received much more than the enlisted men—three shillings a day after all the deductions—his expenses were much higher. His servant, a sturdy Yorker, cost him too much, but no aspiring officer could do without a servant. Also, he paid for his own lodging when at Detroit, and the care for his horse, now eating comfortably in the fort's stable, added to his daily expenses.

Many men from the British Isles would stay here and settle down when discharged in North America. But regular soldiers were universally disliked by civilians, and few would be able to find a better life outside the army, even though half were American-born. Many remained soldiers all their lives—they could do nothing else. After years of rising at command, of stepping out without question at the bark of a sergeant, and fighting whomever he was told to fight, the longtime soldier was often unable to shift for himself after becoming a civilian.

Sutherland looked around the camp, where six small fires burned and smoked in front of the tents. The men moved easily and comfortably about their chores. For all their misery and the thanklessness of their task fighting elusive Indians, these men were satisfied with their lot. The camaraderie, the daily gill of rum, the infrequent fling with whores or gamblers, the supreme glory of living through a great battle—all these were the fiber of a soldier's life.

Perhaps, Sutherland thought, they were no worse off than the poor borderers, who struggled in the soil day after day, with guns across plow handles, and an eye on forest shadows. Perhaps the soldier could say he had more security and just as full a belly as the farmer trying to bring in the harvest with the threat of a tomahawk always hovering over the heads of his wife and children.

Perhaps. But Sutherland was not sure. He had chosen a totally different life, one that promised danger but also rich reward if he were successful. He did not labor the winter through to trap and skin hundreds of furbearing animals, nor did he trade for goods which kept him alive only until the next round of trading. Sutherland was an entrepreneur who risked everything, including his life, in the hope of great wealth. One day, if all went well, he would be a controlling force in the northwestern fur trade, and he would be a very rich man.

In the tent, Ella still slept soundly. The smell of dinner was in the air, and Sutherland felt the urge to ready himself for the coming confrontation with the Pennsylvania borderers. From its case in his baggage he took out the claymore that had served him as an officer in the Black Watch Highland Regiment. He rubbed it with a little polish, and the blade gleamed. Others in the group noticed the sword and asked its history, but Sutherland simply said it had seen a few things.

The men knew his own story, and they regarded him as the foremost fur trader in the northwest. Though Ensign Parker was in command of the escort, Sutherland was looked to as the leader—and by the ensign, also. It was a long way to Pitt, and a longer way to Philadelphia. Some of these men would be making the entire journey with Ella and Sutherland, and they knew it might be dangerous at times.

However, Sutherland was not thinking about the trip to Philadelphia, but of the journey back. He and Ella would return as soon as the borderers were convinced to go home and live in peace with the innocent Indian tribes. That would be early in December, he hoped—about seven weeks from now. He could not endanger Ella with a later journey, in the dead of winter.

He had asked the old Ottawa, Mawak, to pick the dogs and sled for him. Mawak had learned much from the northern Indians and knew how to train dog teams. It was he who had shown Sutherland how to master a team and sled. Through Gladwin, Mawak would see to it that the best dogs and sled available were sent east for Sutherland, and that would make the journey home possible even in the coldest weather.

A few days later Ella and Owen sat with the soldiers at breakfast fifty miles down the trail. The whaleboatmen had returned to Fort Detroit, and the main party had marched through the dark, noiseless forest, where the only sound was an occasional woodpecker's rattle. They were following a French military road, now mostly overgrown. Hundreds of French soldiers had labored on the road during the critical years of the French and Indian War, and many had died of sickness and hunger. Here and there Owen had pointed out rotting crosses planted along the way, and after a few miles of travel, Ella could spot graves without any help.

They had passed the ruins of forts Le Boeuf and Venango. They had been part of what was termed the "Fort Pitt Communication," the line of forts that had connected the interior with the lakes. Now that harsh part of the trip was past, and they were camped above the mighty Allegheny River. Its sound filled the misty air, and Ella felt refreshed. They were only few days from Pitt, where they would journey once more by water on birchbark canoes.

Also past was the initial pain of walking long distances. Again the soldiers had been considerate of Ella and had not pressed on too quickly the first couple of days. Her feet had blistered only slightly, for she had a good pair of shoes, though they were not meant for forest trails.

She and Owen sat next to each other on a fallen log, drinking tea and huddling close to the fire to drive out the late-October cold. For a fleeting moment, the two of them might have been alone in the forest. Gathered at a little distance, most of the men were packed and ready to go, taking these last few minutes to themselves to rest and enjoy a pipe or a cup of hot, strong tea. Ella noticed that for some reason they were not departing as early as usual, but she thought nothing of it. She was grateful for the rest, and she savored it.

As Owen got up and walked away, Ella thought how much she loved him. It occurred to her that she really knew very little about the small details of his life. What was his favorite food? Was there anything at all that repelled him? Would he care if she arranged her hair differently? When was his birthday? Even that last important fact she did not know about him, just as he did not know that today was her own birthday.

After getting hold of the passing days and making sure it was October 25, Ella decided not to bother Owen with the news that she was thirty-two today. What difference did it really make, anyway? Birthdays were of no real use to anyone out in the depths of an endless forest—though it would be nice if he knew.

She drank her tea, not noticing her husband return until he gave her a small cloth-wrapped package tied with a blue ribbon. She looked up at him, amazement mingled with joy.

"Happy birthday," he said.

She jumped up, threw her arms around his neck, and hugged him. The soldiers drifted away to give them privacy.

She gasped, "How did you know?"

"How could I not know? You're my wife, aren't you?" He grinned and squeezed her tightly, and she gave him a huge kiss. "Besides, Lettie told me she'd have my hide if I forgot."

She laughed, and Sutherland turned to call the soldiers back. Almost shyly, they shuffled to the campsite, grinning like little boys. Ensign Parker stepped forward, saluted Ella, and said, "On behalf of the detachment, Mrs. Sutherland, permit me to offer our sincere congratulations and many happy returns of the day."

"Thank you ever so much, Ensign," Ella said, giving a little curtsy, then turning to the men and thanking them as well. She fumbled at Owen's package until it opened, revealing the most beautiful pair of moccasins she had ever seen. Soft and pliable on top, they were decorated with colored beads and porcupine quills.

He said, "They were made by Lela." That meant much to Ella, because Lela was the sister of Sutherland's dead Ottawa wife. As the squaw of Tamano, Lela was expected to be civil to Ella, but this gift, which Owen had asked the woman to make, was an expression of genuine approval. Also, Sutherland had made it clear that Ella should have the very best moccasins in order that she make this journey successfully. He wanted her to learn the ways of the forest! Then he said, "Mayla had begun them, before..." He said no more.

Ella unabashedly embraced him, and the silver pendant she wore flew out of her blouse, dangling on its chain. Sutherland touched it, and Ella looked down. It was the cylindrical pendant Sutherland once gave to Mayla. Later, when he and Ella fell in love, he gave the pendant to her as an expression of how much she meant to him.

He said, "Lela made them with the best materials she could find. The beadwork is the sun symbol of A-ta-hen-sic, the first woman. It is a blessing from Lela, bestowing fertility to its owner."

Ella blushed when some of the men grinned to hear Sutherland say that. But the embarrassment was broken off when an elderly corporal named Mullaney stepped forward, offering Ella a small green bottle.

"If you'll permit me," the corporal said to Sutherland, who nodded. "Ma'am, I thought you might want to use this here stuff as long as you'll wear Injun footgear. This is Injun remedy for sore feet, an' it's capital on blisters or whatever ails your tired dogs. I hope you don't think I be impertinent."

He gave a grin as Ella thanked him, then he touched the ragged brim of his tricorn to her and to Sutherland. She looked at Owen, who was smiling, aware of Ella's painful feet in spite of all she had done to hide her discomfort.

Ensign Parker said, "Well, now, it seems fitting that we should mark this occasion with some sort of ceremony! What say you, Mr. Sutherland, to resting one more hour here before we set off? I've got a tin of fine English biscuits I was saving for a friend at Pitt, but I reckon it'll go just right with another pot of tea for the lady and a spot of rum for the lads!"

The soldiers cheered to hear Parker suggest they tap the keg of rum, and Sutherland welcomed his offer to delay their departure a little longer. Ella hurried to her tent, the only one not yet struck, and massaged her sore feet with the lotion. They felt better immediately, and when she donned the supple moccasins, she thought she could run all the way to Fort Pitt if she had to.

Sutherland came into the tent and knelt beside her. They kissed, while outside the fiddler started up a bright tune. Then Sutherland admired the moccasins.

"These will do better than your shoes. I have to say it took all my power to keep from giving them to you as soon as we took to the trail. But I wanted to wait for your birthday. How are your feet?"

"Wonderful! This lotion is very soothing."

"Is it?" He picked up the bottle and looked it over. "Let's give it a try."

He sat down and took off his own moccasins. When he spread the lotion over his feet, Ella saw he had blisters, too—even worse than she had.

Sutherland noticed Ella looking at his sore feet, and said, "I haven't done much walking lately, either. Why do you think I always walked behind you? I didn't want you to see me limp."

In Montreal a letter was brought by messenger to the Cullen home, causing excitement almost as great as when Toby ran amok two weeks earlier. Emmy brought the envelope to Mr. Cullen in the parlor, and he immediately noticed the official red ribbon of the government wrapped around it. When he identified the wax seal, he bounded from his chair and called out, "A letter from the deputy paymaster general for the army!" That brought his wife and Linda scurrying downstairs, because the Cullens had been hoping for a contract to supply the army that would go after Pontiac's northern followers next year.

As Cullen stood up and tore open the letter, his wife hovered near. "I knew they would recognize you, Mr. Cullen! I knew they would come to you! Read it! Go on!"

"Do hurry, Father!" Linda chimed in, her mind full of how she would spend her family's earnings.

"'It is our honor, sir,'" he began, "'having recognized your past good service to the government and armed forces of His Majesty in the province of Quebec during these years of British rule, to compliment you on your meritorious conduct. Furthermore, we wish to inform you that the house of Cullen is being considered most seriously as the premier contractor for military campaigns in the coming year!'"

Linda whooped, and Mrs. Cullen clapped her hands, elbowing her husband to keep on reading.

"'Furthermore, it has come to our attention that your firm would be the best we might select for supply of all the posts of upper Canada, as well as for Niagara and Oswego!'" Another squeal from Linda, and by now Mrs. Cullen was giddy as well. Mr. Cullen, smiling broadly and standing straight and proud, continued: "'We ask, then, sir, that your firm hold itself in readiness for the delivery of all necessaries, subsistence supplies'... et cetera, et cetera... 'not less than two thousand men'... Ah, listen to this... 'and, sir, we doubt not that your firm will have its hands full meeting our needs, much to your profit, of course!'"

Mrs. Cullen shouted, "Of course! Of course!" She hugged Linda. They would be rich beyond all expectations; theirs would be the most important merchant house in Canada, perhaps even in all North America!

Cullen read further. The letter promised nothing definite, and told him merely to prepare for great things, but it puffed him up as much as if he had just been told by King George himself that he would definitely be awarded the coming contract.

Arriving at the final paragraphs, he read aloud in tones of infinite self-importance: "'... but before we may be permitted to conclude any final arrangements, sir, we must make it clear to you that this office has a certain sympathy for the heir of your late partner, Mr. Hamilton. Since Mr. Hamilton was a personal friend of ours, and since his delightful daughter is left alone in the world because of his unfortunate death, we must request'"—his voice gradually became sluggish—"'that the young woman continue on, as did her father, as your associate in this contract. We must further request that Miss Hamilton, whom we are pleased to note is the guest of your most generous family'"—Cullen's voice dwindled to a hoarse murmur—"'be afforded thirty-five percent of the contract—'"

Mrs. Cullen shrieked and collapsed into a chair. Linda anxiously patted her limp hand, but Mrs. Cullen could not move. In a slow, plodding voice, her husband read on:

"'Knowing your family's feelings for Miss Hamilton, we doubt not that you will be happy to afford her such an opportunity to make her way in the world.'"

Mrs. Cullen was weeping, her head on Linda's shoulder.

"'Of course, if for some reason your firm has legally terminated your business relationship with Miss Hamilton, or if you have satisfied any financial obligation to the young lady, then please consider these contracts as the property of your own house, and none other.'"

After reading the formal closing, Cullen tried unsuccessfully to decipher the scribbled signature near the deputy paymaster's official seal. But he was able only to make out that the letter came from the army's New York headquarters.

Cullen's hands were trembling as he laid the letter on a table. "What are we going to do?" he moaned.

Mrs. Cullen already knew the answer. Gathering herself, she cleared her throat and said firmly, "We have to find her immediately! We have to find her and get her to sign an agreement severing all ties and obligations. We can give her a few pounds and she'll sign! Then she'll have no right to anything we contract with the military!"

Cullen was worried that Mary might have left the city. Then he would be unable to do anything with the military unless she were a partner. "But we may never find her! Where is she?"

A voice behind them said, "The Grey Sisters." Emmy stood at the door of the sitting room. She had heard everything. "I walked there with her, when you sent her away."

The Cullens flurried around the room, finding paper, pen, ink, and the firm's official seal. Mrs. Cullen stuffed all these things into a small satchel while Linda hurried her father into a blue serge coat. He was propelled out the door, and as he bustled away, his wife called to him:

"Get witnesses! The abbess and a nun or two will do! And don't date it if you can get away with it! We'll date it last week, before we ever got this letter!"

In the middle of the street, Cullen stopped and asked, "How much shall I offer her?"

"Whatever she wants! Go as high as twenty pounds if you must!"

Cullen was off, and his wife and daughter went back into the sitting room, where they slumped into chairs. Neither had noticed Emmy pick up the letter and take it into the kitchen. Now, as the two women sat pondering the fortune to come, Emmy was seeing to it that the letter, written in the hand of Mary Hamilton, burned up completely in the fireplace. Emmy smiled to herself, the glow of the flames bright on her face. Never before had she felt so warm from such a very small blaze.

So it was that Bradford Cullen got his signed and sealed document releasing him from any obligation whatever to Mary Hamilton. And Mary, with Peter at her side, counted out sixty pounds, New York currency—enough to feed, clothe, and house her and the baby for many months to come.

chapter **9**

SWAIN

Four days' travel west of Philadelphia, a small log cabin stood in a clearing near a lively stream. Sunlight falling through the branches of an oak tree dappled the homestead's yard and warmed a yellow dog sleeping there. Beyond the cabin, bathed in light, an acre of stumps waited to be pulled. A little to the right of this field lay another acre, this one covered by withered cornstalks. Next year, if all went well, the stumps would be burned and uprooted, and both fields would yield Indian corn, enough to trade for goods at the general store in nearby Carlisle. When a third field was cleared, the settler might harvest enough to earn a little hard cash if he could cart it to the landing on the Susquehanna River and then send it by flatboat down to Baltimore. That day was two years off, if all went well—if Indians did not drive the family away or burn the cornfield, and no blight struck the harvest. Also, the farmer must be able to work day and night without being injured or seriously ill.

In another few seasons, this peaceful cabin, with its wisp of gray smoke rising from a dried-mud chimney, would be the home of a prosperous family, by frontier standards. Perhaps the windows would even be glazed, and a lean-to room might be added for the children.

Laughter came from inside the cabin, but the yellow dog did not stir. Ignoring flies that buzzed around its floppy muzzle, the hound seemed fast asleep, until suddenly it came alert, lifting its big head and staring at the forest, where a path opened into the clearing. The dog growled low in his throat. The laughter continued in the cabin, but when he rose and took a few steps toward the trees, barking fiercely, the laughter stopped. Someone slammed the door, and shutters were jammed closed on the windows. A hush came over the clearing. Even birds stopped chirping. The hound was silent, watching movement on the trail. Then he growled again, the hair bristling at the back of his powerful neck.

The dog kept his nose pointing at the path, so whoever was approaching on the trail was not attempting to circle the place. A musket pointed out through a loophole in the door, aimed at the path. Now the dog was barking and bounding back and forth, warning the stranger to approach no farther.

Then a whistle, sharp and high, came from the woods. The dog's ears went up, his head cocked, listening. The whistle came again, and there was a shout from the cabin. The musket was yanked inside, and the door opened suddenly. A strongly built redheaded man in an undershirt and drab breeches came out, the musket loose in one hand. He watched the yellow hound scamper clumsily toward the woods, where another man, tall and wearing worn buckskins, emerged from the path and began to feint playfully with the dog as it leaped and barked in recognition. The newcomer also had red hair, but unlike the man at the cabin, the fellow approaching had an enormous beard that hung down his massive chest.

"Thought you was a Injun, Jubal!" shouted the settler. At his side was a slim woman, dark and intense, whose features recalled earlier beauty. She was in her mid-twenties, her husband about thirty.

She stared at the newcomer, thinking how much alike these two brothers looked. Jubal Swain was older than her husband, Matthew, by five years, and he was a head taller, though not as broad. As she watched Jubal approach, Lucy Swain brushed her black hair back and smoothed her plain linsey dress, and her heart beat faster. She had not forgotten the thrill Jubal fired in her back in those long-ago days growing up in eastern New York.

But that was more than ten years past. She was Matt's wife now, though she and Jubal once had something strong and unforgettable. They had not seen Jubal in a year, but every time he showed up, Lucy found herself wondering what her life would have been had he not become a wild adventurer roaming the woods, lusting after danger and excitement.

Matthew rested the musket butt on the ground and shook hands firmly with his brother, though with little real warmth. Then Jubal hugged Lucy hard, squeezing the breath out of her, almost giving her a kiss but holding off when he saw she expected one. Matthew did not miss that bit of teasing. He had not forgotten that Lucy once had been Jubal's girl, and he knew there would always be a spark between them. He said nothing as Jubal stood back to look over the cabin and fields.

"Place looks better'n it did last year," Jubal said in a rough and husky voice. "Looks stronger—an' it better be, way these Injuns is bustin' out here."

Through the cabin door darted two little redheaded boys of five and eight. They shoved aside the hound, shouting their uncle's name. He laughed and picked them up as though they weighed nothing. "Whoa, now! Lookee here! Joe an' Willie! Now yuh rascals be nigh as big as your Uncle Jube! An' you're good-lookin' as your ma! Be yuh as smart as your pa? Yuh better!"

"Come inside, Jubal," Matthew Swain said. "You come at the right time. We're fixin' to eat dinner."

"What there is of it," Lucy said glumly. "With the Injun troubles we ain't been able to bring the corn in to trade at Carlisle. We ain't got much else."

"Hell, Lucy, girl, that's all right." Jubal grinned and set the children down. He held up a large deerskin pouch. "I got a few tidbits! I come with grub; I ain't a-beggin'."

They walked into the dark cabin and sat down at the table, which was set with four wooden trenchers and spoons. Lucy laid another place, adding clay mugs for each of them. In the wide hearth, a fire crackled, and over it hung a pot steaming with squirrel-and-corn stew. Jubal searched inside his bag and pulled out a salted beaver tail, holding it up proudly. This was a delicacy in the mountains, and the children's eyes popped as they stared at it.

Lucy looked at Matthew. "Your favorite, husband! We ain't et beaver tail since wintertime."

Matthew grunted. "Obliged, Jube."

Jubal said, "Cook it fast over the open flame, girl! Your boy here likes it that way, ain't that right, Matt?"

Matthew Swain nodded and tried not to stare as his brother searched through the bag again. It had the look of a Delaware traveling pouch, with colorful quillwork and embroidery all over the front.

Jubal said, "Got the tail same place as this!" He hauled out a bulky, cloth-wrapped package and tossed it to Willie, the older boy, who quickly opened it.

"Honeycomb!" Willie yelped in joy and scrambled to break a piece off, but his father snatched the sticky comb from him and offered it to Lucy. She was slow to respond.

"Save this to sweeten up the parched corn," he said severely. "Obliged again, Jube. We ain't had no sweetener here for some time." He noticed the disappointment in the boys and glanced at his wife. Then he broke two small pieces from the comb and gave them to Joe and Willie, who grabbed the honey with a gasp of thanks and scurried away.

Matthew Swain said, "You been tradin'? This bag looks Injun-made to me."

The elder Swain guffawed and said, "Yeah, little brother, I been tradin', yuh might say!" He reached once more into the bag. "I jest traded a few musket balls for all this stuff, an' the Injuns what traded me threw in these!"

He slapped two dried black scalps onto the table, roaring with laughter at his joke. Lucy shuddered, and from where they sat near the fire the children stared in awe at the scalps.

Matt handed the honeycomb to his wife and said soberly to Jubal, "Put them things away. They don't belong on no eatin' table."

Jubal gave a snort. He left the scalps where they lay and turned back to rummage in his bag again. The children had come to the table and were gazing at the scalps. Then Willie reached out to touch one, but his hand flew back as Matt Swain struck the scalps from the table onto the floor. Getting up, Jubal whirled in anger, his eyes meeting his brother's, both men hard as steel about to snap.

Lucy stepped quickly between them. She picked up the scalps, tossing them into Jubal's bag. Wiping her hands on her apron, she spoke without looking at either one.

"Is this how you act when you ain't seen each other for a year? For God's sake, sit down, Jubal! Matthew, it's over an' done! Let's talk while I do up this beaver tail. You know how much you like beaver tail, Matthew."

The woman implored her husband with her eyes. She had

had to come between the brothers too often before, and she was sick of it. She saw the fire in Matthew cool a bit, and she turned to Jubal, staring at him until he sat down sulkily.

After a silence punctuated by the clattering of pans near the hearth, Matthew began to fill his stubby corncob pipe with dried herbs and chickory. Tobacco was too scarce and expensive to be bought by poor farmers such as he. Jubal watched him, shaking his head. He reached down into his Indian sack again, and Matthew observed from the corner of his eye.

Jubal muttered, "Little brother, how kin yuh smoke that stuff? I swear I don't know why I'm so good to yuh, but blood's thick, I guess."

He triumphantly held up a foot-long rope of twisted tobacco, and Matthew eyed it with guarded interest. Jubal grinned to see his brother's uneasiness at being lorded over, at having his poverty thrown in his face. All the same, Matthew took some tobacco, crumbling it up in his callused hand. Jubal grinned at Lucy, who was busy with the tail, pretending not to notice her brother-in-law's wealth.

"See, girl!" Jubal scoffed, but she did not look around. "I tol' this man o' your'n to come into the woods with me last year! There be more where this come from! No sense yuh both scratchin' like chickens in the dirt for a bare livin', hopin' scalpin' parties'll pass yuh by! Matt, yuh kin come with me as a ranger, an' do some tradin' an' a-fetchin' up goods such's I brung yuh! Little Lucy kin set out the Injun trouble in Carlisle with the boys!"

Jubal was well aware of Matthew's determination to farm, and this invitation was more a mockery than an offer of a better life. Matthew was solid and honest, and Jubal was mean, savage, and a dangerous enemy. Matt would never go with his brother, but in making this offer, Jubal was telling Lucy that she had picked the wrong brother years ago.

For just an instant, Lucy looked directly at Jubal, and saw a covetous man—a man much taken with her, one whose burning eyes spoke his every thought. She looked away and finished coating the beaver tail with cornmeal paste, then jammed an iron spit the length of the meat and set it up over the flames to roast. Involuntarily she looked at Jubal again, and he smiled as he turned away from her. Matthew was lighting his pipe with a taper, but he missed nothing.

Ten years before, Jubal had left Lucy behind and had gone

into the wild, promising to come back to marry her. But he did not come back that year, nor the next, and Lucy's heart broke. Matthew had always wanted her, and he asked for her hand, but she refused, holding out for Jubal. Two and a half years after Jubal had left, she heard he was living with the Oneida and had taken a squaw. That was when Lucy succumbed and married Matthew. Jubal appeared a few months later, just before winter.

Jubal still wanted her, and he said so. How big and strong he had become! But he was wilder than ever. Three years living in the woods, where a man's strength of arm was law, had hardened Jubal Swain and made him dangerous. He was a man who took what he wanted, and was seldom refused. He had met no match in strength, cunning, or ruthlessness, and to this day he was without an equal in fighting. Jubal had a savagery that made other men shun him; only Matthew was fearless enough to stand up to him. When Jubal came for Lucy that day, a killing fight was about to begin, but Lucy stopped it. Pregnant with Matt's first son, she stepped between them, a butcher knife in hand, and faced Jubal down, threatening to stick him if he fought Matthew.

That had worked, and later the brothers tried to make peace. Over the years they seldom saw one another, but it was always the same between them—cold and wary and simmering with dislike. Jubal was free and easy, bold and fiercely handsome. Matthew was quiet, dogged, and not much given to talking— Lucy wished he would say more once in a while, if only to tell her he cared for her, though she knew he did.

Through the years, Matt and Lucy labored with every ounce of strength to build a home in the wilderness. But they remained very poor. They had come from New York to the Pennsylvania backcountry late in the last war, and the French and Indian raiders had driven them out twice, both times burning their cabins. Friends and neighbors had been brutally murdered, whole families wiped out, but still the couple dared to return when the French were defeated.

There had been no war parties for almost two years; then Pontiac's tomahawk fell, bloody and cruel, from the upper Susquehanna River south to the Monongahela. Hopes were dashed again, and this little farm on the edge of a nameless creek was once more a lonely outpost in a dangerous land.

Yet, they hung on. Massacres had been reported to the

northwest; traders had been attacked and killed to the east of them; and several nearby settlements had been abandoned by poor families now huddled in fright around Carlisle. What would happen next? No one knew.

Jubal Swain understood the dread that haunted his brother's tiny home. Brimming with success and self-confidence, free of the anxiety of a man waiting for a war party to fall on his family, Jubal made the most of his superiority. When the food was on the table, he asked why they stayed here when it was so perilous.

Matthew swallowed a juicy chunk of beaver meat and said, "If we go, there'll be nobody to protect the place. We'll lose it; it'll get burned down for sure."

Jubal shook his head. "This little patch ain't worth your lives, is it?"

Matthew glared at his brother, who continued calmly eating. "We stay. Nobody's gonna drive me off. So while you're under my roof, don't talk of me runnin', hear?"

Jubal grinned without humor and looked at Lucy. "Good food, girl." Then he pointed at Matthew with a piece of tailbone and said, "Boy, I come here to hear what your plans was. If'n yuh was gonna run, I was gonna tell yuh there's a better way . . ." He sucked at the bone, then tossed it to the hound lying under the table. The children, sitting with Lucy between them, were noisily gobbling down the beaver meat.

"So yuh say yuh'll stay, an' I'm right proud a brother o' mine has the gumption! Now, I'm gonna tell yuh *how* to stay." First he gulped a swig from the jug of corn liquor Lucy had set on the table. It was their last, and had been saved for Thanksgiving, but she did not want Jubal to know just how poor they really were.

Jubal shoved the jug over to his brother. "Matt, yuh know it's best to go after 'em Injuns afore they come after yuh! Right?"

"That's so." Matthew drank some liquor. "But a man can't leave his family unprotected an' go out huntin' Injun war parties. There ain't enough menfolk here to form a ranger company an' defend the cabins at the same time."

"Right!" Jubal took the jug back. "Yuh can't get up rangers an' haul your arse all the way to 'em villages up on the Scioto River or on the Maumee where hostiles be thicker'n flies on shit, yuh—"

"Jubal!" Lucy scolded. "Keep your language clean afore the children, hear?" She got up and took away the greasy trenchers from her sleepy boys. "You 'uns wash up and get to bed."

"Brother, everybody knows 'em raidin' parties don't come from this neighborhood, but I ain't suggestin' we go out after 'em."

Matthew was watching his brother, waiting for him to continue.

"Listen, how is it raidin' parties know just who to hit?" Jubal began. "How is it when a man's out cuttin' wood far enough from the house for 'em to git at his family, that's when they come in? How is it these strange Injuns kin raid a farm right after the corn's been parched an' git a mighty haul o' supplies in one swoop? An' ain't it been said that 'em bloody bastards—okay, Lucy, okay—them murderin' rats even know where a man's firewater's hid an' kin snatch it outa a burnin' house like it was their own? Answer that, kin yuh?"

"Sounds like somebody's lettin' on to 'em what they need to know, I guess," Matthew said.

Jubal slapped the table, and the children sat up on their pallet in a corner high above their parents' rough bed.

"Right!" Jubal exclaimed. "Yuh ain't so thick as these other farmers round here! Yuh be a Swain all right!"

"But who's tellin' 'em?" Lucy asked. It was getting dark outside, and the room was lit only by firelight, for the family could not afford candles or even tallow.

Jubal had another pull on the jug. "I'm comin' to that, girl. Now listen close." He began in a whisper, compelling Lucy to sit down at the table and lean forward as he spoke. The children hung over the edge of their pallet, the younger one clutching a cornhusk doll that had seen much of the farm's red soil.

"There be only one way these Injuns know what they know, an' that's by bein' told by their cousins an' brothers what pretends to be peaceable! I mean these Moravian rats, and these others what claim they be Christians! That's right! Yuh can't believe it, kin yuh? Well, it's true, b'God, an' any halfwit kin see it!"

He gulped a hasty swig. "Look for yerself next time yuh pass 'em Moravian villages. Go in an' see 'em fine blankets they got! See the white man's clothes an' tools. See the stock an' chickens they got! Even the richest white farmer would admire to have that! And how do they get it? By gettin' paid off for tellin' the hostiles who to hit!"

"Hold on, man, hold on!" Matthew rumbled, shaking his head slowly and dragging the jug across the table. He started chuckling and said, "The reason Moravian Injuns is well off is 'cause the German missionaries teachin' 'em is even smarter than a Quaker! 'Em Moravian Germans taught their Injuns how to farm, gave 'em good land to do it on, an' they been at it a lot longer than any of us!"

"Right!" Jubal roared. "They been at it a helluva long time because they ain't been raided year after year by hostiles—"

"They got hit in the last war; they jest recovered fast, bein' as there's so many of 'em."

"Hell, they didn't get hit like the farmers!" Jubal belched and excused himself to Lucy. "Tell me why the hell 'em hostiles leave Moravian Injuns alone if Moravian Injuns be so cozy with us whites? Tell me that! Why, 'em hostiles could git more'n one raid on a damn Moravian henhouse than they could tearin' apart a hundred settlers' cabins like your'n! 'Em hostiles could get rich as princes cleanin' out just one nest o' peaceful"—he spat into the fire—"peaceful Injuns!"

Again Matt Swain's voice was calm and slow, a sharp contrast to his brother's voice, which had lost its huskiness and now sounded shrill, with an excited twang. Matt said, "Hostiles don't raid just to get what they can carry off, you know that."

"Yuh don't say? Then jest what do they want?"

"They want us off what they claim is their land. They want to drive all white settlers out, an' that's more important to 'em than raidin' for scalps, I guess."

"Hah! Yuh guess so!" Again Jubal slapped the table so that it jumped. "Yuh talk like a goddamn Quaker, boy! Believe me, 'em goddamn Moravian Injuns an' every other so-called peaceful Injun in these parts is the eyes an' ears of every raidin' party from the lakes to the Ohio River an' out to the Delaware! Believe me, every time a Christian Injun drifts by here sayin' his prayers, he's lookin' yuh over so he kin tell his pals if you're worth hittin' or no. Only reason yuh ain't got hit yet's 'cause you're too damn pore, an' yuh ain't got nothin' worth takin' but your scalps—"

Matthew was on his feet, fists clenched. The children gasped, and Lucy jumped up. Jubal was calm—ready for trouble, but calm. He looked at Lucy and said with a soft voice,

"Touchy, ain't he?" Then to Matthew, he said, "Set, boy. I didn't mean offense. I'm jest riled up's all. Set now. Have a drink."

But Matt was angry, and he towered over his seated brother. Jubal looked at Lucy again and said, "Get your man to set, girl. I don't want him to start nothin' we'll be sorry for."

Lucy was frightened. Now Jubal was staring back at Matt. Carefully putting her hands against her husband's heaving chest, she pleaded, "Please, Matt. Please let it be."

Slowly, Matthew Swain recovered and sat down. Jubal acted apologetic and said, "Look, boy, if yuh don't believe me, come out with me to that there Moravian town down to the creek an' take a look for yerself. We'll walk right in an' take a close look. I got a few ranger boys in a camp not far from here who'll go along. Then yuh'll see what I mean. Yuh'll see the only way you're gonna be safe is by rootin' out 'em Moravian varmints. Drive 'em out! Kill 'em if yuh gotta, but do it quick, afore they send a raidin' party here!"

Jubal turned to Lucy. "I'm sayin' this for your sake an' the youngsters'. I know how stubborn this brother is, but mebbe yuh kin talk sense to him. It's the only way yuh'll sleep at night."

The fire burned low, leaving the room dim, with the faint hue of sundown touching the western window. After some time, Matthew Swain spoke.

"I've heard such talk about Moravian Injuns, but I ain't believed it, though lots o' folk talk way you do, brother. But much as I want to stop all this worry an' git on with buildin' this place, I don't go for doin' what some folk want to do."

Jubal leaned forward, his eyes dark coals in the firelight that flamed in his red hair and beard. "Do what?"

"You know—raise enough men to burn out the Moravians." Matthew shook his head. "No, I won't be a party to murder."

"Murder?"

"That's what it'd be, an' you know it! All 'em Moravian Injuns can't be helpin' the hostiles! But if a lot o' angry bordermen git together an' go after 'em Injun Christians, there'll be blood, an' when killin' starts it's mighty hard to stop. The wrong people get rubbed out."

"Pshaw!" Jubal declared and sat back, folding his thick arms. "Nobody wants to rub out 'em what don't deserve it, boy! We just want justice done, is all."

Lucy, fumbling with some knitting, spoke quickly. "Why you want Matt in this?"

Jubal spoke with distaste. "Because Matt's—looked up to by most o' these dirt farmers here. I've talked this 'round some, an' most o' these settlers asked if I talked to Matt yet." Jubal gave his brother a grudging look of respect. "Seems none o' 'em want to take steps less'n Matt Swain says it's the right thing to do. Don't ask me why they think so much o' the boy, him bein' so hot-tempered an' all."

Jubal noticed Matt's pride in this backhanded compliment, and he knew he was on the right track. He kept on talking about settlers, how they needed a leader like Matt. He said Matt could get this matter straight once and for all; if the Moravians were innocent, they could clear the air and tell everyone what was what as far as the Christian Indians were concerned.

Matthew was persuaded at last. He said, "All right, I'll go with you to this Moravian village. We'll take a look around. But no trouble unless it's necessary, hear?"

Jubal put his hands up, palms showing, and he grinned pleasantly. "You be in charge, boy." Then he looked at Lucy, who saw how charming he could be when he wanted to. "Don't worry about Lucy an' the boys, 'cause I'll have a couple o' men rovin' the woods around here, keepin' an eye on 'em."

"They better be good men," Matt said.

Jubal laughed. "They're good. In fact, those boys an' me picked up this little bag o' trinkets by cuttin' off a couple o' hostiles sneakin' through the trees not far from here, probably headed this way."

Jubal's eyes twinkled as he spoke, but Matthew was deep in thought. Lucy noticed the bag where it lay near the table. Its decorations were unusual, having been painstakingly embroidered with fine thread. She looked closer and saw it was certainly not a Delaware design, or any she had ever seen on an Indian pouch. The embroidery seemed to be in the form of strange words, and below them was the unmistakable symbol of a cross. The pouch had been made by a Christian.

"Like it?" Swain asked, seeing she was staring at the pouch. "It's yours if yuh like it. Just leave me the doodads an' the Injun hair. It's yours."

• • •

Late that night, lying awake in the grass outside the cabin, Jubal Swain contemplated Lucy. He was wrapped in a blanket, his head on the Indian pouch, which she had refused. He thought of her, and he thought of the past. He turned on his side, imagining Lucy naked beside his brother, and it galled him.

She should be his. By rights Lucy *was* his, just as she had been his years ago before his brother sweet-talked her at a time when she needed a man. But things would change soon. One way or the other, Lucy would be his, and that damned self-righteous fool of a brother would have nothing to say about it. Swain laughed to think that Matthew could probably work a week on his little patch of dirt before he ever noticed his wife was gone, if it wasn't for the food she cooked him—the food, and her naked body at night.

He ached inside to think of Lucy, as he did every time he thought of her. He could not stop thinking of her. The first chance he had, he would take her, and no one would be able to stop him.

chapter **10**

THE SHADOW OF DEATH

Jubal Swain found his sleeping followers just after dawn, camped in the forest half a mile from his brother's cabin. All six were wild, tough men, living outside the law but governed by Swain. When he saw them bundled in blankets, the morning's frost lying thick on their gear, Jubal swore loudly and kicked one of them in the ribs. Another he spat on, and a third, who came up with a knife, found himself staring at the muzzle of Swain's long rifle.

"Jube . . ." this fellow mumbled weakly, unable to look away from the muzzle. He was a chunky, short man, with a scar running along his cheek from his sandy hair to the point of a weak, unshaven chin. "What'n hell—?"

"Shut up, Morgan," Swain snarled, putting up the rifle. "Yuh varmints jest be glad I ain't some buck, or I'd be eatin' your vittles an' admirin' six scalps on my belt."

"Aw, Jube," another began. Hurley was a tall, lanky woodsman, the eldest of the bunch, and the only one with a mustache. "They ain't no sculpin' parties for miles around, Jube." He rubbed his side where Swain had kicked him.

Swain sneered and looked away at the dead campfire. "Rustle up some eats, somebody. We gotta make some distance this afternoon, so git grub in yuh afore we go."

"Whar?"

"Moravian town."

Every man turned toward Swain, because he had just said

122

what they had been waiting for weeks to hear. Morgan asked, "We gonna hit it today?"

"Mebbe." Swain tossed his travel bag on the ground. "First we're gonna look it over. I got my brother to throw in with us—leastways he's gonna make a visit to 'em Moravian Injuns with us, an' he'll size things up. If'n he thinks 'em Moravians's helpin' hostiles, he'll git us a passel o' settlers to run 'em out—"

"An' git what we kin git in the runnin'?" Hurley's grin showed a gap in his front teeth. "I gonna git me a sweet little Moravian squaw!"

But Morgan was not so sure of all that Hurley anticipated. After holding his musket lock close to dry tinder and firing it to start a blaze, he asked Swain, "Your brother gonna let us have our way with 'em Moravian Injuns?"

Swain respected Morgan's brains. Unlike the others, he thought things through, and that was why the man was the group's leader when Swain was not around. He shook his head. "I'll convince him 'em Moravians need a lesson. One way or t'other, he'll help us rile up these settlers, an' there won't be nobody kin keep us from havin' our way with every Moravian town in Pennsylvania."

Hurley drawled, "I don' see why the hell we gotta convince nobody o' nothin'. What the hell do it matter if'n settlers jine us or not?"

Swain gave Hurley a long, withering look. "Because, yuh slug-brain bug-tit, if'n we hit 'em Moravians without settlers on our side, we'll git the army on our tails! But if 'em settlers is with us—hell, all we be is honest scouts along to help out! If 'em settlers is with us, nobody kin say nothin' about Jube Swain an' his boys robbin' poor helpless Injuns." He laughed and hunched down near the fire Morgan had got going. "We's jest doin' our patriotic duty!"

They all laughed, though Swain was already thinking about something else. He had another plan to convince the country-folk that the Moravians were hostile. He wondered whether he had the stomach for it. Then Lucy came to mind, and he felt the fire flame up inside. Yes, he could do it.

Peter Defries and Mary Hamilton had never been happier. Even Mary's interlude with Duncan McEwan had not brought her the joy she felt in the days with Peter after she received the sixty pounds from Bradford Cullen. She and Peter met Emmy later that first day and had a picnic lunch on the pretty bluff overlooking the river. She was delighted to be with her friends on the edge of the moor, dining on pâtés, delicious croissants, raisins, French doughnuts, cheeses she had never seen in the stingy Cullen household, and wines of three different kinds.

There was even a basket of scraps for Toby, who soon lay down, sated, her stomach bloated, though there was enough left for two more Tobys.

They had triumphantly toasted Mortimer Gillis, whose official seal reappeared on his desk the same day that Peter Defries showed up to be paid—one thousand pounds, New York currency. Peter wondered if the secretary had even missed the seal, but he suspected that frequent work was not included in Gillis's normal routine.

For three more days they celebrated. They found Mary lodgings in two small rooms next door to the Devalier home. She would be comfortable there, able to visit with Mrs. Devalier, and assured of a swift response when her time came. At the end of those first happy days, Emmy knew she should come out with them no longer and left them alone. Later, each morning at break of dawn, the couple met in Mary's street and walked together. There was always something to talk about, but often they were content simply to walk or to sit and say nothing at all.

Their favorite spot after the knoll was near the docks, where they could watch ships being loaded. There they both let dreams run free, and the sight of a ship raising sails filled with the west wind brought them close to the water, staring intently.

Peter said, "I'd like to load one of 'em with cargo and take her to the West Indies. I'd trade for molasses, spices..." He was about to say slaves, because there was no more lucrative cargo than human chattel, but he thought of faithful Emmy and did not say it.

Mary added, "I'd like to do the same. Then we'd stop in New York, unload and load up with iron and wheat, and we'd sail to the Azores. What's the product in the Azores?"

"Slaves."

"Oh. Well, we'll go to Madeira instead and get wine."

They laughed. Peter said, "If this thousand pounds was all mine, I'd do it tomorrow. Would you go with me?"

She smiled. "It's not all yours. You've got to pay the families of those poor men, and you have to pay for the goods you shipped."

"Would you go?"

She giggled and teased him with her eyes, not really meaning to. "If you had a ship like that one, Mr. Defries, I might just go with you."

"I don't have a ship like that one."

She shook her head. "Then we can't sail the seven seas. We can't even go down to Trois-Rivières or Quebec."

He was gazing at Mary in a way that made her blush, but she did not mind it. She looked back at him and wondered what she would do if he kissed her. For all his rough and honest charm, his good looks and kindness, Mary was not sure just what it was she felt for Peter Defries. She knew love when it had burst into her life in the form of Duncan McEwan. Life had been hard but simple then. There was no other way. But things had changed. Now there was a baby. Peter was a man who wanted to roam, to be a merchant, and to return to Albany soon. Indeed, now that his knee was healing and he had been paid, he would be leaving any day. Dare she let herself fall in love with him? Anyway, was it love, or was it the need for someone to marry, to share life with, to be a father to her child?

Suddenly her happiness left, and Mary looked away at the river, where the ship's sails were blooming with the glow of sunset. Peter sensed her uneasiness. The wind gusted, lifting whitecaps on the broad river. Mary pulled her shawl closer, and he took off his watch coat and put it over her shoulders. She smiled at him, and for a moment seemed to be seeking something in his eyes. He wanted to tell her he loved her, that he would marry her, but before he could gather up the courage to speak, she looked away at the ship once more, and he lost his nerve. Now he looked at the ship, too.

She said, "It's a beautiful sight, isn't it?"

"Yes," he replied. Then, "Do you want to stay in Montreal?"

Her voice was soft, and he could hardly hear her. "I don't know where I want to be, Peter." The docks were deserted now, the workers finished for the day. Seagulls wheeled overhead and cried in their restless way, diving to the surface and skimming along it before whirling upward again to wheel and cry.

Defries felt a little like a gull just then: skimming across the surface when he spoke to Mary, but unable to tell her what he felt. They stood there a little longer, then they turned and walked back into the city.

Jubal led his six men to Matthew's farm, and when they shambled out of the trees, the yellow hound growled and ran at them, his hair standing on end as he snapped and barked. Lanky Hurley took a swipe at the dog with his musket butt, and the animal yelped in pain. Hurley laughed, but he was cut short as Matthew leaped out of the cabin and caught him by the throat, hauling him off his feet and stopping his breath.

Jubal stood back grinning as Morgan came in to help Hurley. But Morgan walked into a savage kick in the groin that dropped him to his knees. Hurley flew through the air like a rag doll, colliding with another of Swain's gang, and a fourth made a move to jump Matthew, then hesitated and thought better of it when the big settler swung around to face him.

All the while, Jubal Swain was doubled with laughter. Then he saw Morgan's hand slide down to his sheath knife, and he stepped between Morgan and Matt. "That's it!" Jubal shouted, still chuckling. "We didn't come here to fight 'im. Anyway, it'd take more'n six o' yuh to beat a Swain, even a little one like this." He grinned at Matthew, but his beady eyes glittered coldly. "Teach your dog some manners, brother."

Matt Swain looked Jubal in the eye and said, "Teach your own dogs manners, Jube."

That got a grumble from the others, but a wave of Jubal's hand quieted them. He looked over his men with contempt, then back at his brother. "Let's get down to business. My boys'll back us up when we go to Moravian town today."

Matthew was hesitant. "I don't need 'em. The Moravians know me well enough."

Swain waved his hand. "They'll stay back when we go in. Never know what's on the road 'tween here an' there; word is a raidin' party's out."

Reluctantly, Matthew agreed.

After taking Lucy and the boys to a neighbor's cabin, Matt gave his usual casual farewell, hardly even kissing the woman, though he hugged the boys. It was not that Matthew did not love her, but he came from a life where too much emotion suggested weakness, and he did not need to tell Lucy he cared for her. He presumed she knew it. He left her at the cabin door and did not even turn at the edge of the woods to wave. He would be back by sunset, after all; the Moravian village was no more than ten miles away.

At the rear of the group, however, Jubal looked around. He stared long and hard at Lucy. She did not avoid his gaze. Her pale, weary face even took on a kind of light, a fire from within—or was it from Jubal that this fire came? Then he was gone with the rest of them, swallowed up by the forest.

The slender young farmer who owned the cabin said absently, "That be a rough bunch, I warrant." He spoke to Lucy, who was holding her arms and feeling cold. "'Specially that brother-in-law yuh got! He's tougher'n 'em all, 'cept for your own man, I warrant! Yep, that Jube Swain is some kinda fella."

The man and his scrawny wife went into the cabin, and the children set to scampering around the yard. Lucy stood watching the forest for some time. Jubal Swain was indeed quite a man. She was still warm inside from the last look he gave her, and she wondered just what it was she really felt for him. Sometimes she thought she knew, and it frightened her.

Two hours later the Swain party was within a couple of miles of the Moravian village, walking single file through the woods, no one talking. They looked a formidable bunch, heavily armed, all but Matthew giving an impression of ruthlessness.

As the eight men moved along the trail, they did not notice a young Delaware brave crouching behind a tree less than ten paces away. He counted them as they passed, and he realized the Moravians were in deadly danger. His name was Niko-lota, and he knew something about warlike whites. He was a member of a small raiding party that was about to set off for the western stronghold of Chief Pontiac to join him before winter set in.

Niko-lota was a stocky youth not yet seventeen, but courageous and skillful in war, for all his lack of years. He had been at the bitter defeat of Bushy Run, and had found himself looking death in the eye until the one called Donoway spared him and let him run for his life. He hated whites, though he longed to repay the debt Donoway had laid on his shoulders. As much as he strove to drive whites out of his people's country, he wanted as much never to owe a white man anything—not even one who was an adopted Ottawa.

Now, as he watched the last man walk along the trail, Niko-lota felt fear. In the Moravian town lived his older sister, Aleta, who had been converted some years ago. She was given to white ways, and she had begged Niko-lota again and again to bury his tomahawk forever, but he could not do that. He did not understand her, nor did he understand the faith she claimed to have taken into her heart. Yet their bond was strong, for they had been close ever since their parents had died of fever six years earlier.

Now he must go to her before these white fighters reached the town. He must tell the village they were in danger. Trouble had been unfolding between whites and the Christian Indians for three months; just the other day two Moravian Indians were found murdered in the forest. Niko-lota left his hiding place and ran through the trees on a shortcut to the village.

He found the campsite where two cousins waited for his return. Soon they were running as fast as possible for the village, and in a few minutes they burst into the clearing, where eight stout log cabins stood amidst neat, well-tended fields. Dogs barked as the three young warriors ran through the middle of the village, shouting warnings to everyone. In a moment, the village was a confusion of jabbering squaws and worried men. There were about forty people here, most of them children. They had lived for weeks in dread of an attack by angry whites. Now they were sure it was coming.

They knew Niko-lota, though they had asked him not to come among them when he was raiding. They feared to be linked to him, but now as he ran through the village crying out that they must flee, they knew he was wise in the ways of war, and they obeyed.

Men gathered up what few wordly possessions they could carry, and women quieted and collected the children. Here and there a donkey and cart appeared, and friends shared this means of taking with them what was precious.

Moravian Indians were peaceful. Converted from several tribes, they collected under the shepherding of German Moravian pastors. They worked the soil and built cabins as fine as the best white dwellings. This settlement worshiped in a good church a few miles away, where a larger community of their kind lived and where they would now go for refuge. If their pastor had been at hand, he might have persuaded them to stay in their own village, and then he would have met the approaching whites. But there was none among them who would risk that gamble, and they chose to fly before something happened.

Niko-lota knew these people were not cowards, for he had often seen them stand up to danger, fearlessly confronting angry Indian war parties that had threatened to wipe them out if they refused to give up their white ways and fight with their own kind. He respected them for their faith and their courage, yet he despaired for the safety of Aleta.

He found her helping an elderly man and woman onto a donkey cart. She was a tall, large-boned girl, with long hair braided down to her waist. With strong, quick movements, she tossed bags and boxes of goods into the cart with the old folk. Niko-lota helped with the last sacks, then he took her aside as the cart lurched away.

"Sister," he said breathlessly, "it is time I go to Pontiac."

She did not show her disappointment. She had known this moment would come. There was nothing more to say, though he ached to take her with him, and she prayed for him to give up the warpath. Aleta's dark eyes were soft, her voice firm. "God go with you, brother."

They held one another's forearms. For a few seconds their eyes filled with one another; both would remember how they once stood in this place.

Niko-lota's cousins called to him that the whites were near. He hurried his sister away, and she followed the flight of her people. When she was gone, Niko-lota joined the two warriors in a hiding place on the edge of the village.

A little while later, the whites came into the clearing, walking single file, flintlocks held ready. It took great restraint for Niko-lota and his friends not to shoot at them, but that would have brought terrible retribution on the Indians who had fled. The three young men watched silently as the whites drifted into the village.

Moving together from cabin to cabin, two redheaded backwoodsmen took their time searching the place. Then the others came into the village and went inside cabins. A vase of flowers was thrown from a window to smash on the ground. At another cabin, the invaders came out wrapped in fancy cloth, dancing like women.

One of the two big redheads in the lead shouted to the others, who stared at him angrily. Niko-lota sensed this man was commanding the others to stop pillaging. Then the other redhead, the one with the beard, called to this fellow, beckoning him into a cabin.

The rest stayed outside, coming close together, watching the door where the redheads had gone.

There was a rifle shot.

The men in the village did not move. They kept watching the cabin, obviously very tense, until the bearded one came to the door. There was a heavy silence. Then he motioned the others to come in.

The warriors watched as the man without a beard was carried from the cabin, blood covering his face. One of the whites, a short fellow, dropped to his knees near the body and yanked out a scalping knife. But the bearded man shouted and kicked him away.

The whites divided up, stealing what they could from the cabins and filling big sacks with their booty. Flames soon leaped from the window of the cabin, and Niko-lota had to hold his cousins back from opening fire. It was too late for that. There was nothing Niko-lota could do—nothing but wreak vengeance on all whites, wherever he found them. For they were all guilty, as far as he was concerned.

Peter and Mary met the next morning on the road to the bluff. They would walk together, as they had done every morning for almost two weeks. Each had something in mind, but neither spoke about it. Peter was in love with her; he had no doubt about that. But though he longed to tell Mary, he feared she would refuse him. Now, while they walked quietly, talking now and then, there seemed no need to confirm ties, to ask for promises. Their relationship was too special to jeopardize; Defries thought if he pushed things further, Mary might slip away and leave him forever.

He knew she was worried, with the baby to think about, and he also knew she had to go slowly, to act deliberately. He would not press her, but he would find the right moment to speak his heart, and he had to do it before going back to Albany, where his business drew him.

He should have left for Albany long ago, but despite its attraction and the demands of business, he could not leave Mary until he had spoken his mind. As they walked along the lane, watching Toby scouring bushes ahead of them, Peter knew that this morning was the one. He would tell her when they reached the bluff. He sorted out his thoughts, arranged phrases and sentences, and readied himself for whatever might come when he told Mary Hamilton he loved her.

As Mary walked, her linen cap hiding her face from him, she sensed something. Peter was quieter than usual this morning, obviously thinking hard. Mary, too, suspected that they could not continue this way. She cared very much for him, but she was not sure she could become his wife, could spend the rest of her life with him.

Peter thought they would never reach the bluff. He had not realized just how long the path was; now that he had resolved to speak when they got to the bluff, he was impatient. He looked at her, and she turned to him. They smiled, then found they had stopped walking. He was close to her, his heart pounding. Hers skipped.

Toby came to their side and stood staring at them, expecting something. Mary felt like laughing. Peter could wait no longer.

"Mary—"

"Yes?"

"Mary—"

"Yes, Peter?"

His mouth was dry, his palms moist. He wanted to take her in his arms, but his hands were ridiculously wet. He rubbed them on his breeches.

Mary said again, "Yes, Peter?"

He cleared his throat and carefully took her by the shoulders. She did not resist.

"Mary . . ."

She dared not say anything, lest they go on and on without getting anywhere. She gazed at his blue eyes. He was so very handsome and honest.

"Mary, I ain't much good at this. I mean, I ain't done this sort of thing ever before, but—well, you know I ain't the kind beats around the bush. You know?"

She nodded, flushing.

He said, "So, my—I mean, what I mean is—Mary Hamilton, I'm right happy bein' with you."

She waited for more, but he simply stared at her.

"Peter?"

"Mary?"

"Peter, I'm happy with you, too."

He smiled, and swallowed clumsily. Wind gusted down the

lane, and his mind seemed to clear as though by magic. He realized where he was, and how foolishly he was talking, and how beautiful Mary was, and he knew there was nothing else to say except, "Mary, I'd like to make you my wife."

She was ready for it—until he said it, and then she might suddenly have been in quicksand. All her composure and self-assurance melted. The baby kicked hard, and her hands went to the spot. Peter noticed her hesitation, and he put his hands on top of hers. The wind blew her cap back, and her hair struggled free.

"I want you to know that I understand your position, Mary, and I ain't tryin' to take advantage of a weak moment, if you know what I mean."

She nodded quickly and felt a silly tear in her eye. She wiped it away, then put her hands back on his, which were still against her tummy. The baby kicked again, and he looked surprised to feel it.

He asked, "Does that—does that hurt you?"

She shook her head, looking at him as though he were completely new to her. Whatever it was she felt, it was strong and it was good.

He surprised her by saying, "Mary, one day you'll love me, I promise—"

"Peter! I—"

He put his arms around her and kissed her gently, drawing her against him so that the bulge in her middle pressed close, and the baby kicked them both.

Peter said, "I'll make you happy. An' I'll love the baby like he was mine."

Mary closed her eyes, her head on his shoulder. "He?"

"Why, even if it's a girl, I'll be a good pa to her. Though maybe a mite strict."

Mary laughed and pushed him back. She looked into his eyes. He understood her, and he was willing to grow with her and give her love for him time.

Her love for him! Yes, it was love. Different from her first love, but love, indeed. Perhaps even deeper and more poignant.

Now Mary Hamilton was happy. Relief and joy surged through her. Then his lips were on hers, and she felt like crying and laughing at the same time.

A drizzle of light rain brought them back to their senses. Lightning flashed, followed by a loud clap of thunder. They

looked about for shelter, but there was only an empty hay
wagon in the field nearby. Mary motioned to it and started to
run, but Peter grabbed her, pulling her back to him. Raindrops
became larger, splashing the road into a quick rush of mud.

"Peter!" she cried. "We're getting soaked!"

He said, "You haven't answered me, and you'll get wetter
until you do!"

She nearly knocked him over then, crashing against him
and kissing him with ardor, until he squeezed her tight and
kissed her, oblivious of the rain that spattered over them. The
wind blew hard, but they kissed until a thunderbolt shook them
apart.

Mary shouted to him, "I love you, Peter Defries! I'll be
happy as your wife!"

He whooped for joy, picked her off the ground, and ran
through the wet grass, Toby bounding behind, to take shelter
under the big hay wagon until the storm passed.

Peter and Mary were married in a private ceremony at the home
of Dr. and Mrs. Devalier. The only other witness was Emmy,
who spent enough tears of joy for a hundred guests.

The couple moved into Mary's lodgings next door, and there
they made ambitious plans for the future. Their first days together were full of bliss, but after a week, they knew Peter
must finally go down to Albany. He would return in midwinter,
he promised, in time for the birth. She understood, particularly
when he said his men had left families who desperately needed
their earnings to get through the cold months. Mary accepted
what her husband had to do, but she wished he could stay.
Now that she had given herself to Peter, she needed him more
than she had ever imagined. When the baby came, she had to
be with him. He promised to return no matter what stood in
the way, and that was enough for her to let him go with her
blessing.

"They're back!" shouted the older of Lucy Swain's two sons.

Everyone dashed out of the cabin to see the men return. It
was almost dark, and they had been gone much longer than
expected. As Lucy stared toward the shadows of the forest, she
saw two figures moving toward them, and realized that one
was a horse and the other was Jubal. Willie was running toward
his uncle, the yellow hound loping alongside. About forty yards

from the cabin, they reached Jubal and the horse. Lucy heard the dog begin to whine, and then her son screamed. Shock went through her. She gasped and dashed from the farmyard.

Whimpering "Matthew, Matthew?" Lucy flew along until Jubal caught her, his hands on her arms. She trembled, feeling faint.

"Matt?" she said weakly. The boy was hugging his father's body as it hung over the horse.

Jubal said slowly, "He's gone, Lucy. Injuns got 'im."

Little Willie was trying to shake the life back into his father, and the yellow dog was on its hind legs, whining sadly.

Numb, Lucy pulled away from Jubal and went to the body. Jubal came to her side and tugged back the wailing boy. Lucy touched her husband's face and shuddered. The body was cold. She broke down, falling to her knees, tears streaking her cheeks. "Matt, Matt."

The neighbor and wife appeared, he with his gun. Swain asked them to keep Lucy and the boy there; he would dig the grave that night at the Swain farm. They could hold a funeral in the morning.

The neighbor muttered, "Goddamn murderin' heathen! Was it the Moravians?"

Swain nodded.

"Goddamn murderin' heathen! They'll pay! Call 'emselves Christians, they do! Well, let's see what kind o' Christians they be when they gotta pay for this with their own blood. Eye for an eye's what the good book says! An' gettin' even for a man like Matt's gonna cost a lot in Injun blood, it is!"

Swain nodded again, saying he would tell a full story tomorrow, when there were more settlers gathered for the funeral.

He added, "We druv 'em out after they got Matt."

"Shoulda burned the goddamn heathen village to the ground!"

"We did," Jubal answered, but did not add that his men had borne away everything of value they could carry, and stashed it in the woods. Later they would cart it all to Philadelphia or Baltimore and trade it for goods or sell it. But first there was more to be had at other Moravian towns. One big trip with all the booty would make them rich quickly, so they would wait until they had enough.

"Listen, Jube," the settler said as Swain led the horse away.

"Listen, with Matt gone there ain't nobody kin head us up. I mean we need a leader."

Swain stopped and listened.

"Well, Jube, what d'yuh say? Will yuh lead us agin these red devils?"

Swain paused a moment, then said, "Count on me, friend. We'll talk tomorrow when the folks come in."

The man slapped his leg with excitement. "I be proud to know yuh, Jube Swain! Proud!"

Swain lay on the floor of Matt's cabin late that night. Lucy had been brought back by the neighbor because she wanted to be at her own place. Now she was up in the pallet with the children, and the bed she had shared with Matt was empty.

Jubal had not slept more than a few minutes all night, and he was sick of it. Lucy and the boys had been crying ever since they got back. Swain wanted to tell them to shut up, but he had to try to close out the dismal sound.

He hadn't expected Lucy to take this so hard. But a woman who had lived with a man all that time must get used to having him around, especially at night. She would get over this before long. When she did, he would be there. He could be patient sometimes, and this was one of those times. If only they would stop that damned sniveling and go to sleep.

He turned on his side and covered his head with the blanket. If there was one thing he could not stand it was whining kids.

At the larger village of Moravian Indians, Aleta knelt in prayer. Everyone else was asleep in the big one-room log house where she and the old couple had been taken in after their desperate flight. Aleta had been praying constantly since nightfall, but she had found little solace and no answer to the question of why her people should be persecuted for their faith.

"Why?" she whispered to the stars at a window high above her bed. "Why are my people to suffer so, when they have wronged no one, have hated no one? Why, when they have done all in their power to be devout Christians, must they be attacked and driven away from their homes, when all they long for is to live in peace with all men?"

For generations the Indians converted by the Moravians had made their way in a world of hate and prejudice. While the

German brethren and ministers of the faith were the kindest, most gentle folk she had ever met, many other whites were poisoned with hate for all who were different from them. In years past, Moravian villages had paid the price for neutrality and pacifism, being attacked by both sides in the French and Indian War, the people murdered time and again.

Now Aleta's village was in flight, with no one to help her folk. The town they had lived in had been looted and burned to the ground. How would they survive the winter? The other Moravian villages would take them in, but what if they, too, were burned to the ground?

"But why, dear Father in heaven, must we suffer so? What have we done to be punished?"

She thought of Daniel in the lion's den, and it came to her that Daniel had overcome fear of death through faith. "Faith works wonders," she whispered. Was that the lesson she must learn? Must she conquer her lack of faith by being unafraid in the face of death, in the very den of the lion? Was pacifism, loving one's neighbor, the path to resurrection? Must she still learn how to turn the other cheek?

Kneeling on the hard floor, her hands folded in prayer, Aleta looked up at the stars in the window, the faint light glinting on her tears. Those in the crowded room who were unable to sleep were watching her, though she did not know it at first, not until she began to recite: "The Lord is my shepherd, I shall not want . . ." Her whispers were heard by some who sat up in bed, a few now kneeling. They joined her, speaking in a hush that united them in hope and reverence. "Yea, though I walk through the valley of the shadow of death, I shall fear no evil . . ."

Niko-lota and his cousins sat in camp on a bank of the Juniata River. They ate some dried beef and drank from the stream. No fire was possible here—there were too many white settlements, and there was always the chance that patrolling rangers might spot them and slip up in the darkness. The other raiders they had traveled with had divided into small groups to avoid detection.

Niko-lota was cold and tired, for they had trotted all that day to reach this spot. Here they had hidden a half-canoe, and they would set out in the predawn darkness to paddle upstream toward the western mountains. They would move on the water only at night, or they would drift close to shore when they dared, making sure no settlers were at hand. It was a long and dangerous journey, but before a week was out they would be up in the mountains and crossing through to Indian country. There were white settlements there, too, but they were few and less likely to be looking for trouble with passing warriors.

Beyond lay the valley of the Ohio River, where friendly Indians would help them on their long journey to the northwest. Out there, near the Illinois country, they would find Pontiac, who was gathering braves loyal to him. Then, in the spring, a flood of warriors would burst upon the English settlements and destroy every cabin and hamlet from the lakes to the Allegheny Mountains.

chapter **11**

MAGRUDER

As she sat in the center of a canoe heading up the Youghiogheny River, Ella was glad to have left Fort Pitt. The three days there were the most unpleasant so far in the three weeks they had been in the wilderness.

For one thing, they were not far from Braddock's Road, where during the French and Indian War so much British and provincial blood had been spilled. This was where John Bently, Ella's first husband, had received the wounds from which he had never recovered. For another thing, Fort Pitt itself was a dismal place. Though just as strong as Fort Detroit, and garrisoned with more regulars, the fort was dirty and muddy and jammed with refugees from the Indian raids. Never had Ella seen so many gaunt and dull children, all looking so hungry that it pained her. The outlying clearings near the fort were thick with tents, scrap shelters, and lean-tos that would not stand a good wind. What, Ella wondered, would these people do when winter came?

She and Owen had traded away most of the fancy goods they had brought down from Detroit, exchanging them for staples from the fort's sutler. Then they had met with the leading men of the civilian population and arranged for the food to be distributed anonymously among the poor people. Barrels of salt pork and bolts of linsey-woolsey were doled out to poverty-stricken settlers.

Now they were in the wild again, heading southeast toward the high Alleghenies, and she understood what it meant to

Owen to be free of settlements. There were nine canoes, twenty-five soldiers, and sixteen canoemen. Ensign Parker and the men of the Detroit escort, except for a few who were going on to Philadelphia, had gone back. At Fort Pitt she and Owen had met Lieutenant Arnault Magruder of the Royal Americans, sent from Philadelphia to lead the Sutherlands across the mountains and down to Philadelphia. In his late twenties, he was a provincial, a native of Pennsylvania. His mother was German and his father Irish, giving him the inheritance of a bulky, strong body with a florid face and pale blue eyes. He had thick lips and a hooked nose that suited his haughty demeanor. The lieutenant was not an unpleasant person, but he was overbearing with those he considered his inferiors—and that was almost anyone who was a provincial, even though he was one himself. Magruder was polite to Ella and Sutherland, but he was hard on the enlisted men, who clearly disliked him.

They were just four days out of Pitt, but already Magruder had set the tone for his detachment. Men must sit up straight in the canoes, must not sing at all except when Magruder suggested it after dinner, and must apply fresh pipe clay every third day to whiten their breeches, gaiters, and belts. One canoe was loaded heavily with Magruder's gear and baggage, and another had a large sack of pipe clay. None of the regulars could sit comfortably in the canoes because their clothing was so stiff with the unpleasant whitener. But they did, as Magruder said from time to time, look natty.

There was a Virginian, a guide, along in the bow of the second canoe with Owen and Ella, but Magruder rarely consulted him. More often than not, the lieutenant used a sketchy map of the river's course to determine how far they would paddle each day. He was sure that the map's indications of good campsites and fresh water simply had to be correct: the map was regular army issue, in which he had limitless faith.

Magruder was not interested in the thoughts of the grizzly Virginian, a wise and silent old fellow who wore a floppy hat and fringed buckskins that looked as though they had never been taken off. But Ella and Owen liked him. He gave detailed and fascinating information on every subject from the river's currents to the weather for the coming day, and he was always correct in his predictions.

The canoes were paddled by experienced men, and there were several soldiers in every craft, plus cargo. It was a very strong escort, but the country around the Youghiogheny was dangerous. The Shawnee and Delaware roved here, and no one was safe traveling in small groups. Chances were good that the Indians had already marked the movement of their flotilla, but with the cold weather bearing down, Sutherland doubted enough warriors could be assembled for a major attack. Yet there was always the peril of an ambush or sniping fire from shore. Paddling upstream, the canoes could not move quickly enough to escape, and losses in such an attack could be serious enough to weaken the escort and ultimately endanger them.

The canoes skimmed along, making excellent time through the autumn wilderness. Most of the leaves had fallen in the last rain, and every wind seemed to rob the world of color and warmth. Still it was lovely here, and Ella thought again how refreshing and peaceful it was compared with squalid Fort Pitt.

Now she knew what it was her husband loved about being out here. Now she knew what he meant when he wrote poems about it and spoke about it in terms of tranquillity and freedom.

Then a ripple of anxiety touched her, and she sat up in the canoe, looking into the forest and thinking how deadly it really was here. Owen had said a marksman in the trees could kill anyone in the canoes he chose. That made her uneasy, and she glanced back at her husband, who with the Virginian paddled this craft. He grinned at her, and some of the fear flooded away. Ella thought she could not be in safer hands than Owen Sutherland's.

But he was worried now, despite the reassuring smile he gave her. Sutherland and the Virginian sensed trouble. The problem was that Lieutenant Magruder refused to believe it. Magruder, in the first canoe just ahead of Sutherland's, had been told by the Virginian that there was a likely site for an ambush three miles upstream. But the lieutenant could not accept the idea of a war party large enough to bother them lying in wait ahead. The Virginian had told Sutherland his thoughts, and the Scotsman had listened. Now Sutherland was planning how the place ahead might be passed safely, but it was a full day's journey to Fort Bedford, a small but strong post at the foot of the Alleghenies. From there the expedition would walk through the mountains and come down into safer country beyond.

The sun was lowering behind them, and the mountains in the east were purple, seeming very close at hand. Suddenly a

Brown Bess went off, and Sutherland saw Magruder standing in the bow of his canoe, musket smoking. The officer gave a shout of excitement as a doe foundered at the edge of the left bank.

Magruder turned to the convoy and shouted, "There's dinner, men! Here's where we'll camp tonight." He waved for the canoes to put in to shore.

Sutherland guided the canoe into shore and helped Ella climb out. Then he and the Virginian went to Magruder, who was admiring the kill. The lieutenant looked up, and his face fell, as though in anticipation of an unpleasant discussion.

Sutherland said, "There'll be a moon tonight, Lieutenant."

The officer looked at Sutherland, waiting for him to go further. When Sutherland did not, Magruder said, "Yes. A moon. It'll be very romantic for you and your lady, I'll warrant." He smiled, but the other two did not. "Well, Mr. Sutherland, tell me what's on your mind."

"The guide tells me the river is smooth from here to Fort Bedford. We could travel by moonlight tonight with no risk of running into rapids."

Magruder's red face deepened in color. "So you and my man here have been making plans without consulting me, eh?"

Neither one replied. Sutherland knew Magruder had been told by Colonel Bouquet to take his advice when it was offered, but he did not want to seem overbearing or insulting, so he waited quietly for the lieutenant to reach the right conclusion.

Magruder looked at the guide, whose nonchalance was clearly profound.

"What's the problem?" Magruder stared hard at the man, who was studying the shadows of the far shoreline.

The Virginian moved his pipe to the other side of his mouth before saying, "Country here don't feel right, Lieutenant. I don't like it."

"Don't *like* this country!" Magruder repeated. "Don't *like* it? Well, *I* like it! There hasn't been an Indian in sight for three days!"

The Virginian simply gazed into the shadows and chewed his pipe.

Magruder went on. "Why don't you like it, pray tell? It's as quiet as a church on Monday!"

"That's why I don't like it." Without taking the pipe from his mouth, the guide spat into the water.

"He's got it right, Lieutenant," Sutherland agreed. "It's too quiet here. We've passed three or four villages close to the river, and they've all been abandoned. No youngsters in canoes, no squaws washing in the river, nobody fishing. Why?"

"Why? Because, sir, these Indians are afraid of a strong force coming upstream! That's simple, isn't it?"

Sutherland nodded. "Maybe. But our guide tells me there's a good place for an ambush—"

"Ambush! Ambush? Tells *you!* He was hired by the army to tell me, not you, sir!"

"What will you do about it?"

"Do about it? Why— Do about it? Damn, sir, let's have our dinner, and then we'll talk if you want. Don't think I am disregarding your warnings. I just don't feel it's warranted to be so afraid now. I'll hear you both out, don't worry! But let's eat, and then we can talk like civilized men, not savages."

Sutherland and the Virginian sat near the water, making plans. Later, when they were satisfied, they returned to the campsite, where Magruder was by then ready to eat his second portion of venison. Looking up from his camp chair, tin plate on his lap, Magruder lost his composure to see these two looming over him.

"After dinner, please, gentlemen!"

Sutherland said, "It can't wait. It'll be full dark in an hour. We've got to be prepared to go by nightfall, with everyone aware of his duty." He told Magruder they should leave fires burning in the camp and then paddle upstream in the moonlight until they were miles beyond where the river twisted through a deep and narrow canyon.

This bothered Magruder all the more. His mouth full of venison, he exclaimed, "Paddle all night! We've just been traveling all day! Be reasonable, man!"

But Sutherland would not budge. "This is what has to be done, Magruder, like it or not."

The men were informed and all unnecessary equipment was left packed in the canoes. Presuming Indians were watching them, Sutherland arranged that every impression be given of making a night camp. But the tents were all empty, and as soon as any equipment was used—cooking utensils, saws, axes—it was returned to the proper place in a canoe so no one would be searching for things in darkness when the detachment set off after the moon rose.

The moon would be past full, so there would be enough light to see the river, but not enough to make them easy targets if they were spotted out on the water. At the right moment, camp was broken in silence. The fires, sunk in pits, were left lit, ringed with stones to prevent them from spreading after the soldiers departed. Nine canoes slid quietly into the river, with Sutherland's in front, Magruder sitting before Ella in the center of the craft. The Virginian guide was in the bow.

The river became shallower and narrower, no more than a hundred feet wide. Soon the moon hung low in the sky, big and yellow above the mountains. An hour passed. It was breathtakingly beautiful and peaceful on the river, and Ella was torn between admiration for nature and fear of Indians. No one spoke or made unnecessary sounds. Sutherland's eyes roved up and down both dim shores. The river grew even narrower. Behind, the other canoes stayed as close as possible. If they were attacked, they would race upstream with all their might. Sutherland worried about Magruder's steadiness. He hoped the man was not out for glory, because that might get them into a situation they could not get out of. Absolute silence was essential until they were far above the ambush site. So far Magruder had been perfect, sitting as mute as anyone could ask.

The less movement and disturbance in the convoy, the less chance an Indian spy would see them pass. It took longer than normal to cover the three miles against the current, because every paddle stroke had to be careful, soundless, and made with as little splash in the quiet water as possible.

Not far now. The water funneled into shadows up ahead. The sheen of moonlight on the surface ended in a point upstream, where the river squeezed between massive black outcroppings. Stillness blanketed the river; the water's murmur was the only sound. Stroke after stroke of the paddles brought the narrow end of the funnel closer. Then the moon was blocked by the high rocks, and the canoes drifted into deep, slow water surrounded by blackness. They had been swallowed up by the dark, and only the guide's sense kept them in midstream. It was difficult to see where the water ended and the steep banks began. Ella felt almost blind.

Far above, she saw dark silhouettes of trees against a sky washed by the light of the moon. But down in the chasm the canoes were obscured completely. Paddle forward and down, and slow. Sutherland could barely make out the guide in the prow, giving hand signals for him to steer by. Ella and Magruder were unmoving. That was good. Paddle forward, down, and back, not the slightest clumsiness to give them away to the sharp eyes of an Indian watcher.

The darkness had no end. Trees above bent over the cliffs and shut out the night sky. Still they went on, the Virginian signaling as the channel twisted through the rocks. The guide kept them in the center of the curving gorge. How he knew where he was, even Sutherland could not tell.

Then he saw a glow in the trees on the right just above the dark water. Then nearby another reddish light glimmered faintly behind the shadows of rock and bush. They were unmistakably campfires. Indians were here.

Sutherland looked toward Magruder. Still the man had control of himself. An ambush had been prepared here, though it was likely there were only a few Indians at these two fires.

Then he saw light on the left bank. One campfire, then another. The fires were well concealed from the water, but Sutherland's sharp eyes made out the glow. He reached forward and touched Ella on the shoulder. She nodded that she also saw them, and she dared not breathe. Onward they went in complete silence. Water bubbled against the canoes. More fires on the left, and there were at least five by now on the right. The canoes slid between the camps, and Sutherland estimated fourteen fires in all in a stretch of a hundred yards. Only ten Indians per fire meant a large war party. This was the ambush the guide had felt in his bones. Now they were dead in the center of it, and the slightest error would give them away.

Paddle up, and deeply down, slow and steady. Sutherland did not dare look behind at the other canoes, which he hoped had not lost sight of his craft. Any awkward movement in his canoe might throw off the Virginian's paddle, causing a splash, attracting attention.

An owl hooted from the bank. Sutherland's hair prickled. He listened for an answering hoot, meaning the Indians knew they were there. Nothing. The same owl hooted again. It was an owl.

Another fifty yards and they would be past the line of fires.

If no one got jumpy or restless—especially Magruder, who had so far impressed Sutherland with his willpower—they would be through.

Tension dug into Sutherland's neck and shoulders and he knew everyone, including Ella, was feeling the same discomfort. Indians had a keen sixth sense, and one experienced warrior with a feeling in his bones like the guide—one man strolling to the edge of the bank and looking closely over the water—would discover them. Shadows moved back and forth near many fires. Warriors were awake, probably excited, waiting for their prey to come paddling upstream in the morning. If the ambush succeeded, there would be a rich haul in booty, scalps, and canoes. The convoy was nearly through.

From up on the bluff came a shrieking howl, and Sutherland froze, his canoe slowing against the stream. He listened, and there was another echoing howl, as of a man angry or hurt. The entire convoy rested on their paddles, each steersman holding the prow steady in the current.

Then loud laughter erupted from a campfire, and the voice of the man who had howled rose above it, cheerful and excited. Somebody was at the end of a funny story. Sutherland pushed ahead. With the sound of laughing Indians reverberating through the gorge, the canoes went on, relief sweeping through the whites. Again Sutherland was glad of Magruder's control at such a critical moment.

Soon the river opened wider, the bluffs now behind the travelers, and the moon appeared off to the left above shadowy mountains. Without a word being spoken, Sutherland and the guide knew this was the time to drive hard, and they paddled as fast as they could away from the gorge.

After half an hour of rapid paddling, the guide turned and motioned for Sutherland to let the others come up. Now they could relax. One by one, the other canoes came alongside in this broad stretch of quiet water, men joking with one another. Magruder said not a word. Sutherland was not surprised at the lieutenant's silence, because the man must have been embarrassed to have been proven wrong.

In the darkness, someone said to a friend, "That was close, Jake. I wish I'd brought a change o' britches, though!"

The men laughed, and the speaker apologized to Ella. It was then Sutherland realized how well she, too, had come through this tight spot. Now he wanted to change places and have someone else steer the canoe. He wanted to be with her to settle her nerves if need be.

He decided to ask the lieutenant to arrange this, saying, "It looks as though our little whim was correct, Lieutenant."

Ella turned quickly, her finger to her lips: "Shhhh!" she said, loud enough for everyone to hear. "He's been asleep since just after we left camp!"

A soldier hooted as loudly as he dared, and the others laughed heartily, some slapping the water with their paddles. Jake called out, "Now I need a change of britches, too!"

At that Magruder stirred and sat up, straightening his tricorn and turning around to see the canoes clustered all around.

"Harumph! What's this, now?" He cleared his throat again. "Why are we stopping, Mr. Sutherland? What's the meaning of this? If you want to travel all night, it's fine with me, but let's not waste any time! Let's paddle! Forward, men! It's a beautiful night for a moonlight jaunt! Forward! Foward!"

chapter **12**

RED SILK

Aleta screamed. Blood! Fire! Death! The redbeard roared and lifted his axe. She screamed again, but the axe did not fall. The redbeard glowed and faded, and then vanished.

She found herself sitting straight up in bed, sweating, shaking violently. In the dimness there was another face—Jane Whitefeather, the woman who slept in a bunk near Aleta. Jane was saying something, her kindly eyes worried and anxious. Then Aleta saw again the redbeard, the hate. She fought away the vision and once more found Jane, who was saying gently, "Wake, sister, wake. Have no fear, sister. Wake."

Aleta, breathing heavily, slowly recovered. The vision, the horror, was a dream, and no more. With a cry of relief, she fell into Jane's plump arms, sobbing, while the woman soothed her and told her that all was well.

It was the darkness before dawn, and Aleta's cries had awakened the dozen people living in this crowded cabin in the Moravian village where they had taken refuge. Some got up, others were on their knees in prayer. Gradually, Aleta relaxed, leaning back, thanking Jane for her comfort. An infant cried, and Jane went to the cradle, where her boy of nine months called for her. Aleta forced the nightmare away, but with great difficulty.

Her heart said it was a premonition, but she did not know what to do about it. She looked around the dark room, colored by the soft glow of a dying fire in the hearth. Wrapping a shawl about her shoulders, she got out of bed, slipped on moccasins, and went to stir up the fire. It was cold outside; frost edged the windowpanes of the cabin. Trying to think clearly, Aleta sang a hymn to herself while laying wood on the fire and poking the embers into a hearty glow. That should have made her feel better, but it did not.

She went back to her bunk to take off her nightgown and put on a dress. This was done quickly, in the privacy of darkness. Normally she would never have changed clothes in the presence of men, but these times required many small sacrifices.

Aleta knelt to whisper a prayer. Later there would be a service in the chapel to begin the day, but first she needed a moment of solace and quiet. Nearby an old man got out of bed and hunched silently before the fire, warming his aged bones. Across the room Jane cuddled her boy, who struggled out of her arms and began to crawl on the floor, much to the delight of other women in the cabin.

As she absorbed the comforting scene, Aleta wondered why it was that her dream haunted her so. Why did it not leave her now that she was awake? It *was* a premonition.

Then she could not resist approaching Jane, who looked up from watching her baby. "Sister, I think we should go away from here."

Jane looked confused, questioning.

Aleta said, "I am unable to say why, sister, but my dream . . . I think we should leave this place."

Jane was not one to scoff at the meanings of dreams, even though she was a devout Christian. Her husband was one of the two men recently found murdered in the woods, and before he had been killed she had sensed forebodings of tragedy. But she shook her head and said with a brave smile, "Where will we go, then? Are the other villages any safer than this one? There is nowhere for us to go."

That penetrated Aleta's heart like an arrow of ice, and she shuddered again. Jane was right.

Aleta said another quick prayer for guidance from the Father, stood up, and took from her bag a red silk kerchief. It was her favorite and would make her feel better. She tied her glossy hair up in it, smoothed her dress, and then said good-morning to everyone. As she went back to the fire, she though they must surely be safe here, where there was a church and white ministers. Surely, they were safe! But then why had she dreamed what she did in the brief snatch of sleep that had come to her last night?

The stillness outside was broken. What was it? It sounded almost like a scream! Then she heard angry shouting. People in her cabin ran to the windows, where a flaring red light glinted on the icy glass. There were gunshots! Glass shattered, and someone at a window groaned and fell heavily to the floor. Women screamed. A baby howled. Outside there was a massive eruption of musketry, followed by savage shouting. Aleta ran to a window and saw dark forms carrying torches hurrying through the village. Many cabins were already aflame. Bewildered, she stared at her nightmare and tried to wake up. She could not.

A tremendous crash shivered the door on its heavy hinges. People were praying feverishly. The baby was still howling. Aleta could not move. An axe splintered the planking of the door. It bit again, the blade glowing in the firelight. The back door of the cabin flew open, and she saw her people running out, boys carrying the old man, women fleeing with children in their arms. Again the door shook under the axe, and one hinge snapped free. Aleta ran, but she tripped and fell over a body. She tried to get up, then saw it was Jane, eyes open, blood on her forehead.

Aleta could not even scream. Paralyzed, she knelt at the body. The door bar cracked halfway, and fiendish voices roared. Aleta reached over and closed Jane's eyes. Then she saw something move on the floor. Jane's baby sat silently gazing at his mother. White men were struggling over the twisted planking. Aleta came to life. She snatched up the babe and dashed for the back door. She heard a fierce oath, and near the fireplace her nightmare confronted her. She stopped before the demon redbeard, who grinned and raised the axe. She sprang away, but the devil grabbed and caught her hair. Aleta tried to pull free. The redbeard laughed. The baby was screaming. She yanked with all her might, but he held on. Aleta reached for a firebrand. She saw the axe gleam. The burning stick was in her hand, and she rammed it at the bearded evil, who bellowed in agony and vanished from sight.

Still holding the baby, Aleta fought clear of other clutching arms, swinging the fiery stick as she shouldered through the back door. Then she burst into darkness, cool and free, throwing away the brand, running for her life into the woods. The baby cried, and she held him close, covering him with her shawl. She hardly felt the thorns and branches that scratched and lashed at her. She ran through the night, stumbling and blind, until she left far behind the flames and tumult of the inferno that once had been a peaceful village.

The village was no more. Aleta's family and friends who survived were totally destitute. Where once there had been a prosperous, happy community, there was now only ashes. Even her pretty red scarf was gone. Aleta kept Jane's son with her, and in the morning she met a dozen others from the village— four children, eight young adults—and they slunk through the forest toward Philadelphia, where they prayed they would be protected. Sometimes they hid in the woods or under trees from gangs of horsemen. They begged at homes of whites whom they knew were not killers, and they went hungry when there was no one to help them.

Philadelphia was where they had to go, they were told by Moravian ministers who met them two days after the attack. They collected into a larger group of Christian Indians, walking the long road to the city. Soon there were more than one hundred of them—some from other settlements that had been hastily abandoned—straggling, broken, and miserable. With them were sixty citizens, mostly Quakers, and a handful of regular soldiers sent out by the governor. They needed a guard to the City of Brotherly Love, for along the way they were threatened over and over again by groups of borderers and other settlers who hated all Indians, Christian or not.

What would happen once they reached Philadelphia, Aleta did not know. But in all the world, there was nowhere else for them to go.

Once, as she lay huddled under a blanket beneath the stars, Aleta thought about Niko-lota and wondered where he was. If hers had been a village with warriors instead of peaceful Christians, the attack might not have happened. But then, it was her faith to live as she did, and her faith gave inner strength, even at times such as these. Though Aleta did not understand why she and her folk were to be so cruelly oppressed, she knew the same thing had happened time and again to God's people throughout the ages. Why should this age be any different? Yet how she wished it *were* different! She was overcome with mourning that night as she held the sleeping child against her and listened to the wind lamenting in the trees.

Jubal Swain sat in his brother's cabin nursing his burned face. A little closer to his eye and the Moravian wench would have blinded him. He leaned back in Matthew's old chair, holding a poultice against his cheek. He could barely see from this eye, and it would take days before it really began to heal.

It was just as well for the next Indian he met that Swain had not been blinded because that would have made him wild. As though he were not wild enough the other night! He was satisfied, for the moment. His men had ransacked the cabins in the confusion, while honest settlers in his party were busy running around aimlessly and shouting. The settlers had no idea that Swain's men were stockpiling a small fortune in Indian booty at their camp in the woods. Those ordinary folk, incited by the death of Matthew Swain, were simply angry and eager to kill Indians, but Swain's gang was organized and had a plan every time they struck a Moravian village.

Swain had done some killing, just for the sport, but mostly he had left it to the farmers, some of them murdering Indians while they quoted the Old Testament: "And when the Lord thy God shall deliver them before thee, thou shalt smite them and utterly destroy them; thou shalt make no covenant with them; nor show mercy unto them."

Another raid or two on the few remaining peaceful Indian settlements that had not picked up and run, and Swain's men would be fat and comfortable for the winter. He intended to stay here with Lucy, and so far she seemed not to object. He had been working on her for the past few weeks, and she was coming around. Lucy was not the kind to rush, if only for the sake of appearances, but Swain was ready to take her. Pretty soon now Matthew would be just a memory, and she would lie next to Jubal at night instead of above him in the children's bed.

Swain drank corn liquor from a jug, getting numb enough to ease the pain of his face.

The door opened, and Lucy came in with Joe and Willie. She had been chopping wood, and they all dropped armfuls near the hearth, where a good fire blazed. Looking at Lucy as the fire lit up her face, her hair, Swain felt a burning inside that had nothing to do with the drink. However, the woman and children still had a dejected, tired look, and that annoyed him.

He said, "What in hell yuh all so glum about?"

The boys looked at him, but Lucy went on with her work, taking potatoes from a sack and tossing them into a pan of water on the table.

Swain took the poultice from his face and said to the boys, "Open that pouch there, young 'uns. There's somethin' sweet in it fer yuh."

That got a quick response. The youngsters rummaged through old knives and some new tufts of Indian hair, and then found a cloth package that had to be what Swain meant. They opened it to find some big lumps of maple sugar. The boys cried out in excitement, and Lucy started to say they should wait until after supper. But Jubal was standing next to her, and when she looked at him, her breath caught.

He said, "You 'uns take that sugar outside, now. Eat it all up, an' don't come in till your ma calls."

As he spoke, Swain stared at Lucy, who could not take her eyes from him. The boys went out happily, slamming the door behind them.

"Here, girl," he said, "check my eye."

She stood close to him, examining the glaring injury, her breath coming in short gasps. She could feel the heat of him, but he did not touch her.

"It looks better," she said nervously. "But it'll be weeks afore it's right."

His face was near hers as he said, "How many weeks afore you're right, Lucy?"

Trembling, she moved away.

Then she saw a flash of bright red, and she swung around, giving a soft exclamation when she saw he was holding up a red silk kerchief.

"My, Jube," she whispered. "It be right beautiful."

She dared not reach out for it, but he came to her and slipped it around her neck, tying it at the side. Then he stepped back and admired her, smiling. "It looks awful good on yuh, girl."

She was tremulous with excitement. Never before had Lucy owned anything so striking. She adjusted it better and found a small bit of mirror glass near her bed. She looked at herself, all the more smitten with the lovely kerchief. In the mirror, she hardly saw the plain linsey dress she wore, the dark lines below her eyes. Lucy contemplated the kerchief and how its color illuminated her thin face. She was not as homely as she thought she had become.

Lucy had to ask, "How do I look, Jube?"

"Like a princess." He grinned and took another swig of liquor.

"Oh, go on!" she exclaimed. "Go on!"

He grinned and slapped his thigh: "Hell, girl, that ain't enough for the likes o' yuh! You're still Lucy Gable, the prettiest thing in Albany County! The girl that used to belong to me!"

"Stop, Jube," she said lightly, spinning around so the kerchief flew up a little, all the while gazing in the mirror. "This is too much for me!"

"I said it ain't enough, girl! That's silk! That's what yuh oughta be wearin' all over that good body o' your'n!"

"Jube!" She knew where he was going with this, for she had not forgotten how he had charmed her so long ago. She laughed carelessly, but when he came and pulled her against him she stared at the floor, saying, "Jube...Jube, not now! Not yet."

"Ain't yuh the Lucy Gable what always wanted a fine house an' fine clothes an' a man to take care o' yuh? Don't yuh recall our dreams, girl?"

"Jube—" She struggled a little.

"Girl!"

"Jube, I ain't got no more dreams! I don't know how to dream no more!"

"Yuh gotta dream, Lucy! All these years I dreamed about yuh, an' now—"

"Please, Jube—"

He kissed her, and she tried to get free. He wrapped her in his arms, and she felt his incredible strength. But she felt guilty, and fought away from him, tearing loose and lurching to the table, where she leaned forward and found herself crying again.

From across the room, Jubal said tonelessly, "Whatever yuh say, Lucy." He went for his jug of liquor. It would not be long now before she would weaken. "You're still a hell of a beautiful woman!"

She felt a thrill to hear him say that. Jubal Swain did not need her and the boys. He could have many a woman. She was moved to hear him speak so, but when she looked up at him, she felt uneasy to see his eyes blazing with desire. Summoning her strength, Lucy took off the kerchief and folded it carefully before laying it on the table. Then she looked at him and took a deep breath.

"Thank you, Jubal. I'll wear it on special days."

She went outside to the children. Swain sighed heavily and kicked the stool out of his way, then went to bed carrying the jug. He was too frustrated even to eat dinner, and too aroused with need for Lucy to do anything but drink himself to sleep.

The next morning, Ella and Owen Sutherland came on horse-back through the forest near Carlisle. They had been given mounts at Fort Cumberland, after crossing the Alleghenies. With them were a dozen mounted soldiers commanded by the portly Magruder, who proved himself a graceful rider. No one had said much to the lieutenant about their close call on the Youghiogheny River, and Sutherland was in no mood to em-barrass him further. He expected the officer would learn all the details in due time.

Now Sutherland's mind was full of Ella, who rode in front of him, just behind Magruder. He was amazed by what she had accomplished in the five-week journey from Detroit. Not only had she held up, she had become steadily stronger, as though she had been made for the forest. He could not have been happier with her.

She knew it. Now, riding sidesaddle, she made the most of a chance to prove herself better on horseback than Owen. Even though she had occasionally felt a little queasy lately—probably the result of their unrelieved diet of army fare—she enjoyed charging ahead over desolate cornfields—she and Owen, or she and Magruder. Time and again Ella won their short sprints, with Sutherland unable to match either her or the lieutenant. Owen had the courage to ride fast, but not the talent. Yet he was game, and Ella, who had ridden every day as a girl in England, taught him a few things about riding, until he knew better how to use his legs to control the horse. This last part of their journey was a triumph of happiness for Ella. It was a new stage of their relationship, one that promised a full and exciting life together.

Owen again hoped they would get out of Philadelphia by early December to avoid the worst of winter. Then he would

not worry about Ella so much. She had shown herself able so
far, but that return journey would be perilous if made too late
in the season. Leaving Ella in Philadelphia was something he
did not want to do, but he absolutely must go to Detroit in time
to meet Tamano, who would come back in late February or
early March with the fur harvest.

Not far from Sutherland's approaching party, Jubal Swain was
washing himself in a basin on a bench near the rain barrel. He
felt good this morning: he had slept well, and he knew he was
very close to winning Lucy over. She came out of the cabin,
with the boys bounding ahead of her, and he stood up and
grinned. She smiled back and touched the pretty kerchief
around her neck.

"Special day?" he asked.

She shrugged and looked at his naked torso in a way that
set him off again. He splashed more water on his face and
dried himself with his wool shirt. He stared at her as she walked
down to the stream carrying an empty bucket, the two boys
scampering aimlessly about the yard.

Jubal had waited as long as he could for her to come to him.
He went inside and got the jug. The drink went down hard,
and he growled and took a deep breath. Then he drank again.
He felt good inside, as though nothing in the world could stand
in his way. There would be more hell to pay for those Moravians. In a few days he and his boys would stir up some settlers
and hit another village—if they had not all run out for Philadelphia. Well, that was fine, too. There were enough settlers
mad at the city to form an army to march in there, too.

Then Swain had an even better idea. He chuckled to think
it and drank again. If they could get enough angry borderers
together, they could ransack even Philadelphia itself!

"Why not?" he laughed aloud. Those Quakers did not know
which end of a gun was business and which the butt. There
were not enough regulars to stand in the way of any good-size
army. Who was to stop them? Get these backwoods Presbyterian hotheads mad enough and they would march on New
York if they thought it would avenge the friends and kinfolk
lost to the Indians.

He chortled to himself and quickly downed more liquor. It
went in a rush to his head from his empty stomach. That was
what he wanted. When he heard Lucy return, he stood in the

center of the room and waited until she came through the door. She stopped short to see him with his shirt still off, a grin on his face. She could not help smiling to herself as she lugged the heavy bucket to the kettle hanging over the hearth.

"What's so funny?" she asked, giggling a little.

He laughed. "Wouldn't yuh like to know?"

She shrugged, playing coy. "No, I wouldn't. Jest bein' sociable's all—"

Then he was close behind her, taking the heavy bucket away as though it were empty.

"Jube . . ." Her voice was weak.

He touched the red kerchief. "Soft," he said. "Like you."

Her breathing was heavy; she tried to protest: "Not . . . yet, Jube." But she was tired of waiting, too.

He kissed her gently this time, and she did not resist. At first she was tense, but then she yielded and pulled his head down, the passion rising in her.

"Jube," she whispered as he kissed her neck.

"Lucy—"

The door banged open, and Lucy jumped, jerking away from Swain.

"Ma!" Willie shouted, confused, and seeing red blotches on her face. "Ma! What did he do to you? He hit you!"

The boy clenched his fists and came at Swain, but Lucy jumped between them, shouting, "No, Willie!"

The boy had a Swain temper, and he fought his mother off, because now he realized his uncle had been kissing her, and that angered him all the more. He charged at Swain, who tossed him aside, trying not to hurt him. But Willie came in again, a poker in his hand, and he struck Swain hard on the face. Losing control, Swain swore and slapped the boy down, bursting his lip. Lucy tried to hold Willie, but he was hysterical, and he scrambled away from her, shrieking and accidentally kicking her on the cheek, bruising it. Then he ran outside, his mother behind him.

By now young Joe was crying, and Lucy was shouting to Willie as he ran up the path to the woods. Inside the cabin, Jubal, balked by Lucy at the last minute, was furious. His face hurt where the boy had hit him, and it still ached where he had been burned. Jerking up the jug of liquor, he downed another fierce swallow and went outside.

He saw Willie near the trees facing some mounted soldiers,

and he heard the boy cry, "He hit my ma! He hit my ma!"

Lucy was trying to calm him and talk to the soldiers at the same time. It was none of their business anyway.

Ella and Owen looked down at the woman, who was struggled with Willie and attempting to brush back her hair. They saw the bruise on Lucy's face and the boy's bleeding lip. It was a dismal scene, which neither Owen nor Ella wanted any part of. But if the ruffian standing with the jug in the cabin's door was really beating these people, they would have to step in.

Magruder rode indignantly ahead, not hearing Lucy try to tell him it was all a misunderstanding. Ella and Owen heard her out, and realized it was a minor family squabble, none of their affair. But Magruder was sitting on his horse, scolding big Jubal, who leaned insolently against the doorjamb.

Sutherland looked at Ella, then spurred his horse toward Magruder and Swain, hoping to pull the officer away before there was trouble. But he was too late.

Suddenly Magruder was flying through the air, his horse squealing, Swain cursing loudly. Sutherland cantered over to where Magruder lay, the wind knocked out of him, but otherwise unhurt. The officer tried to speak, but he had no breath, and it was just as well, for he was hissing, "Shoot the bastard! Ride him down!" Luckily all that came out was a whisper.

Sutherland beckoned to a sergeant to help his commander and then rode toward Swain. He had not the slightest idea what he would do, but he started off by saying, "Look here, friend. Let's start over again——"

But he got no further. Swain leaped at him. Sutherland spurred his horse out of the way just in time, and Swain wound up face down in the dirt. Sutherland jumped from his mount and came to the man, who was getting to his feet. The Scotsman could see the fellow was pretty drunk, but he wanted only to reason with him.

No use. Swain grabbed at him, his powerful hands going for Sutherland's throat. The drink in the man slowed his movements. Sutherland ducked away and gave Swain a wicked boot in the soft place just above the belly. Swain's eyes popped, and he staggered a few paces before falling to his knees, only half-conscious.

That was all Sutherland wanted. He saw Magruder was back on his horse, and he took his chance to mount up before Swain got himself breathing again. As Sutherland rode to Ella, who was frightened but tried not to show it, Lucy helped Swain stand up. Struggling for breath, and blue in the face, Swain shook a mighty fist at Sutherland. He had never been humiliated like this before, and if he could only get some air in his lungs he would drag Sutherland from his horse and destroy him. But Sutherland wanted to go before Magruder ordered his men to shoot Swain down.

As the horsemen wheeled away, Lucy shrieked, "Why don't you damned Redcoats leave folk alone an' mind your own business!"

Just before Sutherland rode off, Swain managed to blare, "I'll get yuh!" He sucked in a wheezing breath and shouted, "I'll find yuh! An' I'll break yuh in two!"

Sutherland turned on his horse and said without rancor: "Sleep it off, friend. You won't see me again."

Then he galloped away, not knowing that Jubal Swain had marked him for death.

PART TWO

The City of Brotherly Love

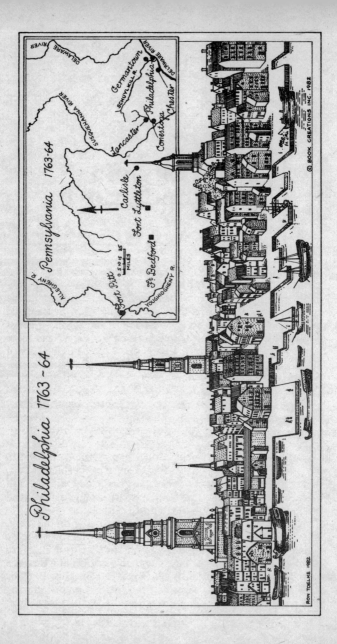

Philadelphia 1763~64

Pennsylvania 1763-64

DELAWARE RIVER
SUSQUEHANNA RIVER
ALLEGHENY R.
Fort Pitt
YOUGHIOGHENY R.
Ft. Bedford
Fort Lyttleton
Carlisle
Lancaster
Conestoga
Philadelphia
Germantown
Schuylkill
Chester

0 5 10 15 25 35
MILES

RON TOELKE 1982

© BOOK CREATIONS INC. 1982

chapter **13**

GATEWAY TO
THE NORTHWEST

      Four days later, Sutherland's party drew near Phila-
delphia, and except for the bruise to Magruder's pride, the
episode at the Swain homestead had been forgotten. At the
moment, how could Ella and Owen think about that squalid
cabin when they were on the outskirts of the second-greatest
city in the British empire? Only London was larger and more
prosperous. Twenty-three thousand people lived in the City of
Brotherly Love, founded a bit more than eighty years earlier
between the placid Schuylkill River to the west and the broad
Delaware to the east.

      They rode toward Philadelphia on the deeply rutted highway
from Lancaster, crossing the Schuylkill on a scow guided by
a rope slung from bank to bank. They were on a thronging,
busy road crowded with folk heading home from the city. It
was almost sunset, and those whose business was finished in
Philadelphia were making their way back to cabin and mansion,
to fertile farm and thriving commune. Compared with the still
vastness of the northwestern forest, this swarming, narrow road
reminded Sutherland of an anthill just burst open.

      As they remounted their horses after crossing on the ferry,
Ella and Owen watched people pass, and Magruder kindly
waited until they were ready to go on. At Fort Detroit, every
newcomer was commented upon and observed from a distance
long before his whaleboat or canoe reached the fort. But this
road was mobbed with strangers who ignored one another as
they passed, each on some absorbing errand. Those Fort Detroit

inhabitants not in uniform wore either feathers or linsey and buckskin, but these people of Philadelphia were dressed in many sharply distinguished styles.

There were Quaker men in long gray coats and broad hats, and wearing white falls, or long collars, that lapped over their chests. The women of the Society of Friends, as the Quakers called themselves, were also modestly clothed—in long-sleeved gowns and white shawls or drab coats; and their starched white bonnets extended on either side of their faces to blind them from the world. Quaker families generally rode in fine but simple carriages drawn by two horses, and they were mostly going into Philadelphia, where the majority of Quakers lived.

Now and again a smart four-in-hand clipped out of the city toward one of the magnificent country estates owned by wealthy merchants or noblemen. But the bulk of the traffic leaving Philadelphia was made up of empty wagons and carts belonging to German farmers returning from a day at the city market. Even though it was late in the year, these industrious Germans did well on their rich farms surrounding the city. In their baggy, comfortable clothes, they looked the picture of good living and contentment.

Then Sutherland saw a group of Scots-Irish coming from Philadelphia. Magruder said they were probably new arrivals just disembarked at the docks and now on their way to the western settlements. They looked very poor, but proud. Some men wore the kilt and tam, while most women were dressed in linsey gowns, with thick woolen shawls over their shoulders. Their worldly possessions were carried in sacks on their backs, and their children scampered alongside, generally barefoot.

Sutherland knew these folk from the northern countries of Ireland were different from the many Scottish Highlanders who also dwelt outside Philadelphia. The Highlanders generally came to the colonies with some savings in their pockets—often former soldiers discharged in the colonies—and they were fairly independent of one another. But the Scots-Irish were clannish, forced from their homelands by famine and lack of work. They were fierce in anger, but generous to friends with what little they owned. In defense of their liberty, they were unyielding and fearless.

These tough folk would join the other Scots-Irish forced to fend for themselves against the Indian raids, and it was they who composed the Calvinist faction known as the borderers. Without the help of the colonial government or wealthy city people, these borderers had organized a desperate defense of their frontier homes, and they resented—if not hated—the pacifist Quakers and Moravians for being reluctant to fight Indians.

Unlike the sober Quakers and Germans, these Ulstermen were cheerful and abounding in energy. As they trudged along, they were singing a Scottish song Sutherland knew well, and an old man was fiddling as he walked. Their life had always been hard, and it would be just as hard on the frontier, but they were strong enough to put down roots and protect themselves. For a moment Owen Sutherland wondered if they were even strong enough to take Philadelphia.

They rode on another half mile, twice having to leave the road to pass small herds of cows being driven back to their owners, who lived in various parts of the city. Ella and Owen both marveled as they cantered around an enormous wagon laden with hay. It was tilted to one side, where a wheel had broken, and a German farmer was moodily levering it up to replace the massive wheel with a spare. The top of the hay seemed to be twenty feet high.

These were Lancaster wagons, sometimes called Conestogas, said Magruder, named for the towns where they were made. The Lancaster wagon, with its front and back curved up like a boat, was a wonderful example of Pennsylvania's genius and wealth built into one mighty machine. And in this same town of Lancaster, Sutherland's Pennsylvania long rifle had been made.

They drew the horses to a halt at the side of the road to make room for an approaching procession of whites and Indians. There were twenty of them, Moravians, and they, too, were singing, but their music was not like the bouncing, cheerful tunes of the Scots-Irish. Rather it was a magical falsetto harmony that entranced Ella and Owen.

In the group were a number of Indian and white women dressed in dark gowns, with light aprons and shawls, and each wore a tight cap tied close about the head. Their hair was put up inside the cap, and they walked with hands folded before them. The white men looked something like Quakers, with broad-brimmed dark hats and long coats, but they all had beards that had never been trimmed. The Indian men were similar to the whites, but without beards. Plain drab linen collars spread from neck to breastbone, and like their women, these men wore no ornamentation or decoration at all.

Their music, sung by hardly moving the lips, was glorious! It was as though a wonderful blossom were emerging from barren earth. Ella had never in her life heard music more beautiful. Even Magruder did not speak as the Moravians passed by, walking placidly as they sang the hymn. When the group was well on its way toward the ferry, Magruder said:

"Remarkable folk, those, but strange." He reined in his stamping horse, which was eager to get home, for it had been stabled in Philadelphia before being sent out to Fort Cumberland for Sutherland's party. "They've got several communities around here—the most notable are Bethlehem, Ephrata, and Nazareth."

"What kind of life do they lead?" Sutherland asked, as they gave their horses free rein to start toward the city once more.

"Utopian, I believe it's called these days," Magruder replied. "They're doing well at it, too. They've done amazing things in agriculture, and they've built hospitals, hotels, even a city waterworks at Bethlehem! And musical instruments! There's no one else got better pipe organs in all the colonies, and perhaps even in England, and the Moravians built them right here in Pennsylvania. They've composed a thousand hymns, I hear, and they even have a good orchestra. I've heard it—very good, very good."

Ella came alongside, listening to what Magruder was saying. She asked, "Are these really the people the borderers want to destroy?"

Magruder nodded. "Not them, but their Indians. They believe the Moravian Indians are working with the hostiles."

They thought about that, and it depressed Ella. After a while they rode on, until they topped a rise in the road. "Look!" Magruder exclaimed. "There's Philadelphia!"

From left to right, as far as they could see, a low line of roofs and steeples pressed against the darkening eastern sky. Magruder stopped the column so his guests could drink their fill of this impressive sight. Behind was the setting sun, burning the horizon red and purple. Ahead, beyond fields and orchards, lay Philadelphia with the sunset flashing on its windows and brass weathervanes.

With the wonderful sight of the city before them, Ella and

Owen listened to the sound of Moravian singing fading away. They hardly heard Magruder say that among the many spires to the left that rose into the sky were Christ Church, the largest; the statehouse, where the colonial assembly deliberated; and the academy, where young men went for higher education.

"It may seem impossible to you that a city on the very edge of the northwest wilderness should be so wealthy," said Magruder. "But you'll understand when you see the port. There is no finer harbor in the world, the sailors say, and our port has brought us wealth and happiness unmatched by any city in the colonies."

It was obvious that Magruder was a native of the colony. He spoke in glowing terms of Philadelphia's vigor as a trading center as well as a shipbuilding capital; and now in his element, he seemed far more reasonable and levelheaded than he had in the wilderness.

As the lieutenant went on about Philadelphia, Owen saw a one-horse shay come whirling out of High Street—the main artery of the city—and pound toward them. The shay, which had its hood up and was carrying two men, clattered along the road, narrowly missing the soldiers, giving their mounts a start, and interrupting Magruder's speech.

The shay hurled straight for the Moravians, who were still singing. Sutherland felt uneasy as it bore down on the people, threatening to crash into them. Sutherland wanted to shout, but at the last moment the Moravians heard the carriage coming and managed to leap out of the way, their song abruptly shattered by pounding hooves. One of the men in the shay stood up, shaking a fist at the Moravians.

Sutherland jerked his horse around, about to go after those buffoons, but Magruder grabbed his animal's bridle and stopped him, saying:

"Mr. Sutherland, it will do no good to box the ears of those varlets, none at all."

"It'll do me good!" Sutherland replied, still eager to gallop back along the highway, where the Moravians were calmly reorganizing.

Magruder shook his head, saying, "No, Mr. Sutherland. You'll have many a chance to confront the likes of them in the weeks to come, but please do not begin by making enemies of them from the very start. It will be difficult enough to get them to listen to reason, but if you let your own Scottish temper butt against theirs before you meet them in peace, this long journey from Detroit will have been useless."

Sutherland let his anger simmer, and Ella rode up alongside him. She touched his arm, and he steadied himself.

"Listen!" Ella said, and they heard the Moravians singing once again. "That beautiful music comes out of such experiences. It's as though they rise above it by their music."

For a moment, while the soldiers began to show the same restlessness as their mounts, Ella and Owen gazed at the Moravian procession until it was out of sight on its way to the Schuylkill.

"Right!" Magruder called out. "Let's get you to your quarters, and there'll still be enough light to see a few things before we get there!"

They were off again, and within a minute they were entering the broad expanse of High Street. This road ran east-west through Philadelphia, which was spread up and down the Delaware. It was thrilling for the Sutherlands to be riding into this great city. Neither spoke as they passed through the long corridor of buildings that reached as far as they could see toward the east. At first the houses and shops on each side seemed to form a solid wall, but as they rode past they saw that many houses stood alone, surrounded by stone-walled gardens. There were no flowers and few leaves in sight because it was November, but Ella thought how glorious the city must be when these gardens were in full bloom.

There were a few buildings of wood, but most were of brick and two stories, their front doors painted bright red, green, or blue. There were some three-story houses on High Street, but the largest buildings—apparently all churches—stood closer to the harbor. As they trotted through the city, Magruder taking a turn here and there, Ella was impressed with how well the soldiers kept in file despite the hubbub of handcarts, wagons, carriages, pedestrians, and garbage in the streets. When the column swung around a corner, the soldiers stayed close together, and more than once an angry driver pulled up his team to avoid them. When a teamster shouted "Lobster!" at the men, they ignored the insult, but were clearly annoyed by it.

As they rode, Ella realized that all she had been told about Philadelphia's grandeur was true. The streets were between fifty and a hundred feet wide, with flagstone sidewalks and posts spaced to keep traffic and pedestrians apart. She was fascinated by a ponderous Quaker meetinghouse of simple square form, conspicuous for its lack of decoration or steeple; and she thought the new Anglican church just built on Third and Pine was tasteful and lovely, generously blessed with many large windows and adorned with a graceful steeple and weathervane. An old woman was selling fruit on this corner, her table set against the wall around the new church, and Sutherland cried out for Magruder to halt as he leaped from his horse and bought an armful of apples for the men and Ella.

They went on, and in the course of twenty minutes, Magruder led them back and forth through the city. Many folk were confused to see the detachment come thundering back from a different direction every few minutes, and they often gave a few good-natured shouts of encouragement and jest. In the brief tour, the Sutherlands saw the large Walnut Street jail, sullen and gloomy with its dark windows. They trotted through the wide marketplace, seeing the Quaker house of worship at Second and Market Street. Called the Greater Meetinghouse, it was indeed impressive, seventy-three feet long and fifty-five wide. Across the street was the courthouse, as ornate as the meetinghouse was sober. The courthouse had a lofty cupola with ball and vane atop, and three nosy gables peered across the street at the dignified Quaker building. By contrast with the worldly courthouse, the meetinghouse appeared to be in devout repose, and the Friends coming and going from the building looked equally pious.

In spite of the obvious saddle-weariness of the escort, Magruder insisted on showing his charges the grand statehouse on Chestnut Street. When they paused before the huge building, however, Magruder seemed more interested in praising the two-story tavern across the way. The mention of food and drink made the soldiers all the more restless, and Owen told Magruder it was time to find the lodgings the army had provided them.

"Right you are, sir!" Magruder said. "I could do with some dinner myself. Come along, then, we'll dismiss the men and I'll take you to dinner before you turn in."

"Before!" Ella exclaimed. "We're going to dinner in Philadelphia with traveling clothes on? I can't do that! At least I have to clean up and put on fresh clothes, Lieutenant."

Magruder nodded. "Of course, mistress, whatever you say. I'll have dinner sent to your rooms."

With that, he wheeled his horse and led them northward

through the city. The sky was fairly dark now, and sunset lingered on the rooftops and steeples west of them. Before long they stopped in front of a fine brick house. Magruder said it was the usual lodging of ranking officers and other guests of importance to the military who came to Philadelphia.

Magruder let the brass doorknocker fall, and a tall, thin black man in dark livery opened the door. He admitted them with a deep bow.

"Botany," Magruder said to the servant, "this is Mr. and Mrs. Sutherland, lately of Detroit, who have come to Philadelphia as guests of Colonel Bouquet."

The servant was fairly old, though neither Ella nor Owen could tell just how old. His graying, curly hair was cut short, and his narrow face was clean-shaven. He smiled warmly at his temporary masters, half bowed in acknowledgement as Magruder said a meal would be coming along within the hour from the India Queen, then after Magruder bade them good night and left, Botany closed the door.

Ella asked, "What is the India Queen?"

"That, mistress, is the finest tavern in the city," said Botany, smiling as he spoke with a slight West Indian accent. Ella had heard the very best slaves came from the West Indies, where Philadelphia did much of her trading. "Please follow me to your rooms. I'll bring your baggage up directly."

Sutherland, who had been admiring the white marble floors and papered walls, picked up their few bags and nodded to the servant. The old man's eyes glittered keenly, and then he led the way up a marble staircase, moving precisely and elegantly, as though he had been created expressly for this house.

Ella was amazed by their awesome accommodations. Even in her family home in Derbyshire, she had never lived as lavishly as this. As they went upstairs, they looked at the pastoral scenes of foxhunting and picnicking printed vividly on wallpaper from corner to corner. Light sparkled from whale-oil lamps, and here and there beautiful chandeliers hung in the hallway that led to their rooms. Botany paused at the door and noticed Ella studying the pretty wallpaper. He smiled and said, "Some of our guests are uneasy to see wallpaper."

Ella asked why, and the servant said, "It's rumored that arsenic used in the printing is given off as fumes at night." He watched their expression and saw they were more curious than worried. He smiled and said, "Colonel Bouquet himself picked this out, and no one yet has suffered from arsenic poisoning."

"It's beautiful," Ella said quietly, then asked, "Do you know, Botany, how long we're to be here?"

He unlocked the door and shook his head, saying, "No, mistress. I understand—though 'it's not my business, you know—but I understand you're to be here until the borderers attack the city . . . if they do."

Sutherland asked, "Does anyone say when that might happen?"

"Why, sir," Botany replied slowly, "you're asking a simple servant about politics, and that's none of my business, you understand. But I guess the trouble won't come until January, after the assembly has another battle with the governor and nobody agrees to do anything to protect the borderers."

"January!" Ella said in surprise. "We have to wait until January before we can go back to Detroit?"

Humor glinted in Botany's eyes. "It's none of my business, you understand, but the other day Dr. Franklin was in here discussing matters with the officers, and I happened to overhear them say the borderers couldn't get a force organized before the end of the year—and that's more than a month from now. Of course it's none of my concern. Now if you'll kindly follow me, *this* is my business—"

Botany led them into a dim room, and Ella gasped as he turned up a whale-oil lamp to reveal a stunning sitting room furnished with handsome cherry-wood chairs and side tables. A small fire in the brick hearth cast a sheen of warmth over the room. Floors of oak glimmered in the flickering light, which lent a bright patina to everything, from rich drapes at three windows to the pewter and silverware in a glass-enclosed cabinet at the left of the fireplace.

Ella was enchanted by this sudden change in her life. She stood limply while Owen followed Botany to the bedroom door in the far wall. Sutherland was shown another beautiful room, half the size of the large sitting room, with a big canopied bed, a dressing table, and a Turkish carpet. In this room, also, a fire burned. Sutherland wondered how the servant knew they would arrive this evening, but he did not ask just then. The two men went back out into the sitting room, where Ella still stood near the door.

Botany prepared to depart, saying baths would be drawn in small rooms off their bedchamber if they wished. Sutherland looked at Ella, who nodded, though she had lost her power of speech.

"Hold on, Botany," Sutherland said. "Ella, do you really want dinner up here tonight? Could you stand a hot bath and dinner all at one time so soon after the journey?"

Ella came to life and sighed. She thought a moment, then said, "I have no appetite at all. But I would love a bath."

"Same for me," Sutherland said, gazing at her. "I'm not hungry."

"Food is already on its way," Botany said.

"Enjoy it yourself, then. But we would rather not be disturbed after our baths are drawn. You see, this is our wedding trip."

The next morning, it was still dark when a faint knocking came at the door. They sat up, and Sutherland called out.

Botany's gentle, cultured voice replied, "It's nine of the clock, sir. Do you wish breakfast yet?"

They were shocked to hear the time. Then they realized the heavy curtains had shut out all sunlight, allowing them to sleep through the dawn. Sutherland asked for breakfast to be served in an hour, and Botany said the dining room downstairs would be ready at that time. When he asked whether they wanted tea or coffee, Ella lay back again and laughed in pure contentment. Sutherland answered, "Tea," and lay down beside her.

She looked at him and said, "I thought you got up before the sun."

He smiled. "Only when I have nothing better to do." She laughed and threw back the covers, hurrying out of bed to open the thick drapes. When the curtains drew back, bright sunlight streamed in from the east. Their rooms overlooked the Delaware, and if she pressed her cheek against a windowpane, Ella could see the entire city of Philadelphia curve far down the shore. It was a beautiful sight.

Sutherland came to her, pulling over his head a flannel nightshirt Botany had laid out for him. Ella wore a cotton nightgown that shone white in the warm sunlight. She kissed Owen and said, "I can hardly believe the way they're treating us. You must be very important to Colonel Bouquet."

He kissed her and held her close. "This is our wedding trip. No talk of anything else until after breakfast."

He turned to look out at the blue river and the distant Jersey shore. The water was alive with sail of every size and kind. In the middle of the river stood a small lighthouse shaped like a windmill; beyond, New Jersey's coast was crowded with wharves. A steady stream of vessels crossed the river between the two colonies, and at least twenty seagoing ships were anchored or docked.

Ella was examining the window, which seemed unusually constructed—as though it were two separate frames. "What's this?"

Sutherland pushed at it, then pushed a bit harder, and they were surprised when the bottom part slid up and opened. Now this was something special! They shoved the window all the way up and leaned out, the wind gusting fresh and clean against their faces. This was the first time they had seen windows with sliding sashes, and they were like children, hanging out and staring at people passing in the dirt street below. The breeze felt good to Ella, who had been slightly dizzy after first getting out of bed.

Then they saw a phaeton drawn by two horses stop at the house. Its passenger was Magruder, who waved to them, got out, and clumped up the steps. Ella and Owen were brought sharply back to reality. They drew in their heads and looked a little glumly at one another.

"They'll want me, I guess," he sighed, then began to dress, pulling on the linsey hunting shirt and a pair of flannel breeches.

A moment later Ella said, "Wouldn't you like to bathe again this morning?"

He looked at her, thinking, then nodded. "You're right!" He bounded up and yanked open the door, about to call Botany, but the servant was already there, holding a silver tray with china and a pot of tea set upon it. Sutherland stepped back as Botany laid the tray on the sitting-room table. Then he said, "I hadn't expected this."

Botany smiled. "When Lieutenant Magruder arrived I presumed he would ask you to come away immediately, but I told him you wanted to have breakfast first. And I thought you might prefer to have some tea in your chamber before you bathe."

This Botany was clearly a very special fellow, Sutherland thought. "Aye, Botany," he said. "Tell the lieutenant I'll be with him directly—after I bathe. How long will it take for the bath to be drawn?"

"It's drawn, sir." The black man bowed and went to the door, saying before he departed, "There's considerable clothing in the wardrobes in your bedroom, Mr. and Mrs. Sutherland. I think you'll find an ample selection that will fit. Mrs. Sutherland, I don't think you'll tire of the particular variety in your own closet—if you permit me to be presumptuous in saying so."

He started to close the door, then poked his head back in and said, "By the way, sir, if you wish to look the part of a frontiersman when you go out to meet the borderers, you'll be a clean and handsome one if you leave out your usual clothing for me." He gave a broad smile and left, closing the door without a sound.

An hour later, Owen and Ella sat at the breakfast table with Lieutenant Magruder. Ella was wearing a silk gown with a fawn-colored background and flowers of light purple, ruffled in fawn at the elbows. She wore the gown over the smallest hooped petticoat she could find. With the silver pendant at her throat, she looked very pretty. Sutherland thought she could be mistaken for a native of the city.

He had on a linen shirt of natural color under a beige woolen waistcoat. His breeches were also beige, his stockings dark brown. He had even found a pair of buckled shoes that fit well enough, but he did not wear a wig or powder his hair, which was clubbed in a short queue. Somehow Botany knew he would not wear wigs or powder and had not even offered these. The frontiersman made a perfect match with Ella—woman of Philadelphia that she now was. Magruder even commented upon their remarkable transformation, saying he thought Franklin might not believe this was Owen Sutherland, the noted Indian fighter.

"Not Indian fighter—adopted Ottawa," Sutherland corrected, and poured another cup of tea for all of them.

Later Botany came in and told Sutherland it was eleven o'clock. As Owen rose, the servant brought his beige coat and helped him on with it. When Magruder went out first, Sutherland said quietly to Botany, "Let's compromise. You don't spoil us too much, and we'll not act spoiled."

Botany thought about that a moment, then replied, "Let me spoil Mrs. Sutherland a bit, sir. I think after the journey she has made, she'll appreciate it. And there's another reason . . . But

I don't doubt she'll tell you about that before very long."

Curious, Sutherland was about to press Botany, but Magruder was already in the phaeton, and it was time to go. Sutherland kissed Ella on the cheek and promised to take her through the city when he returned that afternoon. Ella stood at the door and waved as the carriage clattered away, then came back inside and instinctively went to clear the table. But a young black woman appeared from the kitchen, curtsying as she met Ella, and started on the dishes. Botany was at hand as if by magic, and he introduced Ella to Clarissa, a pretty, strong-featured girl of eighteen.

"My daughter," Botany said. His face was alight with affection as he watched Clarissa take away the plates.

Ella said, "Botany, I'm quite used to clearing the table. I really think I at least ought to help."

The servant chuckled and said, "This is our life, mistress. You've had a hard journey, and you'll need your rest." He looked closely at Ella, and she felt as though he could see her very soul. His brown eyes gleamed strangely, though with benevolence. Then he nodded and smiled. "Yes, Mrs. Sutherland, you'll need a rest."

Ella did not know what he meant by that, but she shrugged off her uneasiness and said, "Botany, I'm new to Philadelphia, as you know. Will you tell me something of the city, of its people, its life? Will you have tea with me and talk about it?"

Something deep and wise was in his face as he said, "Mrs. Sutherland, I'll be happy to tell whatever I can, though none of it's my business, of course. But if you will forgive me, it would not be proper for me to have tea with you."

It seemed an effort for Botany to get out those last few words. Ella also decided against having tea, and the two of them went into the main parlor, which was furnished with walnut Chippendale—it had a lovely harpsichord, which excited Ella, and on its walls hung portraits of British officers who had served in Philadelphia. A Turkish carpet woven in burgundies and dark blue lay in the center of the room, with matching chairs set around it in a square.

Ella wasted no time learning the history of the troubles between the Penn family and the Pennsylvania assembly— much of which Botany prefaced with the words, "It's none of my business, of course." Yet for all Botany's self-effacement, she could not have heard a more lucid and intelligent explanation of the complicated political situation. In his gentle, soothing voice, Botany ended his talk:

"There are only two companies of regulars in the city—not more than sixty men in all. They don't like Indians any more than the borderers, you see, because they've been beaten by them too often in this uprising—not that I should be the one to judge that, of course, but you can look into those matters yourself.

"So, it's like this, Mrs. Sutherland: there's a revolt brewing in this land, one that might bring our fine city down about our ears. Sixty soldiers can't stop a thousand armed borderers. And the Presbyterian city-folk are siding with the Presbyterian borderers against the Quakers. You see, they have been politically weak in the colony, and now they have a chance to force the Quakers to grant more seats in the assembly to other Presbyterians from the back counties."

He looked grave. "Yes, it's complicated, but it won't be so complicated if the borderers come in here to wipe out the Moravian Indians taking shelter on Province Island south of the city. No, it'll be very simple then, so simple that even our peaceful Quakers will arm and be ready to fight."

Ella was taken aback, for his face was transformed, becoming very grim. "Botany," she said, appealing to his good sense, "Quakers have never taken up arms, not even against Indians. Isn't that what this trouble is all about? The Quakers want to avoid stirring up Indians on the frontier because they feel the Indians are being wronged. Isn't that why the borderers and the Quakers don't get along?"

He gave a rueful smile. "Who am I to know such things?" After a pause, he said, "But perhaps even I, a servant, know about this."

Ella thought him very peculiar just then. He seemed distant, as though meditating on what he had told her. Then he became warm again. "Does Mr. Sutherland know you are carrying his child?"

Ella gasped. Botany was motionless, gazing at her kindly. Lately Ella had suspected something was not quite right with her body, but she could not be sure. Yet how did this man know?

She asked him a little shakily, "Botany, how can you say such a thing? What right have you to say such a thing?" She was almost insulted and shocked at the same time. She even felt she might cry if she did not call up her anger. But then, as she looked at the old man, she saw a compassion and understanding beyond description. She had heard of the magic of the Caribbean, but she knew only a little about it. She was familiar enough with people who claimed second sight, but she had never seen such a remarkable display of it before. Staring at this slave who was more refined and more intelligent than most whites she had ever met, Ella's anger passed. As it did, she felt very close to Botany, as she might to a wise old uncle.

"I have no right, Mrs. Sutherland," Botany said, not looking away. "But you and your husband mean something to me already, and if I can be of any use to you, it would give me great satisfaction. I suggest, with all humility, that you discuss your condition with Mr. Sutherland before you attempt a return trip during the winter."

Ella was surprised that Botany knew about even this, but he added, "Your husband has told me your intentions, Mrs. Sutherland. Once again, forgive my impertinence, but I thought you should make decisions about that coming journey based upon complete knowledge of your condition." He bowed low. "If there is anything I or Clarissa can do for you, mistress, please ring the bellpull you will find near each hearth. If you will excuse me, I'll see to a few matters."

He left Ella by herself, watching the fire spark and crackle. She pondered the new life within, that now—strangely enough—she was certain had come to her.

chapter **14**

FRANKLIN

As Sutherland descended from the phaeton in front of the red-brick statehouse, he was impressed with the building's beauty. He stood on the brick pavement and looked up at the high white tower—a square base ascended to a smaller base that supported two domed cupolas, one atop the other, ending in the sharp needle and wind vane high above. To the right and left, arcades led to small annexes. The impression Sutherland had of the place was one of solidity, prosperity, and intelligence. By now he had no doubt that Philadelphia was the greatest city in the American colonies.

Magruder led him inside, where numbers of men were coming and going on apparently urgent business. There were wealthy, dapper gentlemen attended by bodyservants and retinues of political lackeys. There were grim Quakers in deep discussion with other Quakers just as grim; and here and there there were country representatives wearing their best cotton and linsey, hair brushed down, hunting knives at their belts, and calluses on their strong hands.

As Sutherland followed Magruder down a long hall, he sensed an air of tension. The colonial assembly was sitting in a special session, trying to hammer out a proposal to fund a militia to join Colonel Bouquet's campaign in the spring.

Stopping at a closed door, Magruder said, "Dr. Franklin came back early this year from England, where he presented the assembly's case to Parliament. As a representative of the Pennsylvania assembly he spoke out against the Penn family, saying the colony was unable to make laws for its own welfare because the Penn family would not allow passage of any bill that would tax their estates. Be sure the old fellow created quite a stir in London—enough to compel the Penns to yield! They agreed to be taxed after all, rather than be commanded by the king to sell their proprietorship! Yes, it was quite a triumph for the assembly, and Dr. Franklin's a hero in Pennsylvania, as you'll soon learn. But he was accused by some in England of trying to foment revolution here!"

"And what did he say to that?"

Magruder answered, "That no such idea would ever come into the heads of Americans—unless England abuses them!"

Sutherland liked that. He had read much of what Dr. Franklin published—and wrote himself—in his periodical, the *Pennsylvania Gazette*. As a Scotsman whose own country was poorly governed from London, Sutherland understood how Franklin and the Pennsylvania assembly were struggling to get free of being ruled by a proprietary noble family.

Magruder knocked and entered, followed by Sutherland. It was a large room, with good natural light, and comfortably furnished. A small fire counteracted the chill of the rain now pattering against the window. At first, there seemed to be no one in the room, then Sutherland noticed movement near some shelves of books. He saw a short man, overweight and balding, whose remaining hair fell to his shoulders. The fellow looked up from a book and peered over a pair of spectacles at his guests. Then he snapped the book shut and gave a warm, welcoming smile.

"Dr. Franklin," Magruder said, standing ramrod straight and motioning to Sutherland, "permit me to introduce Mr. Owen Sutherland of Detroit, the Indian fighter you asked to have brought to you."

As Franklin approached, Magruder went on. "Mr. Sutherland, permit me to introduce Dr. Benjamin Franklin, renowned agent for the Pennsylvania assembly, postmaster general for the American colonies, inventor, philosopher, publisher—"

"Pish tush, Magruder!" Franklin grumbled, then grinned at Sutherland as they shook hands. "Mr. Sutherland did not come all the way through the woods to hear you read a litany of my weary life. Welcome to Philadelphia, Mr. Sutherland." He led them to chairs near the fire.

Franklin and Sutherland looked each other over, and did so

with no false politeness or deviousness. Sutherland liked this man already. Even if he had not admired Franklin from all he knew about him, Sutherland would have felt immediately comfortable in his presence.

Franklin said, "You look like a Philadelphian, not a frontiersman, Mr. Sutherland."

Sutherland grinned. "I imagine there's many a Philadelphian on the frontier who doesn't look like a Philadelphian, Doctor."

"Ah," Franklin said, touching an ear. "By your brogue, I can hear you're a Scotsman after all. Colonel Bouquet told me that, but I'd forgotten. Yes, now I remember, you once served as an officer in the Black Watch, is that correct?"

Sutherland nodded, and Magruder looked startled, for no one had told him this before. He had a whole new perspective on Sutherland now, and he was struck with respect.

The Scotsman said, "Did Colonel Bouquet tell you everything about my service in the Watch?"

Franklin's keen eyes narrowed just slightly, as he took stock of Sutherland. "Yes. Everything."

"Then you'll understand that I came here as a civilian, not as a soldier. I came at Colonel Bouquet's request because I have had close connections with several nations, and I hope to protect these Moravian Indians. But as for a plan, I have none."

Franklin waved that away, then asked Magruder to get them some Madeira. Magruder hurried across the room to a cabinet with wine and glasses. Franklin said, "Did Lieutenant Magruder tell you the history of the borderer trouble?"

"He told me much about this affair, as did the letter I received from Colonel Bouquet," Sutherland replied. "I understand you wanted me here because these borderers are mostly of Scottish descent."

Franklin nodded. "Also because you're a respected frontiersman who led many of these borderers against the Indians last summer. They'll listen to you. And they'll listen to me, because I went out among them in the last war and organized the building of forts. I like them, for all their bad tempers and stubborn vengefulness. I daresay they like me, and they trust me, as they trust you."

Magruder served the glasses of wine. Franklin toasted to peace as Magruder sat down. Quickly draining his glass, Franklin asked Magruder pleasantly, "Will you be kind enough to give us another round, Lieutenant?"

The doctor rubbed his right shoulder as though it ached, while Magruder poured more wine. "This changing weather," Franklin said with annoyance. "I hurt my shoulder in two falls from horses recently, and it acts up every time the weather changes." Then he nodded to Sutherland, who toasted their health, and another round went down.

As Magruder offered to fill their glasses again, Franklin waved his hand and said, "None for me, Lieutenant. I'd rather we go to the India Queen; we can get both dinner and a private dining room there." He went to the window. "Good. The rain is light. We can walk to the tavern."

Magruder fetched the doctor's cane and broad hat, and they went out into the hall. To Sutherland it seemed that everyone was suddenly attracted to Franklin. The man was surrounded by a flood of humanity, all bowing and cheerfully greeting him. Franklin did not break stride, nor stop to talk to anyone, and he seemed calm in the center of so much attention. As they went out the statehouse door into the drizzle, a dozen people trailed in his wake, all jabbering at once. Sutherland hung back a little and listened, as Franklin gave replies with the utmost patience to everyone who sought his ear. By the time Franklin reached the phaeton that had brought Sutherland and Magruder, it appeared he had changed his mind about walking and intended to ride. Standing before the carriage, Franklin gave a wave of his cane and dismissed the hangers-on, saying, "Our driver is waiting, my friends."

The people doffed hats, bowed, and backed away, all of them apparently satisfied with the answers Franklin had given. He turned to Sutherland and said, "Before I went to England, I was just an aging colonial printer, but now I cannot walk through the statehouse without being..." He sighed heavily, waved his cane at the driver, and said, "Meet us at the India Queen in three hours."

The driver, a soldier, touched his tricorn and pulled away. With Magruder trailing them, Franklin and Sutherland walked through narrow cobbled alleys and along flagstone pavements of wide streets, talking all the way. Conversation flitted to politics, then quickly to natural philosophy and the arts. Never before had Sutherland met a mind that so engaged his own. They hardly touched on a subject before it led to another more interesting one.

The India Queen House was dark and intimate, and Franklin was immediately greeted by the innkeeper, who led them to a private room on the second floor. It was heated by a fireplace of iron, standing free of any masonry hearth. Sutherland remarked on it, for he had never seen such a thing before.

Franklin went to the fireplace and demonstrated how its doors could be closed to convert it into a stove that would burn slowly and use less firewood.

"Very clever," Sutherland said. "We have few enough iron stoves at Detroit, and I'd like to get one of these. Who has the rights to make them?"

"Oh," Franklin said casually as he sat in a leather chair near the table, "I can arrange for the manufacturer to supply you with one. It was invented by a fellow in this city, you know, but he did not keep the rights to it—he couldn't be bothered with such annoyances."

A waiter came with a jug of hard cider, the colony's favorite drink, then left after filling three pewter mugs.

Sutherland took his mug and sat down at the table opposite Franklin. "I'm a great admirer of your *Gazette,* Dr. Franklin." He lifted the mug in toast before drinking. "I thought your arguments to persuade Parliament to free Pennsylvania from the dominance of the Penn family were well thought out. Lieutenant Magruder tells me you have had partial success in that, but I think your opinion of the rights of British subjects will be lost upon most members of Parliament."

Franklin looked at Sutherland over the rim of his own mug, waiting for him to go on.

"How can members of Parliament understand that the American colonies are determined to exercise their rights, when the people of Britain are so docile? How could any member of Parliament believe that a colonial would want self-government rather than a proprietary government under the Penns, when—"

"—when Englishmen are not interested in liberty?"

"Exactly!" Sutherland finished his cider as Franklin thought through his reply.

"My friend," Franklin said, "members of Parliament cannot grasp the American colonial. On the whole they care nothing for the rights of British subjects anywhere in the world. But the day is coming when Parliament will understand that millions of Americans will not be led by the nose from field to shearing house just to enrich the mother country! The time has long passed when the American colonies were a slender tail on the English lion. In a few years, the tail will wag the lion, and God help members of Parliament who don't know how to hold on tight!"

Sutherland chuckled at the image, then grew serious. "This conflict in Pennsylvania between proprietors and the elected assembly proves how little understanding there is in England of life in the colonies. And this bitterness between the borderers and the wealthy people of Philadelphia is more of the same, is it not?"

Franklin agreed. "Those in power today must make way for new forces, for new ideas, and that is not happening in Pennsylvania, nor is it happening in England. The borderer is not properly represented in the colonial assembly, and he is angry because he cannot have laws passed to protect him and his family from scalping parties. It is just the same between England and the colonies. We have no representation in Parliament, yet they insist on legislating for us! They control our commerce, our production, our manufacturers. But there's one thing they cannot control, and that is—"

"Population."

"Correct! You seem to be more of a philosopher than an Indian fighter!"

"Not Indian fighter. Adopted Ottawa!"

"Whatever you say. But you are right! The British government cannot control our population growth, and as we continue to grow at this remarkable rate, how can that little island even feed the millions of sheep needed to provide us with English wool?"

Magruder clicked his mug on the table. "They can't!"

Franklin said, "How can British manufacturers possibly keep up with the growing American market?"

"They can't!" Magruder drained his mug, then refilled theirs along with his own.

Franklin went on. "Nature has put bounds on that petty island, which is no more than a stepping-stone in a brook, scarce enough of it to keep one's foot dry! Bounds on its abilities, but none on its desires. Britain would, if it could, manufacture and trade for all the world. And England would do so for all Britain, and London for all England!"

They laughed, and Magruder was disappointed to discover

all the cider was gone. He went out to fetch more and to see about their dinner. When he was gone, Franklin turned more solemn.

"No, Mr. Sutherland, I am not happy about our relationship with London. I must tell you in all privacy that it frightens me. When I see the determination of the borderer to rise up and threaten Philadelphia itself, and when I see the governor unwilling and unable to prevent such rioters from gathering—as they will soon do—then I fear for the very fabric of our society. Let us pray, sir, that misunderstandings between the colonies and our mother country do not come to such a crisis as that which my unhappy Pennsylvania now faces."

"Do you think it might one day come to an open break between England and her American colonies?"

Franklin replied without a second thought. "If there is no change in the narrow attitude of Parliament, then I believe the colonies might unite and force Parliament to change its policy of treating America as a difficult stepchild in need of discipline. Yes, Mr. Sutherland, I mean *force*."

The printer's face looked drawn and tired after he said this. Magruder bustled back into the room and sat down, banging another jug of cider on the table. Sutherland and Franklin were not thirsty, and both were silent. Sutherland was thinking how the defeat of the French had thrown the northwest territories open to the British colonies, and how all that prevented settlers and land speculators from taking possession of the northwest was the Indian. But how long could Indian tribes hold out against the rising tide of settlement already lapping over the Alleghenies and trickling westward along the tributaries of the Ohio?

As though he had read Sutherland's mind, Franklin said, "One of the most troublesome sources of conflict is your northwest wilderness. Parliament wants to control migration into it and wants to buy land from the Indians instead of throwing them out. Of course that peaceful policy is not simply for humanitarian reasons."

Sutherland said, "If the goverment tried to force the Indians out, it would take armies of twenty thousand men—that is if the Indians did not create one strong force with the support of the French from New Orleans. Pontiac may yet succeed in uniting all the northwestern and Mississippi tribes, if he cannot be brought to a peace council. I understand the government is already bankrupt from the last war; another war would topple it."

"Quite right," Franklin said, leaning forward, chin resting on the top of his cane. "Though, as you well know, *some* funds have have been made available for military campaigns next spring—in order to bring the Indians to the peace council. If these campaigns fail, there simply will be no more money, and the northwest will be lost to us. Few in Parliament realize what vast wealth lies in the northwest, and the government was slow to bargain for the northwest as part of the treaty at Paris. Many would have preferred a rich West Indian island. Englishmen live on a stepping-stone, and they cannot comprehend what an empire is out there! Ah, if only I were twenty years younger, I'd go back to Detroit with you and look for the Northwest Passage to the Orient!"

Sutherland laughed. "If I were ten years younger, I'd go with you to London and meet the great men who live there— the thinkers and the poets, the ones you met when you were there."

Franklin's eyes lit. "Yes," he said softly. "I envy England most its people. That stepping-stone enjoys in every small neighborhood more sensible, virtuous, and elegant minds than we can collect by ranging hundreds of leagues through our forests."

"Someday culture will come to us as well, sir," Sutherland replied. "It is said the arts move westward."

Franklin picked up his mug of cider. He looked at Sutherland. "My friend, be not embarrassed when I say your company has shown me there is already much of value in our mighty wilderness, if men such as you dwell there. I am sorry all the more that I shall never see it with you."

"I hope, sir," Sutherland said, "that from time to time we might correspond, and I'll tell you of the changes and the people. One day I might even write to you of finding the Northwest Passage."

Dinner was served, and conversation continued. Franklin made it clear that he hoped Pontiac's uprising could be put down next year. Otherwise Parliament might indeed abandon the northwest, perhaps by even selling it back to France. "If the Indian uprising were combined with a serious uprising of borderers in Pennsylvania, the numbers of troops required to crush them, and the cost of such an army, would be absolutely ruinous to Britain. The funds simply do not exist to finance such a war unless the colonies are permitted to organize for common defense. But that is something Parliament does not want. Parliament trembles at the thought of a unified America!"

Franklin added that Parliament would have to tax the colonies heavily to put down a major insurrection of the kind now brewing among the borderers. "But further taxes would surely cause an open break between the mother country and her colonies. Americans will refuse to be taxed without being represented in Parliament."

Sutherland nodded. "It is ironic, Dr. Franklin, that the role of the British army in the northwest is partly to prevent settlers from taking Indian lands without legal treaties being made. Yet at the same time, the army must fight the Indians who strike against those same illegal settlers."

"There are many colonials," Franklin said, "who believe Parliament is influenced by powerful fur-trading companies that want the northwest kept free of settlers so it will remain a hunting preserve for the Indians who trade with them."

Sutherland said nothing. Franklin went on, "I know, Mr. Sutherland, that you are a fur trader, so you must be well aware of the hostility many colonials feel. Let me ask you a hypothetical question: What would you do if Indians were driven from the northwest and farmers moved in?"

Sutherland thought a moment. "Dr. Franklin, I admire your writing and philosophy because what you say is very practical. It's pure reason with a practical application. My answer is also based on reason and practicality, not on hypothesis:

"Progress cannot be stopped, only directed and controlled. Settlement of the northwest should be limited to gradual and careful growth that will not destroy the Indians. You see, the Indians are friends of mine, and I like living among them more than I like living among white settlers. I think they belong out there, but I don't delude myself by thinking Indians can resist change. There's too much power in the colonies for the Indians to win by fighting settlers.

"Dr. Franklin, I am no settler searching for land, so I won't say the army should permit free settlement. I'm not a land speculator, so I won't say the government should favor land speculators. I'm a fur trader, and if the Indian is driven out of the northwest, my days as a fur trader are finished. Maybe by then I'll have another way of life, but I tell you there's none other that I love more, and I'll fight to go on living it!"

Franklin asked, "And who is right? Who is wrong? The government? The settler? The fur trader? The Indian?"

Sutherland sat back. "Don't ask me right or wrong, sir. Right and wrong, good and bad—those belong to history. Whoever wins will write out history, and they will claim to be in the right."

"But for you, Mr. Sutherland—what is right for you?"

Sutherland stared intently at the inquiring man across the table from him. Franklin was on a tightrope, always testing, testing, balancing for the sake of the walk itself, and enjoying every minute of it.

The Scotsman said simply, "I'm here, am I not? At the moment it is right for me to help the Moravian Indians and calm the borderers. In the summer I fought against the Indians alongside the borderers. Another day it might be for the government against the settlers."

"And would you ever fight against king and government if it was right?"

Slowly, carefully, Sutherland answered, "To defend what I thought right, sir, I'd fight anyone."

Franklin sat back, as though satisfied, but Sutherland leaned toward him, for he was not finished. "But if it were given to me to change the world, and to right things that need righting, I would be grateful to do it all without fighting." Sutherland sat back, saying, "To me, there is little difference between enemies, whether hostile Indian or settler. So far, I have found no perfect way to live and be, so I am daily forced to choose and choose and choose again. But one day, Dr. Franklin, I will live somewhere beyond the choosing, beyond the right and wrong and all the fighting! There has to be a way to do that, doesn't there? If not, then what is life all about?"

Franklin shifted in his seat and sighed. "What, indeed, is life all about, Mr. Sutherland? If either of us happens to discover its meaning—" he looked at Sutherland, and each had a gleam of humor in his eyes "—then let's promise to tell the other all about it!"

It was not until suppertime that Sutherland got home from his meeting with Benjamin Franklin. His emotions were mixed: on the one hand he was inspired and happy to have spent the afternoon with a person he so much admired; on the other,

what Franklin had told him of the storm building over Philadelphia troubled him profoundly. When first he had agreed to
come to reason with the borderers, he had thought it a local
matter that concerned only Pennsylvania. Now he realized that
the conflict could develop into a terrible battle between the
backwoodsmen and the people of the city. There was no telling
where that sort of situation might lead.

As Sutherland entered the house, taking off his hat and
handing it absently to the waiting Botany, he did not notice
Ella standing on the stairs watching him. When she said his
name he looked up and saw her dressed so beautifully in Philadelphia clothes that he stopped short.

"Well," he said, gazing, "you must be the lady of the
house."

She smiled, trying not to show the disquiet she felt over her
apparent pregnancy.

Botany discreetly vanished, and Ella led her husband into
the sitting room, where they took chairs near the fire, both
deep in thought. Owen was weighing what must be done to
prevent the borderers from attacking the city; Ella was thinking
how to tell him of the coming baby. She guessed she was a
month or two pregnant—certainly not more, since it was barely
two months since their wedding. It seemed nice that it was so
easy to get Owen's child, and she gave a little laugh to herself.

"What's so funny?" he asked, deciding now to let thoughts
of civil war depart for the moment. He stretched his long legs
out before the fire and smiled at her. Ella gave him a strange
look that made him sit up. He asked again why she was amused.

"Because . . ." She bit her lip, and really did not know why
she felt like laughing. Then she realized that she was more
pleased than worried about being pregnant. She would tell him.
But what if she was wrong, not pregnant at all? Well, then she
must tell him at least what she was thinking! But what if that
complicated matters unnecessarily? Anyway, if she was now
only one or two months pregnant, then she certainly could
make a winter journey if they left by early December, about
two weeks from then. He was still waiting for an answer.

"I'm laughing because I—feel good! What about you? Do
you feel good, husband? Was Dr. Franklin as grand as you
thought he would be?"

Sutherland took a deep breath and sat back again. "Much
grander. A week in his company and I could spend a year in

the wilderness without having to talk to anyone at all."

"Not even me?"

He grinned and put his hands behind his head, letting his legs stretch out once more. "Well, I'd talk to you occasionally, lass, just to remind me that thinking is only thinking, and there are better things a man can do with himself."

They let this conversation drift away and went back to their inner thoughts.

Then Ella asked, "How long will it take to do what they want you to, Owen?"

"I'm not sure," he said. "Maybe two weeks or so. I don't think more than that. I *hope* no more than that."

"Botany thinks the borderers won't march until January."

Sutherland chuckled. "Maybe Botany ought to give Dr. Franklin some advice. Even Franklin has no definite idea when the borderers will come.

Ella hesitated, then said, "Will you go back if you are kept here until January?"

He stirred a little and opened his eyes, staring at the fire. "I would go, but you'd have to stay here until spring—"

"Spring?"

"And then go to Niagara and come back out with me after I bring Tomano's peltry down to Montreal." He saw her dismay. "There's no other choice, lass. It's one thing to go through the woods in the autumn, or even in early December, but January and February are bitter cold out there."

She stared at him, and he tried to look away; but she kept her eyes on him until he gave in. "Ella, we said at the start that we would have to leave Philadelphia before Christmas."

She turned to the fire. After some time of silence that was heavier than any she had thus far experienced with Owen, he stood up and walked to a window. It was almost dark now, and outside a lamplight twinkled at the corner of the building. He realized they had been sitting in a room lit only by the fire and by the faint sheen of a cloudy sundown. Trying not to underestimate his strong wife, he struggled with his knowledge of the danger they faced.

He paced the room, hands behind his back, then came to an abrupt stop. He wheeled to face her, and she looked up. Almost hoarsely, he said, "Ella, lass, I don't want you to go through that kind of hardship. You don't know what it can be like!"

Ella's eyes were unwavering. She would not fight him in this, for fear that if she was really pregnant, she would endanger their child by being stubbornly selfish. She would let him make the decision.

A moment later he did. Coming to her and kneeling at her side, he took Ella's hand and kissed it. "All right," he said in a whisper. "We'll go together."

He expected Ella would throw her arms around his neck and kiss him as she had at Detroit when he asked her to come on this journey, but she did not. Instead, she smiled and let her hand run over his face. The fire lit his eyes, her eyes, and the silver pendant at her throat, which was a fiery red. Owen thought she must be a little worried about winter, too, and he was glad she did not take it lightly. She kissed him, and he put his head against her breast. For a little while they stayed like that, resting, calm, and wondering what tomorrow would bring. Both wished it would bring nothing more than peace of mind.

chapter 15

INTERLUDE

As Ella lay in bed that night, she decided she would say nothing yet. She could not be absolutely sure she was pregnant, even if Botany was so wise and her body was so different these days. Instead she would ignore the matter completely, and not even ask a doctor's advice. After all, she was vigorous and healthy, and there was no reason to worry. Now she would be in good spirits, for everyone's sake. After all, she was in Philadelphia, and that was reason enough to enjoy herself.

The following week she was mostly alone, playing the harpsichord, or in the company of Botany. Owen was constantly coming and going to meetings and planning sessions with Franklin and government officials. Ella longed to go with him through the city, to see all the wonderful buildings and to ride in a shay through the countryside, passing the magnificent estates on the outskirts. But there was not yet time for that. Owen was impossibly busy, and despite his apologies to her, Ella found it difficult to be cheerful.

Botany was some solace. When she asked, he told her about himself—and the wife who died bearing Clarissa—but nothing was ever said about his second sight. He was born in the West Indies and brought as a boy to Virginia, where he was educated by a farsighted master who had made a fortune in the tobacco trade. Botany's master had no interest in driving his slaves, nor in forcing them to work like animals as other plantation owners did. This master freed his slaves when they reached the age of twenty-five, and most of them stayed as wage-laborers living on the plantation.

Many of these young blacks were educated in the arts and sciences. When they proved clever as children, they were given the name of what they would study as they matured. Botany had studied botany; other names were Astronomy, Literature, Geology, and even Navigation. They took the master's last name, Lee, so he was Botany Lee.

"It was a good life," Botany told Ella one quiet afternoon as they strolled near the river's edge. A wet wind gusted off the Delaware, and the old man pulled his coat collar up. Ella tied her bonnet a little tighter.

Botany said, "By the time I was twenty I had learned all I could from the library on the plantation. I was ready to go on, and Mr. Lee was willing to help me; but he died suddenly, and the estate was turned over to his nephew. You see, he had no children, having been widowed the year he married."

They walked past a dock, where hammers clanged on spikes, and saws rasped away at massive timbers for a ship skeleton that hung in the ways. They watched workmen swarm over the scaffolding, then Ella asked how Botany had come to Philadelphia.

"Sold," he said. He looked a little sad at first, but overcame his emotions and went on. "The nephew was a gambler, you see, and not a very good one. Though Mr. Lee's will said we were not to be sold, but were to be freed at age twenty-five, the nephew ignored those wishes and sold me to a master who hired me out to the military. I was twenty-four. I have tried since then to buy my freedom—and Clarissa's—but the family we belong to will have none of it."

Ella wanted to protest that it was inhuman, but she saw that Botany Lee had accepted such things. She thought she was selfish to think her own lot in life a difficult one.

When they went back to the house, Owen was home, and she found him in their upstairs chambers, gazing at the river from the open window. He had not yet taken off his watch coat. He hardly turned when she opened the door, and she came to him, seeing something was wrong.

"The borderers have struck again at the Moravians," he said. "More than twenty were murdered in Lancaster—men, women, and children. Franklin told me the city now has two hundred

Indian refugees, but the governor fears the borderers will come for them soon."

Ella waited for him to go on. After a moment, he said, "The Moravians are to be ordered out of the city."

"What?"

"They're to be sent across the river to New Jersey, and from there up to New York and on to Sir William Johnson on the Mohawk River. They'll be escorted by soldiers, but they must walk all the way to New York."

Ella thought of the Moravian Indians she had seen on the Lancaster road, and she felt a terrible sadness to think of what they had endured and must endure.

"Is there any way to help them?"

He put his hand on hers. "Only to go with them and keep them from harm. I intend to do that. I'll return to you after they're safely across the Delaware. I'd like to go all the way, but I have to be back to deal with the borderers. Franklin thinks they will come very soon."

At the statehouse the next day, Sutherland learned that plans to send the Moravians away had been postponed. Franklin said the city was increasingly polarized between those who wanted to be rid of the Indians and those who wanted to protect them at all costs against the backwoodsmen. "Despite the murders at Lancaster, there is no large body of backwoodsmen collecting anywhere yet, so we hope these wretched Moravian Indians can stay in the city until springtime."

Sutherland made a decision. "Dr. Franklin, if there is no immediate use for me, I intend to spend some time with my wife. I've been overlong at your meetings, and if nothing is to be done until the borderers act, I'll take leave of you until I am summoned."

Franklin agreed, then wrote out a letter authorizing Sutherland's unlimited use of a shay leased by the government. "Show your wife our fair city. Just don't take her to Helltown."

"Helltown?"

"A section of Race Street between Third and Front. It's full of the lower sort of characters, a den of vice and debauchery that even one of your toughest *voyageurs* would blush to see. But there's lots else to see around our little town."

Franklin advised him on places of interest, beauty, and good

food, then sent him off with the admonishment not to return
to his sight without bringing Mrs. Sutherland along. That happy
event, the elderly man added, ought to take place at the Franklin
home at the end of the week.

"I've just had my armonica sent over from London, and
you'll both like to hear it!" Sutherland had read something
about this musical instrument Franklin had invented. It was an
extension of the principle of making tones by rubbing the edge
of a wineglass. A number of specially blown glass hemispheres,
of carefully graduated sizes, were mounted on an iron spindle
that ran through a hole in the center of each. A foot treadle
turned the spindle and glasses, and the musician pressed a moist
finger to the rim of whichever glass hemisphere he chose, and
a tone was emitted. These thirty-seven hemispheres were precisely tuned, and three full octaves could be played.

"I have read that your armonica is all the rage in Europe,
and that some important composers have written for it."

Franklin nodded and grinned. "Yes, already there are vir-
tuosos giving performances, and one day a public performance
will be given here in Philadelphia.

"As for myself, I am a mere dabbler, but I think you'll like
to hear it. I can play some of the softest tunes, and with my
daughter Sally on the harpsichord, we'll give you a concert of
some Scottish songs. Why, it's my opinion that Scottish songs
are the finest in the world, Mr. Sutherland—which leads me
to ask you—is it true as I've heard that you write poetry?"

Sutherland smiled. "Sometimes, when a thought has to come
out and won't go away in a less troublesome way."

Franklin said, "Give me the pleasure of letting me read a
few, will you?"

For the next two weeks, Owen and Ella Sutherland made the
most of their stay in Philadelphia. The weather grew colder,
and they were interrupted by messages from Franklin, but there
was plenty of time to ride through countryside or city. They
took horses into the woods and meadowland, followed the
course of the river north, then south, and later crossed the
Delaware to visit the farmlands of Jersey. It would have been
a beautiful time were it not for Owen's frequent visits to Province Island, where the poor Moravian Indians were living in
unused buildings. He found himself overwhelmed with pity for
these people, but there was little he could do until someone in

high office made a decision about their future.

Quakers and Moravian brethren had provided food and some clothing for the Indians, who spent much of their time in religious services. The farms of the Indians were gone, their daily chores and earthly tasks were no longer productive, and every day brought rumors that gave hope or inflicted fear.

In this time, Sutherland met Aleta in passing, but she was always busy caring for the older folk or for the baby, so they knew one another only by sight. Whenever Sutherland came back from a visit to the Moravian Indians he was moody, and Ella found it difficult to cheer him up. Often she played the harpsichord for him, and that helped a little; but for all the pleasure of being in the city, there was always the haunting awareness of why they were there in the first place. Still he had not met a representative of the frontier folk who sought the blood of these Moravian Indians. Little more had been heard from them since the murders at Lancaster, but false warnings often flew about the city, declaring that the borderers were up and on their way.

For her part, Aleta was diminishing. Her physical strength was being taxed daily as she labored to help her brethren. Their ramshackle homes let in rain and cold, and it often happened that Aleta was on the roof of a building with the men trying to lay hay or old sailcloth over the leaks. Later she might sit up all night with an old man suffering from fever, or she would be soothing a woman who had given birth to a baby that died. Aleta cooked and cleaned, washed clothes and pursued little children, keeping everyone's spirits up, and singing whenever and as joyfully as she could.

Still, she did not understand the meaning of it all. Now and again she would linger at the edge of the island prison and sanctuary, and gaze at Philadelphia. Why, she let herself wonder, must this happen to such folk as hers? But that question did not stay with her. There was too much else to do, too many people to help, to nurse, and to bolster with her strength. Aleta was the heart of her little community; without her, many would have given up and died of sorrow.

Lucy Swain's children were fast asleep on their pallet above the double bed. Mending a shirt for one of them, Lucy sat in a rocking chair by the fire. Jubal was at the table, whittling a piece of wood and smoking a cob pipe. She had held out a long time, even after he gave her the red silk scarf now folded away in her traveling chest. He was toying with her now, and she knew it. For days he had left her alone, not kissing her, not touching her, hardly talking to her. But she had no more will to resist him.

He was shaping a chunk of pine into a miniature dugout canoe for Willie. Jubal and the boy had finally come to terms, and that was why Lucy was able to soften. This dugout was Jubal's way of making peace. It needed only a bit of smoothing; the boy would wake up to a ten-inch canoe he could dream with down by the brook.

Lucy watched Jubal's big hands move. They were as clever as he was strong. He watched her, not the wood, as he worked with the sharp jackknife. Again he had that hot, flaming look that she could not ignore.

Lucy decided it was time. She put down the shirt. Jubal watched her as she walked to the chest and took out the Bible her mother had given her so long ago. She came and sat down at the table, putting the worn book in front of him. He took the pipe from his mouth and eyed the Bible suspiciously. Then he looked at Lucy, whose face showed she was up to something.

He asked slowly, "Yuh gonna read?"

"No," she replied. "You know I can't read. But I don't have to read, and neither do you."

He put the pipe back in his mouth and went on whittling.

She said, "You want me, don't you?"

He could not help looking up quickly. For all his backwoods impassiveness, he could not remain unmoved now. He laid the pipe and the whittling on the table, knowing that whatever Lucy had in mind, there was no turning back.

But Lucy was ahead of him. "If you want me, Jube Swain, you kin have me if'n you promise to marry me."

He remained fairly unruffled, though it was not easy. His eyes were penetrating. After a moment, he said, "Anythin' yuh say, girl. Anythin' at all." He took her hand and began to get up, but she clamped his hand onto the Bible. Too surprised to pull his hand back, Swain let Lucy have her way.

"Swear on this Bible you'll marry me in a week, no longer!"

"Lucy—" He intended to make a joke, but saw she was dead serious. A fire was in him. There was indeed no turning back. He tried to be angry, and said gruffly, "Don't push me, Lucy!"

"I'm pushin', Jube Swain. You had me once a long time ago, when I didn't know no better. You promised you'd marry me then, but you didn't swear to, an' you didn't come back when you said you would—"

"Lucy!" He yanked his hand angrily away.

"I mean it, Jube!" Her hair fell raggedly over her face, and through the strands her eyes were like burning embers. "Swear to marry me or get out! But I hope you marry me . . ."

Swain clenched his teeth and sat down to think. He was quiet for some time, but the heat he felt for Lucy did not subside.

He looked up at her, then grinned. Deliberately, slowly, he let his left hand hover over the Bible. All the while, Lucy was like a hooked fish, waiting to be pulled from the water. That was better. Now he was in control again. He laid his hand on the Bible.

"I'll marry yuh soon's yuh git the justice o' the peace, girl! I swear I will, by damn!"

Three days later, it was done. Word had gone out that Jubal Swain was getting hitched, and those who came to the wedding included some who were delighted to go anywhere drink was served, and others who could not resist witnessing the marriage of the toughest, singlest man in the country. Jubal's gang, living in a shack in the woods, came to the cabin overshadowed by dismay and disillusionment. When Hurley made fun of the notion, Swain threw him over the woodpile, and nobody else said a word.

The wedding was a good one, with games, dancing, singing, and lots to eat and drink. Lucy had little to contribute to the food, but much was brought by friends who had liked and respected her late husband, and most thought she was better off being married again than leaving the clearing to go back to New York. Also, Jubal broke into his share of the gang's booty, and had his men organize a grand table of food and liquor, sweets and punches—a table that would have done justice to a wealthy Quaker.

At six o'clock, the women followed custom and put Lucy ceremoniously to bed to await her new husband between fresh sheets scented with lavender. Then only the men were left in the yard, and an uneasiness came over them. Tradition required that they carry the groom forcibly into the cabin to toss him in beside his wife. There were at least fifteen men there, including Swain's outlaws, but no one was eager to make the first move.

Someone whispered to Morgan, who was sitting at a table eating beans and bacon, "Does Jube know we're supposed to rough him up—fun-like—an' put 'im to bed?"

Morgan hardly looked up. "Ask 'im."

The fellow was the slender neighbor who had taken Lucy in the day Matt died. At this reply, he gave a pale smile and went to Jubal, who was leaning back, downing a mighty swig of cider.

The fellow's voice cracked, and he spoke too loudly. "Jube!" That surprised Swain, who choked and coughed up cider, then glared hard enough at the fellow to wilt him. But the neighbor tried another smile. "Sorry 'bout that, Jube, but I jest wondered if yuh be ready to be put to bed." He tried to laugh.

Swain held one nostril closed and snorted out some cider. Then he leered at the neighbor and said, "Why not?"

"Yuh be?" The fellow jumped a little in surprise and cried out to the others, "Jube says he be ready, boys, so let's put 'im to bed!" He spat on his hands and clapped them eagerly.

Nobody moved. The neighbor spat once more on his hands, rubbing them together. All the while he tried to laugh, but he was alone. Then Swain laughed, too, and broke the ice. He downed more cider and then blared, "Well, my Lucy's waitin'! What kinda pals be yuh iffen yuh won't put me to bed?"

That did it. Finally Swain had stirred their fighting spirit. They decided to move cautiously toward him, but only because everyone else seemed to have the same idea.

Suddenly they dived at him, jumped him, wrestled him; there was a mighty uproar, flying shoes and torn clothes, broken cider jugs and a good deal of splattering blood. The skinny neighbor kept a safe distance, hopping up and down and slapping a fist into his palm. Nor did Morgan join in. He calmly ladled out another helping of beans, burped, and paid no attention to the battle.

Before Morgan had finished his beans, fifteen men lay on the ground in various states of destruction and pain. Nobody was badly hurt, but other than Swain none was left standing except for the skinny neighbor, who looked around at the annihilation as though he were witnessing something sacred.

The men groaned and sat up, and a few crawled away for a drink of whatever was handy. Jubal looked over at Morgan and growled, "Join the fun, Morg!"

Morgan nodded and waved his wooden spoon at Swain. "Come over here, son. I'll put you to bed."

Swain was surprised, and he laughed. The others turned to stare at Morgan's insolence. Morgan repeated his challenge, and Swain threw down the jug. Grinning, he strode toward the table where his deputy ate. But before he reached the table, Morgan leaped up quick as a cat and yanked at a rope that was looped in a circle on the ground around the gang leader's feet. At the last moment Swain tried to jump aside, but Morgan had him. The lasso was tight around Swain's legs, and down he went with a bellow of anger.

The skinny neighbor and Hurley sprang to help Morgan, who was dragging the shouting Swain as quick as he could across the ground. Then the others got to Swain, pinning his arms and lifting him in the air. With a great shout they carried him away, and he roared with laughter even when they opened the door by banging his head against it.

December plodded on, with some snow falling. When Sutherland's sled and dog team came in on a cart from the northwest, he and Ella took satisfaction in exercising the team, caring for the traces and the sled, and grooming the dogs. The animals were kept in a stall behind the house, and they came to know Botany and Clarissa well. In those weeks, much of the budget for food in the military residence went to Heera, the pure white lead dog, and his eight mates.

"Mawak has chosen well," Sutherland told Ella one afternoon as they watched Clarissa feeding big Heera, whose wolf eyes were white. "These are good animals, and the sled is strong and beautiful—I've never seen a better one."

Ella admired the bright blue sled, which was ten feet long from tip to brake. It could carry, in addition to the driver, one person and enough food for several weeks' travel in the wilderness. He showed her how the driver stood behind the sled, and when there was enough snow on the ground, they went for practice runs up and down the river. Early one morning just after a heavy snowfall, they dashed across the city, through the marketplace, and past the Quaker meetinghouse, where a line of men and boys in flat black hats were shoveling snow.

Ella was in the sled, and Sutherland mushed the dogs as they slid through the square. The expressions of surprise and amazement on the faces of the Quakers were frozen in Ella's mind as Heera and his companions yapped their way along Market Street.

Thus was December spent in Philadelphia, and in the days before Christmas, life slowed down. Owen and Ella were homesick for Detroit by now, and she missed Jeremy with an ache she could not relieve. Visits to Franklin and invitations to balls did little to alleviate Ella's longing to see her son. Furthermore, she had not yet told Owen that she thought she was with child. She worried now that he might stay in Philadelphia instead of returning to meet Tamano and take the precious load of furs to Montreal. It was important to Ella that her husband carry out his plans for the Frontier Company, and she would hate to be the cause of failure.

Yet she did not know what to do. As the days passed, Ella was torn between her concern for the company and the need to tell Owen the truth. It went on that way until Christmas, but she thought it could not go on much longer.

chapter **16**

CHRISTMAS

On the north bank of the Maumee River near the abandoned Fort Miami, Jacques Levesque sat in a small bark lodge watching buffalo meat boil on the fire. He was a short man, broad and powerful, though the bones of his face were delicate, shaped in handsome lines of refinement that were not overpowered by the healing scar on his forehead, from hairline to left eyebrow. His long hair, tied in the back, was auburn, as was his curly beard. On his head was the red stocking cap of the French *coureur du bois*—the woods runner—and about his thick, solid waist was the scarlet sash of the *voyageur*.

As Levesque stared at the bubbling pot, he thought of Angélique, and how he longed for her. But Angélique was in his past now. He had made his decision, and she hers. In the spring he would go out to fight again, if they had powder and ball. If they did not have ammunition . . . He did not pursue that thought.

He had been here at the camp on the Maumee for a month, and he was not looking forward to spending the winter with impoverished Indians. Pontiac lived in this little village crowded with newcomers—Indians of a dozen tribes, and at least thirty renegade Frenchmen and *métis*. Yet even the presence of this great leader did nothing to alleviate the sorry prospects facing these Indians on the threshold of winter.

There was not enough food because powder and ball were scarce, and that made hunting difficult. Clothes were old and patched, for without British traders, new cloth and shirts were

not available. Also disappointing to the Indians was the dearth
of goods for gifts—an essential aspect of Indian culture. It was
difficult to conduct important ceremonies without presents, and
Pontiac's few hundred followers who descended upon the Illinois tribal league had brought little with them.

The mood was dismal here, particularly because the French
commander of Fort Chartres—a small post to the southwest,
at Kaskaskia—had given nothing to show his love for the
Indians. He had distributed a little black powder, and a few
chiefs had drunk some brandy with him when first they arrived
here in November, but the soldiers had not shown much respect
for Pontiac, even though he led the Indians who were fighting
France's ancient enemy. Pontiac and the other chiefs had even
been told pointedly by the French that the war was over and
the British were brothers. But Pontiac would not accept that—
could not accept it without losing face. Those who were still
at Pontiac's side also refused to accept any declaration of peace;
they were united in their determination to go on fighting.

The people on the Maumee were united, too, in misery and
hunger. French traders had not come upriver from New Orleans
in any numbers, and if they had, there was little enough to be
traded with them. The bark huts in the camp could hold off the
icy winds whipping down from the northern plains, but the
people within were poor and already hungry. They knew they
would be hungrier before spring arrived.

This pot of boiled beef in Levesque's hut had to go a long
way: there were twenty people in the lodge, six of them children, the rest ravenous adults. Near him, also watching the
food, was his friend Henri Tremblay, a *Québecois* who had
come out to the northwest two years earlier. He was a tall, thin
fellow of twenty, with a kind face that belied his fierce courage
in a fight. Tremblay and Levesque were comrades-in-arms, and
they had talked often of finding a better place than the Maumee
to spend the winter. They had decided to stay a while longer
in hopes the Chartres garrison commander would change his
policy and supply at least the French renegades with enough
powder to hunt for the village. The alternative was to go south
to New Orleans, but that decision could wait a little longer,
at least until the first snowfall.

They heard a child crying outside, and Tremblay looked up
at Levesque. It sounded like Sally Cooper, the seven-year-old
English child Pontiac himself had taken as a slave. The old

chief was hard on the child because she was always very sad; she had seen her mother tortured to death. The girl was also ill with dysentery, and more than once she had fouled Pontiac's lodge, infuriating him.

The skin door flew open, and in burst Sally, hands at her dirty face, brown hair straggling and filthy. She ran to Tremblay, who had become her closest friend, and he stood up, catching her. Sally's dress, torn at the hem in order to fit her, was badly soiled with excrement, but Tremblay did not flinch. He hurried the weeping child out to the river, asking Levesque to follow and bring a blanket.

Sadness in his eyes, Tremblay spoke soothingly to Sally and washed the muck away from her dress and legs. When it was done, Levesque wrapped her in the blanket, and Tremblay picked her up. The child could not speak through her tears, but they knew that she had again incurred Pontiac's wrath because of her dysentery, and he had thrown her out of the lodge.

As they brought the girl back to their own hut, the Frenchmen saw Pontiac standing at his door, arms folded, his face dark with anger. He was garbed in a white blanket that hung loosely on his massive shoulders; his scalplock needed greasing, and it hung limply over his head. However, for all the lack of warpaint and finery, Pontiac was a hulking figure, his scowl exaggerated by the crescent bone pendant that dangled from his nose. Both Frenchmen tried to ignore Pontiac, but they knew he was annoyed that they showed an English child pity. This aspect of the rebellion against Britain deeply troubled Levesque. It was one thing to fight men, but he despised the Indian way of punishing all whites, no matter what the age.

They went into the dim lodge and joined the meal, which was just beginning. It was not much more than weak beef broth and corn gruel, but it was filling. Sally ate quietly. Levesque knew, however, that she needed better food to overcome her illness. As long as she was weak, she would suffer from dysentery and from the fury of Pontiac—a man whom Levesque disliked more with every passing day.

Peter Defries was not far from Albany, riding a swaybacked mare he had bought at the fort on the southern tip of Lake George. He had left Montreal two and a half weeks earlier, traveling by canoe up the Richelieu River to Saint John, then up the endless length of Lake Champlain by whaleboat. He was riding through country thick with forest and swamps, on the east bank of the Hudson River. He would continue this way until he reached Albany, where he would cross the river and go home.

The closer he came to his destination, the gloomier he felt. As he rode, every step took him closer to a reckoning with the families of his friends who lay buried at Devil's Hole, and farther from Mary. It had been a difficult parting in Montreal, but Mary recognized the necessity of this journey. In Albany he would first pay the families, then pay the merchants who had supplied the goods this trip. Then, anticipating another military contract—one he hoped would be much larger than the first—he would order selected goods for spring.

But before making final arrangements, he would visit with Sir William Johnson on the Mohawk River west of Albany, to ask the influential Indian superintendent once again to put in a good word for him with military procurement agents. He would also find out what the army intended to do on its coming campaign—the number of soldiers; the kinds of boats; where it would strike. Then, back in Albany, Peter would be able to complete the order, to be shipped to Fort Niagara in the spring. There was much to be done, and Peter had to do it himself, because he wanted to be sure every detail was executed precisely.

He longed to turn his nag around and gallop for Montreal, but Peter Defries was a practical fellow, determined to be a wealthy man before very long. He had left Mary with enough money to keep her comfortable until he returned in February or early March. As soon as the new baby was strong enough to travel, he would take them down to live with his own family in Albany. Then he would head west with another shipment of goods.

But now Peter was uneasy, even though Mary had the Devaliers as friends, and Emmy would be there from time to time. He did not know just what having a baby really meant. He did not know what he was supposed to do. He knew only that he wanted very much to be at his wife's side when her time came. That he would definitely do, even if it meant fighting a blizzard to get back there.

Then he caught himself, realizing he could not think so recklessly anymore. He was a married man, soon to be a father.

No more headstrong risks; no more gambling with his life. He had responsibility now.

At that moment in their small apartment, Mary Hamilton Defries was wishing Peter did not have to go to Albany. Even with faithful Toby as company, she felt painfully alone as she sat eating a solitary dinner. She was getting big now, and it was strange to her. Her tummy was tight and uncomfortable, and now and again she worried about the baby. When it was restless and kicked her awake at night, she hoped it was all right. When it was still, not moving for hours at a time, she felt another kind of anxiety.

If Peter were here it would not be so much to bear. She had accepted Peter's going to Albany, and when he left, they had parted tenderly. Yet there was a haunting feeling within her as he caressed her for the last time. Perhaps that feeling came from losing Duncan—or was it more, something else?

Mary recalled how Peter had promised to return before the baby was born, but she wondered whether he really knew what it meant to carry the child, to feel it grow, to wait and wait for its birth. It was not that he thought being pregnant a light matter—not that at all. It was just . . .

Maybe if he had offered certain small kindnesses when he said good-bye—she felt a little foolish to wish he had simply patted her tummy and told her to take care until he returned. But she was silly! He did understand! It was just that Peter was quite young and sometimes a bit irresponsible, despite his cleverness and brash sincerity. Peter was still inexperienced in the ways of women and marriage, but he would be a wonderful husband, for all that. He loved her, and Mary loved him. She was excited to be making a life with him, and she was sure he would return in time for the birth. He just had to.

In Philadelphia, the Sutherlands spent Christmas with the Franklins, and there was no talk of politics or civil war. Only a few close friends were invited to the gathering with the philosopher, his wife, and daughter; but there was a surprise visit from Franklin's son, William, and his family.

But even the arrival of the genial and intelligent William Franklin, who was royal governor of New Jersey, did not lead conversation away from interesting subjects ranging from art to literature to science and philosophy. There was much cider and much singing, and Ella and Sally Franklin at the harpsichord accompanied Franklin's armonica. Later, Franklin told Owen of a journey he had taken through Scotland a year earlier.

"I know you well enough, Mr. Sutherland, to say without being accused of flattery that the six weeks I spent in Scotland were among the happiest of my long life!" Franklin and Owen sat with Ella, watching William Franklin standing at a table and brewing up hot buttered rum in a wooden bucket.

"I grew close to several Scots—Sir John Pringle, William Strahan, Lord Kames of Edinburgh. And David Hume, a man I consider the acutest thinker in all Great Britain." Franklin watched a moment as William expounded his recipe aloud and plopped a couple of cups of maple sugar into the bucket, followed by some hot water and a good deal of stirring.

Then Franklin turned again to Sutherland. "Do you know that I sat at the same table with Adam Smith, William Cullen, Alexander Carlyle, and William Robertson—all on the same evening? What a glorious time that was! You would have been at home there, Mr. Sutherland! I wish you could have been with us, but I say in all sincerity that I am glad our young country has you!"

Sutherland, embarrassed by Franklin's kindness, was relieved when William attracted more attention by reaching into a butter tub and coming up with a greasy fistful, which he dropped into the mix. As the guests gathered around the table to receive a nogginful of the finished product, Franklin said, "I met many more Scots such as those, and when I left the country I realized that if strong connections did not draw me elsewhere, Scotland would be where I would spend the remainder of my days!"

Sutherland acknowledged the compliment in the name of Scotland. "Her men have done much for the empire, and I expect they'll do much more in the decades to come." Then he added, "But it's my opinion that the future greatness of the British empire will be founded in America."

Franklin peered at him, and for a moment, the hubbub and happiness of Christmas Eve was forgotten. Ella, who had brought mugs of rum to them, also listened as Owen continued. "The empire's foundations on this continent are little seen—like most foundations—but I believe they are broad enough and strong enough to support the greatest political structure humanity has ever witnessed."

Franklin gave no reply. He merely let a small smile escape, then turned to Ella, who handed him a mug. After a moment, Ella raised her own mug, offering a toast: "To the future of America."

The entire room was quiet, for everyone had been listening to Sutherland's words. Ella had intended this toast to be shared by her husband and Dr. Franklin; she was taken unawares when William Franklin, then the other guests, lifted their own mugs and echoed, "Hear, hear! To America!"

"Once more, Uncle Henry, please?" Jeremy Bently snatched off the fencing mask and slipped the foil under his arm as he followed Henry Gladwin across the living room. "Once more, sir? I think I've got it now!"

Gladwin was laughing as he stepped around overturned furniture on his way to the stairs. Both he and Jeremy were dressed in full-length fencing suits, sweat-stained from two hours of constant practice.

"That already was the once more, Jeremy," Gladwin said and turned at the door, his face showing pleasure with the boy's enthusiasm. "Indeed, I think you almost do have it, but we'll see at our next lesson after the New Year."

Gladwin went upstairs, and Jeremy clumsily staggered amidst the fallen chairs and spilled books that had been inadvertent participants in the fencing exercise.

"New Year's!" Jeremy groaned to himself. "It's only Christmas Eve, I'll forget it all by New Year's!"

There was a knock at the front door, and Jeremy pulled off his gloves as he went to answer it. These days he spent much of his time with his uncle, often living with him here at the commandant's house for a week or more, and they were the best of friends. He opened the door to see Garth and Lettie Morely, both grinning broadly, Garth flourishing a large pitcher. "Happy Christmas, Jeremy, lad! We came to see what's keepin' thee and thy uncle from the feast!"

Lettie and her husband pushed inside, and Jeremy realized suddenly that he had kept his uncle busy all this time while they were expected at the Morelys'. Now he felt very hungry and thirsty, and he accepted a small mug of mulled cider, which just made him thirstier.

"Go on, get cleaned up, lad," Lettie urged. Meanwhile Garth called upstairs for Gladwin, who said he would be there directly after he refreshed himself. Lettie said, "It'll be a grand party! Jean Martine's are fixin' everythin' extra nice-like, an' I promise thee'll have a happy Christmas, Jeremy!"

He hurried off to his room for clean clothes, and Lettie, a little sadly, watched him go. She sympathized with the boy, with his parents away. She and Morely and Gladwin had done their best, but still . . .

There came a rapping at the door, urgent and quick. Lettie let in Ensign Parker, and as the couple was about to wish him a happy Christmas, they saw the sadness about his eyes. The well-liked, high-spirited officer, who had been back for several weeks after escorting Owen and Ella to Fort Pitt, should have been cheerful on Christmas Eve.

"I've got a message for Major Gladwin," he said, his face flushed and tense. "It's serious."

Garth called Gladwin, and when he hurried down, buttoning his scarlet tunic, the Morelys offered to leave the room.

"Nonsense!" Gladwin said, half-smiling. "You know everything that happens out here long before I do, so this won't be anything—" He saw the young officer's troubled face, then asked, "Go on, Ensign. What is it?"

Parker fought back his welling emotions as he said, "The pickets guarding the whaleboats at the lower landing were hit just before dark . . ." He was losing control.

"Go on," Gladwin said, anxious now. "What happened, man?"

Parker took a deep breath and forced himself to speak in cold, mechanical terms. "Six men were attacked just before the change of guard, sir. All dead . . . all dead, and not an Indian in sight, sir!"

Gladwin closed his eyes in pain, and Lettie turned away to stare at the fire. Six men dead. In another half-hour they would have been celebrating Christmas, but now they were gone. All of them had been with Parker on his escort to Pitt, and they had been under the command of the elderly Corporal Mullaney, the man who had given Ella Indian medicine for blisters.

From the top of the stairs, Jeremy watched as Gladwin walked slowly to the window and looked out at darkness and the frame of white snow glistening in the firelight.

The boy heard his uncle say softly, "So we're still under siege after all. We're still at their mercy. It's not over, not at all!"

chapter 17

ESCAPE

By January, nothing more had happened to create fear of an attack by the borderers, and Sutherland was getting restless. He had waited long enough, yet no one had employed him in an embassy to the leaders of the borderers. Franklin said that the only way to deal with the troublemakers was to wait until they were collected and ready for business. Then they would be led by the men they trusted most, and Franklin would go directly to them with Sutherland at his side.

Sutherland understood that logic, and he agreed with it. But how long must he wait? Tamano would be heading for Detroit in another month, his furs laden on dogsleds, and Sutherland wanted to be there when his friend reached the fort.

Yet he was still in Philadelphia. The novelty of the city had worn off, and even the charm of Benjamin Franklin was not enough to calm Sutherland's unease. Ella had not said anything about her pregnancy, but he sensed that she, too, was restless. They could not wait much longer.

The Moravian Indians on Province Island had passed Christmas and New Year's with a brave attempt at some spiritual understanding of their plight. All they could really grasp, however, was that this was a mighty test of their faith.

They knew there was no one in political power willing to return them to their ruined homes, which they would happily have rebuilt. As the weather deepened into winter, the Indians were dependent on charity for everything from firewood to blankets and clothing. They had even grown used to hearing rumors that the governor intended to put them out of the colony. They hardly believed anything they were told anymore, because keeping warm and staying alive were all that concerned them.

Then one evening someone cried that boats were crossing from the city, and an alarm went up in every little shack. Fear swept through the Indians as they collected before the largest shelter, which served as their church. There a few Moravian ministers and a Quaker volunteer spoke to them, saying the boats running ashore were from the army. These were the troops that Colonel Bouquet had managed to obtain for his beleagured city from the commander of British forces in North America, Sir Thomas Gage.

The governor, the Indians were told, had decided to send them away to Sir William Johnson. Although Moravian Indians were better educated than most people of that day, few could imagine just where the Mohawk River was, and only a handful ever had been outside the province. Nevertheless, the thought that they might be safe at last to begin a new life evoked excitement and hope among them.

However, hope faded from a flame to an ember when they were told they had to gather their families and belongings within the hour. They would set off that very night, pass through the city in utmost secrecy under the escort of Highland soldiers, and then take larger boats across the river to New Jersey. From there they would have to walk more than sixty miles to Amboy, then be ferried over to New York. Eventually, they would be taken to Sir William, noted friend of the Indians.

Though many were ill or too young for such a hard journey, the Moravian Indians still did not complain. They accepted this new twist in their destiny and obeyed what the white Christians told them to do.

Two hours later, two hundred shabby, weary Indians trudged through slumbering Philadelphia, the snow cold under worn shoes, the winter wind biting through frail and tattered clothing. From somewhere, a few Quakers appeared and handed out woolen blankets, which were wrapped quickly around the shoulders of those who most needed them.

In the midst of the procession, Aleta carried Jane White-feather's baby under one arm, a pack of belongings over her shoulder. Tonight Aleta had no inclination to sing, not even a melancholy hymn. Step by step they tramped through lamplit

streets toward the docks, with a few dozen kilted soldiers of
the Black Watch scattered up and down among them for an
escort.

But they had not gone very far when windows began to
open and people shouted, some hurling insults. Others came
down to the streets to throw snowballs, but the Indians kept
going, and the soldiers did nothing to stop the abuse. These
same soldiers had seen friends die fighting Indians this past
summer. They had no love for their charges, and they, too,
were cold, and they were irritable. As the Moravians moved
on, more and more people—many carrying flaming torches—
came into the streets, some aggressive, others protective. Now
and again a fight broke out in the growing mob around them,
and Aleta noticed that often it was a pacifist Quaker taking on
someone from another denomination.

The soldiers began having difficulty getting through the
crowd surging in on all sides. When this march began, Aleta
had felt only weary and hopeless, but now she sensed their
danger if they did not soon reach the docks. Then the Indians
were blocked; progress was impossible. There was little co-
ordination among the Highlanders, who were strewn singly and
in little groups over a length of two city blocks. Several hundred
people milled around the Indians, and tension mounted. Aleta
no longer felt the chill of the wind. The baby sobbed sleepily,
and she hugged it against herself. The roar of the mob was
increasing every moment, some people calling for the blood
of the Indians, and others trying to assemble for a defense.

A few white Moravians tried to persuade the soldiers to take
the Indians back to Province Island, but that only caused more
confusion. Aleta saw the burly Scottish captain walking alongside the stalled procession, trying to collect his men. But he
was as rough and rude with Indians who happened to be in his
way as he was with Philadelphians. Clearly he had no sympathy
for the Indians, nor did his men, whose own lives were increasingly endangered.

A stone flew through the air and struck Aleta on the side
of the head. She staggered but caught herself and held on to
the baby. An Indian grabbed her and kept her up. She closed
her eyes and fought away the stinging pain, then began to pray
silently. There was nothing else to do.

Oaths and shouts of hatred rang out on every side. Pacifists,
though not inclined just then to be passive, were outnumbered.

Another stone and then another flew. The soldiers stood by helplessly, and the crowd sensed they would do nothing to stop what was about to happen. White Moravians and Quakers were on the defense, but disorganized. The majority of the mob had one mind—punish these Indians—while the defenders had neither a plan nor the knowledge to organize resistance.

Whistles and catcalls, stones and sticks, bottles and filth from the gutter began to fly. The soldiers looked to their captain, who was arguing face to face with a furious Quaker leader. The mob, united in their herd mentality just then, pushed toward the Indians. Soldiers were shoved aside, at a loss for what to do. Aleta saw men reaching for her, and she prayed frantically, hugging the bawling baby close.

The Indians pressed forward, and Aleta felt relief that they were moving once more. Ahead, some Quakers and a few soldiers were making progress. She felt the crush of bodies as people behind her tried to move up. The baby was squealing in fright. Aleta was borne along in the crush, and she found it hard to catch her breath. People squeezed against one another, without room to turn. Fear rose inside Aleta, fear and helplessness.

The mob was shouting, pelting them harder, but at least they were passing through these hateful folk. Indians began to sing a hymn, and soon the street rang with the high, shrill, haunting sound. Aleta sang with all her might, and it gave her strength. The Indians seemed to move in rhythm to the song, impelled forward, pushing through the devils who cried for their blood.

The mob tried to drown out the hymn by roaring louder, but the pitch of the Moravian hymn was too intense to be overwhelmed by mere shouting. This infuriated the crowd, and some men charged past soldiers, battering indiscriminately into Moravian Indians, knocking them to the ground, and kicking them. Soldiers tried to stop this savagery, but there was no organization. The captain had shoved his way to the head of the line, and that was likely the reason they were advancing. But he failed to protect the Indians by directing his soldiers, and with every passing minute peril mounted.

The hymn came to an end, and a bearded German pastor began another, followed quickly by his flock's two hundred voices, who gave the song all they had. Now they were moving faster, and Aleta thought she could smell the riverside docks at hand. Relief came to her, and she wanted to weep for joy that at last they were almost free of this terrible city, where they were despised by so many who called themselves Christians.

Then she heard much shouting behind. She turned just as bodies bumped into her, crashing her and others nearby to the ground. Legs and feet and falling Indians surrounded her. She struggled to her feet, the baby crying in her arms. The mob had broken through the soldiers and now assaulted the procession, driving a wedge into the center of the Indians and knocking them down right and left. Aleta staggered back, trying not to fall again, trying to protect the infant.

There was a tremendous explosion, and Aleta shook with fright. The crowd hushed as a powerful voice cried out, "To me, men of the Watch! To me or you are cowards and false to your regiment!"

Aleta looked up at the captain, but it was not he who spoke; he was just as stunned as everyone else. The stranger's voice blared again: "To me, lads! Prove yourselves worthy of your name!"

Aleta saw him then, standing high upon a great Lancaster wagon, a big man whose eyes burned with battle madness. He wore buckskins, but above his head he waved a Highland claymore that glittered and gleamed in the light of streetlamps.

As if by magic, the soldiers hurried to his side. Only the befuddled captain stood immobile. On the wagon next to this amazing fellow a tall black man was reloading an old-fashioned blunderbuss. The crowd murmured in surprise and anger. A few tried to reorganize to assault the Indians, but their moment had passed. This man from out of the night leaped down and led the Highlanders into position. Bystanders were swiftly driven from one side of the street so that a brick wall was behind the Indians, and they were not endangered from there.

Owen Sutherland swung his claymore, slapping the flat of it against Philadelphian bellies and rumps, pointing it at the noses of astonished men who backed off quickly. Sutherland was angry enough to use the sword if he was forced to, and that fury showed in his face. With all the authority of a commander, he spoke decisively to the soldiers, who obeyed without question. By now they recognized him, having fought alongside him at Bushy Run when he saved them from slaughter at the hands of the Indians. It took only a few sharp words, a command here, a motion with the sword there, and the soldiers did what they knew by training to do.

Bayonets glittered in the torchlight, and the angry mob, almost as one man, flinched from the sight of cold steel. These were no longer confused individual soldiers; they were a fighting unit, divided into squads of six that trotted alongside the line of Indians, bayonets pointed ahead so that anyone in their way was compelled to leap aside. More than one indignant citizen had a coat slit or a hat skewered from his head before he saw the prudence of backing off.

By the time the captain confronted Sutherland, the soldiers stood with fixed bayonets in line between the huddled Indians and the mob. At the same time, others sympathetic with the Indians had quickly arrayed themselves in cohesive protective groups, and the attackers were foiled.

Aleta and her people moved ahead toward the docks with the soldiers and peaceful citizens protecting them. Though she did not hear the conversation between Sutherland and the captain of the escort, her prayers had been answered after all.

Sutherland sheathed his claymore as the officer angrily approached him. In the dim lamplight, the captain could not see Owen's face, and he blustered with fury, threatening to arrest him, until Sutherland stepped into the light and said, "Captain, if you don't know me, inquire at Colonel Bouquet's headquarters."

The officer stopped short. "Mr. Sutherland, sir! It's you! I, ah, I thought it was just some civilian acting the fool. I mean, ah, sir—"

Sutherland turned to Botany Lee and helped the old man from the wagon, catching the blunderbuss when he tossed it down. Then he turned to the embarrassed officer and said, "You were right, Captain. Just a civilian." He started away with Botany, then turned back. "It's the first time in my life that I've seen a civilian do the duty of an officer of the Watch, Captain. I hope I never see it again."

Back at the residence in the morning, after supervising the safe embarkation of the Indians, Sutherland sat with Ella and Botany at the dining table. After much persuasion on Ella's part, the old black man had decided it would not be improper to join the masters of the house at their table. Clarissa came into the room with a tray of hot tea, honey, and bread. She served them all, then hurried out of the room, but Ella called to her:

"Clarissa, dear, I'm tired of having slaves. Won't you sit with us and have some breakfast? Please do."

The lithe girl hesitated and glanced at her father, who laughed softly and said, "You might not ever get the opportunity again, my child. Sit with us."

Clarissa fetched herself a cup—though not one of the good ones—and sat down. They talked about what had happened.

"But one thing is clear," Sutherland said to Ella. "The Indians are gone, so there's no reason for the borderers to menace Philadelphia. That means we'll be going home soon, lass."

Ella drank some tea. She had been awake from the time Botany banged on their door at midnight, shouting for Owen to come quickly because the Indians were in danger. She was tired, depressed, and anxious to get back to Detroit. She looked forward to being in the wilderness again, where there were few people to make life so unpleasantly complicated. In her mind were endless forests and great mountains, and after a moment she felt at peace.

Just then they heard the door open and slam. Before Clarissa had a chance to jump up—her father did not bother trying—Ben Franklin appeared at the door of the room. He was taken aback to see slaves at breakfast with their masters, but his surprise lasted only a moment. He scurried into the room and with a grin clapped Owen on the back.

"You've done it again, Mr. Sutherland!" he exclaimed. "No, girl, sit down, sit down!" he said to the nervous Clarissa, who did what she was told.

Franklin started to talk to Sutherland about the night before, and Ella asked if he wanted tea. When he said he did and moved to a chair, Clarissa jumped up again, but Ella sat her down and went for another cup.

In the course of the discussion, Sutherland answered all Franklin's probing questions, but asked that the captain of the Black Watch not be accused of dereliction of duty. The officer knew well enough how he had failed, Sutherland said, and the situation had been difficult to handle, almost impossible.

"Yes, almost impossible," Franklin said with a chuckle. "For the captain it was impossible, but not for you, eh?"

Sutherland waved that off. Franklin liked his modesty. Then, unexpectedly, he asked about Owen's poems, and whether he had any more than the small package that had been left off with Franklin some days earlier. Sutherland said he did, and Franklin asked to read them, adding, "Would you permit me to publish one or two in the coming issue of the *Gazette?*"

Sutherland did not know what to say about that, but before he could reply, Franklin thanked him heartily, got up, and told everyone—particularly Clarissa—to enjoy breakfast. Then he was gone with the same gust of wind that had blown him in, and the others sat amused and in better spirits.

Ella and Owen found themselves inundated with letters from the most prominent folk in the city, who wanted to call on them before they left for the northwest. For the next week they had little time to themselves.

Ella took advantage of all this popularity to pay a few return visits to the finest houses and estates in and outside the city. These houses gave wonderful ideas for the home she and Owen dreamed about; and the owners' clothing, furniture, food, and education fascinated her. By the time she was finished—exhausted from all the teas and dinners and chats—she had been filled up with all she ever wanted to know about the life of wealthy Philadelphians.

As it turned out, Ella was generally in the company of the men, while Owen was invariably surrounded by pretty, flirting women. When visiting or entertaining, Ella wore little makeup, and always found the simplest dress possible in her large borrowed wardrobe. This confused the painted and ornamented ladies of Philadelphia's grand society. At least it confused those who paid her any attention at all. It seemed most were much more fascinated by Owen.

At the end of a week they had met enough people, eaten enough rich food, and ogled enough great houses and fine furniture to numb them. They wanted to go home. The sled and dogs were ready, and it was certain now that the borderers would leave Philadelphia alone.

As soon as they could, Owen and Ella said farewell to Dr. Franklin, who meant much to them by now. They promised to return one day, perhaps next year if all went well. Owen and Franklin agreed to correspond, and as the couple left Franklin at the door of his house in a narrow alley, the old fellow cried, "I want to hear more about the Northwest Passage!"

They came back to the residence, where what little they had

brought along was packed and waiting. It was late in January, and all they needed was warm clothing and food and gear to keep them alive for the weeks in the winter forest beyond Fort Pitt; in the first leg of the trip, they could resupply at the army posts.

Ella and Owen felt sad to say good-bye to Botany and Clarissa, but when their servants came into the sitting room, Botany said, "I have to inform you, sir, that something tells me you won't be leaving yet."

Sutherland was surprised, and Ella feared the man was about to tell Owen she was pregnant and could not risk the journey. Instead, he said quietly, "You see, the Moravian Indians have been sent back to Philadelphia."

Ella sat down heavily in a chair. Owen rubbed his chin and went to the window. No one spoke until Botany went on:

"I just heard it from some friends, sir. The Moravians were turned back by the governor of New York, who said they were Pennsylvania's responsibility, not New York's. And the governor of New Jersey—Dr. Franklin's son, sir, yes—has also sent them back, claiming that there is no other choice because the Moravian Indians would be in danger in his province also."

Sutherland turned, his hands behind his back. "Where are they now?" he asked.

"They're being taken to the barracks in the center of the city. I believe the governor has not yet informed the colonial assembly or Dr. Franklin, sir." Botany's knowledge was considerable. The servant had friends on the street and in the estates who knew even more than he did about official business, and they passed the word on.

Owen looked at his wife and sighed with exasperation. "This means we stay in Philadelphia. The borderers surely will make their move now."

chapter 18

THE BORDERERS MARCH

Sir William Johnson welcomed Peter Defries to his mansion with a hearty shout of delight and a bearhug.

"Well, well, my lad, I hadn't expected to see you so soon!" Johnson guided Peter into his library, where a fire blazed and crackled in the hearth. Johnson's great stone house on the Mohawk River was as strong as a fort—it had to be, for over the years he had been threatened with attack from the French and their Huron allies.

As they sat down in comfortable chairs near the fire, the Indian superintendent said, "I thought you'd be off spending that tidy sum you made with your army contract!"

"No, sir," Peter replied. "I can't be wastin' that money. You see, I plan to use it for another shipment, which I hope to contract this spring. An' I'm married now, sir."

At that last news, Sir William roared happily and called for rum. Peter noticed a beautiful Indian woman rise and leave the corner of the room, where she had been stringing wampum beads. This was Molly Brant, daughter of a powerful Mohawk chief, housekeeper here at Johnson Hall. Peter knew, however, that Molly Brant was more than a housekeeper, for she had borne the boisterous Irishman children.

Johnson asked all about Peter's experiences and of his recent marriage. Halfway through Peter's talk, Molly returned with glasses and a pitcher of rum flip. Defries smiled at her and took some flip, then went on with his tale. At the end he came right to the point and asked whether Sir William could help him get a contract for the coming campaign. Sir William chuckled as Defries ran through a long list of questions: Who is the commander? Where was he going? How many troops, and what kind . . . ?

"Peter, you've got the good sense of a born merchant! I don't see anything to prevent you from going far in this country, lad." He leaned forward and winked, his face merry, flushed with rum. "And with my help, you'll go farther than most, I promise!"

Defries felt good now, lucky to have the confidence of the man the Iroquois had adopted and named *Warraghiyagey*— "He-who-does-great-things." Peter downed more rum, which warmed him inside, then listened as Sir William outlined a plan to help him establish himself as a premier military supplier for the northwest.

"First of all, pick the right officers to serve—I mean ones who can win, for they'll be given additional duties with larger forces, and you'll advance along with them."

Sir William promised to write a letter of introduction to either Colonel Bouquet, who would command the coming campaign in the Ohio Valley, or Colonel John Bradstreet, who would lead an expedition across Lake Erie to assault the Indians of the lake country. Bradstreet would strike south from ruined Fort Sandusky against the Miami and the Delaware, while Bouquet would lead the southern half of the pincers northwest to meet Bradstreet in the Muskingum or Scioto valley, laying waste to every hostile Indian town in their paths. About two thousand men would be in each army—half regulars, half provincials from colonial militia.

Sir William said, "I wish you could serve Bouquet, lad, because he's the best there is, and you'd go far with him; but Bouquet will be supplied by Philadelphia Jews and Quakers, and you'll never beat them at their trade. No, you have to go after Bradstreet, though I don't like that overrated ass.

"He won some victories in the French and Indian War, true. But he has to sing his own praise. He writes anonymous pamphlets lauding his grand successes, then has them printed and distributed in England at his own expense.

"He took Fort Frontenac, as you must have heard, splitting the French empire in two—but he had three thousand men against a garrison of less than two hundred! If you ever read

the pamphlet he wrote about that battle you'd think him the
greatest tactician in the empire, but those in the know say he's
a most self-infatuated ass!

"He's brave enough," Sir William said. "But he fancies
himself more than he is; if he spends as much time next summer
writing in his journal as I fear he will, the Indians will let his
army drift past, then they'll fall upon the frontier and pillage
to their greedy hearts' content!"

"Nevertheless, he's in charge," Defries said. He recognized
the great importance of having Johnson's patronage, and
thought he should be able to work with Bradstreet.

Johnson accepted that, then poured them more rum. "All
right, my lad, Bradstreet it is. Now listen—I have a way you
can establish yourself solidly as a military contractor before
next summer!"

The Indian supervisor said he was organizing an expedition
to destroy Delaware and Shawnee towns down on the Susquehanna River, towns in which many hostiles were living. The
raiders would number three hundred and would be a mixed
force of Mohawks and local provincials. Sir William explained
that Defries could supply this expedition, which would set out
in six weeks. If it was successful, everyone connected with it
would be brought to the attention of military leaders, for it
would strike the first offensive blow against the hostiles, a
blow that would be certain to bring them to Sir William's peace
council.

"This expedition has to be noted," Sir William said with a
grin. "You see, it will prove that Indian irregulars and white
rangers are the force needed to defeat the uprising, though
General Amherst did not agree when he was in charge of our
forces here.

"Peter, my own reputation rests on this expedition, and I
will do everything in my power to see that it uproots a number
of villages that have produced scalping parties."

The Indians would be led by Joseph Brant, a war chief and
the brother of Molly, Johnson's mistress. Brant had been educated in a Connecticut seminary, and was more cultured than
most provincials. Yet he was a brilliant, aggressive leader in
battle, the right man to show that the Iroquois League was
against the uprising. The Seneca, the westernmost Iroquois,
would be warned by Brant's campaign that their hostility was

contrary to the wishes of the rest of the six-nation Iroquois alliance. There would thus never be a repeat of the Devil's Hole massacre.

"Yes," Johnson said, "this campaign will outshine even Bradstreet on the lakes! And knowing that the Iroquois oppose the uprising will do more to strike fear into the hearts of the hostiles than even Bouquet's victory at Bushy Run."

Defries thought of what this campaign meant to himself. Triumph would mark him as an able supplier, and he would be well on his way to earning Bradstreet's confidence. Then he remembered Mary and the coming baby. He would have to wait until this winter campaign was over before he could return to Montreal. But if the expedition went as planned, he might still get back to her by March, in time for the birth. If it did not go well, there were many ways a man could die a lonely death in the winter forest.

Before organizing a supply train for the expedition, Defries would find someone to write a letter telling Mary what was at hand. Johnson suggested, upon Peter's query, that Joseph Brant would be glad to write his letter. It would be a good way for them to establish a friendship that would serve Peter well in the coming weeks on the warpath.

It was the afternoon of a cold February day when the ranger called Hurley galloped into Jubal Swain's clearing. Before Hurley had dismounted, Willie Swain was running to grab the bridle of his horse. Hurley leaped down and hurried to the cabin door, where the younger Swain child stood sucking his finger, a cornhusk doll in his hands. Hurley passed the boy and found Jubal eating at the table.

Swain looked up at Hurley, who said breathlessly, "It's time! It's begun!"

"What the hell yuh talkin' about, boy? Sit down an' eat!"

Hurley threw his bullet pouch and powder horn aside, propped his rifle carefully against the doorjamb, and caught his breath. "They're movin' on Philadelphia!"

Swain stopped chewing. "Who's movin'? How many?"

Hurley sat down, accepting the bowl of soup Lucy handed him and digging in hungrily. After a few mouthfuls, he took a deep breath and said, "Matthew Smith's leadin' borderers agin the city—you know Smith, he's the one led rangers agin'

Injuns in the French an' Injun War. Tough nut." He kept on eating.

"How many he got with 'im?"

"Hundred now. They're on the Philadelphia road, an' more boys're joinin' up every mile. Could be a thousand by the time they git to the city."

"A thousand," Swain said softly to himself. A thousand angry frontiersmen marching on a rich city like Philadelphia . . . It excited him to think of the possibilities. As Hurley dipped rye bread into his soup, he saw that Jubal was making plans to go, too.

The two men looked at one another, and both grinned. Through a mouthful of soup and bread, Hurley said, "A thousand sons o' bitches comin' down from the hills!"

"Hurley!" Lucy said sharply.

"What?"

Jubal said a little uneasily, "She don't like the young 'uns to hear that talk."

"What talk?" Hurley asked. "What did I say?"

Lucy took his bowl away to refill it, and Hurley turned back to Swain, who was adrift now, eyes burning.

Swain said, "What they got in the city to stop us?"

Hurley chortled, "Lots o' helpless Quaker sons o' bitches—"

Lucy scolded him again, and Hurley looked around at the two boys, who were staring at him, fascinated.

Swain began to laugh. "Quakers? No regulars? No militia?"

"Some, I hear, not much. Not a thousand, that's sure!"

Swain nodded, thinking. Then he asked, "Where's Morgan?"

"He sent me to git yuh. He's near the Conestoga Road with the boys an' another few rangers he picked up here an' there. We're waitin' for yuh!"

Swain got up and called to Lucy to prepare his gear—a linen smock, leather shirt, moccasins, a blanket coat, some extra food, hunting mitts with the trigger finger free. Lucy hurried around the cabin while Swain got dressed. As he readied himself, he asked Hurley more about the man called Matthew Smith, whom the backwoodsmen had elected leader and spokesman.

"He's a hard man when he wants to be," Hurley said, cutting

another slice of bread and smearing it with bearfat. "He's got a core with 'im, about thirty scouts an' rangers, all of 'em gone through the Frenchy war an' able to chew glass if Smith asks 'em to. They say he's got a petition of some sort that a reg'lar lawyer drawed up an' signed. They're gonna mop up 'em red niggers an' hand over the petition all in one visit. They're hot, an' they're mean enough an' mad enough to kick ass all the way from Philadelphia to the sea if any son of a bitch gits in their way!"

Exasperated, Lucy did not bother anymore to complain about Hurley's language. She stuffed her husband's gear into his deerskin pouch.

Swain slipped the hunting smock over his head and grinned. "That's what I want to hear! There enough boys in this army who'd like to have some sport in the city?"

Hurley chuckled. "I tell yuh, Jube, Morg's picked us up a couple o' sons o' bitches that would like nothin' better'n to kick some Quaker ass and tear hell outa Helltown! An' this here boy's one of 'em!"

Forty miles from Philadelphia, where the rolling hills were snowy and gray, the highway shuddered with the pounding of hooves. Around a bend in the road thundered two hundred horsemen riding three abreast. Farm wagons and carriages pulled out of the way to let them pass. They were grim, angry men, strongly built, and armed with rifles, tomahawks, knives, and pistols. These were the borderers. Most were farmers, but over the years they had learned the ways of wilderness warfare. Fighting a savage, cruel enemy in the depths of the woods had toughened them, seasoned them, and tempered them in the white heat of killing.

For too long they had fought defensively against a merciless foe without the aid of their rich and powerful neighbors in Philadelphia and the city's adjacent counties. These were men of the forest edges, the small clearings, the new hamlets. They were honest men, brave and fearless, and they had collected their families at homes in Lancaster, Cumberland, Berks, York, and Northampton counties so they could ride to Philadelphia and demand their rights. Indians seldom raided in the winter, so the borderers were able to move. If they left their families unprotected in the spring, they would return to ashes and death.

They were not outlaws like those who made up Jubal

Swain's band. When Swain and his men joined them at a crossing in the road, honest woodsmen were not happy to see them. This force riding to Philadelphia to demand equal representation in the provincial assembly intended to compel the Quaker-controlled government to organize a militia to protect their homes and families. They had sworn to make the government drive out all Moravian Indians and any other peaceful Indians from the settled areas of their country.

These men were not ignorant ruffians—they had built schools for their children, brought in teachers and ministers, and raised churches. But they were too angry to care that the army might be reinforced from England and sent against them, nor did they think that their fury against Philadelphia might lead to a bloody civil war.

These fighters—and another hundred who joined them a little farther down the road—were determined to have their way once and for all with comfortable and safe Philadelphia. Too many of their children had been killed by Indians, too many families had suffered, too many homes and fields had been destroyed for them to turn back now without achieving full satisfaction.

For many, there seemed to be only one way to make their point: kill the Indians in Philadelphia, then plant their petition on the stairs of the assembly. Most believed that the Indians now under government protection had conspired with Indian raiding parties. They were prepared to testify on oath that friends had heard Conestoga or Moravian Indians bragging about committing atrocities in the French war. Some had been told that the Indians recently murdered in Lancaster had harbored known raiders. All of them felt there was no place for Indians of any sort in the midst of their white, Calvinist community.

The numbers swelled. They rode up, in groups of three or four, and mile by mile the column grew. Here were another seventy, there two hundred. Across the fields charged yahooing young fighters, leaping mounts over fences to meet the gathering army. The closer they came to Philadelphia, the bolder they grew. When they reached the country just west of the flooded Schuylkill River, some of them called aloud for an immediate assault on the city. Leading this faction were Jubal Swain's toughs, who had pressed themselves close behind Matthew Smith at the forefront.

Smith, a tall man, lean and wiry, with a shaggy mustache, wore a black hat and coat. Sitting on his gray pony, he looked more like a traveling preacher than a woods ranger and Indian scout. But he was a true wilderness fighter, one of the best. The men who knew him would follow him into hell, as some had already done. Yet he was known for wisdom and prudence as much as for his courage and quick thinking.

Matthew Smith was as angry and stubborn as his followers, and he intended to destroy the Indians. He would do it, even if it meant riding down a few Quakers at the same time. Though no one in this army of nearly a thousand expected Quakers to resist their invasion, plenty longed to bloody some Quaker heads, and any Philadelphians who got in their way would suffer.

Most of these men were mild and generous in time of peace, but their blood was up, and heaven help the city if it tried to oppose them now. That, of course, was precisely what Jubal Swain was counting upon.

Singing a popular country song, these proud fighters rode like a storm wind toward Philadelphia. They turned north at the Schuylkill, heading for the upper ford, to cross the river and make camp that night, then enter the city in the morning.

Philadelphia was frantic. Bells rang, couriers galloped through the street, Quakers met to discuss what to do, and the handful of regulars were assembled near the barracks where the Indians were kept.

Inside the barracks—a stout stone building with small windows that let in little light—the Moravian Indians listened to the tumult. But so much had happened lately that they paid little attention. They heard alarm bells ring, but did not know what was going on. Often before, false alarms had caused them to tremble and pray. This latest hubbub did no more than wake a few sleeping babies, including Aleta's foster child, who lay in an old cradle provided by a pitying Quaker matron.

Aleta went to the boy and took him out. He stopped howling as she hugged him. Despite everything that had happened, and all the terrible experiences, one thing had been wonderful for Aleta—her guardianship of the baby boy. His name was Ollie, and he was a happy child, almost always cheerful. He was known to all the hundred people crowded into this section of the barracks building, where the Indians slept on cots and bunks arranged into forms roughly delineating family groups—homes of some sort. Aleta and Ollie had a corner of their own close to a door. She liked it there best, because air circulated while the rest of the barracks was fetid and close.

As the bells rang, little Ollie struggled from Aleta's arms, and she let him down to play. Others called to the child, and he tried to stand up. Aleta, laughing, helped him, and soon he was wobbling, weaving, attempting to take that first step. He reached out with one chubby foot, and Aleta crouched before him, her face alight. Ollie giggled and sat down with a thump that caused everyone nearby to laugh.

Aleta offered her fingers, which he grabbed, and up he came once more. Then she moved away, talking to him, encouraging him. He giggled, but this time did not fall. He lifted that uncertain foot, and it was as though all the people watching held their breath. He wobbled, but put his foot back down again, not taking the step. He tried again. Aleta was sure this time he would do it. However, she got a shock as the barracks door burst open, letting in the noise of the courtyard, and a man was at the door—one of the Moravian ministers. He shouted, "The time is at hand, brethren. Borderers are on the way!"

Women turned their faces from him, and men stood up, ready for what might come. Aleta closed her eyes and tried not to quake. Little Ollie took his very first step, but no one noticed at all.

Early in the afternoon Owen Sutherland and Benjamin Franklin rode through the wintry streets of Philadelphia. For the past three hours Franklin had been busily organizing citizens sympathetic to the Indians into militia companies. According to plan, six companies of militia were distributed at defensive positions at the ends of every street entering Philadelphia. These were citizen soldiers in the extreme, for few had ever tasted gunsmoke. But they were grimly determined to confront the riders when they came. To everyone's surprise, a large number of Quakers assembled in the square opposite the barracks where the Indians were lodged. There, contrary to all Quaker dicta, they armed themselves. They carried muskets and pistols, helped serve small cannon brought to the square, and looked every bit like warriors. The sight of Quakers in arms astonished the rest of the city, particularly those who sided with the borderers.

There was a large faction who wanted the Indians destroyed or thrown out of Philadelphia for good. They, too, were arming and gathering, across the square from the Quakers near the barracks. If the borderers broke into the city, blood would flow between these two factions, and few Philadelphia citizens would be able to avoid becoming involved in the struggle. Where this kind of fighting might lead was anyone's guess, but it was a certainty sections of the city would be left in ruins. That it would cause an uproar across the sea in Parliament was also certain. The animosity and hatred spawned by such bloodshed might endure, and the once tranquil City of Brotherly Love would for generations be divided into armed camps infected with hatred for one another.

There had been a mild spell this early February, and it began to rain as Sutherland and Franklin cantered into the market, where cannon had been emplaced to sweep every street entering the square. It was difficult for the two riders to get through the mobs here, until they were helped by a sudden downpour that sent hundreds of folk scurrying for shelter.

Sutherland remarked that no one had thought to drape oilskins on the guns, and Franklin shouted for the artillerymen to come back and do it. Then the statesman nodded toward a host of Quakers entering their meetinghouse, all carrying guns.

Franklin said, "It would be a comical sight if they were not in such deadly earnest."

Franklin and Sutherland had spent much of the morning in meetings with leading men of the city—men of both factions. A few had agreed to speak to the mobs and try to calm them when trouble was imminent. The soldiers—only two hundred at most—had also been organized; the majority were lined up in the market, separating the pro-Indian and anti-Indian factions. A handful of soldiers had been scattered at key strongpoints to bolster raw militia recruits. Hay bales, carts, and lumber barricaded each street on the perimeter of the city, and nearly twenty additonal cannon stood aimed toward the countryside.

The city hummed with martial excitement, but Ben Franklin did not delude himself that the defense was adequate. When at last he and Sutherland had done all they could to prepare the militia and soldiers, they went to the India Queen for dinner. There, when they were alone in the private room, Franklin spoke his mind.

"We can do precious little with what paltry resources are given us," he said, taking off his wet coat and sitting down at the table. "If a thousand borderers come in, there will be hell to pay, but we cannot stop them. Not with lead alone, that is."

Sutherland joined him at the table, rubbing his cold hands. A waiter came in promptly to serve them a hot meal, and they ate ravenously.

After they had eaten, Sutherland said, "They must be stopped from even approaching the city. If they come close enough, some green artilleryman will blow somebody's head off, and that can end only in slaughter."

Franklin pushed back from the table, fortified for the rest of what had to be done. He got up and went to a window. The rain was still falling, dreary and cold. The streets were almost empty, but in every house men were waiting for the alarm; when it came, battle lines would be drawn for the last time. Even if the borderers were driven back at first, bloody work would have begun in Philadelphia—work that could only result in a bitter defeat for Franklin's forces. Once first blood was spilled there would be no turning back. The province of Pennsylvania stood on the brink of civil war, and of all the men in the city, there was only one who could prevent it: Benjamin Franklin.

The elderly man was already tired from riding around the city. His injured shoulder ached, and he often rubbed it. He was thinking hard when he returned to the table, where Sutherland sat watching him. Franklin took his seat and said quietly:

"You know, Owen, it's ironic, but I like these mad borderers!" He laughed, sadly amused. "Perhaps if I were in their position, I would ride in with Matthew Smith, too. I understand their difficulty, and sympathize with them."

Franklin told of how, during the French and Indian War, he had led the bordermen who built forts along their frontier. "Old fool that I was to meddle around in the wild! I nearly died of the strain." He chuckled. "Though I must admit that a few weeks in the country changed me somewhat—I lay on wooden floors so often that my first few nights back on a featherbed were sleepless."

Thus the borderers knew him well—as well as they knew

Sutherland. He thought that together they could make these men listen to reason before it was too late.

Sutherland said, "They must be made to understand how much blood will be shed if they try to come in. They have to see that it won't be a simple dash to the barracks, a quick killing, and then out again."

Franklin agreed. "I can think of one way—a dangerous way for you and me, but one that just might succeed."

He told Sutherland his dangerous plan. Sutherland would have preferred to carry it out alone, and let Franklin stay safe in the city, but he knew the man would not accept that. Besides, if anyone could debate with the leaders of the borderers, Franklin could. Sutherland might just get angry with them, and there would be trouble on the spot.

So Franklin and Sutherland left the tavern and started off toward Germantown, five miles from the city, where the borderers were camped. Franklin said, "I wish my *Poor Richard* had a clever saying for this occasion—one that speaks clearly and tells us something of value."

Sutherland laughed and answered, "I recall one: 'The first mistake in public business is the going into it.'"

The rain poured harder as they swung onto Second Street, riding through sloppy mud, and bowing their heads to keep the wind off. Suddenly alarm bells began to ring once more. In a moment, the streets came alive with men running to their stations. The cry went up from a mounted courier sloshing toward them and waving his hat: "They're coming! They're coming! Riders approaching from Germantown!"

Sutherland cut the man off and grabbed his animal's bridle. "How many?" he shouted.

"A hundred!" The fellow was frightened. "I've got to find Dr. Franklin—"

"Here, man!" Franklin cried, coming alongside. "Are you certain they're borderers?"

Breathless, the courier nodded, saying, "Armed they are, Your Excellency! A hundred or more, all riding fast. They'll reach the first barricade in ten minutes."

The barricade! The militia manned a cannon at the end of Second Street. If the riders bore down too quickly, they would be cut to pieces, and the battle would be on. They had to be stopped before they came through.

With the vigor of a much younger man, Franklin spurred

his horse, and Sutherland followed. In three minutes they reached the barricade, where thirty nervous militiamen were forming into a firing line. The cannon's oilskin covering had been swept away, and a young militia officer was overseeing a fellow ramming down the charge.

Franklin came up behind the militia, his horse stamping and blowing in the drizzly rain. "Are you sure they're borderers?" he called to the officer, who nodded and said word had just come to him that they were charging all the way in.

"Hark!" the nervous youth said, and they felt as much as heard the hoofbeats trembling through the earth. "They're near! Ready, men!"

The others brought muskets up to the port, the muzzles at an angle to the sky. Next the weapons would come up to their shoulders, and then they would be ordered to fire. The officer jumped up and down as he shouted at the clumsy rammer to get clear. The sound of hooves was louder now, the riders just out of sight behind trees and a farmhouse, where the road bent.

"Hold your fire!" Franklin ordered, but his cry was lost among the shouts of more frantic militiamen running up Second Street from the city and forming into a ragged line with the men already in position.

Sutherland galloped in front of the ranks and waved his hat at them, but already muskets were being trained on the bend in the road. The pounding in the distance was very close. Officers had no control over their men now. Fear and anger were on the faces of many. The young man in command of the fieldpiece held a lighted match above the touchhole. Sutherland could not let them fire first and talk later. Everything he and Franklin had planned hung in the balance. A flash of understanding passed between them; then he and the doctor sprang simultaneously into action.

Sutherland whipped out his claymore and charged along the line of militiamen. Slapping down muskets, riding into men too excited to listen, he drove back squad after squad. Dismayed, they swore at him, and some threatened him, but he acted so decisively that these inexperienced soldiers were thrown into confusion. In twenty seconds, nearly a hundred men were milling about, picking up muskets Sutherland had knocked away, bumping into one another, and trying to reorganize. Cooler heads sided with Sutherland, steadying the militiamen, who now looked like a gaggle of geese, quarrel-

some and disorganized. Sutherland turned and rode through
them again, trying to reach the cannon, where Franklin had
dismounted and was arguing with the excited officer in charge.

"Horsemen!" a man yelled. Around the bend came a mass
of men and horses. The militia struggled to reform. The can-
noneer saw the riders and, with a trembling hand, touched the
fuse. But Franklin was too quick. Snatching off his hat, he
slapped it down on the touchhole, snuffing the ignition. The
officer protested, but not for long, as someone shouted in dismay. "It's the Germans, not the borderers! It's Captain Hoff-
man! They're with us! They're with us!"

A cheer went up from the militiamen, and the militia officer
at the cannon was so astonished that, standing limply, he
dropped his match to the mud. Toward the barricade rumbled
a hundred stout Germans on every kind of horse imaginable—
drays, fine walking horses, stallions, tired mares, plowhorses.
These men were from Germantown, and with the arrival of the
borderers there, they had organized for defense, sending their
families away north, out of the line of fire.

The riders pushed through the barricade and rode on to the
city, accompanied by the wild hurrahs of the relieved militiamen. As the tumult surged around them, Franklin looked up
at Sutherland, who was still mounted. Neither one spoke until
Franklin glanced at his singed hat.

He said, "It was my favorite." Then he clapped it on his
gray head and mounted up. "Well, maybe the powder burns
will impress Matthew Smith all the more! Ride on, Owen!
We're not finished yet!"

Off they galloped toward Germantown, along a broad highway lined on every side by neat, prosperous farmhouses. Soon
they would be in the camp of the borderers.

Inside the dim barracks, the Indians were quiet. They had held
a solemn service, with much harmonious singing and prayer.
They were prepared now for whatever might come, having
made peace with their God, and no one was afraid.

Loud and raucous noise ebbed and flowed outside in the
courtyard. Now and again a rock was thrown through a window,
and jeering could be heard from those Philadelphians who
wanted the Indians out of the city. The shouts of officers giving
orders, the rumble of cannon being wheeled into place, and the
clatter of shod hooves on flagstone pavement—all these om-

inous sounds filled the barracks, where Indians sat quietly on cots or on the floor, trying to distract themselves from what was happening.

Aleta was beyond fear now. She could not flee, for there was nowhere to go. Since the awful trek across Jersey and back, she had lost hope of escape from the impending conflict. Many of her people had sickened, and some had died in the toil of that winter tramp, but the Moravian Indians had not lost heart, nor had they lost their faith. Where they would live and how after all this was over, none knew, but they prayed and they dreamed of beginning again in the spring.

A door opened, and in came Quakers with Moravian whites who distributed food and went among the Indians, speaking words of kindness and comfort. They told of Franklin's embassy to the borderers, and said the city was well defended in case of an attack. The Indians heard them but did not know what to believe.

Aleta prayed they would be protected; but she had believed whites too often in the past. She heard again the surging tide of hatred outside her little prison, and the gentle voices of these Christian whites were drowned out. Right and wrong were muddled in Aleta's mind, but she knew clearly that death stalked her loved ones, and she did not know why.

There was a crashing explosion, and the Indians gasped. Then another bang, and another, and the room was a babble of excited talk. Cannon blasts went on and on until eight had fired, leaving little children howling in fright. But the Quakers assured the Indians that the cannon merely were being tested as a warning to anyone who dared injure the Indians. Everything, they said, would be all right.

chapter 19

REASON AND ANGER

The rain had stopped, but clouds hung gloomy over the countryside north of Philadelphia. Every farm was abandoned, and the road was empty. Crows cawed and flapped from fenceposts as Franklin and Sutherland trotted along, but a ghastly stillness lay everywhere. Even the cattle huddled under trees, and the hamlet of Germantown lay dismal and forlorn.

Riding over a small rise in the road, Sutherland and Franklin smelled woodsmoke. A long grove of trees lined a watercourse below, and they stopped to study it.

They could see the flicker of campfires of the borderers in the gathering dimness of late afternoon. Sutherland counted more than forty fires. "Figuring fifteen or twenty men at each fire, there must be seven hundred to a thousand," he said.

Sutherland let his eyes rove over the landscape. He pointed out a herd of horses on the hillside beyond the trees. At first Franklin found them hard to see because they merged so well with the wintry ground. But when he brought them into focus, he marveled—there were so many horses that they looked like a living carpet moving slowly over the slope.

Franklin set his jaw, "There are more borderers than I would have imagined."

They kicked their horses forward and rode down the highway. Trotting purposefully, they soon were through the outer perimeters of the camp. Here and there campfires were nestled in hollows where there was water and a tree or two for shelter. As they passed, men watched them, some standing up and staring.

Sutherland got a good look at these backwoodsmen as he reached the campfires grouped in the center of the grove. Now and again he recognized someone who had been with him at Bushy Run, and a greeting was exchanged. Most were friendly, though all seemed surprised to see him here. Men such as these might listen to reason; but if not, Sutherland was prepared to carry through Franklin's dangerous plan to the very end. He was counting on the men he recognized to support him. If they did not, neither he nor Franklin would see another sunrise. For just a moment he thought of Ella, who had bidden him farewell at the door of their residence. Whatever happened, Botany would be at her side, and Lieutenant Magruder had promised to go to her if Sutherland did not return. Then he put the image of his wife out of his mind, for they were at the very heart of the camp now, and several hundred men had gathered around them.

Franklin, too, knew a goodly number of these frontiersmen, and they welcomed him civilly, if with suspicion. He asked directions to Matthew Smith's fire, and they were led to where the leader of the borderers was camped near a big, naked willow at the edge of a half-frozen stream. As they dismounted, Sutherland saw potential trouble in the form of at least twenty mean-eyed men. By the look of them they were not farmers—farmers usually wore simple linen shirts and smocks, with flat wide hats and heavy shoes. But these men gathering nearby were woods rovers, with greasy buckskin shirts over their linsey, and dirty leggins. They were heavily armed, grimy, and unkempt, and as they glared at Sutherland, jugs of corn liquor were passed among them.

Someone took charge of the horses, and Sutherland and Franklin were brought before Smith, who was sitting near a makeshift lean-to, with a dozen others of his stamp nearby. Smith stood erect and dignified as Franklin approached him. Sutherland liked his looks as much as he disliked the looks of the toughs close at hand. Franklin shook hands warmly, and Smith showed considerable affection for the elderly statesman. When Franklin introduced Sutherland, Smith stopped short, then took the Scotsman's hand in a firm, honest grip.

Smith said, "I've wanted to meet you, Mr. Sutherland, after all I'd heard of what you did for our folk at Bushy Run. I'm honored."

Sutherland could not help but like this tall, clear-eyed man who held his head so nobly. He replied, "I've heard much about you and your rangers, Mr. Smith. It's my pleasure to meet you, sir."

The crowd of borderers kept growing as the three principals sat down on logs by the fire. Smith knew just why they had come, but he took his time getting to the subject and offered them tea from a big kettle, which was gratefully accepted. Whispers drifted through the audience, but most were silent, waiting to hear what would be said.

"Ah," declared Franklin as he sipped the tea, "that's better!" He looked at Smith. "It will be difficult for us to remain enemies after we've supped together, Mr. Smith."

The borderer sat back and stared at Franklin. "Doctor, you're no enemy. Of everyone in Philadelphia, you must best understand our desperate situation. We are indebted to you for standing by us during the last war. We have not come here to trouble you, sir."

Franklin slurped a little, saying, "My, that's hot." Then he looked at Smith, who was watching him closely. "Do you think, Mr. Smith, that you can ride a thousand strong into my city and not trouble me?"

Smith was silent, but he did not take his eyes from Franklin, who went on. "Mr. Sutherland and I have come to you as an embassy from Philadelphia. I am here to listen to what you have to say and then to express the sentiments of the people of my city."

"You know why we're here, Dr. Franklin."

Franklin was grave. "Yes, my friend, I do. But do you know why I am here? Do you know what I am about to tell you? I think not. But first, do me the honor of laying your case before me, and I give my word that you shall present it in person to the assembly."

"If I state our case to you now, what good will it do?"

"I want to advise you of what can and cannot be done to satisfy your demands. In that way, Mr. Smith, you and I shall clearly know why we are fighting one another."

"Fighting?" Smith cried and sat back. "I did not come here to fight the likes of you. Or Mr. Sutherland. We've come for the Moravian Indians, and we'll harm no one who does not oppose us."

Franklin raised a finger. "Ah, now we come to a point that stands between us. Mr. Smith, you shall not have your way with the Moravian Indians. That is something we'll fight about."

A rumble went through the borderers, and they began talking together, some angrily, some making jokes about the old man's spunk.

Smith looked around, and they hushed. Then he said to Franklin, "I've always thought you a practical and wise man, Dr. Franklin. Sensible, and knowledgeable in the ways of war. I say again, our business is with the heathens only. You do us honor to accept our petition of grievances against the colonial government, but beyond that, there is nothing you can do for us."

Franklin's voice was cold. "Then you'd better give me that petition now, sir. And if you have delegates among you who are your spokesmen, keep them at the rear of your army when you come to the city."

Smith was clever, and he knew Franklin was leading him on, but he played the game, saying casually, "Since when do the spokesmen and leaders march at the rear of those they represent, Dr. Franklin?"

Someone quipped, "Is that a maxim of Poor Richard's? If it is, he's got a yellow streak!"

That evoked a few chuckles, but most listened for Franklin's reply. He said, "I presume your column has come here to accomplish something other than fighting?"

Smith said, "We've come to bring the assembly to its senses, yes! We've come to tell them what must be done to protect our people!"

Franklin nodded, but his voice was still cold. "Then let those who must live to present your case ride at the rear of your army, Mr. Smith. Because the first of your force that rides against us will be wiped off the face of the earth."

There was a surprised stillness for just a few seconds. But it was broken when someone let out a stifled high note of hilarity. Then the entire mass of countrymen erupted into hearty laughter, joking about Quakers bayoneting themselves in the posterior, and about Philadelphians not knowing the business end of a musket from its butt. But when the laughter died down, Matthew Smith saw that Franklin's calm features had not changed.

The leader of the borderers sighed and said, "Just who, Dr. Franklin, will wipe us off the face of the earth? The Quakers?

The Moravians? Perhaps the shopkeepers—"

"Usin' brooms!" someone shouted, and the men roared again.

But Franklin held Smith's eyes until the right moment. Then he said, without malice in his voice, "I will wipe you out, Mr. Smith."

The crowd grumbled. Smith showed no emotion, save for a slight twitch at the side of his nose. But Sutherland saw he was growing angry at Franklin's belligerence. In the tense moment that followed, Franklin poured himself another cup of tea and offered both Sutherland and Smith a refill. Sutherland accepted. Smith said nothing.

Franklin went on, "I know very well your grievances, my friends, and it is my intention to do all in my power to persuade the assembly to defend your homes. Plans are being made for an army of two thousand men, regulars and colonials under Colonel Bouquet, to march against the Delaware and Shawnee towns of the Ohio, Miami, and Scioto. Another two thousand under Colonel Bradstreet will invade Indian country via Lake Erie and then sweep southward against the hostiles. We shall not make peace until every white hostage taken in this war, the last war, and in every war ever fought against Indians is returned safely to the families who have lost them."

Franklin's voice rang out. "The time has passed when our province borders will be ignored by the legislators of the inner counties. Yes, gentlemen, I admit that your show of force here today has done much to persuade us of that. I admit that you have been compelled to take drastic and sometimes cruel steps to protect yourselves against the depredations of the hostiles. I admit, further, that the city of Philadelphia trembles to think that your mighty force will sweep down on them tomorrow and take vengeance on all who have permitted your families to suffer!"

The borderers shouted in agreement at that.

"But understand, gentlemen, that for all the fear in our hearts, and for all the power of your arms, for all that you have the strength to burn our city to the ground if you wish—understand that you will not do so without a terrible struggle."

Silence. Some men shuffled their feet. The toughs nearby snickered, and a few drank from their jugs.

"There are six companies of militia, two of artillery, and two companies of regulars waiting for your attack, which I pray will never be launched. If you approach Philadelphia in force, you will be fired upon without being challenged first. Your vanguard will be met with grapeshot and chain shot. We have thirty cannon emplaced at the entrances to Philadelphia, and at every cross street there is a strong barricade.

"Yes, you may very well be brave enough and numerous enough to reach the barracks where the Indians are lodged, but I doubt that many of you will fight your way out. The city may burn down about my ears, but I will fight you for it until my last breath."

Smith had no words equal to Franklin's. Every man listening was grim, silent, though angry.

Franklin said slowly, "Yes, my friend, even the peaceful Quakers are in arms, and that tells you something of the reception you will receive when you attack."

Franklin was done. Smith stretched out his long legs and looked over at Sutherland. He asked, "And where, sir, do you stand in all this?"

Sutherland thought a moment, and it seemed the mass of men pressed even closer to hear what he had to say. Then he tossed a stick into the fire. "If you march on Philadelphia, I stand at the side of Dr. Franklin; I've come here to see justice done, for everyone concerned. Attacking the city won't get you justice—it'll just get you regiments of Redcoats sticking you with bayonets, or billeted in your farms the way they occupied my Scotland after the rising of forty-five . . . when they drove the clans from their homes and killed those who resisted.

"There's no justice won by lying bleeding in the gutter! And that's where many of you will be by nightfall tomorrow if you strike us." He paused, and not a sound was to be heard. "I pray, gentlemen, that I am not compelled to spill anyone's blood, especially the blood of men whose cause is just, even though their means is cruel and misguided. Aye, cruel and misguided you are to murder innocent Indians, and if you come tomorrow, look for me at the barracks. I'll be there, and I'll have my own justice to deal out."

Sutherland felt a cold fire within that molded such words in the face of these angry men. Yet he was convinced of the rightness of his stand, and he did not flinch. For a restless moment, no one spoke. Then a heavy, savage voice snarled, "I know him! I know this dirty government lackey!"

Sutherland turned to see Jubal Swain, looming huge in the

light of the fire illuminating the gathering darkness, and recognized him from the cabin. Apparently Swain had not had a good look at Sutherland until the Scotsman spoke. Swain's hand was on his knife, and he moved forward, his men at his back. Sutherland was on his feet, claymore sheathed, but ready.

A quick movement from Smith sent twenty men into action, and they came between Sutherland and Swain.

"Bastard!" Swain hissed, blocked by Smith's men. "Don't let that bastard out of this camp, Smith! Tie both of them up and let's move on the city now, tonight!"

A number of borderers shouted in favor of Swain's plan, but Smith stood up and spoke to several key supporters. A large number of loyal men collected at Smith's back, as he looked at Swain and said, "This is a council between me and Dr. Franklin. Anyone who doesn't like it can get out now!" That got a grumble from Swain's followers. Smith went on, "Choose for yourselves, lads. March on the city tonight if you wish, but you'll do it without me."

Then he turned soberly to Franklin. "Doctor, I have made no decision yet. For now, I'll give you an escort back to your people." Then he saw that Franklin, standing, was shaking his head. "What do you mean by that?" Smith asked.

Franklin said loudly, "Gentlemen, I will not leave this camp until Mr. Smith gives me his word not to attack Philadelphia!" He and Sutherland stood back to back now, as they had planned, hands on their weapons. Franklin said, "If you intend to begin your attack, then do so now! But you will march on the city only over our bodies!"

Momentary silence, then Swain roared, "Get 'em!"

"No!" Smith shouted, leaping to the two men and pulling a pistol from his belt. "Anyone wants a fight, come on!"

Another man, then another came to Smith's side until it was clear that most borderers had faith in their leader and would stand with him in this. Only Swain and his surly pack of cutthroats were angry.

After the crowd calmed down, Smith shouted to them, "To my mind, Dr. Franklin speaks straight. I won't harm him or Mr. Sutherland! I've heard what has been said about the city, and I won't lead you into a slaughter. We didn't come here to start a war, and from what the doctor says, that's what'll happen if we go in there tomorrow."

The crowd rumbled until Smith held up his hands. "I vote

for taking our petition to the assembly. Then we go home. But we'll be back if we get no satisfaction! If you agree, say so now!"

A tremendous shout went up from nearly the entire thousand men jamming around the campsite. Smith then called for a vote from those who disagreed, but Swain's men were too furious to say anything.

Smith shouted, "I'll put my trust in Dr. Franklin! Tomorrow I'll go to the city with a delegation, and I'll warn them that if our grievances are not resolved, we'll return to Philadelphia and we will burn it to the ground."

Another great shout of agreement. Then Smith said to Franklin, "My men will see you back to the city, Doctor. I'll come in through Second Street in the morning. Please arrange that your Quakers not fail their faith and shoot me out of the saddle."

Franklin smiled warmly, faint beads of perspiration on his forehead, and shook hands with Smith. Sutherland did the same, and they got on their horses once more. As they turned to go—twenty men riding alongside—Sutherland saw Swain glaring from a distance. He ignored him but wondered if they would meet again, sensing that the big, red beared man would have it that way no matter what it took.

They cantered off into the night, and Sutherland quietly asked Franklin, "Do you think the government will give them what they want?"

"If not, Mr. Sutherland, I'll never again bare my breast in the presence of an armed Matthew Smith. By the way, who was that big fellow? He wanted to get at you."

Sutherland replied, "I don't really know who he is. But as for why he wanted my hide, anger is never without reason, but seldom with a good one."

"What was that? The part about anger . . ."

He leaned toward Franklin. "I said anger is never without reason, but seldom with a good one."

"Hmmm. Very good, yes. Is that your own maxim?"

"No, Doctor. I read it in *Poor Richard*."

Ella sat at the harpsichord, idly touching notes, trying to assemble a melody that would release her tension. Now and again she found something tranquil that eased her troubled heart, but it never lasted long enough, and her fear for Owen's safety mounted with every passing hour.

When he came home early that evening, she held him close, letting the stress of this long day flood from her trembling body, and neither spoke until she was calm. Botany brought food to the dining table, was told by Sutherland what had happened, then left them alone. Though her husband was hungry, Ella was not. The time had finally come for them to leave the city. Was it also time to tell him of the baby? She was at least three months pregnant, though she showed very little because she was tall, and her body firm. Had he noticed anything? If so, he said nothing. Perhaps it was better to get home to Detroit first.

Once again Ella put off revealing the truth, though it troubled her to do so. But she thought it prudent, because she was certain she could make this trip and was unwilling to put unnecessary strain on her man. If he knew nothing of her condition, he would be better able to cope with the difficulties of the journey than he would if he worried about her. She was fit and ready for a month in the wilderness—as fit as ever she would be. But if they waited any longer before going, she would have to tell him everything, and their life would suddenly be very complicated.

Ella was glad when Owen said they would leave within the week. As soon as the borderers broke camp and went home, they, too, would depart. First, though, Franklin had invited them to dinner the next night, and Ella was excited by that, for it would be her last big dinner in Philadelphia, and she wanted it to be memorable.

The following day, near sundown, Ella was finishing her dressing at the mirror in their bedroom, with Owen seated nearby, watching her. One leg thrown over an arm of a comfortable chair, Sutherland was already dressed in brown breeches and waistcoat. He smoked a long clay pipe, contentedly following his wife's every movement. There was reason for him to be relaxed, because word had come in that the borderer camp in Germantown had been abandoned.

As he watched Ella fasten the silver pendant around her neck, Sutherland mused that she fitted well into this world of wealth and elegance. She glanced around at him, and her smile set him afire within. She stood up and looked herself over once more in the mirror, and he saw the fine lines of her neck and arms, the suppleness of her body, which she held as graciously as any noblewoman. It was amazing that she could be so adaptable, so pliable, and yet so very strong. She stood before him, asking how he liked her burgundy gown.

"You look beautiful in it," he said. "Tell me, would you like to live in Philadelphia, lass?"

She laughed and was about to reply when suddenly alarm bells began to peal, and the street below became a hubbub of excited shouting. Sutherland ran to the window and threw it open to hear a man crying:

"The borderers! The borderers are riding in!"

"Where?" Sutherland yelled down to him.

"From the west!"

Sutherland turned away from the frantic scene in the street and faced Ella. She was pale, trying to maintain her composure. Without a word, he opened the wardrobe door and took out his claymore and belt, buckled it over his evening clothes, and said, "I'm going to Franklin's. Stay indoors. If fighting begins, get the servants up here with you and extinguish all lights." He kissed her roughly, then tenderly. "I'll come back as soon as I can." He grabbed his rifle, bullet pouch, and powder horn, then left.

A moment later, Sutherland was running through the streets toward Franklin's house. In this neighborhood, lamplighters were calmly going about their task of igniting the candles in each streetlamp, but the rest of Philadelphia was swarming with anxious people, many of them armed. At Franklin's, Sutherland found half a dozen other guests, also in dress clothes, deep in conversation with the statesman.

As Franklin greeted the Scotsman, another messenger came to the door, panting that it was a false alarm after all. "It's only thirty or so of them," gasped the young man. "They just came in to see the city, and to spend some hours in Helltown! The watch took their arms, so there's no danger."

Everyone in Franklin's house felt immense relief to hear this, and soon they were joking or departing to fetch their wives—all of whom, like Ella, were sitting at home in their dinner gowns. Franklin insisted that his own carriage be sent for Ella, and he said to Sutherland, "Now, my friend, if you will kindly hand my servant your rifle and sword, we'll have something to drink, and there'll be no more talk of borderers until tomorrow!"

One by one the rest of the guests arrived. A score of the

most notable and interesting Philadelphians gathered in the parlor, where a violinist played soothingly.

The evening passed in good spirits, and after they sat down to dinner, Sutherland leaned over to his wife and whispered, "You still haven't answered my question: would you like to live here in Philadelphia?"

He thought Ella inexpressably beautiful as she held her wineglass to her lips before replying. She said quietly, "I'd be happy anywhere with you." There might have been no one else in the room as they gazed at one another. He smiled, and then Ella said, "But you'll be happiest at Detroit, and now we've got lots of ideas for a new house at Valenya, don't we? We can always visit Philadelphia."

They looked around to see Franklin on his feet, glass in hand. He was grinning at them; then he spoke to the guests. "I have been told, to my sorrow, that our friends the Sutherlands will leave us in a few days and return to their wild and untamed—".

A stone crashed through the front window, and women screamed. Every man was on his feet as a fierce voice from the street shouted Sutherland's name. At once, all eyes were on the Scotsman. Ella touched his arm. The voice shouted again, and Sutherland left the table. Men cautioned him to stay and let the watch handle this, but he moved past them and opened the front door. Stepping out into the alley, which was lit only by a few dim lamps, he closed the door, and in the dark saw at least ten mounted men packed close together. He wished he had put on his sword.

From the mass of riders, one moved his horse forward, and Sutherland knew it was the man who had become his enemy. Standing with legs apart, Sutherland saw the red bearded man's eyes glitter in the glow of streetlamps. At that moment, the door to Franklin's house opened, spilling yellow light into the alley, bathing Swain and his mount. The women were pressed against the windows of the house—except Ella, who had come out and was being restrained by several of the guests who had followed Sutherland and were gathered behind him near the door.

Swain remained mounted. He grinned wickedly, and Sutherland smelled the stench of liquor on him. The man had no weapon, but there was a stone in his right hand.

Swain hissed, "Ain't we invited to the party? Ain't we good enough?"

Sutherland stared at him but said nothing.

Swain leaned over his horse's neck while his friends whooped and joked behind him. He said, "Ain't yuh gonna speak? Too tongue-tied, boy?"

Sutherland said, "Make your move."

Swain sat up and laughed with contempt. He looked back at his men, as though about to say something, then he heeled his mount, and it jumped forward at Sutherland. But he was ready for it, and his big fist caught the horse squarely on the nose. It reared with a terrified whinny, and Sutherland drove into its belly with all his might, throwing it off balance against the other horses.

The animal went down heavily, squealing and kicking, but Swain jumped clear, just avoiding the flying hooves. Instantly he was on his feet, charging Sutherland, who quickly ducked under the attack and lifted Swain bodily into the air. With a sudden whirl, he used the impetus of Swain's rush to keep the borderer going and rammed him to the cobblestones with a resounding crack. Swain grunted in pain and rolled over, holding his head. The light of the door showed blood on the man's hands.

Twice now Sutherland had used skill to down this giant, and Swain was as dismayed as he was stunned. He got to his knees and shook his head, then began to laugh, blood pouring down over his face. He tried to focus on Sutherland, who saw he was dizzy.

Swain said, "You're a sneaky son of a bitch! But it'll take more'n that." He struggled to his feet, a little wobbly. He mustered all his strength as the two men circled, each in a fighting crouch. Ella, her hands to her face, felt cold fear to see how powerful this man was. She had to do something. Then she saw that Franklin held her husband's claymore, and a pistol bulged in the doctor's waistband.

Swain seemed about to spring, and in the mingling shadows and lamplight, he loomed huge compared to Sutherland. Then, when everyone was tensed for his leap, he hesitated and stood up straight. He spat, and with his sleeve wiped blood from his eyes. To Morgan, who was mounted nearby, he said, "No more shit, Morg. Give me the 'hawk."

In an instant, Swain had a steel tomahawk in his right hand and a scalping knife in the other.

Franklin cried "Owen!" and the claymore still in its scabbard flew through the darkness. As Sutherland flicked it clear of the scabbard, the blade gleamed hungrily. A stifled muttering came from the mounted men. But Swain was unruffled. Teeth bared, the cords of his neck bulging and covered with blood, Swain tested his enemy's swordsmanship. Tomahawk and knife darted back and forth as he moved in. Sutherland advanced and retreated, moving from side to side just enough to make Swain less certain. Swain feinted to Sutherland's right with the knife, then came straight ahead, the tomahawk chopping down. Sutherland recovered from the fake, and the claymore parried the tomahawk blow. Swain slid fast to Sutherland's left, the tomahawk already low and hacking at the Scotsman's legs. Sutherland hopped and struck, knocking the tomahawk from Swain's hand. But the man's knife was there, slashing Sutherland's right shoulder, tearing his coat, cutting a shallow gash, and he skipped back. Following up his swift move, Swain had the tomahawk again, and threw it. Sutherland saw it flicker. He ducked as it whisked past his face and clattered against a stone wall.

Now it was Sutherland's claymore against Swain's knife. Almost blinded by blood, Swain went into his crouch, and they circled.

Sutherland said, "Give it up now, man, and you'll live. If you don't, I'll split you in two."

Through clenched teeth, Swain growled like a cornered wolf. "You're not the man to do it."

Then, so rapidly that no one saw him move, Sutherland laid Swain's chest open, from left shoulder to breastbone. The cut was no deeper than a nasty nick, but it ripped the man's buckskin and drew a good deal of blood.

"I'm the man," Sutherland said.

At the far end of the alley, shouts from the approaching city watch were heard. Then came a howling whoop, and Morgan's horse sprang forward, crashing into Sutherland from behind, knocking him flat. Struggling under the hooves, Sutherland was kicked a glancing blow that stunned him. Then he saw Swain's bloody face and the glint of the hunting knife above him. A shot rang out, and Swain staggered backwards, dropping the knife.

With a roar of defiance, the ruffians dragged Swain up behind Morgan, and they pounded away down the cobbled alley, nearly riding down a dozen men of the watch as they escaped. In a moment, they were gone, and the alley was filled with babbling people. Ella stood trembling, both hands holding Franklin's smoking pistol. Franklin helped Sutherland to his feet and, with Ella, guided him into the house. In the bright light, Sutherland saw only vague images at first, and his head rang from the horse's kick.

Franklin had him taken up to his own room, where he was bathed, and Ella treated his head and shoulder with compresses of comfrey leaf and alcohol. The cut on his shoulder was stitched by a doctor who was an invited guest, but it was not serious, and it did not take long for Sutherland to come to his senses. Ella's face regained its color, and she sighed, relaxing as she sat down in a chair near him.

Another shirt and coat were brought, and the Sutherlands went downstairs to find that no one had left, though it was nearly midnight. Owen was surprised when the guests applauded him. He smiled wanly and tried to quiet them with a few gestures of his hands. Then he saw Franklin standing near the head of the table, where dinner had been cleared and desserts of apple pie in pewter dishes had been set.

"Come in, my friends," Franklin said to the couple. "Let's enjoy the rest of the evening. Violinist, something cheerful, if you will."

A few minutes later, Sutherland and Ella were joking together at how they could be eating pie at a time like this, and Owen tried to ignore the pain of his shoulder and head. Franklin stood up and addressed his guests once again, raising his glass as though nothing had happened since he began this toast two hours earlier.

"And furthermore . . ." Everyone laughed warmly. "My dear friends, I give you Owen Sutherland."

"Hear, hear!"

A woman said, for everyone to hear, "A few more men such as he and we need fear no borderers!"

Another woman looked straight at Owen as though she would pierce him with her eyes. "And to think he's a poet too."

Sutherland, embarrassed, could stand no more. He got up, a little stiffly, and raised his own glass. "Good people," he began. He felt slightly dizzy, but kept control. "Good people, there have been enough compliments directed to me tonight. I am grateful to have been of some small service to this fine city. But—" he took a deep breath before going on "—but everyone in Philadelphia should know that it was not I who prevented what might have been." Franklin looked down at his plate, his face red.

Sutherland lifted his glass higher. "It's a pity that the publisher of the *Gazette* is too modest to tell the story of what really happened in the camp of the borderers. Perhaps, one day, someone will do him justice. For now, let it be sufficient to say that I have never had the honor to stand at the side of a greater man. Ladies and gentlemen, Dr. Franklin."

The day before they were to leave the city, the Sutherlands were paid one last visit by Franklin. It was purely a social call, and the statesman insisted on seeing the sled dogs at work. There had been a good snowfall the night before, so Sutherland demonstrated the sled, even letting Franklin try it out. Yowling like a little boy, Franklin set the dogs to trotting around the house, but he did not remember how to stop them, and Sutherland had to dash out after the third circuit and head off Heera, the leader.

Laughing as they went toward the house, Sutherland and Franklin were met by a young fellow in a long gray watch coat, who bowed deeply and said, "Dr. Franklin, permit my boldness, but my name is John Blair from New York, and I am a great admirer of yours."

Franklin shook the youth's hand and said, "Pleased to meet you, my boy. What can I do for you?"

"Do? Why, nothing, sir. I was passing by, and merely wanted to tell you that I am a great admirer, and that I have read everything you have ever published!"

The fellow gave a broad smile at this, and Franklin chuckled, turning to Sutherland and then back to Blair. Peering over his bifocals, Franklin asked, "Everything?" The young man declared it was so. "Well," Franklin muttered, "in that case, I am sorry for you. But it's nice to make your acquaintance, Mr. Blair."

Franklin shook Blair's hand again and turned for the door of Sutherland's residence, but Blair asked eagerly, "Dr. Franklin, I'll be in Philadelphia for some time, and I wanted to know whether I might visit you and talk about some things that interest me—particularly natural science, which I have studied at the College of New Jersey in Princeton."

Franklin peered over his glasses again and said kindly, "Certainly, my boy. Come next week, say Tuesday, after dinner." Then he leaned toward the man and said, "Anything in particular you wish to discuss?"

"Why, yes," Blair said. "Flora and fauna of Pennsylvania, and if you can direct me to anyone in the northwest who might give me advice on a naturalist's expedition, I would be in your debt."

"The northwest," Franklin said, eyeing Sutherland. "How far northwest?"

Blair laughed lightly, in an engaging sort of way. "As far northwest as anyone can go, Dr. Franklin! You see, I intend one day to find the Northwest Passage."

Sutherland said to Blair, "If you're ever in Detroit, lad, ask for me—Owen Sutherland. I'll do what I can for you."

Blair's eyes opened wide, and his chin dropped. "You . . . you are Owen Sutherland? The Indian fighter?"

Franklin corrected, "Adopted Ottawa! Now you have two invitations, son, so if you'll permit us to go about our business, you can be about yours, finding that Northwest Passage. I'll see you on Tuesday—and by the way, you can come for dinner at one of the clock. Then you can even *eat* some of the local flora and fauna. That's better than talking about it, anyway."

They said good-bye to Blair and went inside for a last visit with Ella. When Franklin left for home in his chaise, Ella and Owen stood at the door, waving until he was out of sight. More snow began to fall, laying a white hush over the city and river. It would take many years for their memories of Philadelphia to dim. And as for Benjamin Franklin, Owen and Ella Sutherland would never in their lives forget him.

Later in the afternoon, a messenger delivered to Franklin a poem Sutherland had written:

To My Friend, Ben Franklin

A sage man, yet simple (simple, too, is truth).
A humble man, for humble is the proof
Of inner strength beyond the brittleness of pride.

A warrior, inventor, man of peace,
Philosopher, statesman—these are the least
Of all his lofty callings, he, when asked, replied.

Nay, printer is the foremost, so he'll say;
Free press means liberty! (What's more, the writers
    pay,
And printers prosper most when paid by every side!)

PART THREE

The Conquest

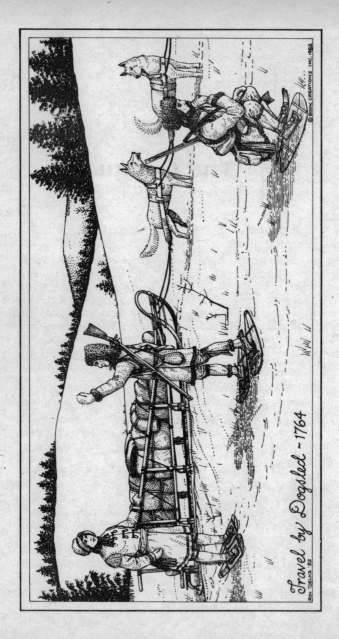

Travel by Dogsled ~ 1764

RON TOELKE '82

© BOOK CREATIONS INC. 1982

chapter 20

WINTER TRAIL

Sutherland was paid for assisting the province, but it was only a small sum. Their stay in the luxurious military residence, however, had more than made up for the token payment. Their time with Botany and his daughter had been one of mutual pleasure, and after Sutherland had loaded the sled and taken leave of everyone else, including Lieutenant Magruder, they said farewell last of all to their servants.

"Perhaps we'll meet again," Ella said to Botany, but she had difficulty believing it. "Thank you for all you have done for us."

Showing nothing of his sadness in parting with the Sutherlands, Botany smiled and bowed slightly, saying to Ella, "Take care...of everything." Then he shook hands with Owen, and their eyes met. Much was left unspoken between these two men, much that addressed the irony and madness of their world.

"One day, my friend, we'll come back to Philadelphia to see you."

Botany replied, "Perhaps one day I will come to Detroit."

That surprised Sutherland, and Botany noticed. The black man grinned, further disarming Sutherland, and something good passed between them.

They left Botany and Clarissa at the door, took one last look at the icy Delaware, and departed. With Owen standing on the back, Ella bundled in furs in the sled, they surged away in a rush of yapping and the hiss of runners. Through the city they mushed, under a crystal-clear sky that gave Ella the impression of magic, of a fairyland. Philadelphians everywhere stopped to watch them pass, many waving in recognition, others staring with interest at the unusual sight of a sled and dogs. Blue, green, and yellow doors passed in a bright blur. Faces of every form and color appeared and disappeared in Ella's view. It was the realm of gabled roofs, red brick, and tall spires. Women washing windows in the bright sunlight, great Lancaster wagons lumbering along, shopkeepers shoveling and brushing to clear snow from flagstone walks—all this soon would be only a memory, something to be recalled as a time of youth, when everything was possible.

They left the city from the north, running northwest along the near bank of the Schuylkill River, making five good miles every hour. Behind lay Philadelphia, now safe from civil war. Beyond the horizon lay the snowbound mountains, and then the deep forest, silent and secret. It was a long way home—perhaps six weeks or more. Ella felt uneasy and she felt decisive, both at the same time. Emotions spun round in her heart until at last she took a deep breath and lay back. Letting restlessness leave her, Ella conserved her strength for the test yet to come.

The sled's rhythm, the steady trotting of the dogs, and Owen singing a Scots song to himself quieted Ella. Soon she was deep asleep.

For Aleta, the passing of immediate danger led into another time of hardship—smallpox ravaged her people. The city quarantined them, and they were not permitted to leave the building at all.

In the dank, confining quarters, the disease raged out of control. Everything possible was done to ease the suffering of the Indians—short of permitting them the liberty they needed. But weakness of the body and soul left them open to infection, and though Aleta felt pain in her lower back, she fought to keep on caring for the sick.

At least little Ollie was healthy. Aleta had given him the best of care, and he seemed strong and immune to the pox. She feared for the baby, but she did not worry about herself. Even when her dizziness became so intense that she could hardly stand up without holding on to something, she worked hour after hour to comfort her people.

The earlier warm spell had broken, and the weather was cold
as the Sutherlands traveled up the valley of the Schuylkill. It
grew colder with every day they pushed deeper into the heartland. Nights were spent at occasional inns or at farms, where
they stopped well before darkness. Usually they slept in barns,
paying the owners some small sum in exchange for a hot meal
and a bed of straw. Now and again they found themselves far
from village or farm, so they slept in the shelter of an evergreen
grove, or at the southern base of a rocky windbreak. After a
few days they swung across the frozen Schuylkill and cut
through wooded, fairly level land toward Harris's Ferry on the
Susquehanna.

This was the country of the borderers who had threatened
Philadelphia, and it surprised Ella, after all she had heard about
these warlike folk, to find them kindly and hospitable. The
weather held clear and cold, and that was good, for a slushy
trail would have made the sled sink and drag, taxing the strength
of the dogs. They followed the beaten track of hunters or riders,
finding the going easy on the hard-packed snow. Frequently
Sutherland took the strain off the team by running alongside
on snowshoes, or broke trail ahead of the dogs when the snow
was deep.

It was a spacious and lovely country. They journeyed to
Carlisle, a hundred miles from Philadelphia, in less than a
week. By the time they reached this sleepy little town of stone
houses and big barns, Ella thought Owen's warnings about
winter travel must have been exaggerated. She was as warm
as pie in the bearskin, and even though she took her turn
driving, she felt more exhilaration than weariness when evening
drew near.

To prevent snowblindness they often wore sheer gauze over
their eyes; to keep off the dry cold wind, Ella regularly smeared
her cheeks with a fine cream made of cucumber essence, bought
in a Philadelphia apothecary. This cream—ten jars of it—was
the only luxury she brought with her from the city.

Owen let his beard grow, and by the time they reached Fort
Loudon, a small post at the foot of the mountain barrier, he
had a dark and curly growth that Ella thought delightful.

The dogs were tireless, though they ate prodigiously. Now

and again Owen would rest them for a day and go off on snowshoes to hunt. At those times, Ella was glad for the company of the lead dog, Heera. Owen had told her that there would be few if any Indians outside their villages at this time of year, so it was safe to move now; yet she felt tense when he was gone, and did not relax until he came back. She knew that as long as the uncertain feeling remained with her at such times, she would not be a true woman of the frontier. Still, she made a point of calling Heera to her and spoiling him with a snack that attracted the envy of the other dogs, but the animal's warmth at her side was reassuring.

In the company of a squad of soldiers and a supply train of packhorses, the Sutherlands crossed over the first chain of ridges until they came to tiny Fort Lyttleton. The weather turned warmer, and it snowed for a few days, stranding them at the post, where they were guests of the young lieutenant who commanded it. They asked whether there had been any Indian trouble with them recently.

"Trouble?" the soldier scoffed, but there was no humor in his voice. "How could there be trouble? They're all sick with the smallpox."

"Smallpox!" Ella gasped.

The lieutenant explained that before he had gone back to England, Lord Jeffrey Amherst, commander of the British army, had ordered that infected blankets be sent as presents to the Shawnee and Delaware in this region. "It's a bad business, Mr. Sutherland," he said. "I was against it from the start. The Indians are losing people every day, I hear. It's not my way to fight a war, sir, but I daresay it'll be effective."

The villages were also suffering from lack of food, he said; they had little ammunition left for hunting. He rose from the table and went to the roaring fireplace, putting one hand on the mantel and bowing his head.

"They'll be half-beaten by springtime," he said. "They'll attack the settlements with a few scalping parties, but they won't have the strength in men or ammunition to hit hard. Last summer was their high point. Unless Pontiac can work some magic and bring the western tribes of the Illinois under his sway, we won't see another Indian force capable of meeting the army in a pitched battle—maybe not for generations to come."

He strode back to the table and sat down wearily. His eyes

revealed the loneliness of a winter command on the edge of a vast wilderness. "No, the conquest of these hostiles will be achieved largely with starvation and smallpox infection."

They set off again, making for Fort Pitt, less than a hundred miles away. Sitting in the sled, Ella felt the harsh winter wind, and buried herself in the bearskin. Now that they were west of the ridge line, they would feel the teeth of every storm that blew down from the frozen northwest.

There were no warm cabins within easy reach of one another. West of Fort Lyttleton were forts Bedford, Ligonier, and Pitt. The largest break between forts was fifty miles—or two days' travel—between Bedford and Ligonier. Tonight they would rest at Bedford if all went well.

She felt uneasy sitting in the sled, and she realized that something alive was in her womb. It came as a sort of surprise, for even though she knew she was with child, until now there had been no real sense of life independent of her own. The baby did not kick, and Ella had not had much nausea. Yet, in this remarkable moment of revelation, she became conscious of the baby. It was a wonder she was unprepared to experience—a mixture of excitement, happiness, and indescribable poignancy.

She sank deeper into the covers, burying all but her eyes, which she closed to think happily about Owen's child.

Except for dark pine forests, the world was a wash of bleak grays and dull white. When they first came out from Detroit, Ella had thought the autumn forest quiet, but now it was deathly still. Only the sound of the sled, the rattle of branches in the wind, and Owen's voice calling to the sled dogs could be heard; and when they stopped to rest, the wilderness seemed a lonely place.

Yet there were enough signs of life if one knew how to look. Owen showed her tracks where mice skittered into the brush. They passed deep hoofprints leading off into a thick stand of pine, and he said moose were yarding in there. Later on that day they crossed a frozen lake against the wind that whipped icy particles against their faces. Here Owen indicated a strange patch a little ways off, which looked like the shadow of a cloud. When they came closer, he said these were the prints of a milling wolf pack gathering to hunt. A little farther they saw a blotch of red in the snow. As they approached, it became the carcass of a young moose, killed and half-eaten by the wolves so recently that it was not yet frozen.

Sutherland drew the sled to a stop, and the slavering dogs were excited by the scent of blood. He took his rifle from its scabbard alongside the sled and told Ella to come and bring the tomahawk. In a few minutes he was hacking off huge chunks of flesh for the dogs, and he sliced a few steaks for his and Ella's dinner as well.

Tossing the meat into a burlap bag, Sutherland and Ella went back to the sled. For just an instant Ella felt wary of the dogs, because they were staring at her so hungrily. But Owen simply threw the bag into the front of the sled and helped tuck Ella in.

Then she saw something move at the edge of the trees. She motioned to Owen, and he looked to see shadows drifting along the tree line.

He said, "That's the pack. They've been watching us ever since we stopped."

"Isn't it dangerous?"

"Not especially," he replied, getting onto the back of the sled again. "Wolves won't bother us, even though we've helped ourselves to their grub. They're more afraid of us than we are of them, though that sounds hard to believe."

Indeed it was, thought Ella.

Sutherland spoke to Heera, and off they went, dashing along the crusted snow of the lake. As they reentered the forest trail, they saw more animal signs: the chain pattern of snowshoe hares, broken at intervals of six feet or so where the hare took an extra-long hop. There was also a gliding mark on the snow where a flying squirrel leaped from a tree. Beyond the skid were the creature's double prints, still fresh. Owen said one could tell how old these prints were by observing the amount of snow blown over them—though if it was a windy day, it took a deal of experience to know what the signs said. But it was fairly simple, once you got the hang of it.

Fascinated, Ella listened mile after mile to Sutherland talk about hunting and traveling in the wild, explaining what to do and what not to do. He rambled easily and with enthusiasm over every subject that came to mind.

As Owen talked, Ella tried to remember everything, but naturally she became confused. She learned much, but there were moments when she was unsure—whether new moose-skin shoes should be worn first with the smooth side or the grain side out for instance. She knew that one way made the shoe last twice as long, but she couldn't remember which. That, however, was a minor maxim. Others, such as never to make a fire under a limb laden with snow, and never to cut firewood from a swamp, where water would be frozen in the sticks, were easy to grasp.

Ella was determined to prove to Owen that she could learn these things and be as capable as any squaw. Perhaps she might even be as good with him as Mayla was. But she stopped this line of thinking, accusing herself of trying to live up to an ideal she could never match. She was not Mayla. Yet, could she not learn to be just as skillful, just as wise in the ways of the northwest?

Sutherland interrupted her reverie by saying, "Look! A beaver lodge!"

Ella had learned something of beaver on their trip out to Philadelphia, but now she could make out nothing at all. Then her husband pointed to a large white pyramid set among saplings. "They're in there, and they'll stay in until some trapper breaks it open. But it better be done soon if their fur's to be worth anything. Beaver who hole up all winter don't get much light or air; they lose weight, and their fur is ruined until late summer, when they get strong again. They might even die in there if winter's too hard and long."

The beaver's fur was the mainstay of the northwest trader and hunter. Because of beaver pelts, the French had colonized the endless Canadian wilderness, and fortunes had been made in the Indian peltry trade. Beaver was first, but there were other important furs, including muskrat, otter, fox, raccoon, mink, and sable. Fur buyers and hat manufacturers in Europe were on the verge of bankruptcy just then because the northwest—the greatest producer of furs in the world—was sealed off by Pontiac's uprising. Ella and Owen knew the Frontier Company was in an ideal position to make the most of the fur shortage.

On they pressed, up hills, where Owen got out and ran in snowshoes alongside the dogs. There were tricky curves where Ella had to get out and drive the sled while her husband broke trail with his snowshoes, so the sled could get through. Then there were long downhill runs, easy and free, with the wind swishing in her face, and Owen ducking under low branches, braking the sled so it would not come too close behind the team.

They followed the military path most of the way, taking the road Sutherland and Colonel Bouquet had followed on their desperate march to relieve Pitt last year. He knew it well enough, though there were moments when the lay of the land tricked him, or the drifting snow sent him in the wrong direction. Yet always he found the path again, causing Ella to marvel at his remarkable sense of direction.

When she asked him how he did it, he explained a few things about the position of the sun and about the growth of moss on the north side of trees, as well as about branches being thicker and longer on the south side.

"But there are other things that are hard to explain, though they're simple enough to a woodsman or Indian," he said. "You see, everything has some meaning, or tells a story, and when you've been through a place, you remember what you see— a sloping path, a blasted tree like that big one over there that lightning hit, a cut in the hills, like that one in the distance. That's where we're headed, and we'll get there by tomorrow.

"Even odd-looking stones that I don't think about until I see them again on the same trail—they can't ever be forgotten if you see them once."

He said that when he was first learning the ways of the wild he followed an Indian guide over a trail nearly three hundred miles long. To test himself, he had asked to be the guide on the return journey, and to his own surprise, was in doubt only once:

"We were standing on the ice looking at a tongue of land that pointed out toward us. The portage leaving the lake was at the other end of one of those two bays, but which one? Well, the Indian had stopped right behind me, enjoying my confusion. But I stood there thinking and passed over the entire start of the trip out, and then there was no doubt in my mind which was right."

He laughed to recall that day, and Ella thought he seemed still proud of it. She asked, "What did the guide say?"

Sutherland said with feeling, " '*A-a-ke-pu-ka-tan!*' That means, 'Yes, you are able!' That was one of the best moments of my life."

Sometimes the things he talked about were too much for Ella to follow, though she enjoyed listening. She was secure being with him, lying cozy and warm in the bearskin. She let the rhythm of the sled sliding over a long, straight buffalo path lull her to sleep. Now the wild in winter did not seem quite so forbidding.

The howl of a wolf woke her, and she sat up quickly. Owen spoke softly, saying she should sleep again, for they would stop soon and make camp. The weather was milder now, the wind blocked by trees growing on both sides of the trail. She lay back once more as the sled skidded onward, rocking her to sleep as though she were a baby.

As she slumbered, Ella dreamed of Philadelphia and its colorful doors. She then saw Detroit, rough and solitary on the rise above the straits—there was Jeremy. Images in her mind were happy and pleasant. The boy was growing—

Then her dreams ended in Owen's fierce shout. Ella felt herself falling, and there was a jarring crash, hard snow, ice over her. She was sliding, face down, the sound of yowling dogs loud all around her. Her breath was knocked away. She came to a stop. Fighting to her feet, trying to breathe, she saw the sled was overturned, the dogs tangled, struggling in their harness, and Owen was nowhere in sight.

She shouted his name and stumbled back up the steep trail, which ran through a narrow defile surrounded by dark ever-greens and clattering, naked maples. "Owen! Where are you?"

The dogs were barking and snarling in their excitement. She turned to go to them and free them, but then felt terror for Owen, and she ran clumsily up the trail. She saw a movement where the trail rose and fell sharply, as though crossing over a drifted log. It was Owen! She reached him after struggling through knee-deep snow, and fell at his side. He was trying to sit up, and like Ella, was covered with snow. Feeling his head, he shook it angrily and looked up at an overhanging branch.

Ella touched the nasty bruise on his forehead, and he laughed ruefully. She asked whether he was badly hurt, and he mumbled something about his pride and added, "The smart sled-dog driver avoids tree limbs whenever possible." He got to his feet, saying, "I just wanted to demonstrate that maxim to you in a way you wouldn't forget." He grimaced and rubbed a handful of snow against the swelling lump on his head. Ella tried not to giggle, but it was hopeless.

Then, just inches away, came a terrifying roar. The snow

was exploding as in an earthquake. Ella fell back, but Owen was on his feet, pulling his tomahawk free from his belt. A giant black bear crashed out of the bump on the trail, ferocious and angry at being disturbed during hibernation. Savage, but still woozy from deep sleep, the animal lunged at Sutherland, who retreated a few feet and struck hard at the bear's head with the tomahawk.

The bear snarled and lunged again, dropping on all fours, slashing with its claws. It nearly had him, but Owen ducked to one side as the animal charged. The bear turned to catch him, then stumbled as the tomahawk cracked down on its head again. In a blur, the bear whirled for Sutherland, who kept it off balance with a third terrible crack on the skull. It went at him blindly, and he darted aside, then tipped backwards over buried wood. Ella screamed. The animal, bleeding from its head, tried for Owen, staggered, and collapsed heavily beside him.

Owen got up carefully, easing around the fallen bear, and Ella ran to him in a flood of relief. He tried to wave her back, but it was too late. The bear rose, roaring madly, just a yard away from her. Unable to move, Ella, smelling earth and animal and fresh blood, saw yellow fangs and eyes of rage. Shouldering Ella aside, Owen leaped against the wounded bear, striking again and again with the tomahawk. The bear was stunned, and it went down again, breathing, but bloodied and dying. Sutherland stepped back slowly, one arm pushing Ella away.

"Get the rifle," he said, not taking his eyes from the bear.

Ella came to her senses and ran for the sled, yanking the rifle clear and hurrying back to Owen. In a moment, it was dead, shot through the brain. Sutherland sank to his knees, head bowed, sweat pouring from his face. The tomahawk lay in the bloodstained snow. Ella took the gun from him and put her hand on his shoulder. It was then that Owen noticed she was not wearing her mittens or hat. Suddenly transformed, he looked as furious as the bear.

"Woman! Where the hell are your mitts? And your hat!"

"Owen—"

"Put them on! Find them, for God's sake! Hasn't enough happened for one day?"

She wanted to say they had fallen off when the sled went over, but he would not hear it. "Put on your gear, woman!"

"Don't shout at me that way! I'm no squaw to be shouted—"

"If you were a squaw, you'd know enough to keep your gear on! Do you want frostbite?"

She was just as angry as he now. She shouted, "I'm all right! It was only a minute!"

He stood up, breathing hard, but trying to calm down. He came to her and took her hands, turning them palms up for her to see. The skin was torn and frostburned where she had held the frozen steel of the rifle. Now Ella felt a tingling from the pain, and she thought herself a fool to have made such an error. Then Owen took her hands to his lips and kissed them where they hurt.

"I'm sorry, lass. Come on, we'll put on some salve and camp here tonight." He smiled and kissed her lightly. "We'll have some bear steaks. But keep your gear on—and if I ever get angry at you again like this, just talk about overhanging branches."

They held one another a moment, and then she went for her gloves and cap. Though her hands hurt, Ella insisted on cutting evergreen boughs for a lean-to and bedding. As Sutherland set about skinning and butchering the bear, he looked up now and again to see Ella struggling with a small hatchet, trying to chop away branches. He thought to help her, but then understood she would rather do this alone, and he admired her for that.

While Owen went about his business with the bearskin, Ella scorched for firewood, remembering to get it from high ground, where the sticks would be dry. She got enough for that night, then realized she should collect enough for the next day, too, just in case it snowed and they were forced to stay here longer. When she thought there would be enough firewood for several days, she gathered and hauled it back to camp.

Owen finished with the bear, cutting meat for the dogs, and dragging the enormous skin under the trees, where Ella was cutting frozen potatoes and onions into a pot of snowmelt. Soon there would be bear stew.

Ella knew by now it was squaw's work to clean and dry skins, but she was not eager to do it. She knew, however, she would never prove a capable mate for Sutherland unless she could endure such chores. She looked at Owen, then at the skin, then at Owen again. He sat back to light a pipe and rest, his hands clean now from wiping them in snow and in meltwater near the campfire. He knew what was in her mind, but said nothing, simply puffing away and taking his ease. Just like an Indian, she thought.

What was the right thing to do? Ella did not know, but she made up her mind and took the scraping knife from their gear. She went to the skin and began raking off the remaining flesh. It was hard work, her hands stinging from the frost burn, but she did it without a word until Owen came and knelt next to her.

"Your hands," he said. "I'll do this after we eat. Let your hands heal, lass."

She was grateful for that but did not show it. In a nonchalant way, she looked at her sore hands, already stained with muck from the skin, then nodded. "Of course," she said, and left it at that. She washed her hands in snowmelt and applied more salve to them. Then she boiled fresh water for tea, and they sat quietly, listening to wind in the evergreens and the noise of dogs crunching bear bones. Darkness was setting in, the forest dim, and the last light of afternoon shimmered cold and dull through the treetops. Ella felt good here. They had come through another adventure. How many more, she wondered, would she have to go through before she would qualify as an experienced frontierswoman? She saw Owen begin to scrape the bearskin and knew that she would at least have to learn how to prepare a pelt. But that would wait until her hands were cured.

After a good dinner, they snuggled under blankets laid on top of the old bearskin from the sled, which was spread over soft evergreens. They could not have been warmer. Ella lay on her side, with Owen against her, arms about her waist. For just a moment, she thought he was investigating her tummy, which she knew had grown a bit. She held her breath as his hands caressed her and slipped inside her clothing to feel her middle again.

"Ella," he said.

"Yes?" She answered more loudly than intended, then coughed to mask her tension.

"How do you feel?"

"Feel?" She laughed. "Don't I feel fine to you, husband?"

He murmured and kissed her ear, then she once more felt his hand examining the vague bulge at her middle.

She sighed and said, "I feel fine, dearest. But I was so

hungry tonight that I ate too much stew. I'm positively stuffed, you know."

He lightly rubbed her tummy and said a little sleepily, "Yes, I was going to say that myself."

"You're stuffed, too?" she asked.

After a moment, he said into her hair, "No. You ate a lot tonight, it seems."

In the distance a wolf howled, eerie and mournful. Ella pressed back against her husband and listened as another wolf answered somewhere closer. She thought of the shadows that had followed them from the frozen lake, and she hoped Owen was right about wolves not being as dangerous as many folk thought.

Plaintive, haunting wails lifted on the wind, and Ella lay awake, trying to tell how many there were. The sled dogs answered now and again, sending up their own melody. This little grove of trees was far from everywhere, but in her husband's arms, with a fire blazing at the entrance to their lean-to, and Heera sleeping peacefully nearby, Ella felt safe. Perhaps, she thought pleasantly, feeling safe out here was one step toward belonging here. She thought it must be so, and strangely the cries of hunting wolves were no longer frightening. Like her, they were part of this wilderness. Like her, they had a place here. To their lingering song, Ella slipped into a deep, dreamless sleep.

chapter **21**

THE ISLAND

Snow fell on Philadelphia, and the city lay ashen and still. In the courtyard near the barracks, where not long ago there had been hundreds of angry citizens, lumbering cannon, and nervous soldiers, there was now only a lonely sentry pacing back and forth. For the moment, the Indians were ignored by the city. As long as none of them tried to break the smallpox quarantine by going outside, they were left alone.

A melancholy wailing drifted from the barracks, as a squaw lamented a lost loved one. A third of the two hundred souls jammed into the barracks had died during the weeks of epidemic. But the worst was over now, and only one person had died recently—yet that death took light from the Moravian Indians, and with that light went much of their hope for a happy future.

In the dimness of the barracks, an old woman released her grief in an ancient, echoing song of her people—a song not taught her by the Moravians, but one she had known since childhood. It came back to her now, unbidden, to be sung over the shrouded body of the latest death. In the old woman's wrinkled arms lay Ollie, sucking his finger and gazing at the white sheet that covered Aleta, the one he had come to accept as his mother.

Fort Pitt was much quieter than it had been on the autumn journey. Many of the soldiers had been sent east for the winter, because there was always a shortage of food during the cold months, and there was little danger from Indians. The boredom of winter hung heavily over the post, and smallpox had struck the refugee hovels, leaving those who survived weak and listless.

At Pitt Owen and Ella were told more of the awful conditions in the villages, learning that smallpox and starvation were ravaging the Indians, killing them off more efficiently than an invading army. Sutherland wondered whether Bouquet and Bradstreet would even have to fight next summer.

The Sutherlands did not stay long in Fort Pitt, resting only two days and trading the fresh bearskin for some essentials. They set off in early morning, heading north into a country empty of posts and settlements.

Indians were also rare in this next stretch of country, and there would be no big villages until they reached the western portion of Lake Erie's southern shore. It was good that there were few Indians there. Pontiac's truce would mean nothing to roving hunters who might come upon Ella and Owen.

It was still two hundred and fifty miles to Detroit. If they made between twenty-five and forty miles a day, they would get there in time to meet Tamano, who would return with his furs by early March. Sutherland would surely be weary from this overland trip, but he was determined to set off as soon as possible for Montreal with Tamano's harvest.

Since the furs were so important and because every penny the partners had was invested in the trade goods Tamano used to procure the peltry, Sutherland would not trust anyone else to get the harvest to Montreal. He also knew how to barter with the best of the eastern merchant houses, and he was determined to get cash, not goods, in return for the pelts. Cash would give the company a solid basis that no one else could match.

He was amused to think how the Montreal merchants would howl when he demanded cash for the furs. But they would pay. The market was sky-high in Europe just then, since so few furs had come through last year, and a canny Montreal merchant could make a fortune by supplying London furriers this spring. The merchant with furs could name his own price, and so could the Frontier Company when Sutherland brought in Tamano's harvest.

Sutherland thought over what faced them before they reached Detroit. They would follow French Creek north after they left the course of the frozen Allegheny; then from French

Creek they would cut sharply west to Lake Erie. Following the
shoreline as far as they could, they would swerve across the
lake, making for a scattering of islands north of the ruined Fort
Sandusky. He estimated they could reach those islands in one
full day's travel after swinging away from the shoreline. However, it was dangerous, because they must not be caught in a
blizzard on the open lake, where they would freeze to death.
But it was the only way, because near Sandusky were several
large Wyandot Huron villages, where hostiles were wintering.

They would have to get as far as possible along the Erie
shoreline before taking off across the ice, but if they went too
far they might be seen by people in the villages. They would
be hunted then, and they might not be able to stop at the
sheltering islands. As quarry, they would be compelled to over-
shoot the islands and spend the night out on the ice. Then they
would have to make the second part of that run toward the
mouth of the Detroit River with an enemy at their backs, and
with tired dogs.

Many Indians along the lakeshore had small teams of sled
dogs, and it was even possible that they might pursue the
Sutherlands that way. Determined men in snowshoes could
catch them eventually, for their dogs must rest sometimes, and
there were Indian warriors capable of outrunning dogs.

At that moment Pontiac was asleep in his lodge near the Maumee River. Jacques Levesque and his friend Tremblay were
glad for that, because it meant the English child, Sally, was
safe from the chief's outbursts of hatred. Sitting in their lodge,
Levesque, Tremblay, the child, and a few Delaware Indians
were listening to a tinkling, chiming music box that was an
heirloom in Tremblay's family.

The *Québecois* had wound up the pearl-inlaid rosewood box
and opened it, revealing a carved ivory rose, and at the same
time releasing the sweet music. It was a bizarre scene, these
six fierce men in a circle, sprawled happily around the little
girl, whose face was alight with pleasure, gazing at the box
and listening to its music.

Nearby, several cheerful squaws were watching, thinking
also how strange was the sight. When the music stopped, Sally
cried out to Tremblay, *"Encore! Encore, Tremblay! S'il vous
plait! Encore!"* He had been teaching her French, and she got
something from him only when she tried to speak his language.

Tremblay feigned weariness of it all, but the Delaware laughed and cajoled him; the one named Niko-lota was the most enthusiastic, growling in jest, *"S'il vous plait! S'il vous plait!"* The Frenchman laughed, delighted that this memento of his childhood in Quebec should please so many others as it still pleased him. Holding up his hands as though won over despite his pretended weariness, he handed the music box to Sally and told her to wind it up.

The excited girl brushed hair back from her eyes and held the box as though it were gold. Then carefully turning it over, she wound the key until it stopped. Sally longed to open the box, but thought better of it and gave it back to Tremblay. He shook his head and smiled, indicating that Sally should open it. Eyes wide, her pinched, sickly face aglow as never before, she lifted the lid. When the music came, she squealed, and all the warriors laughed with her.

Early one morning, Peter Defries sat huddled under a huge pine tree, trying not to tremble. Perhaps it was the bone-chilling cold before the sun rose, or perhaps it was the anticipation of what soon would happen, but no matter what caused Defries to shake, he fought to keep the others from seeing it. Nearby a dozen of Sir William Johnson's Mohawk warriors stood so silently in the shadows that he would never have noticed them had he not seen them take up positions.

These Mohawk were painted black and red, the colors of death—disguised so their victims would not recognize them and could not haunt them afterwards. They were part of the force Sir William had organized, and were encircling a large Delaware village on the Susquehanna River. Defries looked through the haze of a gray morning and saw at least thirty big lodges, each with four or five smokeholes, clustered in the center of a clearing. He estimated six or seven hundred Delaware lived here, and that meant more than two hundred fighting men. It was a gamble to strike such a formidable enemy with only three hundred men, but the element of surprise lay with the attackers. From this village many war parties had ravaged the frontiers from New York to Maryland. Even in this faint light Defries could see the tall scalp poles thick with racks of hair.

As the light increased, he saw a few people walking through the snow-covered village. Then he looked at a broad and sturdy

Mohawk standing motionless a short distance away, the breeze
flicking an eagle feather at his ear. This was Chief Joseph Brant
from New York, leader of the expedition—also leader of the
few-score Yorkers whom Johnson had sent along. Brant would
decide the moment to strike. Defries presumed he wanted
enough light to keep the attackers from firing on one another.
Also, good light would make it easy to pick off warriors as
they sprang from the doors of their lodges.

Defries shivered again. How he wished there had been no
need for him to come on this accursed mission. He did not long
to shoot down anybody, even though he had seen the Indians
massacre his teamsters at Devil's Hole. Let the fighting be
done by men trained to it, or born to it, or who enjoyed it.
Defries wanted to be home with Mary. He would just be waking
up at her side, or still sleeping while she busied herself in the
kitchen. He stifled a yawn. The musket he held in his folded
arms was loaded, but he was not especially proficient with it.
Actually, he had no intention of using it at all if he did not
have to. He was only the quartermaster, the supplier of Brant's
expedition, and when it was over he would go back to Albany
and be paid off by the provincial government. Then back to
Montreal and Mary.

Brant moved! Or was it just the wind flicking his feathers?
No, it was a signal given to the subchiefs and provincial leaders
hiding in the woods on the far side of the village. The Mohawk
braves near Defries tensed, and he looked at them to see
whether they, too, might not be nervously thinking about
squaws at home in their lodges. He presumed not.

The wind swirled, blowing smoke around the village. Defries thought that the people down there were not moving quite
so casually as before. Was that possible? Could they sense
danger? It seemed as though the women were drifting together
in one direction. There were more men outside than previously.
A dog was barking and barking. Defries saw it yelping at the
forest near the other side of the village. Someone moved
quickly in the village. Brant gave the signal, and the morning
was blown apart by musketry and rifle fire. The attackers
shrieked and fired again and again into the village, and figures
collapsed in heaps. Yowling dogs, neighing horses, and the
screams of attackers and defenders mingled in an awful tumult
that turned the peaceful clearing into hell.

Then Brant and the Mohawk were gone, and Defries stood

alone on the little rise, watching the attackers drive into the clearing below. Hand-to-hand fighting broke out everywhere, but every time warriors tried to get out of lodges, men stationed to mark them shot them down. Defries watched the slaughter, seeing the Delaware, ringed by a circle of fire and musket smoke, utterly defeated at every turn. Within fifteen minutes, most of the defenders were dead, wounded, or surrendering to Brant's forces.

The fighting then focused around a small knot of stubborn Delaware just below where Defries stood. These warriors had no intention of surrendering, and they fought savagely, cutting down Mohawk or Yorkers who came at them. They were led by an old, burly fighter, who kept them resisting until their numbers were reduced to a dozen. Then, with a fierce cry, they burst through the tightening ring of attackers and crashed into the brush—heading up the hill where Defries stood.

He was directly in their path, and heard them charging wildly through the brush below him. There was a clearing of forty feet or less between where he stood and where they would appear when they came through the trees.

He ducked behind a slender tree. He would not fire if they did not discover him. His heart beat furiously. Sweat made his hands sticky. The panting fugitives were close, almost at the edge of the trees. He clicked back the musket hammer. He was ready.

They burst through—running madly right at him. He could not get out of the way, and there was nothing else to do. Leaping from cover, he gave a bloodcurdling scream that sent most of them scattering. He brought his musket quickly to bear and fired at the big leader. For a moment, the smoke obliterated his target, but there he was, running hard at Defries, apparently untouched. Using his musket as a club, Defries met the warrior and swung. The fighter ducked and caught Defries a glancing blow on the side of the head with his tomahawk. The Dutchman staggered back against a tree, dropping the musket, momentarily helpless.

He saw the hatred in the warrior's eyes as the tomahawk was lifted for another blow. Using all the strength he could summon, Defries sprang away, crashing backwards into a thicket, vanishing from the angry Indian, who hacked at the bush. Then the pursuers broke out of trees, and the old fighter darted away, leaving Defries bloody and stunned.

•　•　•

Awakening after long cold hours, Defries dragged himself from the bush, but he could not get untangled. He ached, sure he was frostbitten. Then he realized he was not in bushes at all. He was in blankets, lying near a fire. The cold he felt was in his mind, and the aching frostbite was actually the pain of his injured head. He looked around and found he was in an Indian lodge. He heard the voice of Joseph Brant and then saw his friend nearby, a bowl of hot broth in his hands. The terrible war paint was gone from Brant's face, and now he looked the intelligent, educated man he was.

"So you live after all, Defries," Brant said and began to feed him small sips of broth.

"Where are we?" Defries forced himself to sit up and take the bowl from Brant.

"In the lodge of a Delaware chief—the one who laid open your hard Dutch head. You were lucky he did not kill you. It would have been better if you had let that tough old bull pass. But as it was, this belongs to you."

Defries saw Brant holding a scalp stretched on a hoop, already dry from the fire. He was shocked, and asked what the Mohawk was talking about.

"You fired—I saw it myself—and hit the old fighter in the chest; but he was tough, and he nearly got you. I saw him flee as my men came up, and I thought he had escaped, but we found him farther down the trail, dead. I took the liberty of fetching your trophy."

Defries put the soup bowl down. He refused the scalp, trying to be polite, but Brant understood his squeamishness and laughed a rolling, deep laugh as he tossed the hoop aside.

"There is more to be done," Brant said. "We sent the Delaware away from here, and tomorrow we'll burn this village to the ground. It pains my heart to see Indian fight Indian, but it must be done. If the Delaware invoke the wrath of the English king, then the king might, in his anger, tread on the toes of the Iroquois. That, you see, would anger us in turn, and there would be war between our peoples."

Defries sighed and took up the soup again. He said, "You Iroquois know what side to choose, I guess."

"Yes, my friend. Why else would I be willing to burn Delaware villages?"

The campaign went on for another few days, with a Shawnee town being struck in the same way—destroyed, without even the orchard left standing. Now the fear that the ferocious Iroquois had always fired in the hearts of other tribes would once again be kindled. By this expedition, Joseph Brant had reasserted the position of the Iroquois as ruthless, fearless conquerors who had held sway over the northwest country for decades. Later when the Iroquois commanded hostile tribes to make peace with the English or risk obliteration, this winter expedition against the villages on the Susquehanna River would be well remembered.

Another significant step had been taken in the conquest of Pontiac's uprising. At the same time, Peter Defries had proven himself a capable supply contractor. That, thought Peter as he touched his tender head while trudging back to Fort Johnson, had made this hazardous venture worth it. He hoped Mary would understand why he could not come back to her sooner.

Ella sensed a change come over Owen. He was less talkative, more watchful, even when they were stopped for the night. They had been in this camp since early yesterday afternoon, and now it was midmorning of a bright and cold day. Owen was resting the dogs in preparation for the first leg of their sixty-mile journey across the open ice of Lake Erie. They would leave the following morning, after their animals were readied for their hardest pull yet. Ella knew the dogs could run tirelessly with fifteen-minute rests every two hours. But even those brief respites would be shortened, Owen had told her, because they could not linger out on the ice. They had to reach the first small island before nightfall in order to set up camp, which required shelter and firewood, and those essentials would be difficult to get if they made solid ground after dark.

But it was not only the coming journey, the desperate dashes across the ice that worried Sutherland: it was the nearness of Wyandot Huron villages. While Ella slept or read Shakespeare's sonnets under the bright winter sun, Sutherland stood guard almost constantly. Their camp was sheltered from the lake by a knoll, and they had made it well off the beaten track, so that stray travelers would not come close enough to smell the woodsmoke. From the edge of their camp they could stand up and see the windswept lake, and Sutherland often paced the campsite and sometimes went into the woods. In these short scouts, he made sure no roving Indians had come near and observed them. He saw only the tracks of a wolf or two, a fox, and a couple of young deer—no Wyandot hunters.

Late in the afternoon, they sat together eating a meal in silence, when Owen hissed, "Turn very slowly and look at the top of the knoll."

At first Ella thought they were in danger, and it took all her self-control to turn and see what Owen meant. It was nothing more than a red fox jumping up on all fours and thumping hard back down on the crusted snow. Nothing more? Ella suddenly realized that elusive red foxes were seldom seen in the wild, and this one was acting so curiously that she laughed softly to watch it hop up and plop down again.

She whispered, "What's it doing?"

"You'll see."

Then, after a few minutes of leaping up and pounding down with all its slight weight, the fox suddenly poked its snout into the snow. It gave a quick shake of the head, came up with a small creature, then pranced away to have its dinner.

Intrigued, Ella followed Owen to the top of the knoll, and saw where the fox had caved in a maze of tunnels in the snow belonging to a mouse or a shrew. Carefully, Sutherland dug out the top layers of snow to reveal the remarkable network of passages well worn by tiny animals who lived in these snug dwellings throughout winter. Moments such as these brought Ella closer to nature, and she was always learning something new, something fascinating, which gave her another perspective of this northwest country. When she looked across the white, silent snowfields, she understood how it was alive and changing all the time. She had learned only a little about the wilderness, but it was enough to open her mind, and she would never again see winter as a time of inactivity and loneliness.

The next morning, before the sun was up, they set off across the ice. Sutherland had explored their first two miles on snowshoes the evening before. He drove the dogs fast, following the darker line of his own tracks that showed up in the faint light of false dawn. By the time the sun was up, they had covered seven miles, and were well out of sight of the Huron villages on the distant, gray-blue shoreline behind them.

He relaxed again, and talked of what they would do when they reached home in less than four days. Ella sensed his

excitement, as she had earlier sensed his concern. She was also
relieved, her hands on her growing tummy. She would tell
Owen tonight that she carried his child. There was no more
reason for him to worry about her.

Giving the dogs only five-minute rests every two hours,
they pushed across the snow crust and brought the bulk of a
good-sized island into view. Here they would camp. There
were others in the distance, five miles away, all like this one,
hilly and white with snow, washed with the gray of bare maple
trees. Sutherland approached the island in a straight line, then
when they were a couple of hundred yards away, he swerved
to the right, heading for the northern end.

At the shore Owen left Ella by the sled and scouted around
to make sure there were no Indian lodges in sight. Satisfied,
he led the team to a sheltered, frozen cove where a thick stand
of balsam made an ideal windbreak. It was not likely Indians
would choose the cold north side of the island to make camp.
If any were here, they would be on the southerly side, facing
the warm sun and protected from the north wind.

They ran the sled up onto shore, unharnessed the dogs, and
left them in their traces; the animals were glad for the rest.
Then they set about making camp. By now Ella was skillful
at collecting balsam branches for their bed, loading them criss-
cross on her axe, and Owen complimented her. Camp was set
up swiftly and without a wasted motion. Ella truly felt she had
achieved something, and had proven to Owen and to herself
that she belonged out here with him. The only thing she had
not done yet was to skin and prepare pelts. That work did not
appeal to her at all.

Leaving the dogs to rest, Ella and Owen put on snowshoes
and went for a stroll an hour before sunset, drifting along the
shore of the island, and looking west toward the sun and Fort
Detroit. She felt happy now, and he was content, his rifle in
the crook of one arm. Soon she would be with Jeremy again,
and except for Owen having to go east almost immediately,
their life would be perfect.

Then Owen grabbed her arm and stopped her from moving.
They listened. In the distance someone was calling—a strange
cry, as of one injured. Sutherland told Ella to wait and went
to the top of a ridge. There he looked down a long slope,
through crowds of gray maples, and he saw the tracks of a

man. The cry sounded agonized. He motioned for Ella, and they slipped through the trees, following the sound of the voice on the wind.

When they stopped behind the shelter of large boulders, the sound of despair was very close. It was human, that was certain, but who could be out on this lonely island? She dreaded to think the Indians might have caught a white traveler and tortured him, leaving him for dead in the bitter cold.

Owen looked past the rocks, and after a moment he stepped out into a clearing, where an old, ragged Wyandot Indian hung upside down, caught in a sprung snare trap. The man's face was blue from the strain, his left leg caught at the ankle by the slipknot attached to a strong sapling that had whipped him off the ground after he stepped in it. The old Indian saw Sutherland approach, knife in hand, and he wriggled with all his strength, trying to get free.

Then Sutherland told him in Wyandot that he was not in danger. The Indian stopped wriggling, and let himself go limp, waiting until he was cut down. Then Ella came out of the trees, and she joined Owen, who was cutting the rope from the man's sore leg.

Sutherland said to her, "He was calling for someone else, so keep an eye out while I get what I can out of him." The weakened old man was bundled in a patched blanket coat, wearing breeches and leggins stuffed with straw. Handing him a battered beaver hat that lay nearby, Sutherland asked how long he had been up there.

"Too long."

Sutherland said his name was Donoway, and was passing in peace through the Wyandot land, heading for Detroit. The Indian, who had gaunt cheekbones, a hooked nose, and most of his teeth, said he knew the name Donoway. His own name was Ido-lana, and he was hunting with his two grandsons, who were at their camp across the island.

"Maybe," Ido-lana said, "they have looked for me already, but in the wrong places; my grandsons are very young, and it was they who set this trap that caught me." He chuckled and rubbed his leg. "It was a good trap."

Sutherland considered what to do. The old man was barely able to walk, but he had to get back to his grandsons. Furthermore, Sutherland and Ella could not rest easy knowing there was a camp of Wyandot hunters at the other side of the little island. There was no choice but to take the man back to his people.

They found the camp two miles around the island, and the Sutherlands were surprised that the two boys who jumped up in surprise were no older than nine or ten.

A bit frightened to see Sutherland and Ella with their injured grandfather, the boys fingered small bows hanging at their sides. There were no firearms in sight, and it did not take long for Sutherland to learn the tale of these three Wyandots. Sharing a sparse meal of squirrel and parched corn with them, Sutherland was told their village was suffering terribly. Nearly every male old enough to hunt, who had not gone south to be with Pontiac, was ill with smallpox or had died already. In the summer there had been two hundred Wyandots in the village; now there were only ninety. Sitting across the fire from the children Ella saw not only their beautiful, dark eyes, but also the pockmarks on their skin, evidence they had survived the same disease. Unlike their grandfather, whose head was shaved, save for a bristly scalp lock, the boys had long black hair, for they were not yet warriors entitled to shaved heads.

Smearing a salve on his sore leg, old Ido-lana said slowly and with dignity, "It has been many seasons since Ido-lana was a hunter, and this is the first hunting season for my grandsons." He stared at the two boys, who crouched on their heels and gazed back. "Never before has Ido-lana called such young ones companions on the hunt, but times have changed."

The sun was low in the sky now, and the Sutherlands wanted to go back to their own camp. Sutherland saw that Ido-lana was finished talking for the moment. He said, "If Ido-lana will forgive the interruption of his tale, Donoway would ask him and his grandsons back to our fireside. We have food and drink aplenty, and it would do us honor to share it and our fire with you tonight."

Ido-lana looked up, his eyes deep and impenetrable. He said, "It shall be so."

They returned to the Sutherlands' camp, where Ella made a meal that was extravagant compared to most they had eaten on their journey. But this was a special occasion, and she brought out a part of everything they carried, including some butter, maple sugar, and the last of their dried bear meat, which she knew was regarded as a delicacy by Indians. As she roasted the meat over the fire, the two boys stared hungrily. Sutherland ceremoniously shared a pipe with Ido-lana, and gave him a few noggins of rum to ease the pain of his injured leg.

After the meal, which was eaten in silence, and of which not one morsel was left, Ido-lana sat back and smoked another pipe with Owen. Then Sutherland asked, "Will there be more war in the Green Month, brother? It is said the British have two great armies ready to march when the ice leaves the lakes. Will the Wyandot fight?"

After waiting the appropriate ten minutes to answer such a grave question, Ido-lana said slowly, "There will be war as long as the English crave our lands, Donoway, and you know that well." He thought a moment longer. "But I understand your question: Will there be warriors left to fight?" Again he hesitated. "There are a few who will never surrender. But our dead are many, and their bones cannot be covered without numerous presents from the English—presents the English will not give, I think."

He looked at the feeble bow at the side of one of his grandsons. "I tell you, Donoway, this child can use that bow better than I. It was never my weapon, for war or for the hunt. Now, without powder or lead, with no one to repair our guns, we have been forced to return to the bow of my grandfather's father, to the leg-hold snares—and we cannot do it."

He sighed, a hint of his despair, though he did not break down. "We cannot learn old ways fast enough, and we cannot bring back game to feed the village, where there is only food for a week or less. Not one hunting party remains out, for all have failed. Some have starved to death trying to keep their promise to bring back food, and have not been heard from again. It is for us, and for our bows, to save the village."

The Sutherlands were four days from home, and desperate to get back, but when Owen translated for Ella all that Ido-lana had said, both of them knew what must be done.

Owen said to the old man, "If you will do me the honor, brother, I will offer my rifles and my eye, and together we shall teach your grandsons the way of the hunter." Hardly comprehending at first, Ido-lana looked up, unable to speak. Sutherland said, "These islands are rich in game, and we'll bring down enough to feed your people."

chapter 22

SNIFFER

The next day—after Ido-lana prayed—Owen and the Indian, whose sore leg was better, went out to hunt for elk and deer. They were not disappointed, and found plenty of tracks. Sutherland had no time to waste in a prolonged hunt, and he intended to work quickly and depart soon. When Sutherland and Ella were safely on their way, Ido-lana could fetch more people from his village and come for the game, which would be gutted and hung from trees to protect it from scavengers.

Ido-lana's eyes gleamed with anticipation, for he had Sutherland's spare rifle. The two boys carried their bows. They had found the deer yarding in a grove of small firs, and they decided on their strategy: the boys would hike up behind the deer and drive them toward the hunters, who would wait on a rise above a ravine through which Ido-lana predicted the game would flee. The men would open fire as rapidly as possible.

Ella stayed in camp when the men and boys went hunting. She again was glad for Heera's company, and she took advantage of the rest. It surprised her that she sensed no twinge of fear or loneliness as there had been on their first days out. That, she thought, was another small achievement, and it made her happy.

Ella also felt a pleasant kind of poignancy to think of Jeremy, who was now so very close at hand—only a few days away. She wanted her son to know something about the world before he permanently settled down, particularly if he was to stay on the frontier, where formal education was virtually nonexistent.

She wanted him to have the kind of education that would enable him to choose his future; she did not want him ignorant of everything but wilderness living. Ella thought the boy would be best off to return to Britain for his education, with her brother Henry as his guardian. It pained her to think of losing him, but it would be in his best interest. After all, he might come back, and that would be wonderful. It meant much to think of Jeremy coming back out here, where Ella's heart belonged more and more with every passing day. With her and Owen he could help mold the future of the northwest territory, whatever it might be.

That afternoon, the men returned to camp, having brought down five deer and an elk in one onslaught. The two boys were doing their best to haul the carcasses to a new camp they would have to make that night near the kills. Ido-lana went back to help the boys, and the Sutherlands quickly struck their present camp and took the dogs and their gear to the new site.

By the time the sun was down, they had built a large lean-to against a stone windbreak. A fire blazed under roasting venison steaks, and they sat contentedly sipping rum flip, the hunters well pleased with their day's work.

The next day, Ella and Owen went for a walk on a path near the ice. They spoke of leaving in two days, after more hunting. Ido-lana and the boys were happily stringing up the gutted deer, and they planned to start back for the village as soon as they could. Sutherland stopped Ella and said, "Beaver." He saw a half-dozen snowy pyramids, where beaver were lodged.

"Ido-lana could use this catch if we can break into their lodges and clean them out," he said eagerly.

Then there was a strange snuffling sound nearby, and Ella jumped around to see a movement in the brush. Sutherland threw himself between her and the rustling branches, his rifle cocked. He handed her his tomahawk, and she backed away. Carefully, Sutherland used the muzzle of his gun to pry the frozen branches apart. Ella was afraid, ready for a mass of black savagery to fling itself at her husband.

Then Owen leaned forward. The snuffling had become a kind of whimper, and Ella saw him reach into the bushes. In a moment, he held a squeaking, whining baby otter, no more than ten inches long from whiskered snout to pointed tail. It snuffled against his arm for warmth, its enormous, plaintive eyes gazing up at him.

"Barely weaned," he said, grinning, as Ella came to him and touched the helpless thing's smooth body. It sniffed and snuffled at her hand.

"Hey, little sniffer," she said softly. She took the otter from Sutherland and held it close, murmuring as the animal poked up its curious flat nose. Ella cuddled the creature, and Sutherland searched behind the bushes. There he saw the otter's mother, torn to pieces by some vicious animal—a wolverine, no doubt. Blood was everywhere, as were tufts of black fur from the *carcajou*. It had been a savage fight, for no doubt the otter had inflicted serious wounds as it died to protect its young. Badly injured, the wolverine had been too weak to kill this baby otter in Ella's hands.

They returned to camp, and Ella sat near the fire, the trembling baby otter huddled in her arms, afraid of the excited boys who were poking at it out of curiosity.

Ido-lana, seated at the mouth of the lean-to, said something to the boys, and they darted away to get some whitefish from the pot boiling on the fire. Soon the otter was struggling with a piece of fish almost as big as itself, tearing at the flesh with all its might, but not getting much because it was weak and still very young. Ella had another idea, and ladled out some broth from the boiling fish. That was easier for the hungry baby to consume, and it soon lay on its back, bloated, paws up.

Sutherland knelt near Ella. "So, the little sniffer has found a home. These boys will make a good pet out of him; I've seen Indians teach otters to fish and even scare up beaver, who are their natural enemies—"

"Wait," Ella said, loud enough for the otter to take fright and struggle into her arms. "Why don't we—I mean, why don't I keep him . . . her, whatever it is."

Sutherland smiled. "It's a he, and I can see you like him. Listen, otters are smart pets, but they're trouble, always in some sort of mischief."

"Mischief?" Ella cuddled the baby close and kissed it. "He'll be good—won't you, little sniffer? You'll be good, and I know a boy who would like to teach you to be good. Oh, Owen, let's keep him ourselves. He'll be wonderful for Jeremy!"

Sutherland realized he had forgotten he was now the father of a growing boy. Ella was right; Jeremy would have a lot of pleasure with an otter as a pet.

They smiled to see the otter lean over and sniff at a bowl of whitefish stew Sutherland had brought for himself and laid on the ground near where Ella sat. The otter was more curious than hungry, so Sutherland dipped his finger in the broth and let the baby lick it off. A moment later, it was lapping the stew, forefeet on Ella's leg, its snout in the broth. More often than not, it got more broth up its whiskery nose than down its gullet, and it kept snorting and sniffing to blow the liquid back out its nose.

"He's a real little sniffer, isn't he?" Sutherland said absently. "Now, that's a good name: Little Sniffer!"

Little Sniffer looked up, his shining eyes seeming to adore Owen. Then he sneezed and sniffed again. Ella laughed and dragged him away from the food, smiling contentedly as she held the otter in her arms.

"Sniffer," she said, and the trusting baby lay on his back once more, legs apart. Sniffer soon was asleep in Ella's arms, and she thought it amusing to feel already so much like a new mother. How would Owen feel when he knew about the baby? She had not told him because of all the activity and excitement since they had met the Wyandots. She could wait no longer.

Setting Sniffer down on her blanket, Ella said to Owen, who was stirring up another bowl of stew, "Walk with me, husband. I have to tell you something."

He looked directly at her, trying to fathom what he could from her face. Ella saw his own expression change and become thoughtful.

Then she was up, lacing on her snowshoes, and he did the same, without speaking. In a few minutes they were sitting on a log, looking out at Lake Erie and the distant islands. They leaned against one another, and Ella sighed, searching for the right words. She put her head on his shoulder, and his arm went around her back.

Before she knew it, Owen's cold hand was inside her coat, inside her shirt, and touching her slightly swollen middle. She held the hand against her, and they looked at one another. Ella felt tears of happiness, unexpected and welcome. He kissed her softly and put his other hand behind her head, tangling his fingers in her hair and bringing her close to him.

Ella whispered, "I've known about our child for some time,

darling, but I didn't tell you, because I was afraid it would make your decision to go back too difficult." She looked at him, questioning. He smiled and kissed her again, lightly, without speaking.

She said, "I'm four months or so with child, and I feel good, strong. I knew I could make this journey, but I thought you might not agree, and you would have left me behind, or—"

His kiss silenced Ella, and she drew him against her, still not knowing what he was thinking, but aware that he was happy.

After a while, he said, "I would not have taken you with me—you were right. Perhaps I would have stayed in Philadelphia, but I think not. But I'm grateful you've done it this way—for we're nearly home. At first I didn't think you could do all you've done. No man could ask for more from his woman than you've given me, Ella. And now, this. We're blessed."

Ella kissed him, and they stayed together until the sun was high, and it was already late for Owen and Ido-lana to continue hunting.

For the rest of that day, as Sutherland hunted with Ido-lana, the ideas and snatches of a poem worked through his mind, though he could not write them down. By nightfall, the hearts of verses had taken form, and when he returned to Fort Detroit they would be put on paper in this way:

With Child

To my woman who's with child I send the sun
To keep her woman's soul and light aglow,
And in her deepest thoughts she'll feel the love
And life within her heart
That helps the other soul inside her grow.

To all women who are with child I touch the earth
And feel it touching me in sharing life:
Bringing us together under wind
And blessed rain,
Compelling us to stand and giving life.

And to my woman's child I send my fire
Of hope and living joy and joyous giving,
The fire that glows inside us, every one,
And kindles in the heart,
Flaring, blazing, with the joy of living.

Sitting outside his lodge on the bank of the Maumee River, Jacques Levesque heard the distant screech of Chief Pontiac in a rage. He looked up from polishing his rifle, took the pipe from his mouth, and listened. He heard the name Little Eagle— his friend Tremblay—shouted loudly. He went to investigate and found a group of curious onlookers standing before the chief's dwelling. Pontiac's face was contorted with fury, and nearby, huddled against Tremblay's leg, young Sally quaked in fear.

Sally's dress was smeared with excrement, and Levesque realized the sick child had once again fouled the war chief's lodge. Never before had Levesque seen Pontiac in such a wild temper. His fists shook as he shouted at the girl and then at Tremblay, who seemed in a trance. Finally, to Levesque's shock, Pontiac grabbed the howling child away from Tremblay and stamped down to the water's edge. Sally gave a shriek of terror as the chief cast her into the icy water. Tremblay and Levesque dashed for her, but Pontiac roared at them to stop.

Levesque hesitated and gaped at the chief. Tremblay also stopped, and he appealed to Pontiac for mercy. The child was standing in freezing water to her waist, shivering and soaked.

Pontiac glared at both Frenchmen and said to Tremblay, "Little Eagle, drown her!"

Tremblay reeled. "She is but a child—"

"Drown her!" Pontiac roared and put his hand to his scalping knife. "Or you shall die with her."

His hard face immovable, Pontiac stared at Tremblay. The shoreline was crowded with Indians. Some thought this a hideous act, but others cared nothing about an English child and were amused by the scene.

Levesque could hear Sally's teeth chattering. He knew this atrocity must not happen. Tremblay, his face pale, raised his hands in appeal, but Pontiac snatched out his knife, and three other warriors appeared around the Frenchman, all holding tomahawks.

"Now, Little Eagle!" Pontiac commanded. "Prove your

courage as a warrior! Prove you have the strength to drown her, or *you* shall die!"

Levesque was armed with only a tomahawk, and Tremblay only a knife. Between them they could not defend Sally for long. Then, to Levesque's horror, Tremblay walked slowly, stiffly down to the water, gazing ahead like a blind man, not seeing Sally.

The child began to wade to her friend, but then she saw something in him, and she backed away. Blue with the cold, she struggled aside, but Tremblay caught her and lifted her close to him. Levesque, unable to move, saw Tremblay talking to Sally, soothing her, stroking her long hair. The girl was trembling, but then she began to calm down. She put both arms about Tremblay's neck.

He submerged her suddenly. All Levesque could see were her feet kicking, kicking helplessly. She thrashed, but Tremblay held her under, and as he did so, he emitted a long wailing howl of anguish that was taken up by the squaws, many of whom covered their faces and turned away.

"No!" Levesque cried out and ran toward the river. A big Indian stepped in his way, tomahawk raised. Levesque felled him with a savage punch to the throat. Another Indian leaped into his path, but went down the same way, choking and coughing.

Levesque leaped at Tremblay and knocked him aside, grappling for the child, who was no longer kicking. Tremblay wrenched himself away, covering his face and weeping. Levesque threw the girl's limp body over his shoulder and turned to face another warrior splashing toward him, tomahawk lifted. In a flash, Levesque's own tomahawk was out, its blade aimed at the surprised warrior, who stopped short.

Brandishing the tomahawk, his face streaming with water, Levesque moved past the man and up onto the beach. He glared at Pontiac and said, "If you will not keep her, then she is mine."

Four other Ottawa were moving to the chief's side, ready to spring. Tremblay stood helplessly in the river. Levesque, his tomahawk ready for blood, strode up the beach. He knew Pontiac would not accept such humiliation, and was aware he was a dead man if he stayed in this camp, but for the moment he counted on enough people in the village disliking Pontiac's murderous intentions.

As Levesque carried the girl to his lodge, he saw the four warriors near Pontiac make their move. He spun, and the water soaking him and the girl sprayed as he confronted the fighters. They came in, and the people on the beach tensed. Levesque had not a chance. He laid Sally at his feet. The men were circling him.

"Enough!" someone shouted.

The warriors hesitated as out of the crowd stepped the Delaware Niko-lota, hand on his scalping knife. Behind him came his two cousins, both as angry as their leader. Things had changed, for Niko-lota was well known as a fighter, as was Levesque. Also, Pontiac risked a feud breaking out between the tribes, and that would mean the end of his uprising.

Niko-lota said, "I have killed many whites—yes, their children, too—in the madness of battle." His face was sad. "But I am not in battle-madness, and there is no need for this child to die. And it is not right that my brother Levesque should die. I will not let him be killed, Pontiac. Nor will my Delaware."

In a heavy silence, Pontiac and Niko-lota stared angrily at one another. This was not the first time Pontiac had been challenged by another leader during the war. There were those who thought his strategy against Detroit had been faulty, and his ability to make medicine was in doubt. And tribal differences had created conflict within the Indian forces. Pontiac intended to lead his Ottawa and their allies out against the English in the spring, but he knew that would not happen if serious fighting erupted between his people and the Delaware.

Pontiac called his men back. "It is enough!" he said. "Let us not fight among ourselves over an English dog. Levesque, if she lives, bring her back to my lodge, and you will not be harmed. Do this tonight—if she lives."

The chief spun and strode back to his hut, and his warriors reluctantly did the same. Wasting no more time, Levesque dashed to the warmth of his own lodge, where he stripped the wet clothes from the unconscious child and wrapped her in blankets. She was pale, her lips blue. There was a suggestion of breathing, but not much. Levesque was alone in the lodge, for no squaws dared hazard Pontiac's fury. He toiled over Sally, rubbing her hands, massaging her chest. He did not think she had swallowed much water, but rather was stunned by cold and fear.

Levesque built up the fire, heated water and a little brandy, and forced some of the liquid into her mouth. He thought so much of the child that he ignored his own condition, and left on his wet clothes. The brandy trickled through her lips, and soon they were not so blue. Her breathing became a bit deeper. She coughed once, then lay back, color coming into her face. Finally she seemed to be sleeping.

Levesque let himself go, and slumped near the fire, closing his eyes and thinking what he must do next. Pontiac wanted the child back, for she was his slave. But the girl was doomed if Levesque returned her to him. If he did not, Levesque was doomed.

Later, Tremblay came in, his clothes wet and half-frozen, matching Tremblay's bedraggled, shamed countenance. Saying nothing to Levesque, he knelt at the child's side and put his quaking hand on her forehead. She stirred in her sleep and reached up to take his hand, holding it tightly with both her own. At this, Tremblay broke down and wept bitterly.

By now, Levesque had made up his mind. He changed clothes and hurriedly assembled his gear. Taking what food he could find, he prepared to flee, intending to get Sally to safety. Tremblay looked up, his eyes full of tears, and he was not surprised to see Levesque preparing to leave.

"Where will you go, brother?" he asked.

"I do not know." Levesque had warm clothing, food, rifle, ammunition, and a pair of snowshoes at hand. He began to dress Sally as warmly as possible, hoping she would not awake before they fled at sundown.

Tremblay hesitated, then went to his own bedding and dug through his possessions. When Levesque had the child wrapped warmly and had slung rope and a blanket around her so she could be carried hanging at his chest, Tremblay came back. Holding the rosewood music box out to his friend, Tremblay said, "For better times, brother."

Levesque looked at him, but said nothing. Then he took the box and tucked it into Sally's clothing. It was growing dark outside, but still the dwellers in this lodge had not come back to make their dinner, fearing Pontiac might come for the child and see them helping Levesque. Burdened with Sally and his gear, Levesque would need a good head start if Pontiac sent men after him. He planned to run all night by the light of a quarter-moon and the stars. Then he would run all day if he had to.

Tremblay came to him suddenly, his eyes aglow. "I have a plan, brother." He snatched up his own blanket coat and snowshoes. "I will go in another direction. They will not know which is I and which is you and the child."

They shook hands, and Tremblay hugged Levesque. Then he kissed the sleeping Sally again, fighting back tears. But when Tremblay looked up, it seemed there was new hope in him, new strength born of this determination to help his friends escape.

They went quickly out of the lodge, then slipped through the gloaming until they came to the edge of the woods. Tremblay would cut south—perhaps, he said, he would keep going all the way to New Orleans. Like Levesque, he had no love for making war on children, and he had sickened of this uprising. Levesque would head northeast for Detroit.

"God go with you, Levesque," the young fellow said desperately. "I'm not the man you are!"

Levesque slapped him on the shoulder, saying, "And with you, my friend. May we meet again—in better times!"

Then they parted, Levesque dashing along an old hunting trail he knew so well that even gathering darkness could not hinder him. The child was cumbersome, but Levesque was a *voyageur,* and strong; he could trot like this for days with little rest if he had to. He only hoped he would not have to. However, Pontiac was not one to be treated so scornfully without a fight, and there were many Ottawa who would take what Levesque had done as an insult to their whole tribe. No man stole away an Indian's prisoner. As he ran, settling into a steady dogtrot that consumed mile after mile of snowpacked trail, Levesque knew in his bones he would be pursued until they caught him or he killed his hunters.

Ella and Owen Sutherland sat in camp after a good dinner. In the lean-to, the Wyandot boys were fast asleep, with Sniffer snuggled between them, each filled with beaver tail and stew— a stew like none of the Indians had ever tasted before, because Ella had cooked it to perfection. Owen puffed on a pipe, thinking as he gazed up at the starry sky. Ella, however, felt uneasy, because Ido-lana was peering at her as though trying to puzzle something out.

Finally, Ella could stand it no longer, and she asked her

husband why the old man stared at her so. Sutherland said, "He has never met a squaw like you before."

Ella was somewhat flattered, and she pressed. "What do you mean?"

Sutherland puffed and said, "He is amazed that Donoway would have a squaw who does not clean his beaver pelts for him."

Ella sat up, the shawl falling from her shoulders. She glanced at a dozen big gutted beavers suspended from trees at the edge of camp. Ido-lana had caught them; he had given the skins as gifts to Sutherland, but wanted the meat for himself and his village. Again she looked at the old warrior, who was still scrutinizing her with profound interest. Ella was troubled. In this moment all the sureness and confidence born of what she had accomplished in the wilderness vanished, and she was helpless, alone.

She lay back and looked up at the balsam roof of the lean-to, then closed her eyes. A vision came to her, one of arms streaming with blood and filth, and of a dozen pelts to be cleaned, scraped, stretched, and dried. It would take hours to prepare so many pelts—long hours and sickening work. Ella had cleaned rabbits before, but never beaver. Yet something inside her insisted she must do it. Then another voice said she was no squaw, for better or for worse—she was merely a white woman, inexperienced and squeamish!

Ella tried to sleep, but when she did, it was a restless sleep consumed by dreams of beaver pelts, beaver blood, beaver hats. As dawn touched the sky, she lay awake, listening to Sniffer clinking around the forks and spoons and turning over the empty broth bowl he had used the night before. She sat up, looking for the otter, but her eyes went directly to the frozen beavers. Owen stirred, then got up to stoke the morning's fire. The boys tried to sleep late, but Ido-lana soon wrestled them out of their blankets, telling them to fetch some snow for melting down into drinking water.

Ella had no desire to make breakfast that morning, so she let Owen prepare the batter for johnnycake, and she busied herself repairing a broken thong on his snowshoe. Again she sensed Ido-lana's curious gaze on her. She knew it might be only her imagination, but every time the Indian looked at her, Ella felt accused of inadequacy.

After a little while, she could stand it no longer. She grumbled a faint "All right, I'll do it!" then rose and stamped toward the beavers.

Ella struggled with the first carcass, which was stiff from the cold and weighed at least thirty pounds. She tried to undo the rope, but it was frozen as well, and she could not get it free. Then Owen was at her side, his hand on her arm. She looked up into his sympathetic eyes and felt a flood of relief, sure that after all he would not let her do this.

"Let me help you get them down," he said. "Have breakfast, and these will thaw by the fire so you can skin them easier."

Without meeting her astonished eyes, Sutherland took down the carcasses and set them one by one near the fire to thaw. Before long, Ella was drinking hot tea and staring at the mass of blackish brown fur near the blazing fire. It was as though she had fallen into a very deep hole—one that would take all her strength to escape.

After an hour of toil she freed the first skin from the beaver flesh. Uncomplaining, Ella was struggling at her task when Owen and Ido-lana left to hunt more deer. The boys stayed behind, for they were too tired to hunt. Sitting with Sniffer in the lean-to, the youngsters lorded over this white woman just as Indian braves lorded over their own squaws and sisters. Ella cleaned and scraped the first skin, then stretched it on a large hoop of willow, and hung it at the back of the lean-to to cure, just the proper distance from the fire. She was surprised that this work took so long and was so exhausting. Surely Owen would come back soon and tell her to stop because she was pregnant.

But he did not come back early, as she had hoped. By late afternoon, eight beaver skins were hanging in the lean-to, and Ella's hands were so bloody and dirty, fingernails broken and grimy, that she wondered whether they would ever be pretty again. On she worked until she realized with shock that she had not prepared a meal. She tried telling the boys what to do, but they did not—or would not—understand, preferring to play with some sticks at a gambling game. But Ella was angry now. With a clap of her hands, she got their attention. Then she picked up a stick and wagged it, insisting they collect firewood. She tossed the empty bucket at the boys and said to get snow for more water. Surprised, and a little haughty at first, the boys looked in question at one another. But when Ella rapped one of them on the leg with the stick, they got the idea and jumped up to do what she wanted.

She swiftly tossed chunks of meat and vegetables into a pot of water to boil, set a second pot on for tea water, then went back to her fatiguing chore. These final four skins came off fairly quickly, and she fancied she had learned something and was capable of preparing a beaver pelt in one tenth the time it took her to do the first one.

Finally, as night was coming on, she hung up the last hooped pelt, and stepped back to admire her work and to rub her sore legs. Her entire body ached from the labor, but it was done! She could hardly believe it herself. In a moment of self-satisfaction, she thought about what Owen had said yesterday—that she was everything a man could ask. Trying not to be proud, Ella had to admit that she had done more than even she had ever expected.

As she stood admiring the pelts, she heard the barking of sled dogs. The weary hunters came back, trudging alongside a sled laden with deer carcasses. In the front was old Ido-lana, happy as a young boy, who waved his rifle in the air and fired it for delight as they came in. The boys ran to their grandfather, and Ella stood watching, bloody hands on her hips. Yes, she was proud; she was satisfied! These last days had been worth much to her. She saw Owen, his face alight as he led the dogs to their place and released the traces from the sled.

He turned to Ella and untied his snowshoes as he called out, "We've done it! There's enough meat in here now for two villages!" Panting and exhausted, he came to her and she held out her hands for him, but he stopped short when he saw the caked blood and dirty fingernails. Surprised, he said, "Just what—How many did you do?"

Ella showed him the twelve skins drying in the rear of the lean-to. He stood there, a grin on his face, beaming with pride. "Remarkable, lass," he said. "Aye. Remarkable!"

Ella felt a chill, and her body released an involuntary shaking sigh, yet she did not want to show how exhausted she was. With a greasy hand she wiped sweat away from her face. She did not care about the filth anymore. It was accomplished. Her arms were so tired that they trembled as she filled another bucket with snow for her wash water. Out of the corner of her eye she saw Ido-lana next to Owen, examining the work of the white squaw. Even he seemed impressed, and that pleased Ella very much.

She lugged the bucket to the fire and laid it on hot stones to melt the snow. The pot of water for tea was already boiling, and the stew was bubbling and smelled delicious. Ella had come through a great and difficult struggle; truly she had mastered the final challenge.

As she watched the snow slowly melt in the bucket, Ella was content. Absently, she added tea leaves to an empty kettle. The fire crackled, the snow gradually became cold water, and the stew simmered cozily. Everything was just right with Ella Sutherland's world. Moreover, they were leaving for home tomorrow.

Owen came to her side and slumped down wearily on the blanket. Again he said, "Remarkable, Ella."

A little smugly, she said, "Remarkable for a white woman, you mean?"

He lay back, saying, "No, remarkable for anyone."

There was a pause. She could not help herself, and said carefully, "Anyone? Mayla must have been very good at preparing pelts."

Sutherland yawned and replied, "Mayla? She hated to do it. She was always too proud of her pretty hands. No, as far as I can recall she never did clean pelts. Too clumsy at it."

Sutherland heard Ella catch her breath. He spoke her name, but she did not reply. He leaned up on his elbows, realizing what had driven her to accomplish all this. "Ella? Lass?" No reply. He tried to find the right thing to say, but all that came out was "Ella?"

She turned to look at him, but what he saw was not the frustration and contained fury he had expected. Rather, Ella had a bemused look, a look of one who had been foolish, and knew it.

With a sparkle in her eye she bit her lower lip and said, "Husband, I'll get even with you for this."

He tried to smile, but did not know what to think. Then he wanted to laugh, but restrained himself. However, he knew Ella was angry, because she used not only the pot of warm wash water but also the entire kettle of boiling tea water for washing up, and took more than an hour before she served herself a bowl of stew. Served herself, no one else.

chapter **23**

A DANCE AND A SONG

Jacques Levesque was exhausted but not defeated. He had been running for days, taking no more than an hour's rest from time to time. Pontiac's men were after him. He had seen them in the distance from the top of a high ridge . . . how long ago? He could not remember.

Sally was stronger now, though he still carried her in the sling across his chest. By eating very little she had recovered somewhat from her dysentery, but like Levesque she was very hungry. Their food was almost gone, and they seldom ate. Now and again he would find some evergreen cones to munch on, bitter and harsh, but better than nothing. He offered the child what little pemmican and parched corn remained. She was old enough, however, to realize he was giving up his own nourishment, and she refused his morsels, insisting he eat them himself—it was Jacques who must keep up his strength. She was right, and he ate.

One day he had shot a stringy old snowy owl, and they ate it half-raw, for they dared not linger over a cooking fire. On and on they pressed, and this afternoon he estimated they were fifty miles southwest of Detroit, where he would leave her. He did not know what would happen next, but he did know Angélique had been right. This war had nearly destroyed him, as it had come so close to destroying his friend Tremblay. Levesque knew if he had let the girl be drowned, he could never have abandoned the war trail. He could never again have looked Angélique in the eyes. His heart surged as he thought how near he was to her.

His snowshoes felt like lead, his legs had no feeling at all. The winter cold bit at him but on he ran. Pontiac's warriors could move fast, not being encumbered with a child; Levesque was certain Pontiac wanted him killed.

Levesque trotted along the trail, his eyes suffering from the start of snow blindness, but he could distinguish the soft face of Sally before him. He thought of how she had lost so much, had suffered so much, yet had done nothing to harm anyone. He felt a stabbing remorse for all the evil that had been done in the name of justice. It was not the open warfare that sickened him; he could stand the blood and human sacrifice. It was the mode of war, the ruthless slaughter on both sides. No man was better at war in the wilderness than Jacques Levesque. Perhaps that was why he was finished with it—he knew it only too well; he understood precisely what it was, and he no longer wanted any part of it. Somehow, saving this child would atone for some of the hurt he had done in his life. If only he succeeded—if only he could get her safely back to her own people.

He plodded along the shore of a frozen lake, his lungs aching, throat raw. As he ran, he glanced back from time to time. He would have preferred the shelter of the woods, but no trail was cut there, and the ground sloped too steeply. Right now Levesque needed to make time, to cover ground. They would follow his tracks with ease unless it snowed, so it was better to move quickly rather than to try concealing himself as he ran.

New snow was what he needed. A good hard blowing snow that would obliterate his tracks. If he was far enough ahead of his hunters when a storm hit, it would take them days to find his prints, and he would be gone by then.

Clouds hung in the northwest, but above him the sky was blue. Maybe tonight, maybe tomorrow, they would bring snow. Levesque wished they would move, but they lay dormant and gray on the horizon above the far end of the lake.

Then he hesitated. There was something back there, not more than a thousand yards away. He stopped and peered back, but the sun flashing on the snow hurt his weary eyes. He shaded his face and looked closer. Yes, it was movement. Deer, or elk? Maybe a bear shambling along the trail?

No. It was a man! Then another, and two more. They were close enough now to catch him if he dared rest for even a moment. He began to run again, and Sally stirred, her every movement an extra strain on him, but he did not complain.

She sang softly as he ran, his eyes half-closed, thin gauze shielding his face from the painful whiteness tormenting him. He ran and ran. Sally stopped singing, and then Levesque heard the sparkling music box, playing a song about a silly duck and a ball that keeps on rolling. He could not help laughing to hear it again, for he was a *voyageur*, and this song gave him strength.

Before Sutherland and Ella departed from the Wyandots, Ido-lana invited Owen to smoke with him. Ella sat waiting near Heera, who was tethered in the traces with his mates. The two boys stared as their grandfather reached with great solemnity into the small medicine pouch and drew out a beautiful red-stone pipe, inlaid with silver. These pipes were precious to their owners, who had traded away much to get them from the tribes of the west, where red stone was turned into pipes of such wonderful craftsmanship. Sutherland watched the old man ceremoniously fill the pipe with the last of his *kinnikinnick*— tobacco mixed with herbs—and realized Ido-lana had kept back this special pipe until the important moment of leave-taking. It was an honor to be asked to share this smoke.

No wonder Ido-lana was pleased with Sutherland, for together they had killed twenty deer, three elk, and much beaver. Sutherland had given his extra rifle to Ido-lana, asking first that it never be used to kill a man except in self-defense. The Wyandot also had been given a supply of lead and powder that would last through many hunts.

Before lighting the pipe, Ido-lana made an offering to the four winds, standing and holding out the pipe to each one. When he gestured to the north wind, Ella felt a chill, sensing the breeze strengthen. Wisps of snow blew across their clearing; the sky was darkening. A storm was on its way. Owen had said they were seven hours from a landfall at the western end of the lake. There were a few small islands in between; if a storm broke, they could put in at one and sit it out. They were anxious to get home, willing to risk the weather to do it.

Ido-lana and Sutherland smoked in silence until the *kinni-kinnick* was finished. Then the Indian said, "Come back to us, brother Donoway; in the days to come there may be peace between your people and mine. Then we will come back to this island by canoe and hunt the beaver together."

Sutherland shook hands with Ido-lana and the boys, then

tucked Ella and the baby otter into the sled. He climbed on the back and said to the Wyandots, "May your hunting be good, old one; and may your grandsons grow as strong and as wise as their grandfather."

A little while later, they were being whisked across the ice by eager dogs, who were strong and excited to be back at work. Shooting like an arrow through a world of gray and white, the Sutherlands at last were on their way home. Sniffer pressed against Ella and snuggled beneath the bearskin. Sutherland mushed the dogs across the crusted snow, heading northwest, toward Detroit, where the Frontier Company would soon take its first bold step.

Whenever Jacques Levesque reached the crest of a ridge, he looked back to locate his pursuers. Whether he saw them or not, he made sure he was never outlined against the lowering sky, always slipping over the ridge by passing through trees or behind rocks. The country was a mixture of forest and open meadow rising up to stony hilltops that separated ponds and lakes. As he ran, Levesque longed to sleep. Food and drink were beyond comprehension. Sleep was what he needed.

Little Sally mercifully slept. She had not once complained about hunger or weariness, and Levesque loved her as he would his own child. On he ran, and ran and ran and ran. He picked his way between boulders or through blow-downs of trees, lifting his cramped legs with the utmost pain. Flopping along, his *racquets*—as the French named snowshoes—spilled little clouds of powdery snow with every step. He had seen Pontiac's men more than once, and they him. There were four of them, and he knew they were using the timeworn Indian technique of running down quarry: one man would sprint ahead on his snowshoes, forcing the prey to sprint also and use up much strength. Then the next man would take the place of the exhausted first one, then the next, driving Levesque to the outer limits of fatigue.

The warriors had closed the gap from a thousand yards to five hundred. Levesque was a strong man, but there was little left in him. Having reached the western shore of Lake Erie, he turned northward, estimating he was still two days from Detroit. Though he could not be sure, he thought it was late in the afternoon. There was no sun, and that soothed his scalded eyes, but it took a supreme effort to see at all. He managed to hold on to his rifle, but everything else he had cast aside. They had no more food, and the only article of excess baggage was Sally's music box.

He fought his way up a rocky, snow-swept hillside, then stopped to rest. Looking down along a streambed that ran away into the forest, Levesque breathed heavily, the cold air burning his throat and lungs. But before he had caught his breath he saw the first runner break out of the trees, no more than a hundred yards behind. This man was obviously exhausted, for he ran with his head down, eyes on Levesque's trail.

Struggling to move with sleeping Sally before him, Levesque took shelter behind some rocks. The other Indians must be at least a hundred yards behind this one. He recognized the pursuer as one of Pontiac's best fighters, a seasoned man who would not give up until the bitter end. Well, Levesque thought, this was the end for him.

Levesque put Sally down, and she awoke with a start. He clapped a hand over her mouth and told her to be silent. By the time he leaned against a large boulder and brought the rifle to bear on his enemy, Levesque had recovered his breath. The man was trudging painfully up the slope, so close that Levesque could hear him rasping for air. The Frenchman drew a careful bead. The warrior was as good as dead.

Then Levesque thought of something. It was a gamble, but if it succeeded, he would gain three or four hundred yards on the other pursuers. It was worth the chance.

The warrior was seventy-five yards away and struggling up the steep hillside, slipping with weariness, even though his snowshoes should have held him. Levesque found a strong pole from a deadfall and jammed it under the massive boulder, wedging it and levering just enough to free the rock from frozen ground. The stone gave. The warrior was fifty yards away. Levesque heaved down on the pole with all his might.

The rock moved forward. Levesque grunted and summoned the strength to heave it lumbering down the slope. Startled, the Indian stopped short. The boulder bounced right at him, setting off an avalanche that grumbled, then roared downhill. He cried out, staggering backward, and fell just as he was swallowed up in snowy rubble.

Without looking back, Levesque turned to Sally, who huddled in fright, hands covering her face. He lifted her up, hung the blanket sling across his back, where it had worn painful burns on his skin, and hurried over the top of the hill. By the time the other Ottawa dug out their companion and found Levesque's trail, he would be well ahead of them. Down the other side he ran, picking up too much speed, trying to control himself, but the force of his stumbling broke a strap on his snowshoe, and he pitched forward, wrenching his body to the side to avoid falling on Sally. As he fell, he cracked his skull on a rock and passed out.

Sally struggled free of her sling and tried to revive him. Wiping his face with snow, she called to him, but it was no use. The icy wind whipped through her, and she felt cold, exhausted, and hungry. She knelt at his side, seeing the bluish welt on his forehead, praying that he would waken before the other Indians came upon them.

She looked around for a hiding place. They were on a rise that looked eastward over the flat lake. Struggling with all her strength to move the unconscious man, she dragged him behind some bushes, then went back for his rifle. As she dropped to Levesque's side and tried again to revive him, she heard the howl of a wolf. Shivers went up her spine, and she tried not to tremble. Please wake up! she pleaded silently. An answering howl sounded off to her left, much closer. Then the first wolf cried again, and Sally knew these were no wolves. Too often she had heard the young braves practice animal signals.

Sally waited helplessly, and time seemed to drag on, though only a moment or two passed. Then she saw two men at the crest of the ridge they had crossed. They moved down slowly, following Levesque's footprints. A third Indian joined them, and they came on, walking cautiously until they were only fifty yards from where she hid.

Levesque stirred. Sally whispered to him, and his eyes fluttered, but he was still stunned. Sally shook him. He tried to awaken; however, his mind was blurred. It was as though he knew what was happening but could not get back to defend them. Sally saw the Indians drifting ever closer, separated now, for they sensed their quarry was close. The three braves all carried muskets, and from where Sally hid, she could see their faces drawn with exhaustion, their dark eyes filled with pain.

Levesque gasped, and one of the braves heard it, turning quickly, crouching, his musket ready. The others began to circle, careful and alert. Levesque rolled onto his side, and Sally knew the Indians had heard even that faint sound. The wind whipped up snow in front of the warriors, and each lifted a hand to protect his face. Closer and closer they came. By now they had seen that Levesque had fallen. They sensed they had what they were after, but they were suspicious.

Her heart thundering, Sally shook with terror. In her young mind came the awful visions of the raid on her family farm, the cruel torture, the horror. She recalled madness in the eyes of the warriors, and recognized that same cruelty in the faces of these three men coming for her. She could bear it no longer. She would not let them do it again! Sally dragged the rifle from Levesque's side, struggling with its weight, trying to remember what her brothers had taught her—she rested its muzzle against a rock; used all her strength to pull back the hammer; attempted to aim it at the first warrior, who was only twenty yards away.

The hammer came down, the pan flashed, the gun banged, and Sally was knocked backward with the recoil. Fear and gunsmoke, the whistling wind and bitter cold—all a turmoil in the terrified girl's mind, and she shook uncontrollably. She whined and fought to her feet, trying to drag Levesque's tomahawk from his belt. She got it free, expecting the warriors to be upon her any second.

A powerful hand ripped the tomahawk away, and she screamed. It was Levesque. He pushed her to the ground and rapidly reloaded his rifle. When he looked out from their cover, he saw no one.

The clearing on the slope was empty of life, save for the wind blowing snow in clouds that swirled and danced madly. Silence. Sally regained her composure and huddled against a rock. Levesque was watching every sign of movement. He was still groggy, but he was ready now. Peering out at the clearing, he thought he saw bloodstains on the snow as Sally whispered what she had done. Though Levesque thought she had wounded one of them, he could not be sure.

He did know they were being circled. Sally had found a shelter that was protected from the clearing in front, but up behind was a cliff where a marksman could climb and shoot down on them. Just as he told the girl to take cover farther back among the rocks and bushes, he saw something move up above. He brought up his rifle, saw the movement again, and fired.

The bullet ricocheted off a rock; the movement was gone, but he thought he had missed. Soon they were forted up where

their attackers could not get at them without coming through
a tangle of boulders and fallen wood. Between these obstructions was deep snow that would suck a man up to his waist if
he stepped down from the rocks or logs. Coming at them, an
Indian would be exposed on the rubble and logs.

As the sky darkened, the bitter cold filtered into their bones.
It penetrated their hiding place, but they could not build a fire;
its light would make them easy targets. Their hunters could
make a fire if they chose, and wait until dark to slip closer.
There were at least two and perhaps three of them out there.

Night fell within half an hour. The wind picked up, and on
it Levesque smelled woodsmoke. The Indians were getting
warm before they struck. It was almost full dark under a cloudy
sky when Levesque heard something close by. Sally heard it
also, and she sat in silence, fear in her eyes.

The Frenchman clicked back the hammer of his rifle and
stared into the dimness. He saw a shadow move, but it was
gone before he had a chance to fire at it. Silence but for the
wind. The hair on Levesque's neck bristled. He could also
smell his enemies, they were so close. He knew they could
smell him, too.

Listening, he waited for them to jump over the rocks. He
could not shoot both of them—or three, if Sally's shot had not
taken one out. He lay back, his rifle pointed from the hip at
the top of a black mass of stone, which the Indians would have
to cross to get at him. Sally lay off to one side, in case the
Indians fired blindly at Levesque. Silence. A creak in the snow
in front of him. The wind. Whispering? Or just the wind? The
snow creaked again, this time to his right. He faced that way,
tense and ready. Then something scraped on wood at his left.
He could not cover both approaches.

Metal clicked on stone. Was a musket being leveled at him
from the darkness? He peered at shadows. They all seemed to
move. Another sound behind and above on the overhanging
cliff, but from there no one could aim down to fire at him.
Yes, there was someone above, because a sprinkling of snow
fell down. However, above was not where danger lay; it was
in front, where at least two Indians were coming in.

A terrible yell rang out on his right. He swung the rifle, but
held his fire. Sally gasped. Silence. They wanted him to fire
and reveal where he lay. No doubt they were ready to blast
away at the flash of his weapon. His hands sweating, the chill

penetrating his back and legs where he leaned against snow and stone, Levesque kept himself under control.

Another hideous shriek on the right. A click of metal on the left. A shadow on the left. Levesque fired at it. A man screamed in pain. Quick movement on the right, more felt than seen. Another rifle banged, echoing in the stones. Again a scream. Levesque thought he must have been wounded. But he was unhurt. He moved away to another spot to reload, watching the dark line between shadows and sky. Snow fell down from the movement of the one above. Levesque was loaded again. He heard someone up on the rocks making his way down, coming closer. He anticipated a leap and a swinging tomahawk. But what would happen from the front?

Silence. He was ready. He would shoot the first attacker, then go after the other with his knife and tomahawk. A rock clattered down and fell at his feet. The man above would get it first. Levesque trained the rifle on the spot where the man's head would appear from behind the boulders.

Silence again.

Only the wind and Sally's desperate breathing. It was very dark now, and Levesque was numb with cold. He knew Sally was, also, and longed to help her, but he had to keep still. Any movement could attract a well-aimed bullet.

Silence. The wind.

"You there!"

The voice echoed around the boulders, and Levesque jumped involuntarily.

"You there! Who are you?"

Levesque knew that voice! But who was it? "I am called Levesque! And you?"

"Jacques! Jacques Levesque! It's me, Sutherland!"

"Sutherland!"

"Aye! I'm coming in. Don't shoot!"

"Watch the Ottawa!"

"They're finished, all three of them! Don't shoot."

In a moment, Sutherland clambered into Levesque's hiding place. Astonished, the Frenchman was told that Sutherland had seen the fight begin before dark. He was attracted by Sally's shot, but did not know who was fighting whom at first.

"I didn't want to shoot the wrong people," he said. In the darkness, they could just make one another out as he explained that he had been the one above on the cliff and had seen the two warriors moving in. He had taken a position above Levesque—though he knew only that it was a white man and girl under attack—and waited for a target. It had been Sutherland's shot Levesque heard after his own, and it had killed a warrior about to fire from the Frenchman's right. Levesque's bullet had killed the other Indian, and Sally's desperate shot had done for the first.

As they made their way through the darkness to where Ella waited in fear at the sled, Sutherland carried the girl, and explained that Levesque had nearly hit him when he fired up at the cliff earlier on.

"Right then I wasn't sure who I should help," Sutherland joked, and Levesque gave a little chuckle. The Scotsman saw how exhausted these two were, and with Ella at hand, they made a cozy, sheltered camp, fed them, and tended to Levesque's head injury. Within an hour, the girl and the Frenchman were fast asleep, and they stayed that way well into the following afternoon.

Darkness was returning when Levesque sat up painfully and stiffly, unsure at first where he was. Before long, he was eating again, regaining his strength. Sutherland told the Frenchman he had buried the three dead Ottawa and covered them with stones to keep away animals.

"They're my brothers . . . in time of peace," he said sadly. Then Levesque said a fourth lay buried on the far slope.

When Sally awoke, she was quiet but calm. Ella warmed to the child, and Sniffer soon got a laugh from her by lying on his back and flipping up the little music box on his short legs. When Sally opened the lid, Sniffer lay on his stomach, staring with his head cocked and listening to the music.

After night fell, as they sat by the blazing fire under a sky that had cleared of clouds and now was brilliantly starry, Levesque and Sutherland sang some *voyageur* songs, including "À la Claire Fontaine," which lifted their hearts and cheered them all.

> À la claire fontaine
> M'en allant promener,
> J'ai trouvé l'eau si belle
> Que je m'y suis baigné.
> > Lui ya longtemps que je t'aime,
> > Jamais je ne t'oublierai.

Ella and Sally sang, too, and Sniffer slept on the child's lap. The words of this verse of "At the Clear-Running Fountain" meant:

> At the clear-running fountain
> Sauntering by one day,
> I found it so compelling
> I bathed without delay.
>> Your love long since overcame me,
>> Ever in my heart you'll stay.

Ella thought it good that they should sing a song of love at such a time. Love was what had driven Levesque on at peril of his life. After hearing his story, she asked what he would do next. He did not know.

Ella said, "Angélique loves you, Jacques. Can't you go back to her and put all this behind you?"

Sadness showing in his proud, handsome face, Levesque said, "At Detroit I am a wanted man. I will never be thrown in jail!"

"But you saved Sally," Ella protested. "That will speak in your favor!"

He shook his head and said to Sutherland, "Tell your lady that a *voyageur* will die in prison waiting for his trial, even if he knows he might go free one day." To Ella, he said more cheerfully, "Come, madame. Let us teach you more French songs. Speak no more of what cannot be."

In the morning, Ella awoke to find Sally asleep, but Levesque gone.

"Where did he go?" she asked Owen.

"Where? I don't know. But he's gone, I'm sorry to say. He told me to give you his apologies for being so rude, but he has many a mile before him. And he does, indeed."

chapter **24**

BACK HOME

Two days later, under a blue sky, Sutherland and Ella whirled along a trail on the west bank of the Detroit River. In the sled, on Ella's lap, Sally Cooper happily cuddled Sniffer. As the dogs pulled, Sutherland ran alongside, jumping onto the back of the sled for an occasional rest. Sniffer lay on his back, flipping a snowball from foot to foot as though trained to it, delighting Sally.

Since Levesque left the child with them, she had regained much strength. When awake, Sally was a normal, cheerful girl; but when she slept she was restless, tormented by nightmares that caused her to sit up, eyes wide but unseeing. At this moment on the trail, with the sun high and brilliant, Sally's ordeal of the past half-year was only a dream. Now she was safe, and she responded to Ella's warmth.

Shortly they dashed around a bend in the path, and there was Fort Detroit! Ella caught her breath when she saw it. Though no more than a rough outpost in the middle of an endless wild, Detroit was home for her and Owen, who began to sing that *voyageur* song about the duck and the rolling ball:

En roulant ma boule roulant,
En roulant ma boule.
En roulant ma boule roulant,
En roulant ma boule.

302

Ella joined in, waking Sally, who rubbed her eyes and dug the rosewood music box from within her blankets, winding it and holding it up to accompany their song. The timber palisade surrounding the fort rose above the snowy fields, and Ella saw the gable of her old room in the commandant's residence. Sutherland shouted at the dogs, who sensed the excitement and yipped, pulling faster.

From out of a sturdy whitewashed cabin came a bearded *habitant,* broad and squat. He raised his arms as the sled approached, waving at Sutherland, who kept on singing. Some children appeared at the *habitant*'s side, wearing only indoor clothing, but they took up the song and ran with the travelers for a hundred yards or so. Others in French houses looked out of windows or turned from hanging up the day's hunting at their doors. In the space of half a mile, twenty *habitant* families responded to the excitement, and Sutherland's sled was pursued all the way to the fort by laughing, cheering children who did not know what the celebration was all about, but thought it a good idea just the same.

Inside the fort, Ella's reunion with Jeremy was a joyous one. She found him with his uncle Henry in the officer's house, where the furniture of the living room had been pushed against the walls to make a space for practice with fencing foils. As Ella came through the door, she saw the boy and Henry dressed in linen exercise garb, fencing masks over their faces. Jeremy and Gladwin turned and shouted, and the boy ripped off the wire mask and ran to his mother. Forgetting to put down the foil, he caught it in the hem of her dress, but neither of them cared.

Ella pushed him back, amazed at how much he had grown in the past five months. Then she hugged him again and put an arm around Henry as he came to them.

Sutherland entered with Sally at his side. Jeremy gave his stepfather a good handshake and then stared at the girl. She looked back at him curiously, as though she had never before seen a white boy. Something jumped inside her coat, and out popped Sniffer's nose. Jeremy stepped back in surprise, and Sally laughed—a lovely bright sound that filled the room.

Carefully, Jeremy put out a hand to Sniffer, who cocked his head this way and that. When the boy touched his nose, Sniffer sneezed, making Jeremy yank back his hand. Sally giggled again, and asked, "Are you afraid of Sniffer?" Before

Jeremy could answer, she said, "Don't be. He's very nice and won't bite you. Will you, Sniffer? You only bite fish, don't you? And this child's no fish!"

"Child?" Jeremy said, annoyed, and stood up straight, trying to make himself taller than Sally, but failing because she was exactly the same size as he—which she proved by standing tall and proud, her chin up. The Sutherlands were glad to see the change come over Sally, whose dysentery was gone now. Ella urged the children to sit down at the table while the grown-ups talked together. Sally and Jeremy went to the dining room's long table, where Sniffer was placed for Jeremy to examine him more closely.

Owen and Ella sat down before the fire with the major, who offered them tea. Ella noticed immediately how worn and drawn her brother looked. It was easy to see that the strain of continued siege and of isolation out here was eroding his spirit and physical strength. This long and lonely winter was not yet over, and there was no telling when Sir Thomas Gage, Amherst's successor, would send another officer to replace Gladwin. She felt a rush of sympathy for him, but he caught her sad gaze and laughed lightly to cheer her up.

"Well," Henry began as they drank their tea, "you have lots to tell me, and I'm starved for news of the outside world. Nothing much has happened here except that now and again our wood-chopping parties are ambushed; despite Pontiac's professions of peace last year we're still under siege. Our supplies are low and will remain low until the spring convoys come up."

Like anyone who has been confined too long without kindred spirits, Gladwin unburdened himself in a rush. After a minute of good-natured grumbling that veiled only thinly the awful weight of his duty, the major abruptly changed the subject and asked Owen and Ella about their trip.

Hearing how the threat of civil war had been removed in Philadelphia, and how the Indians in the northwest had been debilitated, Gladwin took heart in the possibility of the uprising ending soon. He was further gladdened by the news of Ella's pregnancy. However, when he was told the tale of Sally and Levesque, he became pensive as he said, "Levesque's been a renegade, and I'll have to arrest him if he comes into the fort; then he'll be sent down when the ice leaves the lakes, to be given a fair trial in Montreal." He sighed and stood up to pace the room. "Such a waste of good men this war has been!"

Ella asked, "Won't what he did for Sally count in his favor, Henry?"

Her brother stopped pacing. "Most assuredly. The government wants to put the conflict behind us all, and anything showing that Levesque will be a loyal subject will count in his favor—but first he'll have to turn himself in. He'll have to risk the gallows. But I don't think he's that kind. Do you, Owen?"

Sutherland thought a moment before saying, "I think I have a way of finding out just what kind he is."

Sutherland did not explain himself, but instead turned the conversation to word of Tamano. Gladwin said the Chippewa had sent a message that he would be in within a few days if nothing went wrong. The messenger, Gladwin added, had asserted that Tamano's harvest was a big one, and would easily fill three sleds for Montreal. The furs would be in Detroit in time for Sutherland to carry out his daring plan: to mush across the northern route, where rivers should yet be frozen and would serve as a highway for the dogsleds. Before lakes Erie and Ontario would be free of ice, it would be mid-April, and Sutherland did not want to wait so long to take the furs by canoe down to Montreal.

As usual at dusk Angélique Martine went out to the cowshed beside her small house, a milk bucket in her hand. She sang softly to herself as she approached the cow that stood calmly munching hay. Speaking a few words to the animal, she patted its side and pulled a milking stool into place near the swollen udder. She sat down and pressed her forehead against the cow's ribs, crooning softly as she milked. She heard the cat moving on the hay and called his name, then her mind wandered and she sang.

The cow gave a start and lumbered sideways, nearly knocking Angélique off the stool. She stood up quickly and scolded the animal, glad the bucket had not spilled.

"Angélique!"

Jacques! Her heart fluttered as he stepped out of the shadows and took her in his arms. Without speaking, they held one another, and Angélique wept, though she did not know whether it was for joy or sorrow.

A little while later, they sat in the hay, once again talking of what he would do. He told her all that had happened, but said he refused to surrender and be imprisoned. At least, thought the woman, Jacques was done with war, and that made her glad. But where did they go from here?

They heard footsteps in the yard outside. Martine? Jacques reached for his rifle. Angélique felt terror, afraid her father and Jacques would fight. The footsteps came to the darkened barn, and the creaking door was pushed open. They saw the silhouette of a tall man against the twilight.

"Levesque?"

"Sutherland!" Jacques went to the Scotsman, who came in. "Who is with you?"

"Both Jean Martine and I knew you'd slip into the fort, and we've been keeping watch for you. Jean is waiting in the house until we finish speaking."

"Where is the child?" Levesque asked quickly.

"She is well, and in good hands, my friend. She's glad to have a home. Wouldn't you like a home, too?"

Levesque gave a scornful laugh and turned away, saying, "I can be at home in the forest."

Angélique put her hands on his arm and gripped him tightly. Without words, she was pleading with him not to be so stubbornly fatalistic.

Sutherland said, "A man like you could do much for his people, Jacques, especially if he were in a position of power and influence."

"In case you've forgotten, I'm a renegade with a price on my head!" Levesque held up his rifle and shook it once. "This is my power and influence! This is how I represent my people, Scotsman. There is no other way!"

"There is," Sutherland replied. "Has Angélique told you about the company?"

"Yes."

"We need a Frenchman we can trust as our agent in Montreal. One who can speak English, as you do."

Levesque was listening.

Sutherland said, "We'll have an English agent who will cooperate as an equal partner with a Frenchman to set up our office in Montreal; we need a man who can deal with French merchants and can create the best canoe brigades this country has ever seen. I want the finest *voyageurs* available to man the canoes."

Levesque spoke roughly. "You want Frenchmen to serve

their British master, who will get rich from the strength of French backs—"

Angélique pulled at his arm. "No, no, Jacques, not that at all! Not as servants, but as partners!"

"I want you as a partner, equal with Tamano and our Montreal English agent. Out here you can be arrested, but no one knows you in Montreal. If anyone tries to arrest you, the company will support you, and what you did for Sally Cooper will stand you in good stead—Henry Gladwin told me that himself!"

Levesque moved away from Angélique and went to the door of the shed, staring out at the night and the twinkling yellow lights dotting the fort. He understood the Frontier Company's importance to his people: he could pick the best men available, true French and *métis* who deserved an opportunity in these hard times. He could employ forty or a hundred or more if the company were successful. And he could marry Angélique!

He turned to the others and said, "What about Jean Martine?"

"He approves," Sutherland said. "Go in and talk to him yourself. But I warn you both that Jean won't approve of your marriage until Jacques has proved himself loyal and reliable. Yet, Jean has offered to outfit you with all you need, and to give you funds for a trip to Montreal if you agree to join us.

"Jacques, if you join, I need you to depart right away—you can go by sled or by snowshoes, but we need you to contact a woman in Montreal and convey our offer to her to become our English agent there."

It was said now, and Angélique barely restrained herself from falling at her sweetheart's feet and begging him to try this, to accept the position, to risk being arrested—to trust something more than his rifle!

Levesque breathed a long sigh and looked down at the ground. Then he turned to Sutherland, offering his hand, and saying, "I'll do what I can, my friend."

Sutherland grinned, and Angélique flew into Levesque's arms. The Scotsman went into the house to tell Jean that Jacques would be in soon. Out in the shed the lovers held one another, and Angélique wept again, but this time tears of joy.

Tamano arrived two days after Levesque left for Montreal. Sutherland could not have been happier with the harvest the

Chippewa and Lela had gathered in the north country. All the company's goods had been traded, but the furs taken in return were magnificent. Tamano had traded shrewdly, loading his three sleds with only beaver coats worn by the Indians. Coat fur was the most in demand by British hatmakers because it was the softest and most pliable—having been used for a year or two, it was impregnated with human body oils. When a fur trader went out to the villages, beaver coats were the first pelts sought, but there would not be another well-worn beaver coat northwest of Detroit for at least a year.

Though well packed when first loaded into Tamano's sleds, these furs were unbaled and repacked even more tightly at Morely's. Using a large vise to press down the furs, Morely made the harvest small enough to fit onto two sleds which could be pulled by one team. Both Sutherland and Tamano would take the furs to Montreal, and on the trip neither man would ride at all. Instead, they would run on snowshoes behind or ahead of the dogs, one snapping a small whip over the team's heads, the other in front, breaking trail in the snow. The nine animals would haul furs and scanty provisions over the thousand-mile journey, which would take close to a month.

It was dangerous, but the value of the furs was reckoned at two thousand pounds sterling if they were brought down early. A few weeks later other furs might have come in, lowering the market value of the Frontier Company's haul. The undertaking was well worth the gamble.

Their route across country, over the frozen edges of lakes, would be level and easy, and they would make good time as long as ice remained on the northeastern rivers. The danger lay on the lower reaches of the Ottawa River before it emptied into the broad Saint Lawrence, for the ice might be breaking up by the time they got there in mid-April. But it had been a bitterly cold winter, and Sutherland was relying on this fact to see them through.

They intended to cut along the eastern shore of Lake Huron, swing across a spit of land and then enter Georgian Bay. From there they would go due east on the ice until they reached another landfall. Once back again on land, they would head straight overland for the Ottawa River, or *La Grande Rivière*, as the French called it. After striking the river a little below the falls called *La Grande Chaudière*, or the Great Kettle, they hoped the ice would be solid enough to cross and drive rapidly southeast toward Montreal, about a hundred miles away. Sutherland expected at least ninety of these miles to be solid ice; the other ten miles were rapids, which would be risky. Rapids they would pass by running the sled dogs overland when possible; when not possible, the dogs would be unharnessed and led over rocky portages, and the two men would be forced to unload the sleds and carry the furs. This meant, they knew, hiking back and forth with bundles of fur on their shoulders until everything was brought past the rapids. Also they would be compelled to lug the sleds the same way and then reload them. But compared with taking rough trails over hills and ridges if they tried to follow an overland route, the river highway was the best means of getting to Montreal quickly.

Taking the more southerly route along Lake Erie and Lake Ontario was impossible because of the hostiles—those who had not been struck down by the smallpox—who at this time of year were returning to their villages from the south. Also, it was unlikely those lakes would stay frozen as long as the northern waterways, and the travelers would be forced off the lakes onto rough and broken terrain—always risking ambush from Indians.

It was the only feasible plan, but Ella was nervous when she said good-bye to Owen and Tamano at the gate of the fort. Bundled up warmly, she watched the two sleds shoot across the straits, picking a way through ice floes and jagged barrier ridges where the ice had been driven into pyramids. At Ella's side was Lela, whose expressionless face told nothing of her inner emotions; nearby were Jeremy, Gladwin, the Morelys, Martine, and Angélique. Each one had different feelings as they watched their friends vanish in the distance, but Ella thought she must be most worried of all. No one else knew that Owen had left behind with her his precious claymore—as though he thought there was danger of losing it. This secret she would keep until he returned safely.

Jubal Swain knew he should have slaughtered the old sow back in December, when Lucy first asked him to. If the pig had been killed and preserved before winter, there would still be some bacon and lard left to get them by until he did some hunting. But he had been too busy or too lazy to take the time to wade into the pigpen and slit its throat. Then the bullet wound in his arm he had suffered at Philadelphia had kept him idle. Now it was late March, and they were short of food.

Swain put a leather apron over his clothes and rolled up his sleeves. He picked up the big butchering knife and touched the edge. It was sharp—sharp enough for the likes of that Sutherland! How he wished he could use it on him!

As Swain went out the door, Lucy and the boys, sitting near the fire, watched him go. They were tired of corn and jerked venison, though even that would do if it had not been eaten up already. Pork would be tasty. They had worked half the morning to heat a tub of water in the yard by chucking hot rocks from a bonfire into it, bringing the water to a boil. Now they were eating a hurried meal of milk and bread before going back out to help Jubal. The hog carcass would be scalded by lowering it into the tub by a rope slung over a tripod.

But scalding a hog was the last thing little Willie Swain wanted to do just then. As he supped his mush with a spoon, he held in his other hand the handsome dugout canoe Jubal had carved for him. There was peace between these two now, and the boy was willing to accept Swain as his pa.

As Lucy waited by the fire for the pig's squealing to begin, she wondered what her man would do this spring. She did not miss noticing the restlessness of Jubal's men, who often came to the cabin. They wanted him out ranging the woods again. What if he went?

There was a terrible squeal of fright from the sow, and the sound made Lucy get up and walk around. The awful squealing went on and on. The hog must be running around the pen. Lucy wanted to go out there, but dared not lest she shame Jubal by watching him make a fool of himself. Anyway, she had no stomach to watch a sloppy job of hog-killing.

Jubal's shouts rose from time to time over the agony of the sow, and the boys sat quietly with their mother, no one speaking, all of them wishing it were over. After the killing and the scalding, they would scrape off the hair, cut up the carcass, and render the fat into lard in another smaller kettle already set near the bonfire. The rest of the pig would be brined or ground up—all of it a long day's work that neither Willie nor Joe savored.

The door banged open, and they turned to see a furious Jubal, covered with blood, standing there. The sow was still squealing over in the pen.

"Load the rifle and give it here, girl!" Swain angrily commanded and went to the washbasin to get the muck from his hands. "Never could git the hang o' stickin' a pig." The squealing was hideous.

Willie approached him, the dugout in his hands. "Where's the butcher knife, Uncle Jube?"

Without looking up, Swain said, "In the damned sow's arse! Don't ask me! Take that boat an' play down by the brook; we ain't scaldin' for a while yet." He dried his hands and took the loaded rifle from Lucy, who did not meet his eyes. "Hell, I ain't no use at this damn farmin' work!"

The boys darted out the door in front of their uncle, who went to the pen while Lucy sat down by the fire, hands interlocked. She jerked when the rifle barked. The squealing slowed but did not stop. Swain roared mightily, and a moment later the old sow squealed once and fell silent.

Later, after eating his midday meal, Swain decided to get at the carcass. He went out the door and shouted for Willie and Joe to get more hot stones from the bonfire and heat up the water again. Swain grimly loaded the sow onto a stoneboat and dragged her toward the tub of water. He called again to the boys as he tied the pig's hindquarters to a rope. Lucy came out to help haul the animal above the tub.

"It ain't hot enough," she said. "We need more stones."

"I called 'em," Swain said. "They're at the water."

She cried out in the general direction of the brook, where the boys had gone with the toy dugout, but there was still no answer. After a moment, Swain hesitated. Lucy's face went white. She gasped suddenly, then ran toward the brook.

"Lucy!" he shouted. "No!"

The stream was at the edge of the forest, down a little gully and out of sight of the house. As Lucy raced madly, she called her boys in a shrieking voice filled with terror.

"Willie! Joe! Willie! Answer me!" She staggered to a stop, wailing, as she saw the bloody body of the yellow hound lying nearby.

Up from the ravine came a Shawnee, painted red and black, like a devil out of hell. Lucy screamed. He grabbed for her, laughing and snatching her hair. Another warrior, this one fairly young, jumped out of the ravine, the dugout canoe stuck in his belt as a trophy. As Lucy frantically struggled, she glimpsed her boys being dragged away through the forest, and she screamed again, kicking and fighting, but the warriors simply laughed—until Jubal Swain put a bullet into the older Shawnee's face and killed the second with a tomahawk. Swain had slipped up on them from the ravine, where he had run to intercept Lucy.

His wife fell to the ground in a faint. Swain dropped to his knees, loading his rifle and watching the trees. Struggling for consciousness, Lucy gaped across the ravine and screamed again in desperate horror, crying out for her sons. Swain saw movement in the woods and dragged her down just as a bullet sang past. He pulled her to cover, then quickly hauled her from stump to stump toward the house, which was their only protection. There was nothing they could do for the boys.

Jacques Levesque drew near to Montreal after traveling three long and lonely weeks through the wilderness. From time to time he had found a bed in Huron or Seneca villages, and he sensed a change in attitude among the men there. Previously, these tribes would have welcomed him heartily as a Frenchman, but on this journey he had been taken in more often than not simply because he was a traveler and it was his right to be given shelter.

In their lodges Levesque dared not mention the French king or the uprising lest he evoke anger that might lead to his murder. In one village he encountered drunken braves who threatened to kill him for the lies some French had told them last year, that the Great French Father was coming back to help the Indians in their fight against the English. Levesque slipped away in the night while cooler heads kept these bitter men from attacking him. Indeed, it was a hard trip in more than loneliness and exhaustion, for Levesque had seen that the Indians in the east were very nearly beaten by now.

Levesque had crossed the wide, frozen Ottawa River without much trouble, though there was already some open water. He hoped Sutherland would meet no difficulty when he got here in two weeks or so, but he had lingering doubts about the safety of the ice by then. It was already shifting with the current; a spell of warm weather would send massive floes drifting down toward the Saint Lawrence, and the Ottawa would be a death trap for any who tried to cross it.

He pressed on to Montreal, reaching it by driving over ice at Montreal Island's northern shores. The city was bustling, with preparations for spring already underway. He was sur-

prised at the large number of Redcoats on the streets, then
realized they were there for the coming campaign. Levesque
had not been in Montreal since it capitulated in 1760. Then it
had been full of soldiers in Bourbon white. The sight of these
hated Redcoats struck Levesque as very strange, and it was as
though he were walking through a nightmare—a nightmare in
which his favorite city was occupied and overrun by his archenemy.

It was no nightmare, however, and it took all Levesque's
strength of will to keep from searching out people from the
past, to resist haunting every street and alley in his unhappy
reverie. Finally he pressed on to the address of Mary Hamilton,
which he got from a clerk at the office of Cullen and Company—who also told him she was now Mary Defries.

At the moment Jacques Levesque knocked on the downstairs
door of Mary's apartment, she was finishing a letter she had
received from Peter. Joseph Brant had written for him to tell
Mary that the success of William Johnson's campaign down
the Susquehanna had come to the attention of Colonel John
Bradstreet, who would lead the lakes expedition come spring.
This was a spectacular opportunity for Peter, but he would
have to rush to Albany, order every available item on the
colonel's requisition list, and beat other contractors who were
eager to supply the campaign. Thus Peter would not be back
in Montreal as soon as he had hoped. At first, Mary was too
shaken to hear the knocker, and tears came into her eyes. She
understood what Peter was trying to do, but how she wanted
him there now! How she needed him, no matter what she had
written in her last letter telling him to use his own judgment
and not to worry about her! Despite all her optimism, she
wanted him to forget about the business and come to her.

The knocker sounded again, giving Mary a start. She folded
the letter and tucked it under a book on the table. As she hurried
downstairs to the door, Mary fussed a little with her hair, which
was tied back and fell in curls to her shoulders; then she adjusted
the red-striped bodice under her sack dress.

Mary opened the door and was surprised to see the handsome
voyageur, who bowed with a flourish of his red stocking cap,
saying his name, and adding, "I have come from Detroit with
a message from Monsieur Owen Sutherland, madame. May I
be permitted to come inside?"

"Owen Sutherland! Oh, of course, monsieur, please come

in." She bustled back from the door, and took another look at Levesque, who was wearing a bright red sash about his waist, rough but clean frontier garb—doeskin leggins, a buckskin jacket over a blue woolen shirt. Bearded and weathered, Levesque looked both fierce and adventuresome, but Mary knew anyone coming from Owen Sutherland must be reputable. She went upstairs while he closed the door and followed.

Mary realized that her eyes must be red from crying, so she took a handkerchief from her sleeve and wiped her face quickly before turning to offer Levesque a seat. The room was comfortable, though small and sparsely furnished. The Devaliers had given Mary a few pieces of furniture, including several wooden chairs and a pine table. There was a well-worn carpet on the floor, and Mary had sewn drapes with patterns of flowers in blues and reds that matched the rug. Levesque sat down in a chair washed by a patch of sunlight falling brightly through the room's only window.

Declining Mary's offer of some cider, he handed her the letter, noticing that her eyes were puffy—likely from a cold, he thought—and waited until she had read it all.

She began to read while seated, but when she discovered that Sutherland wanted her as a junior partner, she stood up, still reading, and went to the window, hardly believing her good fortune. Mary was excited, as Sutherland had anticipated. The prospect of joining the Frontier Company was the fulfillment of a dream for her, and she was sure Peter would feel the same way.

When she finished, she returned and stammered, "Why— why, Monsieur Levesque, this is—this is wonderful!"

Jacques smiled, attracted to this young woman's open beauty and warmth. She was like a fair image of his Angélique, and that gave his heart a twinge. Mary declared her eagerness to join the company, adding:

"Mr. Sutherland does not know it yet, but I am married now, and I'll have to make this decision with my husband, who will be back from Albany in—in—" Composing herself, but not until Jacques saw that something was deeply bothering her, Mary said, "Mr. Defries is in Albany and will be busy there for some time, monsieur. But I am sure this offer of partnership in your company will interest him as much as it does me! I will write to him at once!"

"Do that," Levesque said. "Work here must be started immediately. The harvest of pelts is already on its way down; there is no time to spare."

Mary thought about that, gazing blankly out the window. She was certain Peter would jump at this opportunity! Turning to Levesque she said, "As much as I believe my husband will agree, yet I cannot accept the responsibility you require of me." She gave a helpless little gesture at her swollen midriff and said, "I am due at any time. I have not the strength, you see—"

Levesque stood up and said, "Madame, if you will permit me to offer my services, I'll complete whatever needs to be done before the furs come down, and you can consider the partnership sealed between you and the company. When you are able, or when your husband returns to take your place, then the Defries partners may begin to undertake their duties."

"Monsieur!" she exclaimed. "You are most kind, but I wish not to be an added burden to you."

Levesque smiled and said, "Say no more, madame; no one knows Montreal's merchants—at least the French ones—better than I. Leave it all to me."

He stood up and kissed her hand. Mary seemed in a daze just then. This sudden change had come upon her with such force that she was at a loss for words. As she followed Levesque to the top of the stairs, her head whirled with all the excitement. Now they would no longer have to worry about the whims of the military establishment, no longer have to please haughty officers, no longer have to grovel at the feet of petty officials who were always slow to pay. The northwest lay before them, rich and untouched, and Sutherland's new company sounded like an idea whose time had come.

Levesque turned to say good-bye, saw Mary's dreamy expression, and smiled. "I'll return in a day or two with news about storage, shipping schedules, interested buyers. Take care of yourself and the baby, madame, and do not fret about the least thing."

Mary held her big tummy and gave a wince as the baby kicked again. Then she smiled at Levesque. "I will help you as long as I am able, monsieur! Oh, I do hope my husband will agree to join your company!"

Levesque said, "I'm sure your husband will agree; after all, a man with the good sense to marry someone like you must certainly have the ability to see what the future holds for our company!"

chapter 25

ICE

Sutherland and Tamano were cold, and that was good.
As the Chippewa slogged ahead, breaking trail, Sutherland
plodded behind the sled, now and again snapping the short
whip to keep the animals pulling together. The north wind
howled down across Georgian Bay, blowing snow in clouds
that often obscured the bay's eastern shore, only five miles
away. Sutherland was glad the weather was remaining bitter,
because it meant the rivers and lakes would hold them and be
safe to cross.

They were six days from the Ottawa River, and after nearly
two weeks on the trail, making about five miles an hour, they
had been fortunate to have cold, clear days with only occasional
clouds and snow. Sutherland's beard was encrusted with ice.
Both men trudged along with their heads down against the
numbing wind, seldom speaking, resting only every ten miles.
In camp they ate, slept, smoked pipes, and slept again, still
not talking much. It was as though they were saving precious
energy for the next day's toil. Still strong, though pushing
themselves to the utmost, Sutherland and Tamano knew well
how to pace themselves and their dogs. They could accept this
cruel cold and wind, because when they reached the Ottawa
after coursing through forest trails, they expected to find it still
solid. If it had begun to thaw, they might be compelled to run
along the south bank of the river, through flooded marshland
and tangled, unbroken woods with few trails. But what would
they do if they came to the Lake of Two Mountains, the estuary

of the Ottawa, and they could not cross? They would be unable
to get to Montreal from the south bank. They would have to
wait until the ice broke up, then buy an Indian canoe and go
on that way—but this would mean three weeks' more delay,
and their desperate, exhausting journey across the northerly
route would have gained no time and have been for nothing.

As they reached the shore of Georgian Bay and ran the dogs
up the bank and into the trees, where they would camp tonight,
all these thoughts tumbled in Sutherland's mind. The next day
they would begin overland on hunting trails that linked Algonquin villages. From these Indians they expected shelter and
provisions, even though the Algonquin had been allies of the
French in the last war. These days this nation was at peace,
having ignored Pontiac's war belts. Among them Tamano had
old friends, for the Chippewa were also of Algonquin stock
and spoke a language that could be understood in this country.
From the Algonquin the two traders would learn where to find
the best crossing of the Ottawa River. They hoped it was well
downstream, because that would make their journey easier,
that much closer to Montreal.

Mary's letter found Peter at his family's home in Albany less
than two weeks after she had written him about Sutherland's
offer. Her description of the company and what it meant to
them glowed with enthusiasm, but Defries was not pleased.
After all the work he had done, he had no intention of laboring
for or with anyone else. He had his sights on winning Bradstreet's contract, and nearly every merchant house in Albany
had been ordered to prepare supplies and equipment for Defries
to ship to Fort Niagara that spring.

Weary from constant labor, and under the stress of being
responsible for spending nearly a thousand pounds New York
currency loaned him by Sir William Johnson, Peter was angry
with Mary's letter. When he found someone to write her back
for him, he released his tension in a rush of words that were
much harsher than he had intended to be. Though he loved
Mary, he was not about to be dragged into business affairs not
of his own planning. By now, his total absorption preparing
for the campaign had blinded him to all else. Even Mary's
pregnancy was forgotten, and the letter was so stinging that he
neglected to ask for her welfare or to mention the baby.

Peter was ready to go west to Niagara, following the first

load of supplies—only Indian trade goods, ordered by Johnson to be given as gifts at a great tribal council planned for that June at the fort. Johnson's loan had purchased the Indian presents, but Peter would not buy military goods until Bradstreet called on him. When that would happen he did not know, and he was growing even more impatient. Every detail of organization had to be seen to, and there was no one but Defries to do it. No, he did not care a damn about a northwestern Indian trading company—that was a world he knew little about. Supplying soldiers was what he understood, and within five years there would be no one better at it in all British North America.

At the end of the letter he told Mary hurriedly that he loved and missed her, swearing he would come back to Montreal after he established a storehouse at Niagara. He was so caught up in work that he did not even realize that Mary was about to give birth.

Lucy Swain took one long last look at her cabin. She sat on a gentle mare that had been part of the trade Jubal negotiated with the neighbor who bought the farm. Jubal was up ahead, leading the packhorse into the forest, where green buds washed the woods with a hint of color.

There was no one in the cabin. Lucy gazed across the clearing at the small world she and Matt had labored so hard to build, remembering the sound of the boys laughing and fighting, the sight of Matt behind the plow, and the smell of the earth when frost left it. Lucy stared, her face blank, but her heart was deeply wounded.

How had it all happened? How had it come upon her so fast, so mercilessly? She almost thought of Willie and Joey, but refused that, and closed her mind to the agony.

Jubal called. Her horse moved forward on its own, and Lucy did not care to govern it. She cared for nothing these days. Strength and vigor were gone.

They would travel north, Jubal had told her, and soon would join a few hundred Pennsylvania militiamen journeying up to Fort Niagara to take part in Bradstreet's western expedition. It was said the soldiers would be given Indian land in return for their service, and there was a scalp bounty on Indians that could prove profitable to a man like her husband. It had been her idea to go westward, but wherever—Lucy did not care, as long as they escaped the memories.

All that eased her pain was Jubal, in his rough and head-strong way. At his side there was no past and no future, no lost boys or dead husband. But then came morning, and with it the darkness of sorrow. Perhaps leaving the cabin would help her forget. Perhaps the boys would be found when the Indians were finally defeated in the coming campaigns. Perhaps . . . perhaps.

Lucy turned suddenly to look back at the house, but it was no longer in sight.

The wind changed, and Tamano sat up, throwing back his blankets. It was not yet dawn, and the fire was low. As Tamano plied the fire with kindling and branches, he listened to the wind in the trees, gusts that heralded more than morning. The flames shot up, and Tamano walked away from the campfire, standing in the darkness near the dogs, who stared at him, their wolf eyes shining red. Hands uplifted to test the direction of the breeze, the Chippewa knew they were in for snow.

A moment later, Sutherland was at his side, wrapped in his own blanket. Staring out at the blackness, they saw clouds sweeping in to shut out the stars. The gusts blew harder.

"Wind's swinging round to south," Sutherland confirmed.

"Got to go quick," Tamano said and turned back to the campfire, where he began preparing johnnycake batter, jerked venison, and tea for breakfast. Since it was the Indian's turn to cook, Sutherland set about feeding the dogs and harnessing them to the sled. Before the light of dawn was in the sky, the travelers had eaten quickly, doused the fire, and were on their way, mushing through flat wooded land a long two-day's run from the Ottawa River. They had to get there and cross before the snow came down, lest they be stranded, snowbound, for days. The trail might clog and close before they could get out of the lowlands, so Owen and Tamano had no time to spare. Rations were already low, and three extra days in these woods—or maybe more if the blizzard was a bad one—could cost them more than time. Starving dogs were dangerous, and having to kill a dog for food would mean the rest of the team might not be able to pull the full load of pelts.

They hurried through the darkness, and dawn was slow in coming because of the clouds. With morning's bleak light fell the first snowflakes, big and wet. Wind from the south meant warmer weather. The river ice would begin to break up soon, if it had not already done so.

Later that day, in Montreal, Jacques Levesque stood at the door of a warehouse near the Saint Lawrence River and looked up at the sky, steely gray and clouded with snowflakes. Knowing what Sutherland and Tamano were facing out there, he hoped they had already crossed the Ottawa. The fur sleds should be through the lowlands southwest of the Ottawa by now—if all had gone well.

Mary's voice distracted him, and he turned to see her coming out of the warehouse with the old caretaker. Mary parted with the fellow, a Yorker employed by the English owner, and came to Levesque. Smiling brightly, she explained they had been able to lease space in the warehouse for practically nothing, because the city was barren of merchandise and would be so until the military campaign began to shape up.

"They were glad for the chance to earn anything," Mary said as they strolled toward Levesque's one-horse sleigh. "There's not a fur to be had in Montreal. In fact, I don't think Mr. Sutherland needs to hurry here to get a good price for his harvest; everyone's saying there won't be any furs brought in this year."

"I'm not worried about them getting here on time." Levesque stared again at the mighty Saint Lawrence, where patches of black water showed between the ice floes. "I'm worried about them getting here at all."

They had made another appointment at a second warehouse, to hold merchandise bought for trading to the Indians. By the time they finished there, the snow was heavy outside. In the week since Jacques arrived in the city, they had worked hard together, and friendship had grown between them. Amazed by Mary's fortitude despite her delicate condition—she was already past her time—Jacques often had to make her calm down or take rests. To slow Mary down without making her angry or resentful, Jacques usually used a touch of humor, and they laughed quite a lot in those days of enthusiasm and anticipation. Daily, Mary expected Peter's reply to her letter, and each day she had to temper her own delight by throwing herself into hard work—whether housework or work of the Frontier Company.

Today, Mary was particularly cheerful, taking pleasure in the tranquillity of the snowfall and enjoying Jacques companionship. He was by now a true friend, and with the Devaliers and Emmy, he drove away her lonely thoughts.

As they came out of this warehouse, Mary spotted a long, narrow ramp leading from a loading bay down to the ground. It was used for sliding baled furs into carts, and snow covered it from top to bottom.

"Look!" she cried and ran to a ladder leading up to the loading door.

"Hey!" shouted Jacques. "What are you doing?"

"Just watch! Catch me!"

Mary had not had a good slide since her days on the Cullen banister. She went nimbly up the ladder and stepped out onto the platform, about fifteen feet above the ground. Levesque protested, then realized it would do no good. He darted to the bottom of the slide, which ended in midair, and there he waited, calling out for Mary to go slowly.

She giggled, closed the hem of her watch coat and gown, and sat down with a plump in the snow at the top of the ramp. With a joyful whoop she slid gaily down, legs in the air. Levesque could not help laughing, but his laughter was cut short as Mary's coat caught on a bolt, spinning her around and sending her down head first.

Levesque leaped, catching the full force of her slide, and they both collapsed into soft snow, convulsed with laughter. They sat up, dusting themselves and bombarding one another with snowballs. Levesque reached for a big glob of snow and aimed. But he stopped when Mary's expression changed from joy to dismay.

"What is it?" he asked and got to his knees.

Sitting, Mary felt the top of her tummy and said distantly, "I don't know. I've never had a baby before."

Levesque carried her to the sleigh, and they raced through the city toward her lodgings. Mary was calm, but after they reached home, she was sure whatever was happening somehow had to do with giving birth. Yet she did not know what meant what, and it was a relief when Mrs. Devalier came soon after Jacques ran next door to call her. While the doctor's wife settled Mary into bed, Levesque hurriedly assembled towels, extra blankets, prepared some dinner for everyone but Mary, and built up the fire. Dr. Devalier was resting at home until needed.

At first Mary was tense and confused. Having lived in a male world with her father and brothers for so long, she had never seen a baby born. But Mrs. Devalier calmed her, helped her understand what her body was doing, and soothed Mary during her contractions. An hour later Mrs. Devalier sent Jacques for her husband, who arrived glowing with enthusiasm.

Levesque put a kettle of water on to boil, as he had been told, then paced the room. His mind was full of doubt, for he felt that he should have been more careful with Mary, should have stopped her acting so recklessly with the baby due at any time.

In the bedchamber, Mary was in good hands. Dr. Devalier was kind and skillful. After a contraction that lasted an eternity, Mary relaxed, then went into a stronger contraction. She was very close. She was not afraid.

A little while later, Mary lay completely exhausted, with a tiny, black-haired daughter in her arms. A happy Dr. Devalier left the women in privacy and joined Jacques. Mrs. Devalier beamed as though it were her own granddaughter just born. With gentle wonder, Mary held the babe against her breast, and a tear fell, running down close to the infant's lips.

"Now, now, dearest," Mrs. Devalier crooned, "the baby won't like salty nipples!"

Mary looked up through her tears and tried to laugh, but she could only cry. After all this time, the baby was here, was real, was hers. Mrs. Devalier knelt at the bedside, wiping away Mary's sweat and tears with a handkerchief. Gazing at the mother and newborn child, the old woman bit her own trembling lip, then kissed them both.

That evening Defries came out of the snowstorm and took shelter for the night at a disreputable-looking inn west of Schenectady. He was wet and tired as he sat down heavily at a crowded table to order dinner. His mood was as foul as the weather, and by the time he had eaten, he was close to knocking the heads of a couple of drunken cowherds who were boasting too much. But he restrained himself, left them to laugh stupidly at one another, and went upstairs to sleep in a flea-infested bed between two other weary travelers.

Defries was still two weeks from Niagara, where the small fortune in Indian goods had been sent—Sir William Johnson's small fortune, because the military paymaster at Albany had still not paid Peter for supplying Brant's expedition last winter. The slowness and haughtiness of army bureaucracy maddened Defries, and that was one reason he was feeling so surly this night. Add the struggle he had been through trying to bargain with those Albany Dutch merchants, and it was enough to infuriate a saint. Everything had cost more than he had anticipated. Now he understood what folk meant when they said Dutch traders could skin you and hang up your pelt to dry while you were still thinking whether to sell it. Damn, but they were masterful! Yet Defries had learned a few things dealing with them, and he would do better next time around. After all, he had the same blood as they did.

The Indian supplies had been organized and shipped with the utmost care, and Defries hoped to meet Bradstreet at Niagara in April to talk about a supply contract.

Lying in the darkness between two smelly, snoring strangers, Defries thought achingly of Mary. He thought, too, of the angry letter he had sent her, wishing it had not been so severe. Then, with a sudden shout, he sat up and slapped his forehead. The two fellows next to him cried out in fright, and one dived from the bed, half-asleep.

"How could I have been such a fool?" Peter bellowed.

The man still in bed groaned and lay down, deciding against making any snide remark because of Peter's enormous shoulders.

Defries clambered out of bed, muttering to himself, "In all that damned writing to Mary, I never once asked for her health! I never once asked about the baby. The baby!" He stopped abruptly, towering over the frightened man on the floor. "What a lunkheaded fool I am!"

Defries slapped his forehead once more, disgusted and angry with himself for forgetting all about the baby in his labors to please the damned army! Sighing, he returned dejectedly to bed, where the other two were once again trying to sleep.

When Peter's angry letter arrived in Montreal, it was brought upstairs by a cheerful Mrs. Devalier. She had answered the door because Mary was seated in the living room, nursing the baby, now two weeks old. With trembling hands, Mary tore open the folded letter, and the infant slipped from her breast. She deftly guided the baby back to the nipple while she read. But almost immediately, Mary's face fell.

Mrs. Devalier saw the change come over the woman, and sat down, waiting. Mary was shattered by Peter's furious refusal of Sutherland's proposition. At first she could not believe it, but trying to control her tears, she forced herself to finish the letter. Then she let it fall, and began to weep.

Immediately, Mrs. Devalier was at her side, stroking her hair until Mary pressed her forehead against the old woman's frail shoulder. The baby again lost the breast and set up an awful screeching, but Mary did not respond. The little one yowled until Mrs. Devalier reached over and helped her find the right spot. That attracted Mary's attention, and she sighed, compelling herself to stop crying. She put her head back against the pillow and closed her eyes. Mrs. Devalier said nothing and sat down once more, waiting for Mary to tell as much as she wished.

The only sound was the sucking of the hungry infant. Mary opened her eyes and looked at Mrs. Devalier, whose kindly face could not have been more sympathetic.

In a shaking voice, Mary said, "Peter does not want the company. He won't be back for a very long time, and this letter doesn't—even mention the baby—"

She broke off and bit her knuckle, trying hard not to be so sad. Again the baby lost her breast, but this time Mary eased the nipple again to her mouth, and composed herself once more. Mrs. Devalier rose and settled Mary back against the pillow, and the young woman told her everything in Peter's letter.

When she had heard it, Mrs. Devalier patted Mary's hand and said, "There, there, child. Listen to me now: what is important for you at this moment is not a trading company, not even an ambitious husband—and he's a good man, so give him time, give him time. No, child, what is important now is that you rest and care for the infant. Then, when you are calm and know what you want to say to Peter, write him a letter, tell him you have given birth to his daughter, and he'll run home—"

"She's not his daughter!" Mary felt like crying again. She turned away and said softly, "She's not his daughter, Mrs. Devalier, that's why I'm so afraid—"

"Child," the old woman said firmly and took Mary's hand. Mary faced her. "If you love Peter, then this is, indeed, his daughter as much as she is yours. But understand that your husband is young, and he has much to learn about women— about you and the infant."

Mrs. Devalier smiled and kissed Mary, who felt weak and lay back, closing her eyes, with the baby tugging at her breast. Mrs. Devalier was right, and she knew Peter was a loving husband and would accept Jeanette Marie—she hoped he would like that name; "Marie" was for Mrs. Devalier. Mary touched the reddish little cheek. Within herself she felt a surge of warmth. She saw then the beauty that only a mother can see in her child. The baby left the nipple. This time she was full with milk, and Mary lifted the infant to her shoulder to burp. Mrs. Devalier carefully put a napkin between the baby's mouth and Mary's shoulder, then gave a contented sigh, and bade them farewell until tomorrow.

Obscured by clouds, the sun was going down behind Sutherland and Tamano as they stood on the southwestern bank of the broad Ottawa River. What normally would have been a beautiful spectacle—a mile-wide channel, white with ice—was an awful sight to these two men standing beside their weary dogs. Instead of solid ice, the river was choked with twisted, tortured floes buckled into massive pyramids or crowded against one another to obstruct a crossing as effectively as if they were a stone wall. The river ice was breaking up rapidly. The last two days of warmer weather had weakened the Ottawa's brittle encasement, and the river was bursting free of its bondage.

As they stared at the far bank, they heard the booming of cracks opening up. Whenever the wind blew hard, they saw huge masses of ice ridges in the middle of the channel shift slightly. The sky was still gloomy, though it had not snowed much. Yet it was not snow that worried them now. It was how to cross.

"Perhaps lower down . . ." Sutherland said, but his words trailed off.

Tamano spoke after thinking. "We must cross here, my brother, and begin now. If we wait, the north wind will blow the ice until it is too broken to cross. We go now, or we do not go at all."

The sun suddenly broke through at the western horizon, and

the far bank was tinged with reddish fire. Clouds were clearing in the west, and the weather would change tonight, probably freeze again—but that would do more harm than good. As Tamano said, clear weather would bring strong winds to break up the ice floes even more forcefully, perhaps gashing wide channels of open water that could not be passed over by sled.

Sutherland looked at the dogs, who were munching snow in their thirst and weariness. The animals had been pushed hard, having made thirty-five miles already today. The men were also tired, after running every bit of the way through forests glazed with ice and blanketed with deep slushy snow that stuck to snowshoes and the runners of the sleds. The dogs had to be stopped frequently to let them lick the ice from their paws—as they were doing now—while their masters contemplated the next step. It did not take long to decide.

Standing in the shadows of bare, ashen maples, Sutherland and Tamano knew they had to go immediately. The dogs could not be fed yet, because Sutherland did not want them running on a full stomach that might give them cramps. Taking five minutes to peer across the ice, picking out the most likely route to the other side, the two men made their plans. All the while the ice boomed and shifted. Both knew they might have to alter their course more than once, but they hoped it would not be necessary to turn back.

"Heeyah!" Sutherland shouted. He broke trail for the dogs as they gamely hauled the two heavy sleds thumping down the slope and onto the river. Tamano ran behind, whip in hand.

The ice seemed solid enough, and the weary team found a good pace, loping along steadily, following Sutherland, who kept a close eye on the surface ahead.

"Heeyah! Get along!" Tamano shouted from behind, and kept up a steady chatter of encouragement for the team. Heera in the lead had his ears pricked up, and the rest followed his faithful example, leaning into the traces and dragging the sleds across ice covered with wet snow.

Sutherland noticed a sharp rise ahead and swerved them to the right to avoid what might be a sheer drop-off. As they passed this place, he saw that he had been correct: the river rushed and gurgled in the channel like witches' brew in an icy cauldron. After a minute of running, his legs sore and stiff from a hard day's journey, he felt the surface beneath him lurch suddenly, and lost his balance, falling hard. The barking dogs came up quickly behind him, and Heera halted the team as Tamano leaped on the back of the last sled to grind the brake down into the ice.

Unhurt, Sutherland scrambled to his feet. He looked at Tamano, and though neither man spoke, they suspected they were on a vast, drifting peninsula of ice. They only hoped it touched the far shore and was not an island.

"Yah!" Tamano shouted to the dogs. "Get along!"

They were off again, Sutherland still in the lead, stamping his snowshoes to pack down a few inches of snow, making a harder base for the dogs and sleds to follow. It was arduous, and a muscle in his left calf cramped, but he pressed on. Again there was a strange feeling as of the ice moving, and this time it lasted longer. Sutherland looked up at the rosy far bank and saw that his course had changed because of the movement of the ice. He altered it to the left and headed once again for the same spot—a great lodgepole pine sticking up in the sunlight like a tower, now less than a half a mile away.

This grayish mass of ice was so enormous that its limits could not be seen. Perhaps it was adjacent to other great floes so that even if it was pushed along by the river's current, it would remain part of a bridge.

Each time the wind picked up—out of the northwest now— Sutherland felt the ice shift underfoot, and he noticed the dogs often broke stride when it happened. It was a strange sensation, reminding Sutherland of those first days at sea in his youth. Then the new feeling of a rolling deck had been exhilarating and exciting; but now the much gentler lurch of the ice was ominous.

The far bank, however, was close, only three hundred yards away, and danger was passing with every step they took toward solid land. Sutherland swung a little to the left to round a jagged outcrop, then directed them back on course, straight for the lodgepole. When they came within a hundred yards of the tree, he breathed easier. This had been a harrowing crossing, and it seemed to take longer than it actually had. Sutherland glanced back at Tamano, who nodded once and cracked the whip at the dogs. They both felt better.

Fifty yards from the tree, which was in shadow now, the sun having set, they had to swing a little to the right because a low wall of crusted ice ran across their course. The wall was approximately thirty yards long, and Sutherland led his team down to its end. But when he got there, he was annoyed to see open water ten feet wide. To get around the water they had to run another hundred yards farther downstream, but that was not much. They had been only fifteen minutes on the ice, and though it was getting darker, they still had plenty of time to set up camp.

Another hundred yards downstream the open water was bridged by a spit of ice, and Sutherland led them over it, but at the last moment there was a tremendous shudder, and the ice moved. The dogs squealed in fright, and Sutherland lost his balance. The next moment a chasm broke open to the sound of cracking ice and rushing river water. Sutherland nearly slid over the edge of the break, and Heera turned the team on a swift bend to the right, dragging the sleds in a curving maneuver that swung them sideways right for the water.

Tamano shouted and leaped on the back of the rear sled, jamming down the brake, but it would not hold. Sutherland threw his body between the first sled and the open water, just five feet away, and he took the full brunt as the sled crashed hard against his shoulder. Tamano's braking and Sutherland's frantic leap barely stopped the sleds from being lost, and with them the team and every hope of the Frontier Company partners.

But there was no time for relief. The men quickly led the team away from the brink, and stopped a moment to check the dogs. None was hurt, but Sutherland's shoulder ached where the sled had hit him.

In a moment of quick decision they decided to head downstream to find a crossing to the shore, which was only a maddening forty yards off. They knew what lay upstream, and going back to pass that barrier would use up much of the remaining daylight. In about fifteen minutes it would be too dark to see where they were going. If they did not soon get across these last few yards, they could be stranded that night out on the ice. With a cold wind blowing, that was perilous. They might find themselves afloat in the Saint Lawrence River by morning—if they did not freeze to death.

The floe shuddered again. The dogs broke stride, and a few whimpered. Then the ice wrenched even harder, and the team stopped of its own will, whining and yipping, unsure of what to do. Sutherland talked to Heera, who nuzzled him and obeyed the command to go on. Off they went downstream again.

Tamano called out that the ice pack was rotating from left to right, and if they kept bearing northeast, they would likely come to where the floe was jammed against another pack, and thus, on stepping stones, they would make it to the bank. Sutherland agreed, but noticed that the opposite bank was farther away than before, perhaps seventy-five yards now. The river ice boomed and boomed again. The sky was almost dark, but twilight gave just enough light to see by. Still they had found no crossing, being cut off again and again by open water and ridges. The wind picked up, shifting ice and clouds at the same time. Now they steered by the sheen of ice under stars that began to twinkle as the clouds drifted away to the east, but everything was growing steadily more obscure.

As darkness deepened they lit two whale-oil lanterns, one for Sutherland to carry, the other attached to the second sled. The black shadow of the shoreline was very low, and Sutherland estimated it might be as much as half a mile away by now. Yet the southwestern shore was even farther, and there was no going back. They had to go on, or they were lost.

However, a little while later, a strange light came into the sky, and it was twilight once more—the northern lights, the aurora borealis, were bright enough to give them a clear view of the night. Sutherland thought of his home city in Scotland, Aberdeen, which was famous for its spectacular northern lights, that pale, glowing phenomenon that drove away darkness. He laughed to himself to think that the ancient gods of the Scots must be watching over him.

Soon, thanks to the aurora, they had picked their way closer to shore. In the spectral glow of the northern lights the shore seemed only about fifty yards off, and they mushed straight at it. Relieved, Sutherland laughed out loud. When Tamano asked why, he said, "The manitou of the Scots has sent the northern lights to guide us safely across the river, my brother."

Tamano hooted at that, shouting, "It is the Chippewa manitou who has answered *this* Indian's prayers, Donoway! There are no Scots gods in this country!"

Sutherland laughed. But then the ice boomed fiercely. The dogs whined, and Sutherland barely kept his balance as the floe shifted.

He called back, "Let's not argue about it until we're over, brother!" Then he ran well ahead to scout their path.

They were virtually over by now. Only thirty yards from

shore, the dogs were pulling eagerly, sensing safety, forgetful of weariness after their long day's trek.

The north wind picked up, whipping ice crystals and snow so hard that Sutherland had to raise his arm to shield his face from the stinging. Immediately there was another sharp tremor and wrench of the ice, and again he found himself lying on his side. As he tried to stand, he heard the dogs yowling and barking in terror.

"Donoway!" Tamano's voice was muffled and distant. "Donoway, help!" Sutherland turned back, fighting the fierce night wind, trying to see what had happened. But Tamano and the sleds were nowhere in sight.

chapter **26**

NOT BEATEN YET

Again the ice shifted. Sutherland covered his eyes from the lashing wind that prevented him from seeing the sleds and Tamano. He heard the team howling and yipping in fear, and behind that sound Tamano was shouting. Sutherland hurried back, realizing that he had gone far ahead of the sleds, which had been slowed by a crust of ice forming on top of the slushy snow, hindering dogs and runners.

"Tamano!"

"Donoway! Help! Help!"

Unable to see, Sutherland followed the sounds of the Chippewa and the dogs. But the wind foiled him there also, catching the voices and tossing them about so that their direction was difficult to tell. Where was the sled's lantern? Desperate, Sutherland broke into a run, but after only a few steps, he stopped short at the very edge of a break in the ice that had not been there when he passed a moment ago.

"Donoway!" Tamano's voice sounded weaker, though it was more distinct, close. Where was that lantern? Even the aurora was fading.

Then Sutherland saw movement on his right, and he ran against the wind, along the edge of open water. There were the dogs, frantically tugging at their harnesses. Still he saw no lantern. Then his own light revealed the sleds, almost heeled over on a slab of ice that had broken off and tilted fearfully, threatening to spill them into the black water. If that happened, the dogs would be dragged backwards into the river and swallowed up unless Sutherland cut them free. But if he did cut the dogs free, the sleds would surely slide away, and with them the furs. These thoughts flashed through Sutherland's mind as he ran up, looking anxiously for Tamano.

Ignoring the pleading howls of the animals, he searched all around, lifting the lantern so its yellow light would shine farther. The block of ice under the sleds was twenty feet long and about fifteen wide, with five feet of its width submerged. Then he heard Tamano gasp, and saw him in the water, one hand gripping the extinguished lantern from the last sled.

"Tamano! I'm here!" Sutherland shouted and yanked off his snowshoes. He hurried past the yelping dogs, then saw in the faint light that any clumsy move to clamber over the sleds could cause them to slide away and sink. He stopped and called his friend's name, but saw that Tamano was losing consciousness in the freezing water. The first sled's front tipped up at the same angle as the ice, and the second was tilted to the side. Only the edges of this sled's runners kept it from sliding sideways into the water—all six hundred pounds of it.

Carefully, Sutherland leaned over and crawled out onto the chunk of ice, keeping above the canted sleds. He slowly crept along the high edge of the slab, and with his weight it eased down a bit so that its incline was not so steep. Talking to Tamano all the while, Sutherland slid on his stomach the twenty feet to his friend, who hung on at the lower side of the tipping ice. The slightest sudden downward movement by Sutherland toward the Indian would cause the chunk to capsize, taking Tamano, sleds, dogs, and Sutherland with it.

Tamano was just a few feet away, but too frozen to drag himself up onto the sled. It was bitter cold. Frost was forming on the Indian's soaked coat and on his fur hat, which had stayed on his head. He looked up, eyes glazed with cold, and moaned. He tried to pull himself up, but as he did so, the chunk of ice heeled over, and the sleds slid. The dogs barked as they were yanked a bit closer to the water, and Sutherland cried out that Tamano should stay where he was. Tamano relaxed, still gripping the extinguished lantern of the second sled.

After a futile attempt to reach down to the Chippewa, Sutherland lay panting, with no idea what to do. He called to Heera, telling the big leader to stay so the team would not waste strength trying hopelessly to pull ahead. Heera held his ground.

The dog showed courage, his ears pricked up while the others whined in terror.

"Tamano, do you hear me?"

"Tamano is cold, brother." The Indian's shivering voice was weak.

Much longer, and Tamano would freeze to death. He had to come out now! There was no more time for thinking, only for action. Sutherland moved instinctively. He slid back along the piece of ice and carefully climbed onto the main pack. Feeling the traces of the dogs, he saw they were taut. Only the strength of the team kept the sleds from sliding away. However, the next good wind might change all that by further tipping the chunk under the sleds. Tamano no longer had the strength to stay afloat if the sleds went under, and Sutherland could not leap into the water for him, because there was no way to climb out, and with both of them soaked to the skin, they would freeze to death.

Before Sutherland even realized what he was doing, he had cut away the webbing of his snowshoes and whipped out the thongs to make a four-foot line with a slipknot at the end. Then he was again crawling on the top edge of the tilted ice. Tamano's head lay back in the water as though he would let go of the sled at any moment. Sutherland let down the slipknot and spoke to Tamano, who slowly looked around. Sutherland's legs dangled over the high side of the ice, his upper body lying flat as he reached down for the Indian.

"Take the noose, Tamano! Take it and pull it tight on your wrist! That's it! Make it tight!"

Tamano summoned the very last of his strength to do this, and pushed his gloved hand into the noose. Sutherland tugged until it was secure.

"Now, let go the lantern!" Sutherland shouted above the wind and howling dogs.

Tamano at first was reluctant to release his hold. Then he gritted his teeth and let go. His body slipped away, but Sutherland held him, each with one hand tied to the line. The ice tipped down, and Sutherland struggled to counterbalance it by moving farther back to the high side. The Scotsman's other hand held to the high, slippery edge of the ice chunk.

The wind was blowing all the while, but the ice had not shifted much, and that was good. Now Sutherland had to drag Tamano up toward him, hoping the Indian's weight would help counterbalance the tilting ice and sleds, perhaps even causing the slab to right itself so the dogs could pull the sleds free. Sutherland hauled at Tamano, who held the line with both hands, but had not the strength to pull himself up the little incline. He was heavy, and Sutherland was dead tired. With a savage roar, Sutherland dragged his friend a bit more from the water. Inch by inch he heaved. The dogs barked excitedly. Then the ice moved, becoming more horizontal as Tamano came up onto it. As Sutherland had hoped, the sleds were less severely canted. For the first time since the rescue began, he had hope.

Groaning and growling like an animal, Sutherland pulled his friend closer and closer, but as the chunk of ice leveled, the Scotsman's own feet went dangerously nearer to the water. If his feet got wet and froze, escape would be unlikely. Bending his legs at the knees while maintaining the fragile counterbalance, Sutherland strained with all his ebbing power to pull Tamano clear. With one great gasp, he hauled the Chippewa out of the water, then up on the ice far enough that the surface of the slab became considerably less tilted. For a moment they lay together weakly.

The wind gusted, and the small ice block inched downstream, tugging at the harness of the frantic dogs. Sutherland slid painfully along the edge of the chunk, dragging the barely conscious Tamano with him. They were yet on the high side, above the endangered sleds. After an excruciatingly slow crawl, Sutherland was nearly off. Then a strong gust tore at the slab of ice, which yielded. The sleds creaked and slipped downward. The dogs whined, being pulled toward the water. The ice again canted steeply, and Sutherland barely kept hold of Tamano; the dogs could not hold the sleds much longer, either. The second sled was half in the water. The wind howled, and the small ice chunk rotated. Even Heera had his ears down as the second sled began to submerge with a rush of bubbles and a splash as the current pushed against it.

"No!" Sutherland heard himself shouting over and over.

Tamano, too, began to slip away. He moaned. "Donoway, let go of me! Save yourself!" The dogs were hysterical, the last one scrabbling at the ice to keep from being pulled over the brink. The second sled gave a sudden downward jerk, and the first one began going over with it. Sutherland somehow found the power to bite down on the rope tied to his friend's arm, then yanked out his sheath knife. He would not give up the first sled! The end of its runners were in the water, the dog team failing. With Sutherland's strength to help them, the team might be able to save at least one sled, but first he had to cut the doomed one free.

He worked Tamano's body so that it rested against the first sled, then slid down to where the rope connected the two sleds and hacked until it snapped. The ice block became more level again. The second sled and its furs were gone, but at least the first was left, with half the furs, and Tamano safe against it. Sutherland shouted at Heera to pull, and the dogs gave it all they had. But the sled's angle of inclination was too steep. Heera barked, and the dogs hauled again and again, tails between their legs, ears laid back. No use.

Sutherland angrily worked his way to Tamano and tried to get him off the chunk of ice. With the utmost effort, he struggled back onto the main ice floe, and was dragging Tamano toward him when the chunk lurched away. The team went wild, barking and nipping deliriously as the sled sank into the water and pulled the dogs with it. Sutherland bellowed and yanked Tamano onto the main ice pack. He sprang up and grabbed the traces. The rear dog was in the water, fighting for air. Sutherland's knife slashed quickly at the leather harness, but two dogs were lost before he cut away the traces holding the rest. Heera and six of his mates bounded frantically away over the ice, still harnessed together, and Sutherland fell to his knees.

There was no time for regret yet. The furs were gone, and that was that, but Tamano was nearly dead as well. Throwing him over his shoulders, Sutherland found a last reserve of strength, and staggered blindly toward the shore. Heera and the team were already waiting there as Sutherland tottered up from the river. He found shelter out of the wind, laid Tamano on a hasty bed of pine branches, and used his tinderbox to make a blazing fire. Even before the fire was very strong, Sutherland had removed his friend's icy clothes and replaced them with his own beaver coat, fur boots, hat, and mittens. The Scotsman now wore only a warm shirt, woolen underwear, and socks, but the fire was warm. He kept his blood going by massaging Tamano vigorously, working heat into his friend's limbs, and making Heera lie close against the Indian's body. There were Algonquin villages nearby, and he would set out for one in the morning, after Tamano's clothing was dry and he awoke—if he did. He must! Sutherland refused to consider the possibility that Tamano would die.

Far to the west, Ella Sutherland did not sleep that night. She was worried about her husband, and she could not relax. She sat by the fire, rocking and knitting, while Jeremy slept soundly, and Sniffer lay on his back in a basket they had made into a bed for him.

By morning, Ella was so sleepy that she nodded off once or twice, but she was awakened by someone at the door. As she got up to answer it, Jeremy stirred, and Sniffer rose to stretch himself. It was Lela, who looked as tired and afraid as Ella.

After the first greeting, neither woman said much, but they sat down before the crackling fire and stared into it.

As he had every morning for the past ten days, Jacques Levesque went to the Cullen and Company warehouse near the river to ask for any news of Sutherland. It seemed one could learn just about anything at Cullen's well-known offices.

This morning, Levesque was rewarded with the news that Sutherland had come in; but the strange looks the clerks gave him made Levesque uneasy. When the Frenchman asked what was wrong, a young man behind the counter said, "He's been taken to the military hospital—he collapsed as soon as he mentioned your name. Looked like he was half-dead—"

Levesque dashed from the office and raced his *calèche* all the way to the soldiers' hospital in the north end of town. There he was taken into a long room lined with beds and barely heated by a couple of fireplaces at the ends. In one bed lay Sutherland, unconscious, pale, and sickly. The bored supervisor of the ward said he suffered from extreme exposure, and Levesque pulled back the covers to check Sutherland's legs and hands.

"No," the man said, twirling his bushy mustache and talking very fast, as though to himself, "nothing amputated, but it's a wonder. He's been delirious since they brought him over from Cullen's. Keeps mutterin' somethin' I can't make out— somethin' about goin' to a place called 'Mano' or somethin', I don't know, these cases . . ." The man spoke a constant stream of words, most of them worthless. Ignoring him, Levesque knelt at Sutherland's side, knowing that the delirious mumbling meant the name "Tamano." Sutherland was not moving, but he was not in the sleep of a man resting; and that was bad.

"Will he live?" Levesque asked, interrupting the babble.

The supervisor shrugged and yawned. "Might. I never know about anybody's chances. Used to try an' guess who would pull through an' who go under, but . . ."

Within hours Sutherland had been brought to Mary Hamilton's, who had insisted on putting him up in her sitting room until—if—he recovered. Dr. Devalier came to the Scotsman every day for the next week. Yet there was no change in the patient's condition. Often he cried out for Ella or Tamano, but it seemed that the Chippewa was foremost in Sutherland's inflamed mind.

Mary lived in the bedroom, and did not object—it was the least she could do for Sutherland, who had been such a close friend of Duncan's. Toby, too, responded to Sutherland's presence, lying near his bed almost constantly. He had cared for Toby after McEwan's death, and she remembered him. Mary had never seen the excitable dog so downcast, but she felt the same way. Urged to write a letter to Owen's wife, Mary held off in the hope that he would recover. Anyway, no letter could go west until the ice was out of the lakes in another two or three weeks. Day after day, for ten days, Sutherland showed no signs of recovering from his delirium.

Mary and the Devaliers did all they could. Levesque had come in every day for the first five, vanishing without explanation after that. It was on the eleventh day that Mary answered a knock on the door and opened it to find Jacques in company with a bent, seemingly aged Indian. Levesque asked about Sutherland as he helped the man upstairs, and Mary said there was no change. At the top of the steps, Levesque let the Indian limp painfully on his own to Sutherland's bed. Mary began to follow, but Levesque took her arm and held her back, saying nothing.

The Indian leaned over and touched Sutherland's face.

Mary whispered, "Is he a medicine man?"

"We'll see," Levesque said.

The Indian's hands trembled, and he wavered, as though about to lose his balance. But he continued to stand and said, "Donoway." The voice was hoarse, rasping, but deep and powerful.

Sutherland grimaced, his head moving from side to side. He was trying to talk. The Indian knelt at the side of the bed.

"Donoway, awaken, my brother."

Sutherland was more agitated, calling out, "Tamano! Tamano! Where are you?"

"I am here, Donoway."

Sutherland broke into a sweat, struggling through some tremendous barrier, but his face was no longer contorted; it was calm.

"Donoway, brother, come back to us; Tamano awaits you."

Sutherland gave a mighty shout and threw back the covers. Levesque hurried to his side, and Tamano, suffering still from his battle with death and ice, took Sutherland's trembling hands.

Sutherland opened his eyes, and looked at the Chippewa. Mary saw that Sutherland's eyes were clear. He was conscious. He was even smiling! Tamano laughed heartily and gripped his friend's hands. Sutherland lay back, and Levesque put a couple of pillows behind his head. Mary felt tears, and then the baby in the other room wanted her, waking up from all the activity in the small apartment, and crying out. She turned away and went to her child, leaving these three friends together.

After a while, as he and Tamano sipped some weak broth, Sutherland asked what had happened. Tamano told of how the Algonquins west of Montreal had cared for him after Sutherland left him there to get Levesque, and he said he had dreamed of many ancestors in those days.

"But it was not my time to die," Tamano said with a grin; his face was deeply lined, his eyes timeless, as though they had seen eternity the past two weeks. "Nor yours, brother."

Tamano's hair was graying, but he still had his arms and legs—though three small toes of his left foot were lost to frostbite. Sutherland's injuries were much less severe, and he would recover his strength in a few weeks.

"Tell me," he asked Tamano, "will you ever play *bagattaway* again?" Sutherland meant a jest, but he knew Tamano understood the question was intended to probe just how deeply the Chippewa had suffered.

A light came into Tamano's eyes. He was one of the greatest *bagattaway* players in the northwest, recognized by all who knew him as a wonder at this game. The French called it *la crosse* for the crosier-shaped stick used to throw a ball back and forth, to strike the opponent's pole. In that moment, Sutherland gave up the fear that Tamano was finished as a vigorous man. A fierce confidence was in his friend's face, and Sutherland smiled as Tamano said:

"By the time of the berries, I will be strong again—and wiser. What I have lost in the body I will have gained in the spirit."

Soon Mary brought tea with scones and jam. The baby was crying again, and Sutherland said cheerfully, "For a long time I've been hearing a baby cry in my dreams, and it's about time somebody brought it over here so I can tell it everything's fine and there's no reason to complain. Bring it here, will you, Mary?"

Mary called, "It's a she!" as she hurried away for the infant. Later Sutherland lay with the baby asleep in his arms, and he thought of Ella and how she soon would bring him one like this.

"Her name is Jeanette Marie Defries," Mary said, a little shyly. "Marie, for Mrs. Devalier, her godmother."

"It's a good name," Sutherland said, grinning.

"I hope Peter thinks so." Mary's whisper was almost inaudible, but they all heard her.

Little was said among these friends about the lost furs, though every merchant in Montreal soon heard about them. Such a disaster could not go long without rumors being spread, so Sutherland avoided rumors and told the story straight when friends from this city visited and asked. Naturally, news of the fledgling Frontier Company, though not of its secret framework, was spread as well.

Within a week Sutherland was on his feet—though not fully recovered—and had written to Ella, telling all that happened. Not only had the furs and sleds been lost, but Sutherland's Pennsylvania long rifle had gone with them. When the ice was out of the lakes, the message would go back to Detroit. Sutherland was troubled to have to send such depressing news to his friends there, but in the letter he said he was sure he could get credit from the merchants here in Montreal. Also, he was certain to return that summer with enough merchandise to carry through their original plans with Tamano, who would again trade with the northwestern tribes in the coming winter.

For his part, Tamano regained strength rapidly at Levesque's quarters, where both men were now staying, not far from Mary's home. Sutherland learned that Levesque had listened day after day to his delirious moaning of Tamano's name, and that was what had prompted the Frenchman to search the villages along the Ottawa River for the Chippewa. Now the trio was faced with a difficult task, and with each passing day they became more close-knit. Sutherland knew beyond a doubt that Levesque was a perfect partner for this company; however, he was disappointed that Mary and her husband had not joined. Perhaps, he thought, he would meet this Peter Defries one day and change his mind. But first he had to rescue the company by getting enough credit from some supply house.

Before Sutherland could begin his search for financing, he received a letter requesting his presence at the office of Lieutenant Colonel John Bradstreet. Sutherland went to the officer's headquarters and was shown into a large, airy room overlooking the Saint Lawrence. Bradstreet was a tall, elegant man with steely eyes and a firm handshake. Sutherland felt a certain coldness about this soldier, and a haughtiness as well.

Bradstreet wasted no time getting to specifics. As soon as Sutherland was seated, the colonel strutted up and down the chamber, his scarlet uniform ablaze with gold braid. In his strongly nasal voice, he told about the army being assembled at Niagara, saying that before the army departed for the campaign on the lakes, there would be a great Indian council to impress those tribes that were ready to make peace. Afterwards, two thousand men, half of them regulars, would embark across Lake Erie to invade hostile country and relieve Detroit. Sutherland was interested in these details of all that was planned.

He asked which nations were expected to come to the peace council, and Bradstreet counted off friendly Iroquois, the Seneca, Huron, Shawnee, northern Delaware, some Ottawa, some Pottawattami, and some Chippewa. The main body of Ottawa, Chippewa, and Miami, however, had already replied to the colonel's first few peace belts by pounding them into the dust.

"We'll take great steps toward peace with this Niagara council, Mr. Sutherland, but I don't have to tell you that we won't have a lasting peace until—" He gave a supercilious smile and said, "You know what I'm about to say, sir?"

"Until Pontiac comes to terms."

"Exactly!" Bradstreet clapped his hands with delight. "You're the man I thought you would be! Colonel Bouquet wrote to me about all you did for him, and recently I received a letter of recommendation from Benjamin Franklin, who apparently had an idea you would be in Montreal this spring and available. Well—"

"Excuse me, sir, I'm in Montreal, but I don't know what you mean by available."

Bradstreet gave a light laugh and sat down in a chair near his large desk. He gazed at Sutherland, sizing him up.

"Mr. Sutherland, I know everything about your accomplishments with Bouquet and Franklin. I also know of your close association with Chief Pontiac and the Ottawa." He hesitated, collecting his thoughts. "Tell me, can Pontiac raise up the tribes of the Illinois and Mississippi and unite them against us?"

Sutherland answered without a second thought. "Pontiac can raise them, as well as the Cherokee and Chickasaw and anyone else with a red skin who hates the whites. And if he does unite them under his leadership, there'll be fire and blood from Montreal to Charles Town, maybe even to New York and Philadelphia, too." Sutherland stopped before he told the officer how much he disliked British military policy.

Bradstreet pondered what Sutherland said, his slender fingers tented at his lips. "Then, sir, just how can I convince Chief Pontiac that he should come to our peace councils?"

Sutherland gave a little laugh. "You can't, unless you prove to him what you and I both know: that there's no way he can win this war—ever."

The room was heavy with silence. Sutherland already had an inkling why Bradstreet had summoned him.

"Mr. Sutherland, I understand you're a friend to many Indian tribes—"

"I was, until Bushy Run."

"Nevertheless, they trust you, I'm told, and they'd believe you if you were the one who presented the army's case, wouldn't they?"

"They might—*if* I presented the army's case, which is something I won't do. Surely both Colonel Bouquet and Dr. Franklin must have told you I have no interest in the military whatsoever, sir."

Bradstreet licked his lips and looked up at the ceiling. "Quite," he said. "I had heard that, also." Then he stared directly at Sutherland and said, "I have also heard how you sympathize with the savages, and now I have come to believe it. How else could anyone explain why you decline to take an active part in suppressing this uprising?"

Sutherland was angry. "I've already taken as active a part as I intend to take, sir."

Bradstreet said nothing for a moment, unused to such expressions of anger from subordinates—or from civilians he intended to hire. Then he said, with restrained anger, "There is no white man in all America who can walk into Pontiac's camp this summer and present our final terms to him! You, Mr. Sutherland, could nip this uprising and protect your beloved savages if you will accept my commission—a commission authorized by General Gage at headquarters in New York—to take Pontiac our ultimatum!"

The colonel sprang out of his chair and began pacing again. "Sutherland, listen to what I have to say. If Pontiac does not come to terms with us this summer, we'll kill him or have him killed, one way or the other. You're not so much an Indian that you can't see what calamity is about to befall the hostile tribes this year.

"Bouquet has two thousand men, and I have two thousand. The Iroquois are in arms against the Delaware and Shawnee. A British army of four hundred men is poised in New Orleans to strike up the Mississippi at Pontiac's camps. Even French *habitants* have been enlisted in a regiment of their own to crush Pontiac. Eight thousand regulars and provincials in these colonies are ready to advance on every front. The hostiles are doomed! If the army is unleashed there will be no Indians, no Pontiac—and no fur trade, either! If this grim outlook will not bring Pontiac to make terms, then he'll die within one year, I promise you, even if I have to hire an assassin to—"

"Enough!" Sutherland stood up, face to face with this influential officer, a man who would be showered with honors if Owen Sutherland did his bidding and convinced Pontiac to come east and make peace—and admit defeat. "I don't want to work for the army! Get someone else—get Sir William Johnson to send a Mohawk. Send anyone, but don't ask me to get in the middle again! I told you, I'm finished."

Before Sutherland could leave the room Bradstreet stepped in front of him, hands held up to stop him, and said, "You're a trader, I've heard. Well, then listen to this proposition, Mr. Sutherland."

In a few well-chosen words, Colonel Bradstreet explained that Indian trade goods worth four thousand pounds were to be sent to Pontiac and his followers as tokens of good faith. If Sutherland agreed to accept the embassy, the gifts would be bought through Sutherland's Frontier Company, which would profit enormously.

Such practice was common, not considered unscrupulous at all. However, it was not the idea of profiting from such an enterprise that repelled Sutherland—on the contrary, it would be an excellent means of rescuing the company. Rather, he was repelled by the thought of being dragged again into the Indian wars as the representative of a government that he held at fault for prompting the war to begin with. But the temptation was great, and Sutherland stepped back from the door. He went to the window and looked out over the river, where the first seagoing vessels of the spring were arriving. He clenched his fists and unclenched them as he struggled to make the right decision.

Finally, subdued and weary of all this inner turbulence, he turned to Bradstreet and said, "I cannot give you my answer yet, Colonel. Let me think about it a few days, and I'll come back with my decision."

Bradstreet shook Sutherland's hand. Much progress had been made toward winning over the Scotsman. Bradstreet knew about the loss of the Frontier Company's peltry, and he was cunning enough to take full advantage of his opportunity.

Before accepting Bradstreet's offer, Sutherland intended to test the merchant houses. He would rather persuade a merchant to extend credit than become ensnared in politics or war again.

He went to the city's largest trading house, explaining to the principals that he was sure he could bring down a great harvest of furs next year. He avoided revealing anything of the novel partnership network that underlay the Frontier Company. That was a secret he intended to keep lest anyone else attempt to imitate it. Others had dreamed of creating a great company, but none had thought of partnerships, which was the only way independent-minded traders would join any company. Sutherland had laid his groundwork, and no doubt others would follow and copy it, but if the Frontier Company was first, and firmly established with the Indian trappers, latecomers would find it difficult to dislodge them.

However, at the first merchant house he was politely refused credit. The proprietors were short of funds, in dire economic straits; they did not believe anyone could bring furs out of the northwest until the uprising was put down. He went to another, and still another house, but the response was the same. Next winter had been written off by the merchants and traders, because there would be no way to reach the farthest tribes with Fort Michilimackinac destroyed. That base was the focus of the outer trade, where the most furs were to be had for the cheapest prices. No, they told Sutherland, he was gambling, and it was too great a risk to take during a slump. More than once he was tempted to reveal the Frontier Company's partnership system. But he restrained himself when he saw that these merchants were selling to the army what they could get and had no goods for Sutherland, even if they trusted him.

Only one other company was large enough to supply Sutherland and offer enough credit—Cullen and Company. Sutherland had learned of Cullen's reputation as a scoundrel, but he was desperate now. It was already May, and he had to get a load of supplies and trade goods soon so he could return to Detroit in company with Bradstreet's huge expedition, which would offer protection all the way out.

Troubled and weary, Sutherland went to Bradford Cullen's office and explained what he wanted—three thousand New York pounds worth of Indian trade goods, and one thousand pounds in provisions and equipment for his traders.

Cullen was astounded. Sitting smugly at his shiny mahogany desk, surrounded by fine Chinese vases and Philadelphia furniture gleaming in the sunlight of early spring, the rotund man clucked his tongue and laughed. Seated across from Cullen, Sutherland restrained his growing anger as the man made light of the request. Never before had Sutherland felt as though he were begging for something.

"Mr. Sutherland, Mr. Sutherland," Cullen chuckled and leaned back in his chair. "What you are asking for is enough to provision a brigade of thirty canoes!"

"Precisely."

"Thirty canoes? Come, come, my man, there won't be five men daring enough to risk a single canoe in hostile country next season, let alone thirty."

"I'll have those men and canoes."

Cullen paused and looked Sutherland over, trying to fathom this man about whom he had heard so much. "Do you mean to tell me that you, a lone trader from Detroit, can form a brigade of thirty canoes, with *voyageurs*, with Indian trappers who will give you furs for that much trading merchandise?"

"I can." Sutherland sensed Cullen was very curious. But the merchant was touching a nerve. The Scotsman did not want to tell too much, but this was his last chance to supply his company; if Cullen refused, there was no one else in Canada capable of financing it. Many merchant houses in Montreal were on the verge of bankruptcy, and only the hope of supplying Bradstreet's campaign held out any promise for them.

Cullen sighed and thought a while, tapping the desktop with pudgy fingers. Finally he said, "You must understand, Mr. Sutherland, that Cullen and Company is not what it is today because we took rash gambles; other traders have come to me recently and asked for credit, though none as ambitious as you!" He chuckled. "But they've all been refused—for one good reason: the government is forbidding whites to trade with the Indians!"

Cullen stared at Sutherland, waiting for him to speak. Finally Cullen went on, probing more deeply. "Mr. Sutherland, there are stockholders in Cullen and Company to whom I must answer; if I make a loan to you based on what you have told me, and in light of recent past performance, well—"

"What recent performance?" Sutherland leaned over the desk, fire in his eyes.

Cullen held his ground. "My man, you just lost a small fortune in peltry by rash action—by poor judgment!"

"Poor judgment!" Sutherland slammed his fist on the desk, causing a bottle of ink to jump and a quill pen to fall from its stand. "Do you think it was with poor judgment that I acquired a small fortune in pelts when nobody else north of the Ohio River could even catch a squirrel?"

Cullen waved a hand. "Now, now, my man, I meant no insult by what I said, but this business is founded on caution, not blind speculation or flights of fancy—"

Sutherland was boiling now, as he often did in the presence of self-satisfied rascals like Cullen. "Flights of fancy? Blind speculation? Just you listen to me, Cullen, and then tell me if what I've planned is a flight of fancy. Listen, and then you'll see that I have in my hands the ability to transform the northwest peltry trade! You'll see that if you support me I'll buy enough of your wares to make your grand company look like a puddle in a pigpen—"

"Mr. Sutherland!"

"Which is what it is compared to what it might become as the sole supply house to the Frontier Company!"

Sutherland stood up, and began pacing. In the next ten minutes, while Cullen sat mesmerized, he told all about his plans and the partnership framework for the Frontier Company. He believed Cullen would see that it was a guaranteed success and would advance this large sum of credit. Still weak from his ordeal, and angry enough to show this overblown chapman just what kinds of ideas a merchant prince ought to have in his mind, Sutherland had not the force of will to hold back. By the time he had finished, his last card was played.

Cullen was amazed by all he had heard. After a brooding silence, the man cleared his throat and sat back, thinking, his fat hands again tapping unrhythmically on the desk top. "Yes. Well, I must say, Mr. Sutherland, your dream is an ambitious one, indeed. Yes."

Sutherland was on the edge of his chair, waiting. How could any merchant worth his salt deny that Sutherland had the means to do precisely what he said he could do? And why would a merchant house like Cullen's not jump at the chance to be the sole supplier of such a huge undertaking? Sutherland had intended to buy supplies and trade goods from a number of houses, getting the best prices available. Now, however, he had no choice but to offer Cullen what amounted to a partnership. He had even said he would sign a five-year contract.

"Yes." Cullen paused once more in a tantalizing, teasing way, before saying, "What you have told me, Mr. Sutherland, is a very fascinating...dream! A marvelous and entertaining story, I must say, and informative!" He sat forward, leaning elbows on his desk as he smiled, staring hard at Sutherland. "But surely, sir, you cannot expect me to believe that anyone could organize a viable trading company of the magnitude you propose from the wild and dangerous men who rove the backwoods."

"What?" Sutherland was on his feet. "I just told you I've done it! You don't believe me? Are you saying you won't extend the credit?"

Cullen held up his hands and clucked his tongue again. "Not exactly, not exactly. I won't do it this year, but perhaps if you come back to me next year with this same proposal—"

Sutherland again slammed his fist on the desktop, and this

time the ink toppled, spilling over the mahogany. The fat man was too sluggish to get out of the way quickly enough, and the ink ran down onto his lap. When he looked up in mortified anger, Cullen saw the open door, heard the sound of the frontiersman's footsteps in the hall.

Cullen's breeches were ruined, and he should have been furious, but he was not. Instead, he sat down again and tapped his fingers on the desk. He smiled. It was worth it to trade a pair of breeches for the information that Owen Sutherland had so recklessly imparted to him. Well worth it, indeed.

chapter 27

POUNDS STERLING

Feeling foolish, Sutherland returned to Colonel Bradstreet and accepted the task of going once again to Pontiac. Sutherland knew well the danger he faced if Pontiac refused to accept him as the British ambassador. He also knew how perilous a trip to Pontiac's new stronghold on the Kaskaskia River would be for any white man that summer.

However, Sutherland's determination to salvage something for the struggling Frontier Company compelled him to go, to risk his life in the service of a government composed of too many proud, unscrupulous, ambitious men. Yet for all his inner reluctance to accept this post, Sutherland knew that what Bradstreet had told him about the forces gathering to destroy the Indians was correct. Perhaps it was Sutherland's responsibility to go to warn Pontiac anyway, whether or not the British army financed a formal expedition, well equipped and supplied with four thousand pounds in Indian presents.

No matter, the decision was made, and Sutherland signed a contract. At this point he took advantage of the colonel's desperate need for an ambassador: he insisted that he be given the four thousand pounds in cash—in stable British sterling, not the fluctuating New York currency. Sutherland was not sure precisely how he would use sterling, but by the time he had spent it on Indian gifts, he would have done much to curry favor with whatever merchants he bought from. In all of Montreal no one but Cullen had the Indian trade goods Sutherland required, but Cullen would not get one farthing from the Frontier Company. Sutherland would have to go down to Albany for the merchandise and haul it back overland in a difficult, costly journey. Be that as it may, he was willing to do all this to initiate a cash flow for the company. Bradstreet's British pounds would do just that—though not as well as the lost furs would have.

If anyone but Owen Sutherland had so brashly demanded sterling, John Bradstreet would have angrily refused. However, Bradstreet was indeed ambitious, and he had high hopes that Sutherland could bring Pontiac to a peace council. The credit for such a miracle would go to Bradstreet, whose appetite for glory was voracious enough to agree to Sutherland's demands. He stipulated only that a military official take inventory at both Niagara and Detroit. That way there would be no governmental challenge when Bradstreet's accounts were examined by the British Parliament next year.

Later, Sutherland had an idea: Mary had said that her husband was well stocked with Indian presents at Niagara—presents which were intended for the peace council there that summer. Obviously he should buy from Defries, a man on the rise as a military contractor. By the time Sutherland was done with Defries, he hoped the fellow would change his mind and join the Frontier Company—the sight of sterling might just convince the Dutchman that Sutherland's new company was in a perfect position to grow in the northwest, while the military presence there was fated to dwindle to nothing.

The Scotsman told Mary his thoughts, and she was excited. Yes, she said, Peter's mind might be changed after he met Sutherland, who would leave for Niagara with Tamano in a few days. Mary added that she had recently received another letter from Peter, this one apologizing for being so harsh in his first refusal to throw in with the Frontier Company. Though he did not change that position, Peter made it clear in the letter that he was increasingly disgusted with the slow-moving, slow-paying military bureaucracy.

Sitting in a whaleboat entering the Saint Lawrence River from Lake Ontario, heading for Montreal, Defries churned inside with fury at Colonel Bradstreet, who had been expected to come up to Niagara in April. Now it was the first week in May, the ice was well out of rivers and lakes, yet there was no sign of the expedition's leader. Niagara was teeming with soldiers, provincial militia, and adventurers anxious to start west, but Bradstreet still fiddled in Montreal, increasing the size of his army, stockpiling provisions, and looking for additional whaleboats and bateaux. Unfortunately for Peter Defries, none of Bradstreet's purchases were from him. So far, Bradstreet had used his own agents, who did much of their buying in New York and Boston.

Yet such enormous amounts of food and equipment were needed for the undertaking that some merchants in Albany and Montreal were making good profits from what Bradstreet's agents did purchase. At Niagara, Defries had received the bad news from his Albany suppliers that they could no longer hold the additional goods he had requested, for others had put up money to buy them. For all his cleverness that winter alerting his suppliers to what he would order on a moment's notice, Defries had received not one requisition from Bradstreet.

A trip to Sir William Johnson might change things in the future, but that would mean another two months away from Mary, and he was sick of being without her. Angry and frustrated, Defries had thrown up his hands, hired a good whaleboat, and set out for home.

Two days later, Defries stood in the alley at the door to his own house—but if it was his own house, then why did he feel the disarming urgency to knock, as though he were a stranger? He got a grip on himself, realized his heart was pounding with excitement, and took a deep breath before removing his hat and opening the door. Toby was barking furiously, and when Defries stepped into the hallway, he thought the dog was about to attack him as she bounded down the steps.

"Toby!" he cried out, and the dog's barks changed from warning to ecstasy. Toby leaped up at Defries, standing on her hind legs and licking his face. Defries laughed and roughhoused with the dog. "Well, at least you still know me! But my, how you've grown, you—"

He suddenly looked up to see Mary, standing with one hand to her mouth, showing shock mingled with delight. In three bounds he was up and crushing her in his arms. Mary could not speak for joy, though she tried. Then a wail came from the bedroom, and Defries stepped back, listening. Mary watched his face, which changed from surprise to a smile.

Without speaking, they entered the bedroom, where Jeanette

was bawling, trying to find her thumb. Peter went to the cradle
and knelt down, carefully wiping his hands on his legs. He
reached to touch the infant. Jeanette kicked back the blanket,
and Defries took his hand away, unsure of what to do. Then
Mary was at the cradle, gazing from Peter to the baby.

He felt something tumble inside, and could not find the
words to say how good he felt. But when he looked at lovely
Mary, Peter saw her gladness, and that was enough. He put
his left hand against Mary's cheek, and she took it and kissed
it. His other hand touched on the baby's cheek, and Jeanette
tried to get a finger in her mouth. Peter laughed, and Mary
closed her eyes. Life would be just fine now. Just fine.

A few days later, Sutherland visited the Defrieses' home. Peter
welcomed him warmly, for the two men liked one another from
the start. They drank ale and talked of many things, but nothing
was said of the Frontier Company or of Defries's first bitter
refusal to join it. Sutherland asked about Niagara, and Defries
said the place was thick with soldiers, provincials, and hangers-
on.

"What's Bradstreet waiting for?" Sutherland asked, although he was not surprised that the colonel was still in Montreal. The Scotsman wanted to sound out Defries, to hear his
opinions on the British army.

Defries told of his contract with Sir William Johnson and
made offhand remarks about Bradstreet's slowness to act. "It's
the greatest force in the northwest since the French war, an'
there ain't ever been an army this big on the lakes west of
Niagara." He excused Bradstreet's failure to move by saying,
"The man needs equipment an' supplies for two thousand; no
one can expect him to purchase that much so quickly."

"Are you contracting for him?" Sutherland asked.

Defries drained his glass and got up to pour another from
the keg in the kitchen. After a moment, he said, "Hasn't Mary
told you?"

Sutherland replied, "I haven't asked her."

"Why not?"

"I wanted to ask you."

"More ale?"

Sutherland brought his glass to be filled. Then they went
to the fire and stood quietly until Defries said:

"The reason Bradstreet's so slow gettin' his expedition supplied is that he's been to every favorite, bootlicker, an' pimp from here to Boston; but he hasn't come to me. If he had, I'd have him knockin' on the gates of your Detroit by now. But he's got friends, an' I ain't one of 'em."

Sutherland sipped some ale, then said, "You won't be, as long as you're close to William Johnson."

Defries looked up sharply, and Sutherland knew he had found the right approach, though Mary had not told him that Peter was in secret partnership with the Indian superintendent. However, Defries was not sure what Sutherland knew about his relationship with Johnson.

"What does Sir William have to do with Bradstreet not ordering through me?"

Sutherland walked away and sat down. "Johnson and Bradstreet don't like each other—if you're a friend of Johnson's, you'll have heard his side of it."

"Hold on," Defries said and came to Sutherland. "I happen to have seen a letter of congratulations from Bradstreet praisin' Sir William on the winter campaign down the Susquehanna! That shows Bradstreet admires Johnson—why, he even asked Johnson to recommend contractors to supply the army this summer!"

"And did he put your name forward?"

Defries hesitated, but he saw no reason to deny it. "Sir William has been a friend of the family for many years, Owen; he set me up as contractor to the winter campaign, so I could prove to Bradstreet that I know my business."

Sutherland gave a tight smile, then said, "Bradstreet wants to shine, Peter. He wants to outshine everyone else, including—especially—William Johnson. Brant's attack on the Delaware and Shawnee took the thunder from Bradstreet's expedition; already Bradstreet's political friends have been accusing Johnson of staging the offensive just to win prestige and influence with Parliament. No, Peter, Bradstreet didn't ask Sir William for the names of good contractors because he intended to use them."

Defries was confounded, but after a moment's thought, he saw Sutherland's point. "You're sayin' Bradstreet wanted to know who *not* to use? That any friend of Sir William's is no friend of his?"

Sutherland nodded. Defries thought about it, and it made sense. He drank more ale, his eyes distant; then he gave a laugh at the irony of it all and shook his head.

Sutherland said, "If Bradstreet could have cut that Indian-present contract out from you he would have done it just to spite Johnson; but Sir William orders Indian goods—at least he orders them for his special peace councils."

Defries nodded. "That's what my merchandise is for: a council in June with the tribes from Albany to the Ohio."

"In June?" Sutherland did not wait for a reply. "Not June, Peter; it won't happen until August, because there can't be any peace councils without Bradstreet, and Bradstreet won't come out of cozy Montreal until then. He doesn't like blackflies in June, and Montreal is too pleasurable for him in July. Not to mention that all his friends are being paid to feed and supply two thousand hungry men for a summer. No, there won't be an Indian council for months, laddie."

Defries pursed his lips, his eyes troubled. Sutherland suspected he had counted on the army paying for all that Indian merchandise before autumn, but that would only occur if the council was held in June. If Bradstreet waited until August to attend the conference, the snaillike military paymaster would not get around to paying Defries until late winter—or next spring if the bureaucrats could delay it that long.

"I'll buy those Indian presents of yours, Peter."

Defries glanced at Sutherland, who went on. "You can order more merchandise right away for shipment to Niagara in time for the August council; that way your friend William Johnson won't be empty-handed when the friendly Iroquois come in for their English bribes."

Peter was thinking. "How much do you need?"

"The Frontier Company has the contract to purchase four thousand pounds' worth of Indian merchandise for the army to send Pontiac. I imagine that's about how much your Niagara storehouses hold. Am I correct?"

Defries was impressed with Sutherland's astuteness. It was apparent the man had traded with the Indians for years, and knew much about presents and councils of peace.

Sutherland said, "My company must show a profit in the transaction of thirty percent."

"Thirty!"

"Aye, laddie." Sutherland was direct with this young fellow, who understood that this was no attempt to wheedle or gouge prices. "Give me a fair load of merchandise, and I'll offer you twenty-eight hundred, paid in cash. Sterling."

Defries was impressed. "Sterling?" He quickly calculated and estimated that his profit, after Sir William and his suppliers were paid off, would be one thousand pounds.

Sutherland said, "You'll have the cash once you bring the goods to Detroit. We have permission to ship it out on the schooner *Huron,* which is at Fort Schlosser now, so it won't cost you a thing to send it; the army's paying shipment."

"Then why do you want me to come out there with you? Pay me at Niagara, an' I'll be on my way."

Sutherland looked at Mary, who stood at the door to the bedroom, listening closely. He said, "I want to show you where the future lies for traders and merchants in this country."

Defries noticed his wife and saw she was struggling with something he knew had to do with the Frontier Company and him. He gave a wry grin and said to her, "Can you miss me for another month or so, Mary?"

She came to him and sat down in a chair, reaching over to touch his arm. "Peter, I'll miss you terribly, but you know how I feel about all this. Still you know I won't go against your wishes. It's just that you might like what Owen has to say, if you give it a chance."

Defries smiled and patted her hand. Then to Sutherland he said, "For twenty-eight hundred pounds sterling, my friend, I'll listen to you boast of the Frontier Company all the way from here to China."

Sutherland put out his hand to seal the bargain. "Peter, I won't talk about the company or try to change your mind— unless you ask first."

Defries chuckled and drank more ale before saying, "When I've got my share of that much money in sterling, Owen, I won't ask a thing about Indian tradin'. I'll be too busy plannin' to buy a ship an' sail the seven seas with Mary an' the little one."

Sutherland simply smiled. He liked this Peter Defries very, very much.

Lucy and Jubal Swain had been at Fort Niagara for a week. Jubal and ten men who had been members of his gang had come as scouts, as volunteers with the militia. So they were not deserting when they resigned as a body from their unit to take jobs as guides to a botanist who wanted to explore the northwest.

Swain had made that decision, though he intended to follow the army when it moved. He had plans to collect more men of the sort who already followed him, forming a small, tough core of fighters who would move west and establish themselves in a country virtually devoid of law. Except for scattered army posts—and these had been largely eliminated with the uprising—there was no real force of law west of Niagara. The British had confined their traders to the posts for just that reason, and Swain knew it. To prevent the unscrupulous from taking advantage of the Indians, and from robbing honest traders and trappers, the army was empowered to keep whites without permits out of the wilderness.

Jubal Swain watched for his opportunity. With these men behind him, he would establish himself far from Detroit or any other post of strength, and wreak havoc as he chose upon white and Indian merchants and trappers alike. And when John Blair, the New Jersey botanist who had met Franklin and Sutherland in Philadelphia, arrived with a precious license to explore the northwest freely after peace was made, it was just the chance Swain needed to make his way into Indian country under legitimate pretenses. What would happen after he got out there was anyone's guess, but Swain fancied himself a future as a strong man outside the limits of any other authority.

Meeting with Swain in a small cabin that the botanist rented, Blair was charmed by the man—though he did not divulge the real aim of his mission: to discover the fabled Northwest Passage. With Lucy also at the meeting, Blair felt even more certain that Swain was an honest fellow offering to ramrod the expedition.

"Yes, sir, Mr. Blair, sir." Swain grinned good-naturedly, "I got me a bunch o' boys what yuh kin count on to do yuh right—ain't that so, Lucy?"

Pale but still pretty, Lucy sat nearby, gazing at Blair, who was impeccably dressed in a fine vest and coat. Though she was poor, Lucy kept herself clean, and the red silk kerchief around her neck lent a little color to an otherwise drawn face. She hardly replied to Jubal, for her thoughts were in the past; she had become quiet of late, adrift in melancholy recollections of the two lost boys. But she still believed that moving westward would help her escape the memories that relentlessly haunted her.

Jubal was passionately in love with her, though it troubled him that she was so withdrawn these days. Now, as he waited for her to confirm his assertions that his men were reliable, pain came to his eyes. He knew she was wandering in her mind again.

"Lucy!" he said sharply, and she looked around, startled. "Tell Mr. Blair about—"

Blair stood up amiably, clucking his tongue. "Now, now, Mr. Swain, I'm sure your wife is just tired. There's no need to go any further with this interview, for I'm happy with your qualifications as a woods ranger and Indian fighter. Mrs. Swain, it's been a real pleasure to meet you, and I do hope you get some rest—if that's possible in this noisy, dirty place."

Two weeks later, while Blair was busy provisioning and fitting out a whaleboat for the expedition, Sutherland arrived with Tamano and Defries at Niagara. They had left Levesque—and the dog team—in Montreal, where the Frenchman would try to raise more money. These three men wasted no time arranging to load the *Huron* with Defries's Indian gifts. By now, Tamano's health was much better, and all was moving briskly. They were so involved with preparations for their return to Pontiac—and Niagara was so filled with Redcoats, provincials, Indians, and camp followers—that it was not until their last day there that Sutherland met John Blair at Fort Schlosser, on the eastern shore of Lake Erie.

Recalling the young man from Philadelphia, Sutherland greeted him cheerfully. Blair told Sutherland he was heading north on a scientific journey, and the Scotsman said, "You intend going through Lake Huron?" Blair nodded. "I'm afraid you'll need more than a government permit to go that way, young man; you'll need permission from the Ottawa and Chippewa, but as long as they're at war with us, you won't get it."

Nevertheless Blair was confident, and he shrugged. "I'm not afraid, Mr. Sutherland. You see, I've assembled quite a stout body of men to protect me."

He gestured to where Swain's toughs were caulking the upside-down whaleboat, some lying about the beach, sleeping or drinking. Swain had insisted they be on their best behavior at least as far as Detroit; then they could do whatever they

wanted, and John Blair would have not a thing to say about
it. Blair's considerable equipment and supplies were worth
plenty, and Swain guessed the young man would be carrying
cash as well. When the time came, Blair's life would be worth
nothing.

As Sutherland looked at the disreputable crew near Blair's
boat, he felt uneasy. However, he recognized none of them;
Swain himself had noticed him approach and slipped away with
Lucy so as not to be seen.

When Swain had first spotted Sutherland loading supplies
onto the schooner for the west, he wanted to go after him, but
restrained himself. As much as he loathed Sutherland and had
sworn to kill him, Swain must wait until he was across Lake
Erie before taking revenge. For the moment he protected his
position as leader of Blair's group, and when Bradstreet took
the army on its way, Swain's gang would accompany it as
peacefully and innocently as a church choir. Their time would
come, and then, with Swain at their head, they would build
a force of ruffians more dangerous than sea pirates.

Jubal Swain was their captain, and the fur trade—and Owen
Sutherland—would be their prey.

After inviting Blair to join him in Detroit that summer, Sutherland boarded the *Huron* for the return journey. Although
Sutherland's arrival at Detroit would not be the triumphant one
he had expected when he left in March, at least there was the
contract to deliver presents to Pontiac and the western chiefs.
The twelve hundred pounds profit would be enough to keep
the company afloat, though not to stock the new quantity of
trade goods required this winter. Sutherland had not thought
all that through yet, but he was determined to succeed somehow.

For the moment he had to get back to Detroit and make
plans with Ella, Morely, and the Martines. Meanwhile, Levesque would seek new investors in Montreal. The company
needed at least three thousand pounds sterling for trade goods
and provisions for Tamano. The purchases had to be made that
autumn, before winter closed the lakes.

It was a nagging problem, and as Sutherland stood at the
railing of the small ship, with a strong wind filling the sails
and sending them on their way home, he found it difficult to
be optimistic. But in the company of Peter Defries, he was

able to cheer up. Even the stoic Tamano laughed when Defries warmed to telling funny stories, especially the tale of the paymaster's secretary and Albany Crystal snuff.

Ella Sutherland's little cabin was a retreat for her brother Henry Gladwin. In this quiet house he escaped the nagging frustrations that relentlessly plagued him as commander of a wilderness outpost under siege, responsible for the lives of more than five hundred whites in the midst of hostile Indians. Their numbers had been increasing ever since the arrival of warmer weather, and though they were far fewer than the previous summer, and though Pontiac was still in Illinois country the Indians were causing misery at this isolated outpost.

As he sat at Ella's table looking out the window at the sunny June morning, Gladwin was utterly depressed. Ella, growing big with child, busied herself spinning near the open door. Now and again she looked at her brother, wishing she could say something to lift his spirits. She knew that Henry's mood of desolation was caused not only by the situation at the fort, but also by the failure of General Gage to relieve him.

Later, they took a walk through the fort, the smells of springtime filling the air. They went to the council house, where Ella played a gentle melody on her spinet, and the music lifted their spirits.

When her brother took leave of her and returned to his duties, Ella strolled out the water gate, expecting to find Jeremy and Sally, as usual, at the riverside. Each morning at this time they took Sniffer the otter down to play at the edge of the water. It was a welcome distraction for children who ought to have been gamboling in the fields, running free and happy outside the fort. But as it was, they were able to venture only to the riverbank, where vigilant sentries kept watch when the water gate was opened during the day.

Sure enough, Ella saw them crouched by the shore, laughing as Sniffer fought with a wooden ball in the water. Even old Mawak, squatting with a pipe nearby, laughed at the otter's antics. It was a beautiful sound, this laughter. Sally Cooper, most of all, needed to laugh, to forget, to rebuild.

Absently, Ella leaned against the gate, hands on her pregnant tummy, and gazed downriver. She hoped Owen and Tamano would come back on the *Huron* when it returned with supplies and replacements for men whose tour of duty was finished.

Owen's recent letter had given her the bare details of the company's loss. Ella and the others were bitterly disappointed, appalled at the danger Owen and Tamano had encountered, but they were not disheartened. They were not that kind of people.

She watched Jeremy run barefoot up and down the pebbly beach, the otter trailing and leaping up for the ball the boy held just high enough to be teasing as Sally giggled and clapped her hands. Mawak began washing the battered blue tricorn Owen had given him last year at the wedding. The Ottawa seldom washed his clothes, but Indian choir practice was tomorrow, and Reverend Lee had insisted he look presentable, or no practice. Careful to prevent water from splashing on any part of his body, Mawak wiped away grime and dirt from the hat; he worked in that slow-motion way of many men who make such chores last twice as long as any woman would have taken to do it. When he was finished, Mawak held up the hat, and though it looked just as dirty as before, he beamed with pride at having overcome a formidable task.

Jeremy came running by, the otter at his heels, and Mawak looked around, but he should have been more alert. Sniffer darted past and, without breaking stride, snatched the hat out of Mawak's hand, dashing away with it. The Indian and Jeremy shouted and tried to catch the otter, who scampered off insolently, splashing through the ripples.

"No!" Jeremy cried, hoping Sniffer would not leap into the river with Mawak's prized possession. "Sniffer! Come back here!" Sniffer enjoyed the new game and jumped into deeper water.

Mawak stamped into the water, babbling in anger, and Jeremy rolled up his breeches before wading in up to his thighs. All the while, Sniffer swam back and forth just out of reach. Shooting this way and that, the otter kept the hat in front of him. At least he had not torn it to pieces yet, as he usually did when he had a mouthful of his archenemy—the beaver. Mawak, waist-deep in the cold river, hopped and ranted, but Sniffer merely swam farther out.

Staring furiously at Sniffer, Mawak began a sort of coughing chant that got the creature's attention. Sally came close to Jeremy, and asked, "Is that otter talk?"

"Probably," the boy said, watching Mawak scold the otter, which now faced him, just a few feet away, but still out of reach. "It sounds like mad otter talk."

As he spoke, Mawak moved slowly toward the otter, who gazed at him with big eyes. The Indian reached forward, closer and closer, about to get the hat, but Sniffer gave a snort and moved away.

"Fool of an otter!" Mawak shouted, shaking his fist.

Sniffer simply floated nonchalantly on his back, the hat in his teeth. Then Mawak raised his hands to the sky and began another chanting, coughing invocation. He leaned over and peered right at the otter, still chanting and motioning with his hands, as though drawing the animal nearer. Sure enough, the otter came closer—almost close enough for the hat to be caught. As the battle of wills raged between Mawak and Sniffer, Ella was sure the sound of the chant changed, and Mawak began to slap the water with his hand, much as a beaver slaps the water with its tail.

In a twinkling, Sniffer came close. Mawak grabbed his hat, and the otter dived out of sight. As the Ottawa turned and strode angrily out of the water, Sally called, "Was that otter talk, Mawak?"

The Indian glanced back at where Sniffer had vanished, grunted, then looked at the girl and said, "That *beaver* talk! Plenty *big* beaver! That damned fool otter never heard so big a beaver talk, an' he listen, betcha!" Mawak nodded ponderously, and said to Jeremy, who looked ashamed at the trouble his pet had caused, "You tell that damned fool otter this Injun make new hat outa him next time!"

Mawak walked away carrying his soaked tricorn, wringing it dry as he made his way up to the water gate, where Ella was watching, trying not to laugh. As he passed, Mawak gave her a dark and gloomy look. Then he stopped and asked, "You ever try otter stew?" Smiling, she shook her head. "Stink too much an' taste bad, you betcha! But this Injun eat it quick when you make it! You want nice otter hat? Soft, warm! You tell Mawak! Do it quick, you betcha!"

The old man strode into the fort, and Ella watched Jeremy carrying Sniffer away down the shore toward the landing. Behind came Sally, skipping and singing gaily. It was a nice scene.

Suddenly she heard the full clap of several cannon, and she saw bluish smoke far out on the river. Shielding her eyes from the morning sun, Ella saw the white sails of the *Huron* and cried out for joy. Owen must be aboard! Let him be home! In the next moment a cannon replied in salute from the fort, and soon the shore was mobbed with eager folk anxious for news of the east, hoping Bradstreet's army was on its way to Detroit at last.

chapter 28

SWAIN'S ATTACK

Owen's return to Ella was an inexpressible joy. Carrying a canvas bag, Sutherland leaped from the ship's rail down to the dock. He saw Ella running along the shoreline, Jeremy, Sally, and Sniffer behind her, a dog yipping in pursuit of Sniffer. But Sally stopped short, and the otter sprang into her arms for safety. At the beginning of the dock, Sutherland and Ella met and embraced. The children leaped joyfully around them, and Jeremy took hold of the bag. All about the landing the same scene was repeated by returning folk, including Tamano, whose wife, Lela, bounded against him, laughing at first. Then, seeing how he had changed after his awful struggle, Lela stood back, holding Tamano's hands. But even before she asked, the Chippewa said he would tell her later.

Along with Defries, the couples and the children made their way up the slope to the gate, where Major Gladwin met them with hearty handshakes. Garth and Lettie Morely, Angélique Martine and her father, Jean, were also at the gate. As soon as they saw haggard Tamano, now strong again but more gray than ever, they knew their partners had been through hell. Gladwin had to attend to the ship and dispatches; the others, including Defries, went to Morely's warehouse.

Though the loss of their furs had jarred them, none were dejected or pessimistic. Lettie Morely spoke for all when she said, "Thank the Almighty that thee both be back with us, an' alive. That be what counts!"

They sat around the big table in the trading house, and after

Sutherland and Tamano had told the whole story of the mishap,
there was a long silence until Garth Morely scratched his bristly
beard and said, "Well, I guess we've all been in tighter fixes
than this an' come out the other side, an' I guess we'll come
out this one, too! Lettie, darlin', this be the time for that there
good port we been savin' for a rainy day. Yes, this be a rainy
day, so we best be drinkin' some port to warm us up, eh?" He
grinned at Sutherland, who saw a bold fierceness in his friend
and recognized the strength and depth of this old trader.

"Aye," Sutherland said, "get out that port, Lettie, lass,
and—" he reached down into the canvas bag he had carried
ashore "—and we'll see how it compares with some fine Scotch
whiskey." He clicked a bottle of whiskey on the table, then
followed with some excellent French brandy purchased for
Martine in Montreal. He looked at Tamano, who emptied another bag of presents for everyone.

In a moment, the sober mood had vanished in the excitement
of gift-giving. The children all received toys; Angélique flour-
ished a bottle of rosewater and a letter from Jacques; her father
had a book of Voltaire's concerning the English nation; Lettie
put on comfortable sabots; Morely was given three bottles of
port equal to those he so treasured; and Ella received a collec-
tion of John Dowland's songs for her spinet. As he watched
from the end of the table, Peter Defries was impressed and
touched to see these folk so cheerful and unperturbed in the
face of financial disaster.

When the commotion died down, Martine laughed and said
to Owen, "And what, my friend, will you bring back when
your journey is a successful one?"

Sutherland smiled and said, "I haven't said everything."

He explained about the contract he had been given by Bradstreet to supply Pontiac and the chiefs of the Illinois with
presents to show British good faith and desire for peace. By
the time Sutherland told them the company would realize twelve
hundred pounds sterling in profits from the contract, the partners were laughing with amazement. They took Defries into
their circle without the least self-consciousness, though none
of them knew at first that Sutherland hoped Peter would one
day join the company. After it was explained that Peter was
the husband of Mary Hamilton, the one they had sought as
then Montreal agent, the others were full of questions about
him. Defries realized Sutherland had no intention of saying the

Dutchman had refused to join the company.

Morely asked directly, "Well, Mr. Defries, be thee an' thy wife throwin' in with us, then?"

Defries cleared his throat and glanced at Sutherland again, but the Scotsman was gazing at him as though enjoying the young man's uneasiness. Defries looked at Morely and said, "Your kind offer does me honor, Mr. Morely, but you see, I'm committed to supplyin' the military."

"The military!" Morely hooted. "Well, son, I wish thee lots o' luck! I hope thee be patient an' slow to anger. I can see by thy cut thee be no bootlicker or politician, so for thy own sake, I wish thee well, an' a bateau-load o' patience. Yes!"

Soon more friends arrived to welcome back Owen and Tamano, and an impromptu celebration began. Tables were pushed against walls, somebody brought a fiddle, and another came in with a dulcimer and tambourine. It seemed everyone in the fort—including Gladwin and his officers—came in at one point or another, many bringing something to eat or drink. By midafternoon, British, provincials, French, and Indians were rollicking and dancing around the warehouse, which fairly thumped with music and song. As night fell, the memories of defeat were swept away from Owen and Tamano, and they saw ahead only the bright prospect of success.

During all this happiness, Peter Defries did considerable thinking. He liked these people. These last few weeks on the lake with Sutherland and Tamano had also attracted him to the Frontier Company. As he stood in a corner of the trading house, watching the fun and honest camaraderie, Peter thought Mary would like these folk, too. Then he remembered why he was out here. He had fulfilled his part of the bargain and accompanied the cargo of gifts west. Now he would be paid by Sutherland and go back to Montreal, back to Mary and to his aborning profession as a military contractor. Fur trading he knew little about, and even though this country was appealing in its beauty and promise, he had no desire to live here.

Of course—he had not been asked to move west, for the company could use him best in Albany or Montreal, the two traditional competitors for the riches of the fur trade. No, not Montreal. He was a native of Albany, so if he were the supplier of goods for the Frontier Company he would be based in Albany and would make that city the peltry capital of North America.

He caught himself. What was he thinking about, anyway?

He was not about to join the company. He had obligations to Sir William Johnson, and his future lay in that alliance, none other.

By the time the party ended late that night, Sutherland and the other major partners stayed behind to discuss future business in detail. Morely and Martine both said that bringing Indian presents to the tribes of the Illinois might be a blessing in disguise. That country, though now officially British, had never been successfully penetrated by any fur traders other than French. Sutherland had gone up there years ago in company with Spanish traders, but they had been attacked and wiped out—save Sutherland, who was adopted by the Ottawa. The first British traders into that country would be able to establish trading contracts with the Illinois, Ottigamie, and even unknown tribes west of the great river. The company could control trade with northern tribes bringing furs down the Mississippi from the vast peltry-rich country drained by the Father of Waters. By the time they finished their discussion, the principals in the company were excited and enthusiastic. They were on the threshold of a completely new venture, a potentially thriving trade with distant western tribes as yet unspoiled by white goods and liquor.

At the close of their talk, Martine asked Sutherland about young Defries. Owen, cleaning his pipe with a jackknife, sighed.

"I promised not to try to talk him into joining, Jean. He came out here, and now he has seen us. I'll do no more than pay him off and wish him all the best if he returns to Montreal without coming in with us."

Morely said, "He's a good man—the kind we want."

Sutherland agreed. "His wife is right, too. Perhaps one day we'll have dealings with them, but whether we'll ever convince him to join . . ."

The next day passed in rest and relaxation for Sutherland, Tamano, and Defries. Owen and Ella were grateful to be alone again, and he was impressed by her change since he left in March. She had been approximately five months pregnant then, and now she was more than seven, and it showed. Jeremy and Sally spent a lot of time with them that day, and Sutherland thought they were like brother and sister. Weeks ago Ella had sent a letter to Benjamin Franklin, asking whether he could locate relatives of Sally's who would take her in. However, Ella made it apparent to her husband that she grew more attached to the child with every passing day. They did not yet discuss adopting her if no family was found, but it was in their thoughts all the same.

Sutherland intended to go to Pontiac after the Ottawa chief responded to a request for an interview. Jean Martine had arranged through another Frenchman to ask Pontiac for the meeting with Sutherland. By the time Pontiac's message came back to Detroit it would be at least July, and everyone hoped Colonel Bradstreet's force would be at Detroit by then, even though Sutherland had his doubts. But whenever the commander did arrive, Sutherland would consult one final time with him before departing for the Illinois.

Sutherland and the inhabitants of Detroit were not the only ones anxious for Bradstreet to get there; Peter Defries was also hopeful the army would come in soon. He had decided to stay in Detroit, because it was the best place to discuss possible supply contracts with Bradstreet, who, while in Montreal, would no doubt be preoccupied every minute making plans. Even though Bradstreet's agents would have already purchased many of the supplies, Defries knew that a campaign of this size would require a great deal of additional food and equipment. If he was successful contracting for these goods, then he would return promptly to Montreal and fill the requisition lists—he counted on Bradstreet using him, despite Sutherland's insistence that the officer disliked anyone associated with Johnson. In the meantime, Peter lived in a rented cabin near the Martines, idling away his time, intensely missing Mary and the baby.

A warm June became hot and sluggish July, with still no news of Bradstreet. Word came back from Pontiac that he would accept Sutherland's embassy, and that was cause for gladness among members of the company. Still no Bradstreet. Gladwin also was restless, because he expected to depart as soon as the commander of the expedition arrived. He often became moody and short-tempered, but Ella was always there to soothe him. With his good friend Owen Sutherland back to challenge him at chess, Gladwin was able to counter the gloom that threatened to break his spirit.

Sutherland was surprised one day to receive a package and

letter from Benjamin Franklin in Philadelphia. Jeremy had gone to the schooner when it arrived that afternoon, and the ship's master had given him a long, heavy box and the letter. Struggling with his burden, the boy staggered through the fort, in his excitement crying Sutherland's name even before he reached the door of the cabin.

No one could have been more moved than Owen Sutherland when he opened the box and found a splendid new Pennsylvania rifle, even more magnificent than the one he had lost in the Ottawa River last winter. Ella had written Franklin about the misfortune, and she was now delighted with this gift for her husband. With Ella, Jeremy, and Sally at hand, admiring the rifle, Sutherland sat down to read Franklin's letter, one both informative and complimentary.

"For the time being, the borderers seem mollified, because the governor himself has finally given them promises of protection. Whether these resourceful folk will in fact need the governor's protection remains to be seen."

Franklin went on to say that no more outbreaks of violence had occurred against peaceful Indians. Indian raids had recurred during warm weather; but they were not as savage, nor as widespread, as the previous year. Matthew Smith was again ranging the woods with his neighbors, very effectively turning back scalping parties. Colonel Bouquet's upcoming expedition against the Shawnee and Delaware was the talk of the province; if that campaign was successful, the borderers would truly be able to live in peace.

Franklin also said Sutherland's poetry had generated much interest among Philadelphians; he asked to see more poems, adding that the one he liked best was that written for himself and delivered just before Sutherland left the city. "Although," he wrote, "this little show of vanity on your subject's part hints that he may not be as humble as the poem so generously suggests."

He ended by saying he would do all in his power to locate relations of Sally Cooper—though it might prove difficult, since so many frontier families had been wiped out or had fled the region. Reading this last part, Sutherland thought he and Ella might regret it if the girl's relations were found, for she grew increasingly dear to them with every passing day.

• • •

In August, word arrived by the *Huron* that a great Indian council had finally taken place at Fort Niagara. Headed by Johnson and Bradstreet, the council was a success in quelling the uprising among the Mingo, Seneca, Wyandot, Huron and some Shawnee and Delaware. Wielding the threat of his Mohawk hammer, Johnson compelled the Delaware, Shawnee, and Seneca to accept peace. The Indian superintendent had made his point effectively, and it seemed the northern uprising's deathblow would be dealt by Bradstreet crossing Lake Erie and threatening the Maumee villages. That threat, combined with Bouquet's march into Shawnee country, would shatter the Ohio Valley confederacy once and for all, and these Indians, too, would have to sue for peace.

Only the northwestern alliance of Pontiac remained to be beaten, and that included Ottawa, Chippewa, Pottawattami, and now the Illinois tribes that Pontiac compelled to join him. If that force was not broken up, Pontiac would have the ability to bring other tribes of the Mississippi into his uprising—tribes that included the numerous Chickasaw and Cherokee. The northwest was still poised on the brink of a breakout by a huge united Indian force—one that would nullify all former treaties and protestations of peaceful intentions won by Bradstreet and Bouquet. Thus it was up to Owen Sutherland to go into the heartland of the uprising, and in the face of death, to persuade Pontiac to come east to confer with Sir William Johnson, eventually to make a final peace with the British crown.

Unless Pontiac came in, there would be no lasting peace, and there would be warfare on the frontier for years to come. If Pontiac made terms, there was hope that a treaty line prohibiting white settlement could be established once and for all. Without a barrier line there was no hope for the survival of the Indians, who would be hounded, attacked, and wiped out by settlers and by militia forces until the entire race east of the Mississippi was exterminated. This dread consequence of prolonged war was what spurred on Sutherland to go to Pontiac.

That August, the languid Bradstreet and his powerful army finally arrived at Detroit, which turned out en masse to welcome him. Cannon fired, musketry rippled, people shouted and cheered, and the river was choked with whaleboats, bateaux, Indian canoes, and small ships. Bradstreet brought with him an army grown to three thousand soldiers, along with their equipment, supplies, and camp followers. Never before had such a huge mass of humanity crowded around Fort Detroit.

For the first few days, Bradstreet was busy arranging logistical matters with his officers and Henry Gladwin, whose dreams were at last coming true. Gladwin found Ella and Owen in their cabin one afternoon, bursting through the door and laughing like a young boy.

Ella hugged him, and he spun her around after they heard he was soon going back on the new schooner *Victory,* and would be in England by November. For a heady moment, the three friends could not have been happier, but then, as if on signal, they all stopped short and stared at one another, realizing this might be the last time they would be together.

Sutherland said, "It won't be the same without you, Henry."

Gladwin smiled and nodded slowly. "Nothing will be the same again, will it?" Then he said cheerfully, "But you'll both be happy here, and I'll be happy there. Will you come and visit Frances and me, sister?"

Ella's eyes became teary, and she pressed against her brother's chest. "I hope one day, Henry."

Sutherland voiced what Ella and he had thought about for some time now. "Henry, if Jeremy wants it when he's a little older, will you take him in and give him a proper education?"

Gladwin's face lit up, though he knew how much these two would miss the boy. "He would be like a son to me! I would be honored, Owen!"

Ella hugged him again. Her husband shook Gladwin's hand and said, "It is we who would be honored, my friend."

Along with Bradstreet's force came John Blair and his man Jubal Swain, commander of the dozen toughs now in the expedition. Lucy was with them also, but the long wait in Niagara for Bradstreet's army, and the long journey, had been a strain on her already weakened constitution. Swain often worried about her. However, after a few days at Detroit, Lucy showed herself content with this new world and regained her strength. Swain made a point again of keeping away from Owen Sutherland, intending to confront him at the right moment and on his own terms.

First Swain had to get control of Blair's boats and equipment. It was his plan to spend a few weeks at Detroit, then slip away one night with as many men as would join him. He would take the whaleboats and canoes and make for the Maumee River to the south, traveling upstream, trading with villages there, sizing up the country, and heading deeper into the interior. Eventually he would make camp for the winter, build a small fort, and hole up solidly. Then in the month of March he would begin to raid Indian trappers and traders. He would cut off furs going down the Mississippi to New Orleans, or he would send his raiders northeast to intercept peltry bound for Detroit and Montreal.

It was an ambitious plan, but Swain had worked it out carefully, picking many brains for knowledge of the northwest. He would also take Blair's maps to guide him, and he had enlisted fifteen additional men willing to join his dozen now working for Blair. Eventually a force of fifty well-armed fighters could set up a small empire in the northwest, and the battered, weakened Indians could do little to stop them. Within two years, Swain would have many more men, and they would build a stronger fort with a settlement. Newcomers would be welcome to buy land from Swain, enriching him and increasing his power. Between furs and land sales, Swain figured he could easily finance and hold a domain beyond the law of any country. Now, as he lingered in Detroit, planning how to steal a load of provisions and enough equipment, he and Lucy lived in a tent down by the river, well away from the fort and Owen Sutherland.

Now and again Swain would follow Sutherland through the fort, marking the Scotsman's movements, watching who were his friends. Swain moved from cover to cover, nonchalantly pretending to be out for a stroll, but always keeping out of Sutherland's sight. There was always a tomahawk and knife at Swain's side, and they would do well for a sure, silent killing. One night, he knew, he would catch Sutherland in the dark, and it would be over quickly. However, that pleasure would have to wait until Swain's plan was riper and he could flee without botching his schemes, if he was suspected of murder.

More than once the backwoodsman trailed Sutherland simply because he had nothing better to do and it was an interesting, challenging way to waste some time. Also, he saw who could best be killed if he wanted to hurt Sutherland deeply, and he had selected a few likely victims.

Often he followed Sutherland to the cabin of Peter Defries,

which was out of the general hubbub. Peter shared his cabin with John Blair, glad for the company. Swain sometimes had to make up an excuse for not meeting Blair at the cabin and thereby becoming known to Defries, but that was never much of a problem. Peter's company was stimulating to the young explorer. About the same age, they shared a compulsion to achieve a specific goal. Though Defries was uneducated, his quick mind appealed to Blair, who never had known a man so intelligent yet so uncultured. For Defries's part, he liked Blair's confidence, knowledge, and good talk of botany and the North-west Passage. They often sat up late into the night, talking about whatever came to mind. It seemed they could never exhaust the other's interest, and they soon became fast friends.

When Defries finally managed to make an appointment with the busy Colonel Bradstreet, the officer had been in Detroit for more than a week. Though he knew of Peter, both from John-son's letter and from several letters Peter had sent him, Brad-street was not particularly cordial.

Peter stood—there was no chair available—at the far end of a long table in the commandant's house, and Bradstreet sat at the other. Peter mentioned Johnson's winter campaign, when Brant destroyed hostile villages, but Bradstreet was not inter-ested. Several times as Peter spoke about his hopes for a supply contract, Bradstreet drew a pinch of snuff into his nostrils and immediately sneezed hard, swearing as he did so. This cut Peter off, and he stopped talking until Bradstreet leaned back and waved a hand for him to continue. Each time Peter began again, his anger at this haughty officer mounted.

". . . and so you see, sir," Peter said, hat in hand, "I have considerable connections in Albany which can—"

"Albany?" Bradstreet cried out and his chair legs clumped to the floor. "You say you're from Albany?"

Defries sensed he might have made an inroad, and he smiled. "Why, yes, sir, I'm—"

"Wait, wait!" Bradstreet leaned forward and waved a bony finger at him. "Albany, you say!" He looked at the box of snuff in his hand. "Tell me, which side of the Hudson River is Albany on?"

Defries looked at the snuff, and saw it was speckled like salt and pepper, a sort of crystalline mixture. He would have laughed if he was not so disgusted with Bradstreet—with the whole damned military establishment.

"Well, sir," Defries began and rubbed his chin, as though

thinking. "You see, that depends on whether you're travelin' north or south!"

Bradstreet's face was blank. His chin dropped, and the look of his watery eyes told Defries that the mixture his mother had concocted for Gillis's Albany Crystal had considerable potency.

Pretending meekness, Defries asked, "I say, sir, would that happen to be the snuff commonly known as Albany Crystal?"

"What? Why, yes. Yes, it is. Why do you ask?"

"An' did you happen to acquire it through a Mr. Gillis?"

Bradstreet said he did. "Do you know something about it, then?"

Defries grinned. "I guess I know just about all there is to know about Albany Crystal—except what that Mortimer Gillis knows, an' I guess he knows a lot by now."

Bradstreet looked irritated. "He does, the rascal. He knows what side of the river Albany's on—I mean, he knows which nostril to snuff first. Do you, Mr.—Mr.—uh—"

"I do. But I have to say that Mortimer Gillis is *some* kinda man, the way he snorts that Crystal like it was steam from my mama's soup! He's a man like I never met before! I mean he *can* put that Crystal away! But I guess you know that, Colonel, bein' a friend of his an' all."

Bradstreet was even more irritated. "Yes, well . . . hmmm. That Gillis can keep his head when he sniffs Albany Crystal, the rascal. Though he needn't flaunt it so! But it's just because he knows— But here, now, my man, you say you know all there is to know about Albany Crystal. Well, then, be good enough to tell me which nostril goes first."

Defries chuckled contentedly. "Say, there, Colonel, you wouldn't happen to have a chair handy, would you?"

Bradstreet grumbled and called an orderly to bring in a chair for Defries, who sat down with a sigh of relief. He did not like this officer, nor would he ever like him, but he was willing to tell him which nostril first—for a price. "Back in Albany, I'm well-known as a reliable supplier. It would do my heart good to be known that way in Montreal an' Detroit an' anywhere else your troops are stationed, Colonel. But first I need to prove myself by being awarded a contract by you."

They looked at one another, but Defries was not sure he was penetrating. He went on, "What I mean is, Colonel, I'll trade you the answer to your question for the promise of a supply contract."

Bradstreet finally understood. He pursed his lips, squinted, and sat back. "My man, all our contracts are out for the time being. Certainly you can't expect me to cancel one just so you— Certainly not!"

Defries sighed. "I thought surely you'd have saved a contract or two—say for when the troops returned to Niagara—just in case you needed to pay a debt or win somebody's favor."

Bradstreet was livid. Through clenched teeth he said, "Who do you think you are to speak so to me? I'll have you thrown out—"

Defries raised his hands, smiled blandly, and stood up.

Bradstreet demanded, "Where do you think you're going?"

"Back to Albany, on this side of the Hudson!"

"Damn it, man!" Bradstreet smashed his fist on the table. He stood up, pointed a shaking finger at Defries, and hissed, "I'll have that answer, do you hear? Which nostril first?"

Defries leaned forward, his eyes cold. "Promise me that Niagara contract, an' I'll not only tell you, but I'll arrange it that Mortimer Gillis will never be able to buy another box of Albany Crystal again."

Bradstreet stared at Defries. The officer was thinking hard, eyes intense, jaw set. After a moment, he slammed his fist on the table again. "Dammit! You have your Niagara contract!"

Defries stood up straight and pulled his coat down a bit. "Albany Crystal must always be taken in the left nostril first, Colonel."

As though a great burden was released from his shoulders, John Bradstreet sighed and sat down heavily. After a pause, Defries said lightly, "I'll return to Detroit with the *Victory* an' have your goods in Niagara by late September, if that's all right, sir."

But Bradstreet held up a hand. "Not so fast, there." He fumbled at his box of Albany Crystal, nervously looking up at Defries, who was eager to depart. "I'll try this first, and if it works, our bargain is sealed. If it does not—"

He took a pinch. Defries's face showed strain as he watched every small movement the officer made. The thumb to the left nostril. The sniff.

Nothing. No sneeze. Defries was amazed. The colonel's eyes lit—though slightly watery, of course—then he jumped up and came around the table to pump the Dutchman's hand.

"Niagara!" Bradstreet roared with delight. "See my quartermaster in the morning, and he'll give you a full list of what is needed! Now, off you go, and I'll hold you to your promise never to permit that scoundrel Gillis to get his hands on another box of Albany Crystal!"

Defries swore solemnly and bowed as Bradstreet himself opened the door and showed him out.

Outside in the hall, Defries gloated over his success, placing his tricorn on his head. Suddenly the most horrible—most tremendous—sneeze he had ever heard exploded in Bradstreet's chamber. As Defries dashed out the door of the house, he heard another, and then another sneeze, each one astonishingly more violent than the first. Before Bradstreet could catch him, Defries was gone, hurrying for his cabin, to wait for the morning, when, he hoped, it would be safe to see Bradstreet again.

But the next morning brought a message from Bradstreet himself. Defries was not particularly surprised to read that the colonel denied him the contract to supply the army on its return to Niagara. In fact, the letter swore that Peter Defries would never supply a military force commanded by John Bradstreet. Never!

Defries had tried, but failed. For all his efforts he had only the twenty-eight hundred pounds sterling from the Frontier Company—now in safekeeping with the fort's paymaster—but he had no contract to supply troops.

Owen Sutherland went to Defries's cabin late that afternoon, and found him sitting glumly at the table, thinking hard.

He sat down next to Defries and waited for him to say something, but he did not.

Sutherland said, "So you missed a chance to play servant to John Bradstreet, eh?"

"Don't make fun of it, Owen."

Sutherland chuckled. "Sooner or later you would have found out about contracting to the army, lad, and then you would have been sorry to have missed the chance to join us. But now you still have that chance, on the same terms we offered at the start. You supply us, we'll ship goods and furs and carry out the trade. You can stay in Montreal, Albany, wherever you want. What do you say?"

Defries looked up at Sutherland, his face full of both interest and confusion. He thought a bit, then offered, "I've got credit at Albany now, an' I can put in my ready cash—a thousand pounds of what you've paid for the Indian presents. I know Mary would agree to this, too. I'll get it all in the morning an' turn it over to the company to spend the way you want."

Sutherland laughed, and they stood up to hug one another vigorously. With Defries's thousand and the twelve hundred earned from the company's military contract, they would have almost enough to finance the next year's goods for trading. They were again close to success, and all that remained to be done—though formidable and dangerous—was to convince Pontiac to give up this war. Then Indian country would be thrown open to the fur trade, and the Frontier Company would be the foremost trading firm in the northwest.

Sutherland said, "All right, laddie! The *Victory*'s leaving for Niagara a week from tomorrow. We'll give you twelve hundred to add to your thousand, and we'll have Jacques Levesque and Mary do some of the purchasing because they know what to buy for the trade! I'll have the paymaster give it to you, but no one should know you're carrying it, or you'll be in danger. Give the money to the master of the ship, and he'll put it away until you reach Niagara."

When they had made their plans and Sutherland had left, Defries clapped his hands once and lay down on his bed to think contentedly about the company, about Mary, and about the baby. He was too wrapped up in these happy thoughts to notice a man who had been listening all the while at his window. It was Jubal Swain.

Back in Montreal, Mary Hamilton Defries was a cheerful young mother, her child strong and healthy. Jacques Levesque was a close friend, though their bright hope of ever cooperating as partners in the Frontier Company was gone. Levesque was working hard in Montreal, trying to find a few French investors to join the firm. He was successful in convincing Dr. Devalier and his wife to join, adding another dimension to the Frontier Company.

One afternoon, as the Devaliers had tea with Mary and Jacques, the conversation turned to news of the Cullens, Mary's former guardians and owners of the firm that had refused Sutherland credit.

"Now that I am a member of the company," said Dr. Devalier, "I should bring you any intelligence I hear which may be of benefit to you . . . to us!"

Devalier told Levesque that Cullen and Company was trying hard to hire a large brigade of canoes and *voyageurs* for the coming season. It was apparent that the merchant had ideas of forming his own Indian trading company.

"Our friend Mr. Sutherland told him too much about forming such a company, I fear." Devalier said. "This Cullen has the wealth and connections to finance his own firm, but can he get out to the villages before our company?"

"The question is more whether he can buy the trade goods needed, Doctor. Albany and Montreal have been picked clean for the Indian councils in Niagara and for the Pontiac embassy. There might be more available soon, but there won't be enough to supply two trading companies this winter."

Mary asked, "You mean the first company that is able to buy goods when they come in will be the one to control the trade?"

Levesque nodded. "The first company with Indian goods will be the first one out to the villages. This winter there won't be enough prime peltry for two companies to profit because the Indians are still suffering from the fighting and from the government stopping the trade. Whatever they have to trade to us won't go far enough to enrich both Cullen and the Frontier Company."

Levesque thought for a moment, then added, "We have to get the goods first—somehow! Cullen has to be stopped from buying up everything that comes into Montreal, or we'll have nothing to trade and we'll never make up the ground we lose to them."

Devalier asked, "Have we the money to buy such goods soon?"

Levesque shook his head sadly. "If Cullen outbids us in order to break us, we may never have enough, Doctor."

At Detroit that evening, Ella, Owen, and Henry dined together in Gladwin's house, no one saying anything about the officer's departure the following week. Jeremy and Sally were in the company of John Blair, who had become close friends with the children. Blair was also enchanted by Sniffer, and he enjoyed playing with the otter while answering the endless questions put to him by an eager Jeremy, whose capacity for learning seemed insatiable.

Gladwin—recently promoted to lieutenant colonel—would

leave on the schooner *Victory* along with Peter Defries, and they would make their way to Montreal, where Peter would begin work. From there Gladwin would go to New York Town and confer with General Gage, a good friend. Then he would catch a ship for England—at last!

Finding it hard to sit comfortably because she was so far along in her pregnancy, Ella fidgeted in her chair as Owen and Henry spoke about the current situation in the northwest. It was apparent that neither man had much regard for the now absent Bradstreet.

"I have heard from Colonel Bouquet and from General Gage himself that Bradstreet has not even carried out his orders!" said Gladwin. "Instead of marching southwest, to meet Bouquet, he parleyed with a few Shawnee who came into his camp at Sandusky."

Ella asked, "Isn't it better to make peace than to keep fighting, Henry?"

"Of course, if one actually makes peace. But I was told by a reliable junior officer of Bradstreet's that these Shawnee had been caught skulking around his camp, probably spying. Yet when they were brought in they claimed they were spokesmen for their people. They had, however, no more than a single strand of wampum with them."

"But Indians always bring great belts of wampum to their meetings!" Ella said. "They can't have been spokesmen!"

"Exactly. I'm sure they spoke for no one, but they successfully diverted Bradstreet from his duty and spared their own towns certain destruction.

"Futhermore, Bradstreet's actions undermine Bouquet's perilous march through the forest. If the hostiles realize that Bouquet is unsupported on his way to the villages on the Muskingum, and that there is no lakes force turning south, they might outflank him and cut him off!" Gladwin was angry now. "That buffoon Bradstreet has put the lives of two thousand men in jeopardy by his greed for glory! The Indians are laughing at him and call him 'Timid Deer!' He thinks making unauthorized treaties instead of fighting will win him accolades from Parliament, but if Bouquet is smashed—"

Once again this miserable Indian war had depressed the officer. Ella touched his arm and said sympathetically, "Not tonight, Henry. You'll not have to worry about this anymore, dear. Think of it. Soon you'll be back with Frances again."

Gladwin took Ella's hand and looked at Sutherland. "Owen understands why I'm saying this." He turned back to Ella and said, "You see, sister, if Pontiac knows Bradstreet has been fooled, that the Indians have avoided being crushed by such a large army—and one that cost much to create—then Owen might be worthless as an ambassador; he may even . . ."

They were silent until Ella said, as if in a daze, "You mean Owen is in danger."

Sutherland tried to laugh her fear away. "Now, now, lass, you know I'm safe as far as Pontiac is concerned. I trust him in this—"

But Ella burst out: "The way Henry trusted him with the life of Captain Campbell last year?" It pained everyone to be reminded of the fate of the likable Donald Campbell. He had been promised safe conduct by Pontiac shortly after the siege began—but the captain was taken prisoner by him and later hacked to pieces by another war chief. Ella's point was well taken.

Still, Sutherland attempted to steady her. "There is no other choice in this, don't you see? I have to go."

Ella was trembling as she said, "For the company, you mean? Owen, no one in the company wants you to die! If this embassy to Pontiac is so dangerous, then—" She tried to keep from breaking down, and her brother and husband each took a hand. Gladwin apologized for bringing up this subject, but Ella forgave him.

"Perhaps I should leave you two alone," Gladwin said and went into the other room.

Ella and Owen gazed at one another, holding hands. For some time they remained that way, but neither spoke. Then Ella's baby kicked, distracting her, and she felt something strange. All of a sudden she recognized the unusual movement within her body was a labor contraction, and Owen knew it as well. She held her tummy and took a deep breath to relax.

Owen asked, "Is it time?"

She nodded and composed herself. "Before this begins, please know that I understand what you have to do. You must not worry about me." She tried to smile. He kissed her cheek. "Just promise me . . . promise me you'll come back!"

He kissed her again. "I wouldn't go if I didn't think I would return to you, Ella."

She closed her eyes and bit her lower lip, squeezing her

husband's hands, praying silently for his safety. Then she opened her eyes and called out to her brother:

"Henry, will you come in, dear? I'm afraid I won't be able to stay and finish this nice dinner."

The next morning, Ella was delivered of a bawling, black-haired son, with Lettie, Angélique, and Lela as proud midwives. Her labor had lasted ten hours, and she was exhausted at the end. Sutherland was at her side most of the time, departing only when Lettie scurried him away before the moment of birth. Tired and happy, the couple found an hour alone just as dawn broke, before friends would come calling.

"We'll need a name," whispered Ella as she lay back with her head on a pillow. She was pale, but there was a radiance about her that spoke of joy and inner strength and much, much love for her family.

"I have one," Owen said, and they both thought it funny that neither had even broached a possible name until now. "Benjamin Henry Sutherland."

Ella smiled and drew her husband close to kiss him. Then he kissed wrinkled little Benjamin Henry, who lay on his mother's breast without the slightest idea how to get at it.

One week later, the *Victory* was preparing to set sail for Montreal. With all the commotion in the fort over the schooner's sailing, Peter Defries presumed the military paymaster who was keeping his and Sutherland's cash safe might be seeing someone off that morning. To avoid missing the man, Peter went early in the morning to collect the money—all four thousand pounds sterling, which included the Frontier Company's twelve hundred, Peter's thousand, and the money owed Johnson for the original purchase of the trade goods. As Peter walked to the office this cloudy, windy morning, he did not notice Morgan, Jubal Swain's man, following him. As soon as Defries entered the paymaster's office on Rue Saint Jacques, Morgan signaled to Hurley, who was also watching, sending the man off to alert Swain.

Shortly, Defries came out of the office with a satchel and strode toward the Sutherland house to convey his best wishes to the happy parents before he boarded the *Victory* later that day. Excited and happy by the new turn of events, Defries whistled to himself as he made his way along the crowded streets, then entered the quieter section where Sutherland lived. By now there were six men following him, including Jubal Swain, Hurley, and Morgan.

As Defries turned a corner, Swain took a shortcut behind a building and through a stableyard to intercept him. Leaning against the stable wall, tomahawk in hand, Swain waited for the whistling to draw near. As Defries approached, Swain gripped his tomahawk, ready. The victim was close. Just a few more paces. Now!

At the moment Swain stepped out in front of Defries, John Blair, walking with Jeremy, called out a cheerful good morning, distracting Defries, who turned in greeting. This unexpected movement threw off Swain's blow and the tomahawk came down in a glancing whack that rocked Defries's skull and sent him sprawling. The money satchel fell to the ground, and Swain gathered it up quickly. Blair and Jeremy saw this all happen in an abrupt blur of movement. Blair recognized Swain and cried out as Swain dashed away, with five men trailing close behind him. Jeremy ran to Defries, who lay in a pool of blood.

"Get your father!" Blair shouted as he ran up to the boy, who knelt over Defries. Jeremy hurried away, his face white from shock.

Blair tended Defries, who was barely breathing. He had known Defries would be fetching the money this morning, though he had not the slightest apprehension of risk. And his own foreman, of all people!

Within a few moments the post surgeon was tending Defries, and Sutherland, Gladwin, and a dozen soldiers were hurrying through the fort toward Swain's camp by the river. By now Blair had described Defries's attacker to Sutherland, and after asking some questions, the Scotsman quickly realized that the big, redbearded man named Swain was the borderer he had fought with in Pennsylvania. As the men ran to catch the thieves, Gladwin called on others to follow, and when the force reached the gate, there were at least a hundred of them, armed and angry.

The weather was dark and gloomy, with a strong wind blowing and storm clouds closing in, so it was not likely Swain's men would risk the rough river in canoes or even whaleboats. They were trapped, Sutherland knew, but there would be a stiff fight before they were taken.

Then John Blair shouted, "Look there! On the water!"

Sure enough. Swain had gambled on the bad weather that had turned the river into a torrent of whitecaps. There were ten loaded canoes out on the river, making a dash downstream.

The pursuers shouted and ran for the whaleboats drawn up on shore, willing to risk the danger to run down these outlaws. A few sent potshots uselessly at the canoes, and some soldiers ran back to the fort to open fire with cannon from the ramparts. But Swain's escape had been well planned, his people—including a confused Lucy—ready and waiting, and they darted downriver with paddles flashing in rapid strokes. Sutherland stood in fury, while others prepared boats and canoes for the pursuit.

But a fierce gust of wind brought lashing rain, and Sutherland saw two of Swain's craft spun around by the force of the gale and waves. Foundering, they capsized without a hope for the men they carried. Still Sutherland's friends did not flinch, and the boats were readied. Henry Gladwin was the first into one.

"No!" Sutherland shouted above the wind, and everyone turned to him as he waved his arms. "No! It's not worth your lives to chase them!"

They knew he was right but urged him to reconsider. They would go if he asked them to, but he would not ask them. Defeated, they stood on the beach, watching the canoes fly away, taking the only hope left to the Frontier Company. As the wind savagely whipped up water, the men with Sutherland grumbled and turned to go back to the fort, agreeing to take up the chase as soon as the weather let up. By now they all had heard what Swain had stolen, and they swore to stand by Sutherland until the thief was caught. To expect that the money would ever be returned was too much to hope.

Gladwin came to his friend's side. "The wilderness is not so vast that he won't be caught, Owen." His face dark with frustrated anger, Sutherland walked back to the fort with Gladwin. "Word will be sent to every British outpost, Owen. Swain will never get back to civilization without someone waiting for him to arrive. He'll be found."

Sutherland wished he could believe that. The men went to

find Defries, who had been taken to his own cabin. He was conscious now, but in great pain. Over Defries's forehead was a thick, bloodstained bandage. As Sutherland knelt by the bed, the young man said weakly, "It's a good thing I've got such a hard Dutch head, eh?"

"Scots ones are harder, lad," Sutherland said, patting his shoulder. "They turn those blades."

Behind Sutherland the surgeon was washing his hands. A stout, elderly man, he said, "He'll be well again in a few weeks if he looks out for himself."

"A few weeks?" Defries cried. He tried to sit up, but Sutherland pushed him back. "I'm going after that bastard as soon as I can walk!" He groaned from the pain and dizziness.

Sutherland said, "Tamano and I are leaving for the Illinois country in a few days—I have to keep my word to Bradstreet. But when I come back, we'll go after Swain together, Peter." He stood up and again patted his friend's shoulder. "Take care of yourself, and get on your feet soon. You'll be the last one to see our baby."

Defries tried to grin but could not. He looked away from Sutherland. Ashamed of losing the company's money, the pain of his guilt was as intense as the gash on his head, and Defries sighed shakily, closing his eyes as Sutherland left.

At that moment, in the Shawnee country of the Muskingum River, the young warrior named Niko-lota watched as the sachems and chiefs of the Shawnee and Delaware made peace with Colonel Henry Bouquet. In an enormous clearing cut overnight from the heart of the forest by a thousand axes, Bouquet had set up a bower of trees and interlaced branches in which to accept the leaders of the hostile tribes of this formerly impenetrable country.

Niko-lota was astonished by the staggering amount of white power arrayed rank on rank here. Not only were there two thousand men formed up in impressive, menacing files with fixed bayonets, but an entire town had been built in a twinkling by the army.

Niko-lota himself had walked past this place just a little while ago, having been sent out by Chief Pontiac to scout the soldiers approaching the Shawnee country. Where recently there had been gurgling brooks and shady groves there were now mudholes and cabins. The soldiers had cannon, but they had also brought gifts of peace. They had come ready to fight, but Bouquet, their wise and courageous leader, reasoned with the Indians to prove that peace was in their best interest.

Niko-lota felt a wrenching sadness in his heart as he listened to the stocky, clear-eyed Bouquet sternly reprimand the Indians: "The Six Nations have leagued themselves with us; the Great Lakes and the rivers around you are all in our possession; and your friends the French are in subjection to us and can do no more to aid you!"

Bouquet stood imposingly before the chiefs, dressed in his scarlet and gold uniform, backed by officers equally warlike in regular red and provincial blue. There were also hundreds of volunteer Pennsylvania and Virginia riflemen arrayed in loose formation around the clearing, their eyes cold, eager for revenge against the tribes that had shed so much of their folk's blood. By comparison, the Indians looked feeble as they sat wrapped in blankets, listening to Bouquet's eloquence as it was translated to them. Nearby huddled two hundred former white captives waiting for release, another proof of the gradual British conquest of the uprising.

"You are all in our power," Bouquet went on, motioning with his arms as if to enfold the Indian audience, who sat so impassive but listened well. "If we choose, we can exterminate you from the earth; but the English are a merciful and generous people, averse to shed the blood even of their greatest enemies. And if it is possible that you could convince us that you sincerely repent, and that we could depend upon your good behavior for the future, you might yet hope for mercy and peace."

Niko-lota knew these tribes had been beaten—for now. Bouquet spoke the truth: the war in the Ohio country was lost. There was nothing more for this warrior to do but to return to Pontiac again, to carry on the fight until the time came when all Indians were guaranteed their land and their honor.

Niko-lota left with his two cousins, taking a canoe down the Muskingum to the Ohio River, and making for Pontiac's camp on the Mississippi. If Niko-lota and the other sachems and chiefs had known that Colonel Bradstreet had recently been duped by the Huron and northern Shawnee, then Colonel Bouquet's threats would have been empty. The Indians could have slipped behind him and cut off his supplies, and the bones of

Bouquet's army would have bleached in this clearing they had torn from the sacred forest. Jealous manitous would have been satisfied.

chapter 29

TO KASKASKIA

Gladwin's farewell was a mixture of triumph and poignancy. By afternoon the weather was clear enough for sailing, and at long last this brave officer could return to his home after conducting himself admirably in a perilous land. No other British officer in North America had ever endured the rigors of an Indian siege of such duration. Gladwin had stood face to face with the mightiest Indian war chief of all time and had come out victorious. As he stood on the deck of the new schooner, *Victory,* and saw a sailor cast off the bowline, he was grateful to be going home.

In the tunic pocket he carried a brief letter Peter Defries had managed to dictate to him, telling Mary of his decision to join the company but saying nothing of his head injury and the loss of the money. From his bed in his house, he asked Lieutenant Colonel Gladwin to be sure to give Mary and the baby his love, and tell her he would return before the winter.

Gladwin looked down the landing and saw Ella, Owen, the children, the Morelys, and Martines. His officers, soldiers, friends, and fellow sufferers of the past confinement stood by the hundreds before the palisade, waving and singing in his honor. As the schooner eased from the dock, with a whaleboat drawing its bow away from land, Gladwin rubbed at a furtive tear and grinned despite his emotions. He waved to them all, blew Ella a kiss, and heard all the fort's cannon fire in succession.

On the dock stood proud Colonel Bradstreet, now in temporary command of the fort and responsible for rebuilding others that had been lost. The burden was on Bradstreet's shoulders for now, and as far as Gladwin was concerned, he could have it.

The shore fell away. The ship's canvas snapped and filled, and the whaleboat cast off with a final salute from its commander, Ensign Parker, the man who had escorted Ella and Owen to Pitt last summer. Gladwin returned the young man's salute and saw his sadness at the departure. Strange, he thought, but he had not realized just how deeply Detroit and its people had penetrated his own very marrow.

He smiled at Parker, who grinned back, then sat down and ordered the oarsmen to put about. The *Victory* listed in the breeze and creaked as its rudder brought it around to follow the strong current. A sailor ran up the Union Jack, and the ship's two small cannon were fired in salute.

Gladwin walked aft to watch Detroit a little longer. Owen and Ella were already obscure on the landing, and the fort soon shrank until it became only an insignificant, brownish growth on a long, low bluff. It was finished. Detroit was in Henry Gladwin's past. He hoped Jeremy, at least, might come to England one day, but whatever happened, he was sure America would never again have Henry Gladwin back on its lovely shores.

A few days later, Owen and Tamano prepared to go southwest to Pontiac, to his new camp on the Mississippi. They intended to travel much of the four hundred miles by canoe, taking two weeks—first up the Maumee River until they had to portage across high ground to the Wabash River, then downstream and up a smaller tributary until they came to a second portage. This carry would take them to the upper reaches of the Kaskaskia River, which emptied into the Mississippi near Pontiac's village. Behind, moving more slowly, Garth Morely would bring the fortune in Indian presents. Morely would haul the goods in canoes paddled by men hired from the fort.

John Blair had asked to go with Morely, in order to explore some unknown country. Blair knew he could not reorganize an expedition north before winter set in. Also, by now he appreciated the Indian dangers that would continue until Pontiac made peace. Morely was reluctant at first, because the fellow was no woodsman and might slow them down. However, Sutherland vouched for Blair, and Morely was convinced.

Blair had become close friends of the Sutherlands, particularly of Jeremy, who was fascinated by the man's learning. Whenever Jeremy could not be found, he was with Blair, either talking, reading, or playing a kind of skillful chess that Owen Sutherland could not match.

Sally, too, joined Blair and Jeremy whenever she could, though Jeremy more often than not had little time for her these days. When alone, she busied herself with Sniffer, taking over the chores of feeding and caring for him. While Blair was in the fort, the otter became more Sally's pet than Jeremy's, but neither the girl nor the creature seemed to mind.

Those last few days were difficult for Ella and Owen. So often they had parted, not knowing if he would ever come back. They seldom spoke about the journey, rather spending their time with the older children or with the baby. No one could have been happier, nor more aware of the fleetness of time.

The morning of departure came, and a small party gathered near the canoe. All their closest friends, including Defries, who was recuperating well, came to see Owen and Tamano off. After the craft had been loaded, and both Sutherland and Tamano were prepared, the Chippewa bade farewell to Lela and waded through the water to climb into the bow. Jeremy stood in the shallows steadying the canoe as Sutherland and Ella walked toward him. At the final moment, Sutherland embraced his wife, and she held up something before him.

"Take it, " she said.

It was the gleaming silver pendant he had first given Mayla, and later Ella. Sutherland felt a kind of melancholy that he struggled against.

"It's yours," he replied.

However, Ella fastened the pendant around his neck, and it dangled at his chest. She smiled and kissed her husband lightly, holding herself back with difficulty from crushing him close against her. Then she looked at him through eyes brimming with tears.

"Yes, it's mine," she said, smiling. "It will oblige you to come back to me, for it's mine."

It took three days from Detroit to reach the broad mouth of the Maumee River, and in that time, all lingering thoughts of home and family were crowded out of Sutherland's mind. He contemplated the task at hand, and his reflections consumed him day after day. It was September, and the first cold nights had begun to temper the greens of summer, hinting at the yellows and bright orange soon to dominate the world. But Sutherland saw nothing of the changing seasons, even when he took his turn paddling in the stern and was compelled to concentrate on the river and on shifting currents, wind, and landmarks. Jumbled in his restless mind were the words he would use to convince Pontiac to make peace. Yet no matter how he organized his thoughts, how he arranged his logic, he found himself dissatisfied with what he would say. Perhaps the reason was that if he were in Pontiac's position he would find it hard to stop fighting the British.

The windy, rainy weather had changed to mild, sunny days and clear nights, and their passage up the Maumee was swift. They met no hostility, for the Indians along the river had been alerted that Sutherland and Tamano would be making this trip to Pontiac. Now and again the travelers halted at dwellings of Miami, who had made no formal peace as yet. Each village was crowded with impoverished people, surly and dismal. There had been food enough during the abundant summer, but cold weather was on its way once more; game was drifting south, and these folk would be even hungrier than last winter. If smallpox struck again, they would lose many children, and all the misery they had endured thus far would seem light by comparison.

It was in these villages that Sutherland began to understand what must be said to Pontiac. He realized that if he were in the chief's position he would sue for peace under the best terms possible. Sutherland's arguments began to take form and strength, and his mind raced forward as he discarded all the subtle reasoning that formerly had ebbed and flowed in his thoughts. None of that was necessary. He would speak directly, bluntly to Pontiac, even at risk of insulting him and throwing failure in his face. Pontiac had to accept the truth once and for all, its harshness alleviated only by the rich cargo of presents Morely was bringing.

Sutherland's presents included many hunting rifles and fowling pieces, with enough gunpowder and lead for the Indians to hunt this winter. By springtime ammunition would be low, and once again they would be dependent on whites for trade;

they would never be able to go on the warpath unless a great cache of powder and ball were reserved for fighting, and only the French could supply that. However, the French had sworn not to arm the Indians, and Sutherland had learned at his final conference with Bradstreet that Pontiac had been rudely spurned by the commander of the French post at Vincennes.

When Pontiac recently asked the officer for ammunition with which to carry on the war, he laid a war belt at the Frenchman's feet. At first the commander tried to reason with Pontiac, to explain once more what the French had explained again and again to the Indians: the British and French were at peace. But Pontiac would not listen, and he went so far as to threaten the French fort. The angry officer then committed the greatest of insults by kicking the war belt across the room and storming away, leaving Pontiac and his chiefs alone and unheeded.

These British presents would do much to soothe Pontiac's injured pride and, more important, would help the Indian survive the winter. Surely Pontiac, despite his intense hatred of Redcoats, would see the sense in making peace and accepting Bradstreet's invitation to a great peace council planned for Fort Oswego.

Sutherland hoped Morely would have no difficulty bringing the goods through in time to Kaskaskia, a trip of more than four hundred miles. Though the trader was getting along in years, he was the most trustworthy man the company had to direct the shipment. Sutherland was confident Morely would get through, particularly when he saw that the Miami villagers would be willing to let the convoy pass by unopposed.

At dawn the day after Sutherland and Tamano set off on their rapid voyage to Pontiac, Garth Morely began loading twelve canoes with Indian goods, preparing to depart. The weather was fine, and his twenty men were strong and eager to work. Half of them were French and *métis voyageurs,* two were Wyandot Huron guides and interpreters, and the rest were a mixture of British and provincials in need of employment. Morely knew most of them, except for one or two likely fellows who had been hired after being discharged from the provincial militia still camped at Detroit.

In all the confusion and labor of readying the brigade of canoes, Morely had proven himself a rock of experience and skill. Managing men was natural to him, and the group under his authority was chosen for strength and intelligence. Only young Blair could be considered a possible drag on the expedition, but he was wiry and his will was strong, for all his inexperience; and Morely felt certain the explorer would do well enough. In fact, of all the tiresome exertions required of the old trader to form the brigade, only one was really annoying and irritating—Jeremy Bently asked him again and again to be permitted to come along with his friend, John Blair.

At first, Morely laughed at the boy's ambition, patted him on the head, and told him to wait a few years. When Jeremy persisted, Morely was more firm and told the boy he would surely go on such expeditions in the future, but he was just too young for this one. After the third and fourth times Jeremy asked, Morely grew angry and warned him to stop pestering him or he would never be asked to accompany one of the company's brigades.

That apparently worked, and Jeremy asked no longer. However, for the two days of preparation after Sutherland left, the boy moped and sulked around the fort. Blair had told him about the western grasslands, the endless rivers through forest and prairie, the majestic Mississippi, and the little-known tribes of the Illinois country. The boy was burning with desire to go along, to see the notorious Pontiac himself, and to watch Owen Sutherland make his speech.

Ella saw how glum Jeremy was, and she tried to cheer him up. However, all her efforts were to no avail. By the time Morely was ready to depart, Jeremy was apparently so upset that he did not even come to say good-bye to his friend Blair.

The sight of the canoes darting out into the river, the morning's first light gleaming on the water beyond the craft, and the flashing of red *voyageur* paddles thrilled Ella as she stood on the shore, the baby wrapped in her arms. At her side was Lettie Morely, obviously uneasy as she watched her husband leave. Lettie waved a handkerchief, and Garth raised his flat black hat in a dashing salute that made her smile.

The woman said, "There he goes, just like the old days, when he was young. Just like the old days, an' here I be worried about him just like the old days, though this time I be more worried than ever, an' I don't know why, Ella."

• • •

In the center of the last canoe, under a pile of bound-up trade blankets, Jeremy Bently huddled as quietly as he could, hoping he would not be discovered until it was too late for Garth Morely to send him back. The boy knew there was no time to be lost on this expedition, and he was counting on Morely being too shorthanded to spare men and a canoe to take him back to Detroit.

All that day he lay under cover, managing once to slip away unseen from the canoe during a rest stop and answer the call of nature. Before leaving Detroit, he had written a letter telling his mother not to worry, that he would be fine. He had left the note under Ella's pillow, so she would not learn of his leave-taking until that night, hours after Morely's canoes had departed.

He had brought along food and a small skin bag of water, and he was able to sleep soundly on his own blanket under the baled trade goods. He was amazed when, at the end of the first long day, the brigade put in on the shore of Lake Erie, and he was still undiscovered.

Putting to use all the Indian skills Tamano had taught him, Jeremy evaded detection and crept under a bush when the men unloaded and overturned the canoes as shelter that night. He had brought a blanket along, but he was stiff and cold in the morning. Before dawn he made a small fire for himself behind some boulders and out of sight of camp. Having collected sticks and built them up the evening before, he needed only to strike a light in his tinderbox to get a warm blaze going in the darkness. Jeremy knew he had to stay strong and healthy during this trip, for if he was sick when discovered, he might slow them down, and that would have proven Morely right when he said Jeremy was too young to come.

At first light, Jeremy watched the men cooking breakfast and loading the tethered canoes, which were afloat already. Stealthy as a young brave, he slipped through the shadows and into the water, finding his same hiding place, though the load had been arranged a little differently this time. He had just a moment to get under the blankets before the canoemen approached. Tugging his own blanket over his head, he held his breath and did not move as the sternman climbed in, spoke French to his comrade now in the bow, and paddled away. The only problem was that the reloaded canoe had a small bundle of Jew's harps where yesterday Jeremy had lain. They dug into

his back, but he dared not move too suddenly, lest he be found.
For the next hour, he slowly, carefully shifted his weight until
the metal harps were no longer under him. With a sigh, he
settled down once again to await their next stop.

Jeremy stayed in hiding for another night, but that morning,
as he tried to warm himself by his secret fire, he was caught
by none other than Garth Morely. In the red glare of the boy's
campfire, Morely towered over him like a fierce pirate chief.
Behind the angry trader stood the grinning Wyandots, who had
detected the fire and brought Morely to the boy.

   Crouching at the blaze, Jeremy shivered from cold and from
tension. He tried to smile at Morely, whose eyes were alight
with fury—or was it only the reddish flame of the fire that
made him seem so frightening? Jeremy stood up, and the blanket fell from his slender shoulders as he shuffled his feet and
waited for Morely to berate him. Giving a furtive glance at the
bearded man, Jeremy thought he saw something other than
anger in his eyes. Was it—could it be a twinkle of humor? He
looked closer. Sure enough, Morely was unable to conceal the
affection he felt for this daring lad.

   The boy wished he could say just the right thing. He longed
to make Morely understand how much it meant to him to go
on this journey. Over at the camp the men were singing a
voyageur song and loading up the canoes. Morely turned to the
Wyandots and said, "Tell 'em we'll leave as planned. The boy
can go with Blair, an' I'll travel in thy canoe."

   The Indians vanished like shadows, and Morely said to
Jeremy, "If thee be wantin' vittles, get movin' now, for we
won't wait for thee."

   Jeremy's face shone with delight, and Morely gave a deep,
hearty laugh as he clapped his arm over the boy's shoulders
and led him back to camp. Then Jeremy cried out and returned
to his campfire to smother it with dirt. Morely nodded, chuckling, and said, "Thee'll make a woodsman yet, lad, just like
thy father Owen! Come on, then, we've a long way to go, an'
I plan to make thee work for thy keep. Go an' eat now!"

By the time Owen Sutherland and Tamano crossed the ten-mile
portage from the Maumee to the Wabash, they sensed something was not quite right in the villages here. While the communities downstream toward Lake Erie were quiet and somber

as Sutherland's canoe passed, those along the upper reaches of the Maumee, and near the source of the Wabash, demonstrated hostility and anger when they saw Sutherland. Many people gathered on the riverbanks to glare or to rattle muskets and shout threats.

Worried that worse than shouting and shaking weapons might occur if they did not get to the bottom of the troubles, the two travelers put in at a large village on the Wabash, near the captured Fort Ouatanon. There, headmen confronted them and forbade them to enter the village. When Sutherland asked what had happened, he was told that white men were ranging through the country and stealing horses, canoes, food—whatever they could—at weakly defended hamlets or solitary lodges. So far no Indians had been reported killed, but if that were to happen the country would be on the warpath in pursuit of these thieves. Unless someone was murdered, this band of robbers would be considered no more than undesirable transients best attacked or driven off when seen, but it was not likely that a full-scale war party would be assembled to catch them.

Sutherland suspected Swain's party was in the region, though he did not know why they would have come here. When he asked whether a man fitting Swain's description was among the bandits, he was told that, indeed, a redbearded giant was the leader. A few small parties had gone after the whites, but had been eluded. These men apparently knew the ways of the forest well and could cover their tracks skillfully.

Paddling down the deepening Wabash, Sutherland and Tamano knew that a strong body of well-armed white outlaws could be devastating if well led, which Swain's men were. Sutherland guessed that Swain had in mind some larger plan beyond stealing stock and food. But what? If they had the time, he and Tamano would help to hunt these renegades down. After they finished with Pontiac, they would do just that. Once his obligation to the military was fulfilled, Sutherland intended to recover the company's stolen funds, even if it meant hunting Swain all winter long and chasing him to the Shining Mountains in the distant northwest.

Deep in the forest at a hidden camp on a tributary of the Illinois River, Lucy Swain sat before a lean-to and watched Jubal divide his twenty men into two raiding parties.

Just how Lucy's life had taken such an abrupt turn, she did not know, nor did she particularly care. Little interested her anymore. Growing increasingly lonely and more withdrawn, even in Jubal's presense, Lucy tried her best not to think at all. No wonder, for every waking hour found her haunted by the specters of her beloved sons, or by the strong, honest face of Matthew, her dead husband. Thinking was simply too painful for her, so she avoided it.

Eating, sleeping, cooking, cleaning, and satisfying Jubal's desires were what occupied her. However, she found it impossible to sleep very well, often lying awake from sunset to sunrise, fighting off nightmares that came upon her with every snatch of sleep. She was always so very tired, so very sad.

There were five other women, all Indians, in this party. Two of them had been bought from their fathers during the past weeks of travel in the forest. One had been the squaw of Morgan since the group started out at Niagara, and the others were bought at Detroit. None was like Lucy, and they did not interest her. Also, they never missed a chance to ignore her, to shun her because she was white and the woman of their chief. They were all attracted to Swain.

As for Jubal, he noticed none of them. Lucy was the passion of his life, and he would have traded away his share of the loot to see her happy once more. But he did not know how to make her happy. He suspected that if he got her with child it would change her, revive her. That had not yet happened, however much he tried.

As he sent off the small raiding parties to bring back more horses as pack animals, he warned them as usual against any killing. Swain wanted to be stronger before the Indians gathered in force to attack him, as he knew they would when they grasped that he was moving into their country permanently. But first he wanted to pass the winter, to test his followers, and to learn the lay of the land. Let them come after him, but he wanted it to be on ground of his own choosing, and on his own terms.

Swain turned away from the departing men, who ran off northward along a hunting trail, heading for Pottawattami towns near Lake Michigan. He saw Lucy, as usual sitting with empty eyes, and it pained him. One day he would make her happy — they were already rich, though there was nowhere yet to spend it. But he would spend it to make them even richer and more

powerful, and she would rule with him a wilderness domain
as great as a European kingdom! *Lucy,* he thought, *don't be
so far away, girl!*

As if reading his mind, Lucy looked up at him, and their
eyes held. That familiar, driving fire rose in Jubal again, and
he wondered whether she or he was the most dominant—he
really did not know, for sure.

The forests thinned as the land sloped down from the higher
ground to the east, opening up to grasslands, rolling meadows,
and a vast sky. Sutherland and Tamano had portaged two hard
days between the Wabash and the trickling Kaskaskia, passing
through dry, windblown country alive with deer, buffalo, and
clouds of game birds. Here the Kaskaskia River was little more
than a ditch this time of year, and they often had to get out and
carry past mud holes, where black herds of buffalo eyed them
suspiciously. Because the shallow, placid Kaskaskia River
barely offered enough muddy water to float the canoe, it was
the hardest part of their journey. Yet, for all this land's loneliness and scarcity of water and trees, it appealed to Sutherland.
Never had he entered such tranquillity—not even from the top
of a mountain overlooking a sea of forest. It took only a brief
climb up the bank of the narrow river to be standing on a bluff
that viewed serene, waving grasslands, gentle rises, and the
rush of a constant wind.

Dry and hissing in the breeze, the endless, tall grass was
broken by occasional groves of trees and stands of cedar. Sutherland thought that wildfire could obliterate every living thing
here as fast as the wind could blow it. No doubt that happened
often. Then, within a few years, the grasses would be high
again, the cedars sprouting, and the wealth of game would
have found a new way to survive.

The few shabby villages here and there along the way knew
nothing of Swain's plundering gang, and the travelers were
once again welcome in lodges of village chiefs and elders who
had been forewarned that they were coming through.

Late one morning, twenty miles east of the mouth of the
lazy Kaskaskia, they were joined by an escort of Ottawa and
Illinois warriors. Although these fighters had garbed themselves
in their very best and carried many weapons, Sutherland saw
how threadbare their shirts were, and he noticed several muskets with broken locks in need of a white gunsmith's attention.

The first thing Sutherland was asked was whether he had rum.
He sparingly doled out a little, but said the rest was being saved
for after the council with Pontiac. They accepted this, but were
disappointed they could not get good and roaring drunk; they
had not been able to for many months.

It was midafternoon when Sutherland and Tamano came in
sight of the sprawling Kaskaskia villages on the right bank of
the Mississippi. Standing on a broad spit of land, several groups
of lodges were crowded with almost two thousand followers
of Pontiac. Nearby, on the Mississippi side of the spit, stood
the powerful masonry fortress called Fort Chartres. A skeleton
French garrison waited for the British to take charge of the
post, which was deteriorating for lack of upkeep. Sutherland
asked the leaders of the party that escorted him to send word
of his arrival to both Pontiac and the fort's French commander.
This was done, and soon the weary travelers were invited to
Pontiac's lodge for the first talk.

Pontiac dwelt in a rude hut covered with bark and skins,
where he and his family were no better off than any of the
warriors, chiefs, and sachems in the village. However, when
Sutherland and Tamano were brought to the chief, who sat with
thirty elders and war leaders around a large fire before the
lodge, Pontiac's regal bearing was just as imposing as it had
been when the uprising began a year and a half ago.

Sutherland, carrying a large bag full of beautiful wampum
belts, advanced into the center of the circle, Tamano at his
side. The Scotsman would have known Pontiac was the leader
even if he were seeing the man for the first time. Strong of
body, with penetrating, unyielding eyes, the aging chief had
a high comb of greased hair stuck with eagle feathers. Painted
in white and green, the colors of peaceful council, Pontiac held
his large head high, the white bone pendant dangling fiercely
from his nose. The chief said nothing as Sutherland took out
a long belt of green-and-white wampum and laid it before him.

Sutherland began his oration with the usual ceremonial
blessings, invoking open hearts and eyes, washing away the
sadness caused by the loss of loved ones; and with each blessing, he laid another magnificent belt of wampum before the
seated Pontiac.

Then he took a bag Tamano had carried and drew out a rope
of twisted tobacco more than forty feet in length. The Indians
were obviously impressed, and many lost their stoic demeanor,

stirring as they eyed this great wealth of tobacco. Sutherland, with the appropriate good wishes for the ancestors of those gathered here, had the tobacco passed around to fill all their pipes. By now, at least five hundred men had crowded into the village council grounds, and many of them crumbled up tobacco to fill nearly thirty pipes. All the Indians were seated, with only Sutherland and Tamano still standing.

The pipes were offered to the winds, then the chief permitted Sutherland and Tamano to sit at his left. Each man smoked in turn, with Pontiac first and Sutherland second on the same pipe.

After a polite pause of fifteen minutes, Pontiac rose and addressed the gathering. Once again Sutherland felt the magnetism of the man's voice, the calculated, controlled passion with which he enthralled his listeners. In the brief welcome to Sutherland, Pontiac managed to grip every man there, calling upon them to remember the wrongs done them by the English, but reminding them that they must, as Sutherland had asked, keep an open heart, open eyes, and open ears for what the English had to say in this council.

"Brothers and cousins, hear me," Pontiac said, in closing. "Donoway once was a son of our sons, and though he has gone back to his white ways, we have never known him to lie. His companion, the Chippewa, Tamano, is also known to many of you, and he is welcome as the companion of Donoway.

"As long as these two ambassadors of the English are in our lodges, they must be protected and kept safe from insult or harm, because what they have to tell us are the words of the English king. We must decide whether we will permit the English king to become our father, as the French king once was our father."

Pontiac let this sink in, then said, "We shall hear what Donoway has to say, and we shall commune with our ancestors before making a reply."

At that, Pontiac sat down. Sutherland, after half an hour of thought and silence, got up once again. He looked around the great circle, taking in virtually every man there. Their dark eyes watched him closely as he raised his arms and said, in a ringing voice full of power:

"I, Donoway, adopted son of the Ottawa, friend of the Indian, warrior for the king of England, who have fought to restore peace, come to you knowing that you hold my life in your hands.

"Many months ago, when the Indian first rose up against the Redcoats, I spoke against such a bloodletting, and I was warned by Chief Pontiac that I must stay out of this war or fight for the Indian." Silence, and Sutherland let them dwell upon these words a moment. "Pontiac warned I would die if I joined the English against the uprising. Now I have come among you with Pontiac's tomahawk hovering above my head, for I have fought alongside the Redcoats, and I helped them triumph at Bushy Run."

A restrained but unmistakable wave of anger passed through the Indians when they heard this defiance in the jaws of death. But Sutherland did not falter:

"Donoway has come to you despite the peril he faces. He has come to tell what will befall his friend the Indian if peace is not made. He has come to ask the Indian to bury the tomahawk, to wash away the colors of war, and wash away with them his hatred and longing for revenge. He has come to say that a mighty army of Redcoats threatens to assail those Indians who continue this war."

He went on, without softening his language, to enumerate the forces ready to strike at the hostiles—Bradstreet, Bouquet, thousands of provincial militia, the Iroquois, and even a French-Canadian volunteer regiment. The warriors were impassive, but they heard very clearly what Sutherland was saying, and they bitterly knew their final stronghold here would be next to fall. Bouquet's triumph on the Muskingum River was already known; Bradstreet's force staged at Detroit was prepared to strike at them; France had abandoned them permanently, and prospects for continuing hostilities were dim.

But at the key moment, when these Indians were subdued by the raw facts, when they were dismayed by their own weakness, Sutherland changed his tone. He spoke of the future, of peace, of the renewed trade, of honor bestowed on the Indians as they deserved, and finally he told of the rich cargo in presents now on the way to Kaskaskia. This last excited them all.

"I am sent here to convey the opinion of the English king, who desires peace and has no wish to go on fighting such a brave and stubborn foe. The king my father wishes no more blood to flow between us. Instead, he wishes only commerce to flow, commerce in furs and ammunition, in corn and fine clothing. He is sad for the wrongs done his red children, and he wishes them to be happy once again. The English king dreads the thought of his red children enduring another winter such as the last."

Sutherland purposely stopped so the warriors would recall how much they had suffered. Every Indian had bad memories that were soon interrupted by the Scotsman's enthusiasm.

"Already he has sent goods that will make this winter an easy one—guns, powder, lead, warm blankets, shirts. Also he has sent adornments such as beads, paints, thread, and jewelry with which to please your wives, mothers, and daughters.

"Accept these gifts as tokens of the English king's love for you, and let the hardness in your hearts melt away. Let us be glad that peace has come and a time of prosperity is upon us, brothers and cousins. Let us bury the tomahawk. Let us send home the sons of the English king, whose red coats are like the leaves of the autumn forest in their great camps. Send them home and tell them you will make war no longer, for the English king has given you presents as you deserve, and he cares for his red children and wants them to be strong and happy once again."

In veiled terms, Sutherland made it clear that the Indians had only two choices—accept the presents in peace or be driven from this country. He laid honor and friendship at their feet, and if the Indians accepted them, they could return to their former villages and begin a new era under the wing of a benevolent king who would protect them forever against all who coveted their lands.

By the time Sutherland was finished, the sun was low in the sky. He sat down and was followed by Pontiac, who said he would deliver his answer in the morning. The council broke up. Exhausted from his long speech, Sutherland returned with Tamano to where they had left their gear, and were soon given a lodge for the night.

"They understood you well," Tamano said as he lay down on a buffalo skin near the small fire that lit the lodge. "You have left them only one choice, Donoway."

Sutherland sighed and lay back, gazing up at the top of the lodge. "They can always choose to die, brother."

Tamano turned on his side. "They are afraid to die, for they

are weakened by their suffering, and they fear to die as weak-
lings. They will accept peace—for now—but once they are
strong again, in the years to come, they will return to the
warpath."

Sutherland sat up, staring hard at his friend in the dimness.
He was about to ask Tamano why he was so certain of such
things. Then he thought how whites and Indians wanted the
same land, and the strongest would have it. The other would
be forced off.

He said, "If the king will protect the Indian's rights, these
nations will remain peaceful; one day they might even come
to understand the ways of white power and politics, and then
they will carve their own place in this country, a place that
could become the equal of the provinces in wealth and
strength."

They thought about that until Tamano said, "I fear that the
English king has not so long an arm to keep white settlers out
of Indian country, brother. I fear the Indian will have to fight
to protect his borders, and there will be another war and another." He sighed. "The English king will one day have to
choose between red and white. Whom will he choose?"

Sutherland lay back again, not knowing what to think. They
heard the sounds of squaws outside preparing food for them.
After a while, Sutherland asked, "If you feel that way, Tamano,
why have you supported me in this?"

Without looking at his friend, the Chippewa said, "Because
brother, like you, I know there is no other choice for my people.
I wish not to see them destroyed . . . so soon."

It was Morgan's roving party that came upon the convoy of
canoes from Detroit. Camped for the night at the long portage
between the Maumee and the Wabash, Morely's brigade had
just finished the first real struggle of their journey. There would
be only one other long carry, when the canoes would be unloaded and each man would lug bales totaling a hundred and
eighty pounds on his shoulders from one waterway to the next.
That portage was the one from the Wabash to the Kaskaskia,
and it was the last difficulty before sweeping down the Kaskaskia to where, Morely believed, Pontiac's Indians would
welcome him with open arms. It was much like the old days,
before the French and Indian War, when Morely traded in
French-held valleys of the Ohio River tributaries, and every

night was a revelry of rough-and-tumble fun. Back then it had been as dangerous as this trip to Kaskaskia, because there was always the chance French soldiers would come in and take the English traders prisoner. And if the French had Indian allies along, the traders were generally given to the Indians to do with as they pleased.

As Morely sat by the campfire, smoking his pipe and listening to a former New Jersey militiaman sing a cheerful Irish air, he recalled those days long ago, and for a little while he felt young again. Nearby, under an upturned canoe, Jeremy and Blair played a game of chess. The young man exclaimed, "Boy, you're improving rapidly. Either that or you're asking too many distracting questions about botany and nature when it's my turn to move!"

No one noticed the two men watching from a thicket. Morgan and Hurley had stayed behind to observe the convoy while the others were sent back to get Swain and the rest of the men. If this brigade was taken, the renegades would live high and rich for a long time!

The next morning, before Pontiac and his leading chiefs retired to a private council to discuss Sutherland's proposal, Niko-lota was summoned to the chief's hut. The warrior had not been present when Sutherland gave his speech to the Indians, for he had been delivering messages to the nearby French fort. But he knew that Donoway was here, and that this was the man who had saved his life last summer at Bushy Run. Niko-lota despised white men, all the more after learning of the death of his sister Aleta, whom he still mourned. But Owen Sutherland was an exception, and someday he hoped to repay him for sparing his life.

Pontiac dispatched Niko-lota upriver with his two cousins to meet the approaching brigade of canoes. He dared not accept Sutherland's offer of peace without making sure the badly needed supplies actually got through to Kaskaskia. The chief would lose face completely if he recommended assenting to the English terms but the presents did not arrive.

Furthermore, if Niko-lota came back to say there were no presents coming, the life of Owen Sutherland would be forfeit. To Pontiac, sacrificing Sutherland by ritual torture might be the best medicine for magically, mystically reuniting his wavering alliance in the Illinois country. There had been few such sacrifices of captive whites lately, and none of them had the fame of Owen Sutherland, whose death by fire would arouse the warriors and impel them to continue resistance—if the British were lying about these presents.

chapter **30**

DEATH

Garth Morely watched his men trudge off with the first load of cargo as they portaged from a tributary of the Wabash to the upper reaches of the Kaskaskia. Each man would have to carry several loads until the entire cargo and the canoes were lugged over this higher ground, later to be reloaded for the final run downriver to Pontiac's stronghold.

Morely stood near the overturned canoes, which were laid in a line in the long grass bordering the stream. As the men strode away through the dry, windblown grass, he took off his hat and wiped sweat from his face. More tired than he cared to admit, he knew he was not as strong as he had thought, and this journey had taken all he had to give, though it was far from over. Lettie had been right months ago when she said he no longer should traipse through the woods like a young man. Well, this would be the last time.

He searched the border of trees that ran along the grasslands, looking for some sign of Jeremy and Blair. As usual they were off picking leaves or filling canvas bags with stones, sticks, pieces of this and bits of that. Morely chuckled to think how much of interest those two found in places that would not appeal to a hungry goat. He was glad his initial worry had proven unfounded over the ability of Blair—and later Jeremy—to keep up. Both had done well, carrying their own gear and accepting responsibility for checking campsites just before departure to make sure nothing was left behind.

There they were, as always, fiddling with bark or plants,

laughing or staring or talking endlessly about something small that even trailwise *voyageurs* did not notice. Morely had little interest in their talk of nature, but he had noticed a couple of unfamiliar birds on the wing that morning. Likely Blair knew what they were. He would ask him later.

The others would not be back for three hours, so Morely decided to take a snooze under a canoe. He yawned and stretched his stiff muscles, put his hat back on, and ambled toward a good resting place.

The sound of gunfire stopped him short. He looked at the swath in the grass where the men had gone. The firing came from there, and it was heavy. He hurried to where his rifle was leaning against his blankets and began to load it. Jeremy and Blair were staring at Morely as he cried for them to come in. He had no idea who was attacking, but it sounded as though his men had walked into a storm of fire.

There was a shout nearby as Morely drew the ramrod from his gun. There in the grass were three strangers. They were whites, and that confused Morely for just a moment. When one of them aimed his musket at the old trader, Morely instinctively ducked, and the ball whistled by.

Though he could no longer see Blair and Jeremy, Morely shouted their names as he scurried behind a fallen log. "Get away!" he roared, hoping they would understand. "Get away! Save yourselves!"

By now the three whites had taken shelter and were closing in. Morely had only one bullet, for his ammunition and powder were thirty feet away near his pack. He caught the movement of an attacker rushing through the grass, apparently toward Jeremy and Blair. Then Morely saw the boy and his friend duck into the trees. Swinging around his rifle, he sighted on the enemy and squeezed the trigger. It was a difficult shot, for the man was sixty yards away, but he staggered from the bullet's impact and dropped. Morely growled with satisfaction. He was not so old after all.

Sutherland and Tamano were called to the council fire just before midday meal, and there Pontiac told him that the answer to Bradstreet's appeal for peace would be given after the ceremonial presents came into the village.

"Too many times have whites made us promises and then broken their word," Pontiac said grimly. "If Colonel Bradstreet is sincere, then let us witness that sincerity by drinking his rum and holding new hunting rifles. Not before the Delaware Niko-lota returns with the canoes will we discuss peace terms."

When the council ended, after a long harangue by several lesser chiefs, who blamed the British for all that had happened on the frontier, no one had to tell Sutherland that if the gifts did not come through, he would be killed.

Niko-lota should have come back to Pontiac's village within two weeks if, as Sutherland had estimated, the brigade of canoes was already on its way down the Kaskaskia. But it was almost three weeks of waiting, of boredom, and of frequent veiled threats from passing young warriors, before the Delaware's canoe returned from the north. Tamano and Sutherland happened to be sitting on a bluff above the river when Niko-lota came back—without the brigade. Neither the Chippewa nor Sutherland spoke as they stared at the approaching canoe. There were four men in it, one more than Niko-lota and his two cousins. Looking closer, Sutherland recognized John Blair.

He waved to Blair from the bank, thinking the explorer had come on ahead, but when he noticed Blair's head was bound up in bloodstained cloth, his cheerfulness evaporated into icy fear. In a moment, Sutherland was at the water's edge, helping Niko-lota take Blair from the canoe. Sutherland did not recognize Niko-lota from the battle at Bushy Run, and the Indian said nothing for the moment. Blair staggered into the shallows, dried blood on his torn clothes and on his swollen left cheekbone. Sutherland's heart pounded as he laid the injured man on the shore, seeing the pain in his eyes. Niko-lota and Tamano dropped to their knees near Sutherland, who asked Blair over and over what happened.

Struggling to see Sutherland, Blair murmured, "Is that . . . you, Owen?" Then he blacked out. The Delaware brought water, which Sutherland trickled onto Blair's cracked, puffy lips. Niko-lota told what he knew:

"At the Kaskaskia portage we found them, all dead but this one; canoes gone, presents gone, nobody left to talk." Sutherland listened in horror as Niko-lota said, "This one we found at the edge of the woods, hiding and starving. He did not talk much then, either, but he said whites had hit them a couple of days before. The attackers stayed around for two nights, and he was hiding along with somebody else. Before the attackers left, they hunted the woods and found the other one. I do not know more, for he speaks only a little Delaware."

Blair was taken back to Sutherland's lodge, and there tended all that morning by squaws sent especially by Chief Pontiac. Throughout, Sutherland suffered the anguish of not knowing, and he feared for the safety of Garth Morely. It was afternoon when Blair regained consciousness, the injury on his head still painful, but his eyes were clear as he told Sutherland:

"Owen, it was Swain's men...Listen, Owen, they took Jeremy!"

Sutherland nearly burst with fury, his entire body shaking as he barely kept from flying from the lodge and launching his canoe. Struggling to fight back this battle-madness, he got the entire story from Blair. Garth was dead. It could not have been more terrible—except that Jeremy might be dead.

Blair said he and Jeremy had tried to hide in the trees, but the morning Swain's men were about to leave, they were discovered. Apparently the killers did not know there were two persons in the woods when they came in pursuit.

"Jeremy knew I couldn't get away, because I had fallen when the attack began and hurt my head." Blair grunted as a spasm of pain shot through his throbbing head. "They were almost upon us, and the boy showed me where to hide. Owen, he—showed me where to hide, and then led them away from me! He knew—he knew they would follow him. He saved my life."

"What did they do with him?" Sutherland's voice quivered with pent-up emotion.

"Later I saw them put him in a canoe and take him away," Blair replied, shame and sadness in his eyes. "I'm sorry I could not do any more for him, but—"

Sutherland put a hand on the man's shoulder, and comforted him. "We'll find the boy, John. Don't blame yourself. You could do no more. Stay here. They'll care for you."

Sutherland sought out Pontiac and told him what had happened. The war chief immediately gave his consent for Sutherland to go out after the killers and retrieve the presents. Next, Tamano and Sutherland met with Niko-lota, and the Delaware said he had trailed the killers for three days, following them partway up the Wabash. Then he had met some Miami Indians who agreed to pursue Swain's group and to raise a war party, which would go after the whites when Niko-lota returned from Pontiac.

"The whites are well armed and strong," Niko-lota said. "But I have a hundred men who have asked to come on the hunt for them. Already these warriors have begun their war dance, asking for the aid of the manitous."

Within an hour, Sutherland, Tamano, Niko-lota, and the other two Delaware were on their way back up the Kaskaskia. The main body would not depart their villages until the formalities of ceremonial dancing, ritual feasting, and painting were completed. Plans were made to meet them at a Miami village on the Maumee, near deserted Fort Miami.

Pushing hard, Sutherland's party reached the Kaskaskia portage in three days. Though spent from constant paddling, the five men pressed on across the high ground, carrying canoes and supplies in one laborious rush toward the Wabash tributary. The rolling land was in need of a good rain, and the dry grass whispered as they passed through it. Wind whipped around them, cold and arid, as they strode through the grass, laden canoes held above their heads.

They marched through that night, hurrying to where the ambush had occurred. It was difficult to see, but the trail was fairly level, and they did not want to lose a minute by sleeping or resting more than was necessary. It was almost dawn when Niko-lota said the scene was at hand.

Sutherland had seen much in the way of killing in his day, but in that hour before sunrise, as they sat without a fire near the place where Garth Morely and the other good men lay in the darkness, he could not overcome an intense sadness that filled his heart and mind. Sitting in the high grass, in a spot where the wind would not blow at them, no one talked. Worn from their hard push, each knew they had a long way to go, but they were strong and they were willing.

It was then that Niko-lota told Sutherland how they had come face to face before. The Delaware added, "I owe you my life, Donoway. I will help to repay that debt by saving the life of your son. To this I dedicate myself, and I will not waver from my course."

Light was coming, but before Sutherland allowed himself to see the carnage, he, Tamano, and Niko-lota joined in this solemn pact. Nearby, the two Delaware awoke and heard what was being said. They knelt at the side of Niko-lota and offered their own hands in this quest. They were called Shamot and Pay-cus, sturdy youths who had seen much of war; they were wiry and able.

Before dawn, somewhere in the wooded hills north of the portage between the Maumee and Wabash rivers, Jeremy Bently sat on the dirt floor of a half-finished cabin, watching Lucy Swain boil buffalo meat over an open fire. It was almost dawn, and Jeremy had not slept much that night. Confused, frightened, and sad over all that had happened, he was troubled by something else, something he had never expected when first made a prisoner by Swain's men: Lucy Swain had taken him under her care, cooing at him and seeing to his every want as though he were her own son. Earlier, her eyes shining unnaturally, Lucy had protected Jeremy when Morgan wanted to beat him for the fun of it; she had fed him when others refused to share their food, and she talked to him almost nonstop. Last night had been the strangest for Jeremy, however, because Lucy had begun to call him Willie, though he knew not why. She had kept him up all night talking about someone named Matthew, and planning to find another person—named Joey. Tired, aching from the hard journey he had been forced to make from the Kaskaskia portage, Jeremy hardly listened to Lucy jabber about whatever came to mind. But her voice kept at him just the same.

He had seen this robbers' lair in the daytime—a huddle of four small cabins—though he could only guess at where it was. Every chance he had, he thought of a way to escape, but he was closely watched, particularly by Lucy, who kept him by her all the time. Yet for all the woman's eerie behavior, Jeremy felt somehow that he was safer with her than with the others. He had seen his friend Garth Morely killed, and he knew that all the others but Blair had been murdered. Morgan said he had been kept alive because Swain recognized him as Sutherland's son, and that a ransom would be required if he was ever to be returned to Detroit.

"Now, Willie, I know you won't like these here Injun turnips in this stew," Lucy cackled as she stirred the food bubbling in the iron kettle; her hair hung uncombed over her shoulders. "But you got to eat it an' get your strength back. You been through a lot, an' you got to be strong to work in the fields.

We're goin' to have a nice farm one day, an' you'll like it better'n the one we had in Pennsylvania." She mumbled on and began to hum to herself.

Jeremy was on his feet in the darkness, edging toward the door. On a balsam-branch bed in a far corner of the room, Jubal Swain lay asleep, breathing deeply. Slowly, Jeremy opened the door. It creaked ever so slightly, and he froze. But Lucy kept on stirring, kept on humming, and he moved through the narrow crack. Out in the cold, faint light of dawn, he kept to the shadows of the house, sliding along the rough bark of the cabin, moving toward the beached canoes. The sky was no more than a dusky gray. He might get a good start, with luck.

When a horse whickered, he stopped short. He listened as the horse stamped once and whickered again. The animals were nearby in a small corral of woven saplings. As the boy watched them moving about in the darkness, he thought taking one was a better idea than stealing a heavy canoe. He made his way softly to the corral, removed a couple of saplings, and was about to step into the circle when the horses took fright, backed off, and began to whinny.

There was a shout from somewhere, and then another. Jeremy grabbed for a horse's rope bridle, but the animal whinnied and reared. It was too late. The camp was alive with shouting men. He darted from the corral, heading for the canoes, his only hope.

But a shadow rose up in front of him, grabbed him savagely by the neck, and lifted him kicking off the ground. He heard Hurley's harsh voice and saw the flash of a tomahawk being raised.

"Stop!" Lucy Swain crashed against Hurley and wrenched Jeremy out of his grip. "Leave 'im be! Leave 'im be!" Then Lucy was kicking and punching at Hurley, who backed off in surprise and irritation.

Soon Jubal Swain was there, and with him the entire band of outlaws. He demanded to know what was going on, and Hurley said Jeremy was trying to excape. Swain cursed, snarling with anger as he towered over the boy and drew back a hand to slap him. But Lucy again jumped in between, shielding Jeremy and daring Swain to strike her instead.

Swain held off, then let his arms drop. He glared at the boy before turning fiercely on his men, swinging his fists and shouting at them to get away. They melted into the dimness, and

soon only Swain, Lucy, and Jeremy were left. Jeremy thought
Swain was trying to say something to Lucy, but when she threw
herself into her man's arms and hugged him, his fury abated.

"Don't let 'em hurt 'im, Jubal," Lucy begged. "I don't want
'im hurt."

He pushed Lucy back and gave her a little shake. "Lucy,
this ain't your Willie! Understand! It ain't Willie!"

Lucy became a bit coy and tittered. "I—I know it, Jube.
I know it, but—but just for now, let me make believe he is."
She turned to Jeremy and pinched his cheek fondly. "He's
awful like Willie, ain't he?"

Swain said nothing. Jeremy avoided looking at him. Instead
he looked at Lucy, who had that strange shining in her eyes
again.

The burial of what was left of Morely and the others was a
terrible undertaking, though it was done with reverence and
speed. Before they set off down the east-flowing Wabash
feeder, Sutherland bowed his head over the graves and spoke
the Lord's Prayer. He would come back and bury Morely properly one day, but first he must find Jubal Swain and rescue
Jeremy.

By the time Sutherland's two canoes had reached the Wabash and gone upstream to its source, they had traveled for two
weeks with only a few hours' rest now and again. The rolling
country was turning brownish gray as autumn began to lose
vigor and bright color. It was late October, and the world was
brittle, dry for lack of rain. The canoeists were often choked
with windblown dust that laid a film over still water. Prairie-
lands were giving way to slopes thick with trees, and on long,
low bluffs, elk and buffalo were abundant. Denser forest was
at hand now, and the higher lands to the north were suspected
as the haunt of Swain's outlaws.

At a Miami village they were told a band of fifty warriors
in search of excitement had entered the upper country after
Swain. Sutherland had been told by village headmen that all
he need do was to wait until the killers were wiped out. That
was possible, Sutherland knew, but he feared Jeremy might be
killed in the fight.

Though in desperate need of rest, their hands blistered from
nonstop paddling and their legs twisted with cramps from kneeling day after day in canoes, the group pressed ahead on foot.

Leaving canoes and supplies concealed, they made for the hills, hoping to intercept the warlike Miami in time.

Jeremy did not know why he was so hurriedly awakened one night. It was long before dawn, but Lucy, already dressed, got him out of bed and into his clothes. The fire was burning low and had not been stoked up as was usual upon rising in the morning. Lucy said little to him, but she was nervous and urgent as she forced him to dress.

"What's happening?" he asked sleepily.

When she hissed "Injuns!" he awoke with a start.

An hour later, it was still not yet light. Jeremy lay in a small cluster of trees and bushes on a slope a few hundred yards from the outlaw town. Behind the cabins, steep cliffs loomed massive in the darkness. Jeremy was cold, and he shivered uncontrollably until Lucy wrapped him in a thick blanket. Nearby two outlaws guarded the group's horses, which were hobbled close to the bushes and trees.

Jeremy asked Lucy again what was going on, but he was commanded by a ruffian to keep his mouth shut. He tried not to make a sound, though his teeth chattered without letup. Lucy sat with the other women, none speaking, all waiting.

Just before the sun rose, a distant war whoop rang through the forest, followed by a racket of Indian voices shrieking from the trees surrounding the settlement's clearing. Jeremy could make out the flashes of rifles and the movement of many bodies through the clearing. He heard the doors of cabins being broken down, and he saw a cabin take flame, illuminating everything with a reddish light that glowed on the smoke rising into the sky.

Then there was a strange, unexpected silence as the Indians stopped shrieking and firing their weapons. In that instant of hesitation, it was as though every warrior sensed something. In the next second, a wall of fire and smoke burst from the same side of the clearing from which the Indians had attacked. Swain's men had slipped in behind them. Caught against the cabins and the rising cliffs behind, the war party was trapped. Deadly musketry cut them down quickly, and Jeremy watched in shock as the Indians charged first this way and then that, but each time were decimated by rapid volleys. At last, after ten minutes of such slaughter, the surviving Indians burst through the ring of fire and vanished in the woods.

Silence fell once more, save for the crackling of the cabin that had been torched. Then the two men standing with the horses laughed softly and praised Jubal Swain for his brains.

Two days later, Owen Sutherland and his companions met the battered Miami in a camp on the trail leading into the hills. Of the fifty bold men who had gone after Swain, only twenty still lived, and many were wounded. They were tending the most severely injured before starting back for their villages, and most had done all the fighting they wanted. If Pontiac was to re-capture his presents, he would have to do it with others, for these Miami had lost too many friends and brothers going against the redbearded devil Swain.

Sutherland's group pressed on into the hills, led by a Miami who was not ready to give up. They followed the forest trail used by the war party, taking care now not to be seen by Swain's lookouts. Niko-lota had asked the beaten Miami to send someone to meet the main body of warriors from Pontiac's camp at the portage and tell them to follow quickly. No one knew how far behind these others were, but if they came up soon, there would be enough of them to surround Swain and take him. Before the fight, Sutherland had to rescue Jeremy. How he would do that, he did not know.

As they came closer to Swain's cabins, they took a little-used hunting trail the Miami guide knew, and after another day's travel were approaching Swain's settlement from the northwest. They slipped along a creek bed, thickly overgrown and concealed from any sentries. After hard going through the undergrowth, they rested all afternoon just a few hundred yards from the cabins. At sundown, they made their way out of the gully and observed the settlement from the same grove of trees where Jeremy had hidden.

Now Sutherland's exhaustion flowed away, replaced with a new urgency, a will to attack; but he restrained that passion and calculated just how to get down among the shacks and find out which one held the boy.

After full dark, Sutherland crept alone through the trees around the cabins. Using every bit of cover, from fallen logs to large boulders, he approached in silence. The others were waiting on the edge of the clearing. If shooting began, they would cover Sutherland's retreat—with the boy in his arms, he hoped.

It was very quiet in the cabins, and the Scotsman thought it unusual that a tough group of men would be so peaceful this early in the evening. It was cold, yet no fire glowed in the shacks. There was no smoke, no movement anywhere, and that made his skin crawl. He intended to haunt each cabin in turn until he found out which one held Jeremy. If he was unsuccessful tonight, he would hide in the bushes, watching during the day until he marked the right dwelling. He was counting on any guards being beyond the perimeter, with their eyes on the trails instead of on the very edge of the settlement, where the hunters waited.

After half an hour, Sutherland was able to look through a half-open shutter into the nearest cabin. It was dark inside. He heard not a sound, not even breathing. For some time he lingered there, trying to make out how many people were inside, but he could not tell. Within the next hour, he slipped unseen through the camp, yet every cabin was dead silent. Then he realized there were no animals in the stable, no one occasionally leaving a building to use a latrine.

He gave the cry of an owl, and it was answered by Tamano. He gave it twice more, and soon his friends were at his side by the door of the cabin nearest to where they had hidden. Carefully, Sutherland opened the door, and sure enough, the place was empty, the settlement deserted. Swain was gone.

On they went the next morning, though only after searching the clearing for signs of a grave that might indicate what Sutherland dreaded—that Jeremy was dead. There was no grave, and they found the outlaw's trail quite easily. There were many horses in a pack train moving south, toward the land between the Maumee and the Wabash.

Two days later, the Miami Indian who had guided them left Sutherland, agreeing to put men into action bottling up the Maumee River to the east, so Swain could not turn that way. Burdened by a great cargo of goods, Swain's force eventually must find canoes, for the packhorses they used would be unable to get them out of Indian country on the difficult, narrow trails that were adapted to men on foot. Sutherland guessed that Swain had canoes hidden on the Maumee, and he told this to the Miami, who set off due east, heading for his village and hungry for vengeance. The other Miami warriors would be just as savage when they learned of the disastrous defeat of their war party.

At a brief council of war, Sutherland and his friends decided to outflank Swain. Presuming he would be afraid to risk meeting hostile Miami, they guessed he would avoid the Maumee.

Thinking hard, Tamano said, "Swain is a cunning fox. He knows there's trouble waiting to the east. He knows Pontiac would send a war party after him from the west. If he goes north, he can't get away to spend the money and sell the goods. But south, there's the Ohio, and lots of rivers run down to it."

Swain must have known that the country was rising against him; however, there were fewer Indians between the Maumee River in the north and the Ohio in the south. It would be better for Swain to strike due south and then follow the great Ohio west to the Mississippi and down to New Orleans. It was a gamble to anticipate this as Swain's move. If they were wrong and he was already past the Miami villages and traveling east, then he would be beyond their reach.

Shamot, one of the young Delaware, went westward to intercept Pontiac's war party, which no doubt was coming up the Wabash by now. He would lead some southward to meet Sutherland's group at a village of Piankashaw on a south-flowing river. The rest of the war party would bear eastward in case Swain had gone that way.

Sutherland's group went on to the southwest, cutting across grasslands and sparse woods in the hopes of outflanking Swain. It was almost a week before they found his trail—three days old at least. Moving in a long single file to obscure just how many were in the party, Swain's group traveled overland, apparently moving toward the Ohio River, as Tamano had guessed.

They drove themselves on until they knew Swain was making for the source of the White River. That was four days away at the exhausting pace Sutherland was setting. They might catch up with Swain at the river's headwaters and follow him until Shamot brought the other warriors down.

At a section of river deep enough to float canoes, Sutherland and his friends came to the small Piankashaw village of eight lodges near a stand of trees that sheltered the community from westerly gales. As soon as the hunters came to the village, they were met by angry men armed with muskets and bows. There were no more than a dozen in all, half of them too young to have seen much war, but they confronted Sutherland and his companions and told them to be on their way.

Niko-lota stepped forward and asked in a hoarse voice, cracking from weariness, why these people were so hostile. He was told that a group of whites had raided their village two days earlier, driven the people away, and stolen all their canoes. Swain was on water again, and he would move quickly.

Making a sudden decision, Sutherland bargained with the village, offering to purchase horses in return for extra ammunition he and Tamano had carried along. They acquired four mounts, all in very good condition, and left word for Shamot's men to come farther downstream to the next village, where there would be canoes waiting for them. In the meantime, Sutherland's group galloped across the grasslands, following the meandering stream for ten miles, until they came to the village. There they paid for six canoes, trading the horses and much of their equipment, and arranged for five of them to be readied for the war party from Pontiac.

Amazed that a white man would speak for the great war chief, these Indians gaped in awe as Sutherland's troop set off by canoe.

News of Swain was heard at every small village or hunting lodge along the way. Stealing food whenever possible, the robbers were rampaging through the helpless Indian villages. Totally unprepared for this sudden attack, the tribes of this country were unable to defend themselves. Most had never even seen a white man, and when Tamano asked for followers to pursue Swain, these peaceful folk were not interested.

On they paddled, knowing the outlaws were now no more than a day ahead of them. Yet Swain was not slowing down; it was as though the man sensed he was being stalked, and he was determined to break out into the Ohio River before being caught. Sutherland's men pushed themselves as hard as they could, but it seemed Swain was always a day ahead. Then, as the country became more hilly, and the river twisted and turned through steep gorges, an Indian hunter told them Swain was only half a day away. Apparently the gang had encountered rough water, and a canoe had capsized. In the effort to save their booty, the outlaws had wasted precious hours retrieving it from the water. Sutherland suspected that Swain might have lost the money when the canoes turned over; otherwise he would not have slowed down—either that or he felt safe from pursuit here.

Then something else crossed Sutherland's mind: perhaps Swain had laid another trap.

chapter **31**

THE FIGHT IN THE GORGE

It was Jeremy's canoe that had tipped over in the rapids that morning, and he had been spilled into shallow water along with Lucy and Hurley. Swain, who had been in the foremost canoe, stopped his advance toward the Ohio, still a hard day's travel off, and fished out people and baggage that had gone under. No one was hurt, and the gear was recovered, soaked but otherwise all right. Sutherland was wrong to think Swain had paused because the money had been lost; the Scotsman did not know how precious Lucy was to this tough renegade leader. If he had, he would have understood why Swain made camp at the site of the mishap instead of pushing on at all costs. Lucy had to rest and recover from the icy drenching—she had to be more careful. Last night she had told Swain she carried his child.

Sutherland was also wrong in thinking that Swain knew he was being pursued. It was natural for Swain to drive his people hard; however, the thought of spending their share of the money and trading the stolen goods was enough to encourage the ruffians and instill in them a determination that urged them on.

In early afternoon, as Jeremy and Lucy huddled by a camp-fire, the others took this opportunity to patch canoes with birch-bark and pine tar. Blankets and equipment from the overturned canoe were hung up to dry before the campfire. Lighting a fire near Lucy with a watertight tinderbox, Swain made sure she kept warm wrapped in a heavy blanket. Immediately he gave orders to scouts to go downstream by canoe to check quickly

small annoyance became increasingly irritating, because each time he moved, the wind changed as though with a mind of its own, purposely annoying him with smoke.

Lucy saw his distress and clucked her tongue. "Poor boy. Willie, darlin', come sit by me, an' you'll be fine. Ain't no smoke here. Come on, now." She patted the ground beside her, but Jeremy sulked and ignored her.

"Willie!" Lucy said, a little more sharply. "You hear me?" Jubal Swain, leaning back on a bale of blankets a few yards away, looked over as Lucy's voice rose. "You don't ignore your ma, hear? Willie! I'm talkin' to—"

Jeremy threw back the blanket and leaped to his feet, shrieking in a voice that rang through the gorge. "You're *not* my ma! I'm *not* your son! Your Willie's gone! Leave me alone!"

He stood there shaking, his fists clenched, madly confronting Lucy, whose openmouthed surprise, dismay, left her speechless. Swain, his face showing, anger and pain, was ready to sit up. Lucy's trembling hands went to her face, and she crawled away, whining, all the while staring at the boy.

"No," she moaned, the haunting light that had shone in her eyes now out. "No, you ain't Willie." She dragged herself back toward Jubal, as though Jeremy were something dangerous, something that terrified her. She was muttering and whimpering. Jeremy quaked with anger and fear, and he noticed the deadly calm of Jubal Swain.

"Matt," Lucy sobbed. "He ain't my Willie. My Willie's lost. He ain't Willie." Then Lucy stared at Jubal and saw, as though her delirium had passed, who he was. "Jubal!" she gasped and clutched his arm. "Jubal, what's come over me? Jubal!" She wrapped her head in a blanket and curled up, weeping. By now every man in camp was watching, and Morgan, his eyes cold, came to his leader.

Swain motioned to Morgan, who knew what was wanted. Jeremy saw the man touch his sheath knife. In a flash, the boy darted away, crashing into the thicket with Morgan laughing close behind, his knife out.

Sutherland saw Jeremy run, and he leaped with his rifle over the outcrop and down the slope. His first movements careful, he calculated just how to get at the man going after Jeremy, who was tangled in the bushes thirty yards away. Morgan needed only a moment more to catch him. Sutherland closed in, his body tense. It was this unhurried advance that confused the guard who heard Sutherland's leap and got to his feet in surprise, just a few feet behind the Scotsman.

"Hey, Hurley!" the guard yelled casually, rubbing the sleep from his face. "What the hell you doin' back already?"

Sutherland was startled to hear a man so close behind, though he realized he was not yet unmasked. He ignored the guard, giving a perfunctory wave and striding off as rapidly as he dared toward Jeremy, now only a few feet ahead of Morgan, who was digging at the boy through the thick bushes. The guard behind Sutherland was saying something. The sound of Lucy's wailing rose above the river. The man's voice became louder, more insistent. Sutherland felt an icy chill on his back, as though a gun was aimed at it. Did the man know? He dared not turn. Jeremy was struggling only fifteen yards away, Morgan reaching out for him.

The suspicious guard's gun was indeed coming up slowly. Suddenly the man knew this was not Hurley at all. He raised his weapon to draw a bead on Sutherland, but before he could cock the hammer, he was slammed to the ground, Tamano's tomahawk buried in his skull.

Morgan grabbed at Jeremy, who was frantically trying to get out of the bushes. Sutherland dropped to his knee, aimed the rifle, and shouted, "You!"

Morgan stood up straight in surprise, an easy target, and Sutherland's ball caught him in the face, the report from the rifle echoing through the canyon. The sound of Niko-lota and Tamano whooping savagely distracted the other outlaws, scurrying for their weapons. The Indians fired into the campsite, giving some cover for Sutherland, who yanked the astonished Jeremy free of the bushes and raced back up the slope, rifle balls zinging past him all the way.

He clambered over the rock outcrop, and Tamano reached down to heave the boy up to safety. Soon the four of them were under cover, while well-placed shots from the renegades ricocheted off rock and dug into trees.

"They come for us," Tamano said, and nodded at men flitting from cover to cover, sneaking around on their right and left to surround them. Sutherland's group could flee straight back through the thickets and woods and come out on open grasslands, but that would expose them to rifle fire once Swain's men came close enough. They could not use the hunting trail that paralleled the river, because already Swain's men had cut them off there. The outlaw leader was clever, and he knew how to fight. They had to hold out where they were.

Soon the forest was quiet, and only the rushing of the river could be heard. Sutherland discarded Hurley's clothing and put on his own, then he hugged Jeremy close. The boy wept with relief, not caring that they were still in deadly peril. He breathed deeply as he lay next to Sutherland, who was watching the trees for any sign of movement. Jeremy touched Sutherland's pistol, and the Scotsman handed it to him. They lay without a word, grouped loosely in a circle to protect all sides, but if the gang stormed them, they would not have a chance. Perhaps the outlaws would not risk heavy loss by a direct attack. If that were so, Sutherland's men could hold out until dark, when they might slip away. But nightfall was hours off, and Sutherland knew Swain would not go that long without attacking. Each moment of stillness weighed more ominously as they waited.

For ten minutes, nothing happened, yet it was certain the woodsmen were coming in, closer and closer. Jeremy observed Sutherland moving ever so slowly, aiming his rifle at something the boy could not see. Sutherland raised his sights to bear on a man high in a tree—a man whose own rifle was being brought around on Sutherland. The Scotsman's rifle flashed and banged. The man lurched in the top of the tree, and Jeremy heard the sound of a body falling from branch to branch.

Immediately the woods shook with a shrieking, howling yell of fury from many voices on all sides. Jeremy saw someone charge out of the trees, and he swung his pistol, but it was knocked away before he could fire. For some reason, Sutherland had stopped him from shooting. Then an Indian leaped into Sutherland's hiding place, dropping to his knees.

"Pay-cus!" Niko-lota laughed and grasped his cousin by the shoulders. The war party had come!

The forest was alive with the sound of fighting. Within moments, the outnumbered outlaws were shooting their way back toward their beached canoes. Sutherland told Jeremy to stay under cover, and the boy watched as the four men darted over the outcrop and charged against the left flank of the re-treating enemy. In a moment, a dozen more battle-painted Indians hurtled past Jeremy and rushed down the slope.

Swain's men kept cool under a brutal fire. Dragging their wounded along, they stopped behind trees and returned the

Indian fusillade with accurate shots. Pay-cus, running alongside
Sutherland to cut the outlaws off from their canoes, stumbled
heavily. Niko-lota came up behind and hauled his cousin out
of the line of fire, but it was too late. The youth was dead, a
bullet between his eyes. The death wail mingled with the war
cry, and Niko-lota raged ahead through the trees. Swain drew
a bead on Niko-lota, who snatched out his tomahawk, heedless
of the danger. Swain's rifle pan flashed, but in that very same
instant, Owen Sutherland leaped from cover, drove the man
off balance, and the gun fired harmlessly into the air. Swain
fought hand to hand with Sutherland, who had thrown aside
his own empty rifle and swung his claymore. Swain's cheek
bled from a gash Sutherland's sword gave him, and the two
men were spattered with his blood as they fell to the ground
in a tangle of kicking and pounding.

The sword was useless in such a struggle. Swain's power
was greater than Sutherland's, and he threw the Scotsman over
his head. In an instant, the outlaw was on his feet. Half-stunned,
Sutherland saw the man pulling a pistol from his belt, and he
ducked to the side. At the last moment, Niko-lota leaped onto
Swain's back and chopped with the tomahawk at the pistol,
which fell to the ground. Swain roared in agony and whipped
the Indian over his shoulder. Niko-lota bounced to his feet and
turned to fight Swain again. But two other renegades came in
between, and Niko-lota met them alongside Sutherland, whose
claymore slashed and cut. In the confusion, Swain vanished.
More Indians came up to help Sutherland and Niko-lota—these
were Tamano and Shamot, who sprang with a wild fury into
the fight. The outlaws soon lay in their own blood.

Sutherland was fifty yards away from where Swain's men
had left their canoes. The other outlaws had been driven into
a small pocket and were already cut off from their craft. It was
only a matter of time for them, and not much at that. Swain,
however, was the man Sutherland wanted, and the canoes were
Swain's only escape. Sutherland had to get to them quickly,
but before he could race away, he was stopped by Tamano,
who shouted at him to look at something. There on the ground,
still gripping the pistol, was Swain's severed left hand, chopped
off by Niko-lota's tomahawk.

There was no more time to waste. Gunfire pinned down the
three Indians, but in a sprint through the trees, Sutherland made
for the canoes. He was close when a bullet bounced off a tree

near his head and he ducked for cover. As he looked up, he saw Lucy Swain sitting in the bow of a floating canoe, reloading a rifle. He saw Swain, twenty yards away, leaning over a campfire.

Sutherland broke out of cover and made for the man, who bellowed in agony and wrenched out of the fire his smoking stump, savagely cauterized to stop the bleeding. Sutherland's instinct told him Lucy had loaded, and he dropped to the ground as the gun went off, again just missing him. Before he was on his feet and running again, Swain had climbed into the stern of the canoe. Even with his terrible injury, Jubal Swain did not give up. Using his damaged arm to guide the paddle, he stroked with his right hand and forced the canoe ferociously out into the river. Sutherland dived into the water, but the strong current snatched the craft away, and all Swain had to do was guide it while Lucy sat in front.

Sutherland, Niko-lota, and Tamano leaped to another canoe, but found it had been tomahawked. Another and another were in the same useless condition. Then they found one undamaged and took it, knowing no one else could follow to help them. They paddled out into the current, certain they would soon overtake Swain, whose craft had already disappeared around a bend in the swift river.

Faster and faster the pursuers drove their canoe. Sutherland sat in the middle while Tamano steered and Niko-lota paddled in the bow. Sutherland loaded Tamano's rifle, the only gun they possessed, and at his side was the claymore, now in its scabbard. When Swain's canoe appeared momentarily about fifty yards ahead, Sutherland aimed and fired, but he missed. Swain was quickly out of sight once again. The river raged so dangerously between rocks and outcroppings that Sutherland knew Swain could not possibly steer for long in this boiling, white current.

After another few minutes, Sutherland's canoe whipped around a bend, and he saw Swain's craft, upside down, drifting helplessly. Sutherland's own canoe was in the middle of a turbulent rapids, and it was with the utmost difficulty that Tamano kept it from overturning as well. Sutherland searched the whitewater for Swain's corpse, but before he got a good look, there was a shout from Niko-lota over the loud roar of the river. With shock, Sutherland realized they were headed for a waterfall.

The brink came up fast. Beyond was empty space. Driving straight ahead, the Indian paddlers rammed the canoe forward in the hope that the fall would be a small one and they would shoot out beyond the drop. However, the pool was more than twenty feet down, and the canoe's bow plummeted quickly. Leaning back to keep the canoe from going end over end, the three men were helpless as the craft fell with a shattering crash into the water.

Sutherland kept consciousness as he fought to swim to the surface of the pool, the powerful surge of falling water trying to keep him under. Just as his breath gave out, he broke from the water, gasping for air, and struggled blindly to the rocks on land.

Panting and choking, he found he was uninjured save for a welt on his forehead. He heard a voice and saw Tamano at the far side of the pool hauling Niko-lota out of the water. Finding the claymore still at his side, Sutherland stumbled over the rubble of boulders to his friends on the western bank of the river. It was with relief that he saw Niko-lota had nothing worse than an apparently broken leg. They were all alive.

But what about Swain?

Tamano found out that answer. He shouted and pointed to the top of the cliff on the same side of the river as the outlaw camp had been. There was Swain, struggling along a narrow ledge, with Lucy in front. Just before he disappeared from view, Swain turned and stared at his pursuers. Shaking his good hand, he gave a mocking laugh louder than the noise of the waterfall. Then he was gone. Sutherland had seen that Swain was without a rifle; the man must have just barely managed to avoid the waterfall by turning over at the last minute, thus losing their weapons. Sutherland presumed Swain had known about the waterfall and expected his pursuer's canoe to be caught by it.

Without a second thought, Sutherland told Tamano to wait with Niko-lota until the others came down. The two Indians simply nodded, knowing what the Scotsman had to do. Then he started up the sheer cliff after Swain.

After a dizzying climb up the rock face, toiling from handhold to handhold, he reached the top, where scrubby spruce trees crowded close to the edge. He turned and waved to Tamano and Niko-lota far below, then hurried away through the stand of low trees that concealed Swain's flight. The trail was easy to find, for it crashed recklessly through the trees until it met the hunting path that followed the river. Swain and his woman were making for the southwest, where grasslands opened up beyond the trees.

Sutherland trotted along, his senses alert, nostrils flaring. He knew Swain could be lying in wait for him, but he would welcome a final encounter. Swain's physical strength was no match for Sutherland's claymore, and there would be no quarter given the murderer.

His body battered and drained of power from the fighting and the weeks of relentless pursuit, Sutherland found it difficult to keep going. His chest burned with the lack of air. His legs shook with every jarring stride, as though they would splinter under him.

This was a vast stand of small evergreens, and the forest smelled strongly of pitch that oozed from every tree. Above him the sky was bright blue, and the sun glared cruelly in his eyes.

Suddenly, as if someone had swept away the trees and rolled out an enormous grassland, he was at the edge of the woods. He had been careless to run right out of the sheltering trees to stand in the waist-high buffalo grass, but it was done. He paused, chest heaving for breath, and searched for Swain's trail.

He saw it cutting off to the left along the treeline, as though Swain was trying to get back to the river again. He began to follow, but then realized that another, larger set of tracks went west, straight ahead into the long grass, which was pushed down in an obvious swath. Clearly, the woman had gone to the left, and Swain had gone straight ahead. Why they had split up Sutherland did not know, and he was too spent to care. All that mattered was Swain's trail. He trotted ahead into the grassy meadow blowing in endless ripples in the westerly wind.

The buffalo grass crackled, brown and dry, making too much noise as Sutherland hurried through it, so he stopped running and began to walk, listening for any sound that might tell where Swain was. In a moment he was at the rim of a gentle saucer, of meadow that fell away then rose at the other side a hundred yards off. This was a good place to search out Swain's movement. He saw that the outlaw's trail went into the saucer then cut sharply off to the right. Yet when he looked that way, he noticed nothing. Nor was there anything all along the rising slope that drifted back toward the treeline, where the woman had gone. As far as Sutherland could see to the right and left, spruce trees marched along the edge of the prairie. Ahead of him, the grass billowed and shone in the lowering sun. Far off in the distance was the bulk of another ridge, where more evergreens grew thick and dark. The long valley ran from right to left, sinking steadily down and down until it was out of sight below the grasses and bracken. Still no sign of Swain.

He was about to enter the saucer of land and follow the trail when he smelled smoke. A campfire? Swain would not have made camp, but he might have come upon a hunter unawares and attacked him. That would mean the man was armed! Sutherland drew out his claymore, hunched low in the grass, and scurried forward so he would not be an easy target if Swain was lying in wait with a gun.

The smoke was stronger now, and Sutherland saw it rising into the sky in a line at his right. The wind caught the dense smoke and whipped it about until it clouded over Sutherland thick enough to block out the western horizon.

Sutherland's numbed, weary mind warned him it was a prairie fire! He shook himself alert and stood up, but the acrid smoke was thick. He found his eyes running, and it was hard to breathe. The fire was moving across his front from right to left and being blown rapidly toward him by the strong wind. Swain must have set it to drive him off.

He worked his way back along the trail, retracing his steps until he stood again on the rim of the saucer. Smoke was everywhere now, though the blaze was not yet close enough for him to feel the heat. Birds screeched and fluttered into the air. A doe and her fawn sprang out of the grass and bounded away, running past Sutherland, who was trying to decide his next step. It was then he saw Swain. Crouching low, running through the buffalo grass about sixty yards away, Swain was touching off a wall of fire that leaped up close behind him.

Swain's semicircle of fire was coming at Sutherland as fast as the wind. Already the entire sky was blackened with smoke, and it was increasingly difficult to breathe with every passing moment. Sutherland began to run to the left, on a line roughly parallel with Swain's arcing race for the woods. If only he had the strength to outrun the killer, he could catch him at the end

of the flaming wall. Otherwise, Sutherland would be driven
back into the trees, there to be followed by the greedy, scorching blaze, which would pursue him to the very banks of the
river.

But before he ran very far, Sutherland noticed that behind
him was another line of fire and smoke. How did the flames
get behind him so quickly? Then he understood: Swain's
woman was over there, torching the grass in a backfire that,
if it met with Swain's wall of flame, would encircle him.

In a moment of instant decision, he knew he could not run
straight back to the trees before this second barrier of fire cut
him off. There was only one thing to do—run for the sole
opening of the fiery circle in the hope he could break through
before Swain and the woman met. He charged with all his
power for the rapidly narrowing gap between the ends of the
smoky walls. Smoke came down in thick, dark clouds, making
it very painful and difficult to see. Slashing the grass with his
claymore and covering his eyes, Sutherland tried to beat Swain
to the end of the woman's wall, which was a hundred yards
from him, but only forty yards or so from Swain.

Now and again he saw glimpses of his enemy hurrying like
a devil through the grass, firing it with a torch of pitch-pine
root and running on with almost superhuman power. Swain
was closing the circle, cutting off Sutherland's line of escape.
The fire flared up so quickly that the Scotsman was sure his
enemy was only a few seconds ahead of his own blaze. Sutherland tried to run harder. He rammed the claymore into its
scabbard, held his breath so the smoke would not overcome
him, put his head down, and plunged ahead with the very last
of his waning strength.

The fire swept close behind him like a tidal wave of flame,
scorching his back. He could barely see, but he aimed directly
for what little blue sky was left in the gap. Lifting his numb
legs, stumbling over obstructions, and barely keeping on his
feet, he became disoriented and ran into the burning wall. Just
managing to veer to the left, he ran and ran and ran. He was
suffocating in smoke and heat. Dead animals lay all around,
others struggling to their feet, kicking helplessly, and falling.
Still Sutherland ran.

Then unexpectedly, as though he had been lifted out of hell,
he found himself running into sunshine, into pure air and blue

sky. He staggered and collapsed, wheezing and coughing, spitting up painfully, utterly ravaged. The roar of the fire filled the air. For a moment he lost consciousness and thought he was again drowning at the bottom of the waterfall.

Then he came to and knew he had outrun the flames. He had passed through the gap, and the wind was blowing the fire away toward the trees. Summoning what was left of his willpower, Sutherland stood up.

To his amazement, Swain was no more than thirty feet away, running back and forth as though searching for Sutherland in the ring of fire. The man did not know Sutherland was there until the Scotsman unsheathed his sword and shouted above the noise of the blaze, "Here!"

Swain spun in surprise, his face flushed with anger.

It was then that Sutherland saw the horrible stump of a left hand, blackened and sore, clutched at Swain's heaving chest. Both men were charred and dirty from the fire, both spent. This was the end. Sutherland brought the claymore up and advanced. He had no urge to spare the man. Swain was more dangerous with one hand than most men with two, so Sutherland was careful. He moved to within ten feet of Swain, who, for some reason, kept glancing nervously over his left shoulder, as though to flee. If he tried that, Sutherland would not let him go.

Swain slipped to his left, maneuvering Sutherland so he could look into the fire he had set. Sutherland wondered what was on the killer's mind. Fear was in Swain's eyes, but it was not fear for his own life. There came a piercing scream of terror, and Swain leaped around to the fire, crying out, "Lucy! Here!" Lucy had become trapped within the ring. Swain backed up quickly, and Sutherland advanced, but was not ready to strike.

Then Sutherland saw the ghostly form of Lucy Swain beyond the smoke and swirling heat. She was waving her hands, then began to slap at her clothes as they took fire. Swain bellowed like a wounded animal, and she shrieked once more for him. Before Sutherland could move, Swain bounded right into the blaze and through the smoke. Sutherland tried to follow, but the heat was too intense. At the last moment he thought he saw Swain with Lucy in his arms, running back and forth, hopelessly trying to find an escape from the inferno. The flames whipped up as the wind gusted and changed direction, forcing Sutherland to back off and run for safety, leaving Jubal Swain and Lucy to perish in the fire storm of their own making.

chapter **32**

TRADER

What it was that kept Ella Sutherland lingering at the landing on this cold Sunday morning she could not say. Since Jeremy had vanished two months ago, with only a letter to explain where he was going, she had worried as any mother would. But she had refrained from daily haunting the river's edge, from gazing anxiously across the broad water in the hope that her son and her husband would return. Ella had learned not to spend time that way, for there was more, much more, to do—caring for little Benjamin, spinning yarn, knitting winter clothing, and putting up pickled foods.

Yet here she was, for the first time in weeks, walking at the edge of the river, her head down, hugging a shawl about her shoulders to keep off the biting December wind. Most of the soldiers had left the fort and gone back east with Colonel Bradstreet before the end of November. Winter was closing in rapidly, and the people of Detroit were preparing for months of solitude after a bustling, noisy autumn of parading troops, of Indian councils, and endless rounds of parties and balls.

Ella had attended none of these parties, though she was always invited. Staying at home was her only concession to loneliness; and during the times she was with others, she was cheerful and friendly in spite of the anxiety of not knowing about Owen and Jeremy. Not a word had come back in all this time. Not a word.

She first had come to the riverside an hour earlier, when a smart little two-masted sloop came upriver to be greeted by curious residents and soldiers. Ella had come out of her house to see the ship, named *Trader,* which was now tied up at the landing. She had been interested in the vessel, with its black hull and white trim, its rigging and deck alive with sailors, but she was soon dismayed to learn that it belonged to none other than Bradford Cullen, the Montreal merchant who was determined to defeat the Frontier Company. Cullen himself was on the sloop, as were his wife and daughter and the maid, Emmy, Mary Defries's friend.

It did not take long for Ella to learn that Cullen had scoured Montreal and Quebec City for trade goods, which were very scarce these days. Ella had found this out from Emmy, who had accompanied Linda Cullen to the fort's infirmary, where the girl was treated for fever, exhaustion, nervousness, and nausea, all of which might have been included in the general category of seasickness.

While Linda was with the fort physician, Ella took the maid aside—Ella knew about the woman from Owen's and Peter's stories of Montreal—and was told that the Cullens intended to stockpile these trade goods in Detroit until the Indian trappers came in with their furs this winter. That meant that Cullen's agents, who had come with him from Montreal and would stay behind at the fort, would be there first to snap up all the best furs.

As she strolled idly on the shore, Ella thought of all this, aware that Cullen and Company was giving itself a tremendous advantage over her own firm—an advantage that might be impossible to overcome. She thought of the shrewd and diligent Cullen, who had built this ship at the yards on Navy Island, near Fort Schlosser. He was a formidable opponent, perhaps too formidable . . . She struggled against her deepening gloom, turned away from Cullen's ship, and walked with her head down along the shore.

The wind picked up, causing Ella to shiver and pull the shawl closer. She stopped walking and gazed downriver, seeing nothing but the pale light of a cloudy belated sunrise. She began to stroll again, but then stopped short. Something glinted far out on the water. She shaded her eyes to peer closer. It was as though light had glimmered on a dipping canoe paddle. There it was again! There was more than one flash—there seemed to be a line of quick reflections of light, as of several canoes coming in together. Ella was excited, even though she knew her emotions should not get the better of her, for these might be anyone's canoes coming to the fort. She fought down the insistent tension that made it impossible to take her eyes from the rapidly approaching canoes. She counted ten in all, brightly painted, flying sleek and free against the current.

Ella bit her lip, wishing she knew who was coming, wishing she had the force of will to turn away before she was disappointed. She stayed, however, watching the canoes cut across the current, bobbing and bouncing in the choppy water.

Someone in the first canoe waved. At her? Folk were coming down the bank from the fort. An officer near the river gate stood with a telescope to his eye. More waving from the lead canoe; shouts! Could it be? Owen? Jeremy? It was! They had come back! Ella felt her knees go weak, and her body trembled for joy and relief. She waved both arms, her shawl dropping to the ground behind her. Tamano was in the bow of the lead canoe, John Blair in the middle, and there was Jeremy behind them. Owen paddled, grinning, in the stern. Thank the Lord!

The canoes shot toward the landing, where Cullen's sloop was tied up. The vessel's sailors stopped their work on the rigging and cargo to watch the craft—all but Sutherland's paddled by warriors—skim impudently alongside, like so many sharks around a whale. Ella, laughing and crying, wiping away tears and waving, ran along the shore toward the landing. She was too carried away to notice Bradford Cullen standing on the ship's deck, brooding as he glared at the arriving canoes. Ella saw only her husband and son, but Cullen marked that each and every canoe was heavy-laden with prime furs.

Before leaping from his canoe, Sutherland looked the sloop over, recognized Cullen, and realized immediately that the future of the Frontier Company was in jeopardy. Unlike Ella, however, he knew Cullen was eyeing the furs, and he marked the hunger in the man's eyes—the hunger and the envy.

Then Sutherland heard Ella's cry, and he saw her splashing through the water toward his craft. In the next moment he was waist-deep in the river, crushing her against him while young Jeremy sat grinning in the canoe, happily watching his parents embrace.

Owen Sutherland's return to Fort Detroit should have been a triumphant one, for he carried with him the pipe of Chief Pontiac himself. Wrapped in white ermine fur, the pipe was

Pontiac's solemn pledge to attend the next great peace conference held by Sir William Johnson. Sutherland had even recovered most of the stolen money from Swain's camp. However, the loss of Garth Morely made the embassy to the Indians
a bittersweet success. On the way back from Kaskaskia, Sutherland had reburied his friend in a deeper grave and clearly
marked it with stones and a wooden cross.

Furthermore, a fortune in pelts had been given to Sutherland
by Pontiac and by a number of important chiefs, who expected
trade goods in return that spring. Two of the ten canoes belonged outright to Sutherland and Tamano, having been bestowed by those villages that had been glad to see the defeat
of Swain and his cutthroats. The furs would be worth approximately forty-five hundred pounds British sterling when they
were brought down to Montreal. That long journey to Montreal
was on Sutherland's mind, for he knew it could not be made
in time for him to return with trade goods before winter, when
the lakes became impassable. That meant he would be in the
east until spring, in company with Levesque, Mary, and with
Peter Defries, who was now at Detroit, having waited for the
Scotsman to return.

Before taking any other steps—even before delivering the
precious pipe to Detroit's new commander and Bradstreet's
replacement, Lieutenant Colonel John Campbell—Sutherland
went to Lettie Morely and told the news of her man's death.
It was a wrenching, terrible moment, and Lettie broke down.
After some time, Sutherland left Ella with her and carried out
his duty to the army.

Shortly, he was in Henry Gladwin's former residence, standing before the seated Colonel Campbell, a tall, slender, middle-
aged man of stern bearing. Campbell enthusiastically accepted
the pipe and had his secretary record the words of Chief Pontiac,
which Sutherland repeated precisely from memory:

"Father, we have all smoked out of this pipe of peace; it
is your children's pipe. As the war is over, and the Great Spirit
and Giver of Light has brought us together for our mutual good,
I declare to all nations that I have settled my peace with you.
I now deliver this pipe to Sir William Johnson, that he may
know I have made peace with the king of England, whom I
have taken for my father.

"I call the Great Spirit to witness that I speak from my heart.
Now that I have taken Donoway by the hand, I will never let

go, for I see that the Great Spirit will have the English and my people be friends. In the name of all the nations to the westward over whom I am master, I promise to keep the covenant chain of peace bright and strong, for as long as I live."

Leaving Pontiac's pipe with a buoyant Campbell, who intended to send it and a report back to Colonel Bradstreet as soon as possible, Sutherland rejoined his family and his friends. Owen saw very little of his wife that morning, however, for there was much to occupy him as he talked with Peter Defries and Jean Martine. Sitting before a bright fire in Sutherland's cabin, the three men spoke of how they could counter Cullen's apparent success, which threatened to ruin them that coming trading season. They discussed these matters in the quiet of the cabin, while Ella and Angélique comforted Lettie. John Blair, who was with Reverend Lee, planned to stay in Detroit that winter and would renew his search for the Northwest Passage in the spring. Jeremy, now over his shock, played with Sally and Sniffer by the river; and Tamano had gone across the straits with Lela, to spend time alone at Valenya, where he and Sutherland had lived.

Sutherland, Martine, and Defries—whose injury from Swain's hatchet blow was now no more than a thin white scar at his hairline—sat smoking clay pipes as they talked. They discussed every possible way they could think of to meet Cullen's challenge. But the situation was painfully simple: Cullen had trade goods waiting for the Indians to bring in furs; the Frontier Company, for all the four thousand pounds it had as working capital and the Indian peltry in the canoes, could not hope to get goods out to Detroit before late spring, because the lakes would soon be frozen over.

At last, Martine shook his head slowly and blew smoke out his nose. "There is no way to beat him, my friends. We need trade goods now. We need what Cullen already has, but—"

"Yes!" Sutherland exclaimed and slapped his thigh hard. "Yes, we need what Cullen has!"

The others looked at him, their faces blank at first. Then they listened closely as Sutherland explained the plan that had just flashed in his mind. By the time the Scotsman was done, Martine was laughing at such audacity, and Defries was thinking Sutherland might just pull off a coup against Cullen that would make his own affair with the borrowed paymaster's stamp seem child's play.

• • •

"Mr. Sutherland requests permission to come aboard, Mr. Cullen," cried out a sailor on the deck of the *Trader*. A moment later, Bradford Cullen, dressed in an expensive frock coat and tricorn, appeared on deck to glare down at Owen Sutherland, who stood on the landing, a small canvas bag in each hand.

"Mr. Sutherland indeed," declared Cullen, folding his arms and snickering. "And what, may I ask, does Mr. Sutherland want with me?"

Sutherland gave a slight grin and said, "Cargo space for my peltry, Mr. Cullen."

The merchant clapped his hands together and laughed aloud. "Cargo space! Hah! Well, Sutherland, you are as naive as you are insolent! Why, pray tell, should I sell *you* cargo space in my ship?"

Sutherland replied, "Because I'll pay you three hundred pounds sterling to take these furs and my partner back east."

A quizzical look crossed Cullen's face—a look of curiosity and surprise, for Sutherland had just offered an astounding sum in payment for cargo space. Cullen cleared his throat and asked, "And do you have that many furs that you'll pay so dear to have them shipped out?"

"You've seen my pelts from a distance, Cullen, and you know how many there are; but you apparently don't recognize them as exclusively beaver coats and ermine, which in Montreal will be worth— But then, that's not important at the moment. I've made my offer. What's your reply?"

Cullen knew very well that such pelts were probably worth well over four thousand pounds in Montreal. Furthermore, he knew the glory that would come to the first man to haul such a splendid harvest out of the embattled northwest. That prestige was worth much to Cullen, who seethed at the thought of Owen Sutherland winning it. He also realized that Sutherland could take the furs east by canoe, though the trip would be much longer than shipment on the swift *Trader*. Yet by canoe the furs would still get to Montreal in time to catch the last ship to England before the Saint Lawrence froze up.

In a twinkling, these things went through Cullen's mind, and he thought of a way to benefit himself—and outsmart Sutherland.

"Come aboard, sir, and we'll talk further. Perhaps we can

make arrangements that will be satisfactory to both of us."

A few moments later, Sutherland and Cullen were seated at opposite ends of a folding table set up in Cullen's spacious cabin. Sutherland laid the two canvas sacks at his feet as Cullen poured each a brandy, then toasted, "To furs and peace."

After savoring the brandy and wiping his lips with the back of his hand, Cullen leaned forward, folding his hands and peering at Sutherland, who smoothly drained his own glass.

"Let's not mince words, Sutherland; you know the sort of goods I have on board this vessel, and you know what that means for your own ambitions." He looked through narrowed eyes at the Scotsman. Sutherland asked if he might pour another brandy for each of them, but gave no direct reply to Cullen's question.

Cullen drank the brandy too quickly and restrained a choking cough before clearing his throat and saying, "You have furs and I have trade goods. Naturally, my goods are worth twice what your furs are worth, even if your furs are as prime as you claim they are."

Sutherland finished his brandy.

Cullen went on: "I'm willing to give goods to the value of—ah—two thousand pounds sterling for what you have. Add that to the three hundred pounds you won't have to spend to send them down to Montreal, and you'll have made a pretty return on your harvest." He gave a sidelong glance at Sutherland.

The Scotsman grinned, as though genuinely amused, then said, "I'd prefer to pay the three hundred for shipping."

Cullen showed no emotion, though he boiled inside. He watched Sutherland, who said, "We both know the worth of these pelts in Montreal, and it's considerably more than two thousand pounds sterling—even if we were willing to trade them to you."

Both men leaned back in their chairs, Cullen thinking, Sutherland gazing at him, now knowing well how much the merchant wanted these pelts. After a moment, Cullen said, "I'll give you wares to the value of twenty-seven hundred, sterling."

Sutherland said, "That's not enough. Now, let's return to the more simple transaction: will you accept my cargo?"

"No," Cullen said, his lower lip showing the slightest tremble. "I want those pelts. Name your price; we'll strike a bargain!"

Sutherland knew the precise value of the cargo on Cullen's ship, having earlier learned it from his friend, Ensign Parker, the man responsible for the army's merchant affairs. Cullen had been required to present Parker with a bill of lading, declaring the worth of the goods and the ship, which in all was seven thousand pounds sterling, with the ship being five hundred.

Sutherland said, "My peltry will be sold in Montreal for forty-five hundred sterling."

"The value of furs in Montreal is not the same value in Detroit, as you well know, Sutherland. And the value of my trade goods in Detroit is three times their worth in Montreal. Now, come, come. Name your price for the pelts."

At that point, Sutherland reached down for the canvas satchels and opened one after the other on the table, spilling nearly three thousand pounds in sterling notes—the company's cash and Peter's—before the astonished Cullen. This cash, combined with the value of the furs, totaled almost seventy-five hundred pounds.

"By—by Jove!" gasped Cullen. Just then, the sound of Helen Cullen returning with Linda and Emmy from the fort's infirmary could be heard on the gangway above.

Sutherland said, "The peltry and three thousand sterling for your trade goods and your ship!"

Eyes wide, Cullen could not answer immediately. The door to the cabin burst open, and in came Helen, whose face showed shock as she staggered to a halt, staring at the sterling. Linda bumped into her from behind, and Helen Cullen turned quickly to force the young woman and Emmy out of the room, exclaiming, "This is no sight for a child's eyes! Get out! Get out!"

Linda, who had already seen the money covering the table, stood with her mouth hanging open as her mother slammed the door closed. Then Mrs. Cullen turned bitterly to Sutherland, who had stood up. While finding it hard to keep her eyes from the cash, she spat out:

"What is the meaning of this?" She quickly glanced at her seated husband, who was now regaining his composure; then, with her jaw working, repeated her question.

Clearing his throat, Cullen answered, "He wants the trade goods—"

"All of them?"

"All. And the ship."

"And the ship?" Mrs. Cullen was short of breath. For all her family's prosperity, she had never seen so much cash in one place before. Having lived frugally all her life, despite the Cullen financial success, Helen Cullen was unused to such a sight—a sight that made her heart pound and her mouth go so dry that she tried in vain to wet her lips.

"Sit down, dear," Cullen said and stood up, remembering his manners at last. "Can I get you something?"

"Brandy."

"Brandy?" Then he saw she meant it, and he sensed the awful hatred his wife bore for Sutherland, a hatred spawned by jealousy and envy. Cullen poured a little brandy into a clean glass. She drank it without hesitation.

"For how much?" she asked Sutherland.

The Scotsman held out his glass to be refilled by Cullen, then replied, "With the peltry and the sterling, about seventy-five hundred pounds."

She darted an eye at her husband, then demanded that Sutherland leave them alone to deliberate. He went up onto the deck where there was a brisk, fresh wind. He inhaled gratefully. Then he heard a hiss and turned to see Emmy, the maid, poking her head out of a small window, beckoning that he come quickly. No one saw him enter the maid's tiny cabin, and there the woman whispered that she had a letter for Peter Defries from Mary, and she slipped it into Sutherland's hand.

"Tell Mr. Defries," Emmy said softly, her eyes alight with warmth, "that the baby's gettin' awful big and awful pretty! He ought to see!"

From the next cabin, Linda moaned as the ship rocked a little in the breeze. Emmy chuckled, "She's been sick all the way out. Soon as she steps on deck she gets the heaves. Hasn't eaten a thing—"

Just then, Sutherland heard another sound from the other side of the room, and he held up a hand to hush the maid. Voices came from the adjacent Cullen cabin, and Emmy showed Sutherland a chink in the woodword where he could overhear them arguing. Cullen's voice was high and whining:

". . . it means Sutherland's company will have the advantage on us, Mrs. Cullen! What good will this money do if he gets more furs by the spring? I just don't—"

"What good? Why I thought I married a man cleverer and bolder than that! Husband, if you can't think beyond this coming spring, then you're not the merchant I imagined you were! Do you really think Sutherland's little company can keep such an advantage? There are ways to beat them! Many ways! Do you think they'll ever again be able to dictate terms to us? *I* certainly do not!"

Cullen sputtered, but it was apparent to Sutherland that Helen Cullen had considerable say about her company's policy. He had gambled on the Cullen family's lust for quick gain. He knew he had been right in his gamble when Helen declared, "No one else in all Canada, in all the American colonies will be able to offer English furriers such prime peltry this winter. No one else! Do you realize what that will mean to Cullen and Company? What prestige, what importance? Why we'll hold our heads high in anyone's presence this winter, even in the presence of the governor himself! And think of Linda—"

"Linda?"

"Yes, Linda! She'll be the envy of every society daughter in Canada—yes, in New York Town as well! Our name will be held in the highest esteem in the very best circles! The king himself will hear about it! Who else in such difficult times has the genius, the ingenuity, or the ability to do what you, Bradford Cullen, have done to supply the furriers of England? Who? Tell me that?"

"Why . . . indeed, no one—"

"Precisely!" She slapped the table and cried, "Make the transaction! Let Sutherland have his little moment of fleeting success! We'll overwhelm him in a year! We'll destroy him! This is only the beginning for us, Mr. Cullen! Mark my words, we'll break Sutherland's company, and by the time we're through, his name will be worthless in the northwest! Yes, in all Canada!"

A little while later, Sutherland was invited back into the Cullen cabin, where Helen now sat composed and serene in her wrinkled, dry way. Cullen pompously patted his ample stomach and looked once for encouragement at his wife, who stared impassively at the Scotsman. Then Cullen said:

"My good man, we have considered your offer . . . and, it is acceptable. Later today, we shall draw up the proper papers for transfer of the vessel and the cargo to you—"

Just then there was a knock at the door, and in came Linda, green with nausea, begging her mother to take her back to the infirmary.

"I simply must be on dry land, Mama! I can't bear it on board this torture chamber any longer!" The ship lurched slightly, and Linda moaned, hands on her pallid face.

Her parents quieted Linda, and then Cullen finished his speech accepting Sutherland's terms. The Scotsman's heart leaped for joy, though he showed no emotion other than a pleased smile. He had headed off Cullen—if only for the moment. The northwest trade was under his company's control.

As he shook hands with Cullen to seal the bargain, Sutherland said, "The ship will return to Montreal tomorrow; naturally, you and your family will be given passage, gratis—"

"Tomorrow?" Linda gasped and cringed against her mother, who pushed her roughly toward her father. "No! I can't! You promised we could stay a week! Say it isn't so, Papa! I need to recover . . ."

With poor Linda's complaining behind him, Sutherland left the Cullen cabin and went up on deck into bright sunshine. He noticed Emmy's beaming face in the small window and grinned as she clutched her hands together and shook them in triumph. Going down the gangplank, Sutherland saw Peter Defries waiting for him. The Scotsman's mischievous wink told Peter everything, and the young man laughed out loud. But he was cut off when Sutherland pushed Mary's letter at him. Radiating excitement, Defries kissed the letter, and Sutherland smiled, but for the rest he was quiet, thinking about Helen Cullen's threat to break the company. He knew that threat was by no means empty.

Shaking off these thoughts, he clapped Peter on the back and declared, "Come on, lad! Ella can read that letter to you after dinner, but right now we've got a ship to unload if you hope to get home to your family before Christmas!"

EPILOGUE

At sunset in cool mid-April, the Sutherlands joined Tamano and Lela across the river at the place called Valenya. Ice had left the Detroit River, though webs of crystal still lingered at the edges of shady inlets, surrounding wasted cattail stalks and frozen grass. The two families had come here just after winter to plan what one day would be built beside the singing stones that loomed behind them in the reddish sunlight.

Tamano and Lela sat on a log. Ella, with Benjamin asleep in her arms, leaned against Owen as they sat on the sand of Valenya's beach. Playing at the water's edge were Jeremy and Sally, watching Sniffer, who was hungrily and unsuccessfully diving for fish.

It was late, time for these friends to be returning to Fort Detroit. One day—perhaps not until Chief Pontiac went to Sir William Johnson's planned peace council at Oswego in a year—one day Owen and Ella Sutherland would build a fine house here overlooking the river. Tamano would have the best home of any Indian west of Joseph Brant's Iroquois, and the seven great stones would ring with the sound of children.

This past winter, they had done all they set out to do: with Cullen's trade goods, Tamano had paid off Pontiac and the other chiefs for the furs given Sutherland last year. Those goods had also been sufficient to purchase many additional canoeloads of excellent peltry from the Indians. The sloop *Trader,* which had remained in Montreal for the winter, had come back to the fort with more goods and was now being loaded with the furs.

In a few days, Sutherland, Ella, and the children would go east with the ship, as would Angélique and her father, who had consented to his daughter's marriage with Levesque. During their visit to Montreal, Owen would be best man and Ella matron of honor at the wedding, and later they would go to Albany with Peter and Mary Defries. In Albany they would meet Peter's contacts, including the influential Sir William Johnson.

To repay his creditors as well as Johnson, Defries had used the one thousand pounds remaining from his and the company's money, and had been given an additional eight hundred pounds raised by Levesque to meet his entire debt. As a result, he was firmly established with Albany merchants and with Sir William, and when Sutherland brought the latest shipments of furs east, Defries would offer them to the very best markets.

So far, Bradford Cullen had not sent out any new trade goods, and it was yet to be seen whether Cullen could overwhelm the Frontier Company. With every passing day, Sutherland grew increasingly confident in his company's prospects for success. While he, Ella, and the Martines were in Montreal, Lettie Morely would supervise their affairs in Detroit. Already rebuilding her shattered life, Lettie was determined to stay on the frontier, taking her husband's place as a leading partner in the company.

The families went to their two canoes and, in the gathering twilight, pushed them into the current. Before they had paddled very far, they saw another craft skimming toward them, the last light of sunset shimmering on the water behind it. Someone in this canoe was waving, trying to get their attention, so the men headed for whoever was approaching.

To Sutherland's delight, he saw it was Niko-lota and Shamot, and he welcomed them with a shout of joy after these four months of separation. Sutherland's excitement abated, however, when he saw that Niko-lota's face was extremely grave. Their canoes bumped together, and Tamano pushed his close in so they could hold all three against one another.

"I have come from the Father of Waters, brothers," said Niko-lota. "I have bad news for you—for all of us." He hesitated, collecting his thoughts as if trying to find an easy way to say this; but there was no easy way. "Donoway, Tamano, I have come to tell you that a strong force of outlaw whites, English and French, are trying to take control of the fur routes leading south from *Wees-konsan*—the Gathering of Waters. They are evil men, my brothers, and they are very powerful. It is said that they are led by a devil . . . a devil with a red beard. A devil who has only one hand!"

In March 1983 the fabulous saga
of America's Northwest Territory
continues. . . .

DEFIANCE

Northwest Territory Series: Book 3

Here is an exciting preview

Pontiac's warlike Indians in the Northwest have at last been conquered, and the formidable chief himself will attend a great peace council to pledge loyalty to the English king. But the Northwest Territory is far from peaceful as the redbearded giant Jubal Swain and his band of cutthroats loot and plunder through the vast wilderness. Owen Sutherland's burgeoning Frontier Company is threatened not only by Swain but also by wily and corrupt merchants from the East, and a climactic showdown between Owen and the men who want to see him ruined is inevitable.

Meanwhile, America in the years between 1765 and 1774 is torn apart by the conflict between the colonies and the mother country, with men like Owen Sutherland, Ben Franklin, and George Washington forced to take sides. Young Jeremy Bently, Owen's stepson, comes of age as he is faced with divided loyalties. Only Sally Cooper, growing into womanhood, truly knows what is in his heart.

Ella Bently Sutherland, now as much at home in the frontier as she is in the fine houses of the great colonial cities, works with Owen to establish the Frontier Company. Theirs will be a great mercantile empire, and the Sutherlands stand to become one of the most prominent families in the Northwest, even though America is shaken by violence and revolutionary war.

ROMANCE, WAR, HONOR AND ADVENTURE AT THE DAWN OF A NEW FRONTIER!

NORTHWEST TERRITORY

For the millions who thrilled to John Jakes' <u>Kent Family Chronicles</u> comes NORTHWEST TERRITORY, a riveting new series of novels about the men and women who forged out of the American wilderness the vast Northwest Territory, America's heartland and our first great frontier.

NORTHWEST TERRITORY is guaranteed to hold you spellbound with its sweeping tales of love and unforgettable adventure. Discover it for yourself... Order today!

_____ 05738-0/$3.50 WARPATH (Northwest Territory #1) by Oliver Payne

_____ 05532-9/$3.50 CONQUEST (Northwest Territory #2) by Oliver Payne